A PATH TO INNOCENCE, A ROAD TO WAR

A Novel by John V. Wemlinger

2 January, 2005

To Walt,

I hope you enjoy the read and share my hope that this book will always remain exactly what it is today... a work of fiction.

Best personal regards,

John V. Wemlinger
Colonel, US Army
(Retired)

"A Path to Innocence, A Road to War" ISBN 1-58939-376-7 (softcover), 1-58939-377-5 (hardcover).

Published 2003 by Virtualbookworm.com Publishing Inc., P.O. Box 9949, College Station, TX , 77842, US.

Manufactured in the United States of America

DEDICATION

For most of my time in the service, we were lucky. We knew who the enemy was and it was the Soviet Union. Today, Pentagon planners have to ask themselves every day, “Who is the enemy?” The world is full of bad actors whose actions are not bound by even the simplest set of moral principles. Innocent men, women and children are mere incidentals to them. It is the US military that stands as their principal opposition. Yet the number of men and women on active duty today is at its lowest level since before World War II.

This book is a tribute to the remarkable flexibility and amazing agility of the US Armed Forces. It is dedicated to the men and women of America’s Army, Navy, Air Force, Marine Corps and Coast Guard, who everyday have to sift through the political rhetoric and make something happen in places like Iraq, Bosnia, Somalia, the Mediterranean Sea, Saudi Arabia, Kuwait and up and down the Pacific Rim. May our political leaders never overlook the difficulty or the danger of what you are asked to do.

I salute each of you.

ACKNOWLEDGEMENTS

I spent nearly twenty-seven years of my professional life as a soldier. In that time I was privileged to work for dynamic leaders and along side soldiers and civilians whose dedicated service to their jobs inspired me daily. This book could not have been possible without those friendships

When I started to write this book, I was a soldier, not a writer. If it's true that most of us have a book in us, then why don't all of us write one? The answer is simple. We need help. In my case, that help came, first, from my daughter, Brynn, a true military brat, who loves me to this day even though her roots were pulled from under her every two or three years when it was time to move to the next duty station. This book is for you and every military brat like you.

I owe my wife, Diane, much more than I will ever be able to give back to her. She saw a certain restlessness in me after 9/11. She told me to get on with what I really wanted to do. Though I've told you often how important that kind of support is, I can never thank you enough for encouraging me to finish this book. I wouldn't have taken this risk without your support.

I must thank Dr. Rolla Baumgartner, a retired Department of Defense School Superintendent, a friend and mentor, whose encouragement kept me at the computer long after I wanted to turn it off and go do something else.

Finally, I want to thank Sally Ginter, an editor-without-equal. As much as I wanted to get this book out of me, it had to be right. It had to be something that could properly represent me and all service men and women, past and present. Sally has a great eye for what's important...and what's not. She has a marvelous way of communicating her thoughts while keeping the fragile ego of a first-time author in tact. Sally Ginter is last in my list of people to thank because Sally will always have the final word on whether my work is as good as it can be.

Chapter One

The iron door slammed and the noise resonated off the cold limestone walls of the tunnel ahead of him. The light was dim and he took a minute to let his eyes adjust. This was simply one more test of his patience. He'd waited ten years to leave this place; he could take this one-minute delay in stride. Even if the low light hadn't slowed him down, his pride would have. Security cameras were watching him; they covered everything in this place and for the past ten years he'd done everything under their passive scrutiny. This tunnel, his final passage to freedom, would have them as well and he wanted his keepers to see *he* was in control now. When *he* was ready, he stepped off in the practiced, measured cadence of a professional soldier. Each footfall produced an echo down the tunnel that barely had time to fade from his hearing before the next one sent out its reverberation.

The tunnel, carved into the base of the prison's north wall, was cold and stank from an old mustiness. He could smell the moss he saw growing on the walls. It was difficult for him to tell how far he'd walked before he saw the final guard post looming just ahead of him. He tightened his grip on the papers in his right hand. Reassuringly his thumb pressed down on the ID card, which would be the first document the guard would want to see. The guard, a military policeman, saw him coming and stepped out of the heated guardhouse. When he was close enough the guarded demanded, "Your papers, please."

He handed them over. As the military policeman scrupulously checked each one, he fixed his eyes on the door behind the guard. The inmates called it "the freedom door". He'd seen it once from the outside when he'd been part of a work detail. Another prisoner had pointed it out to him. "Gonna' make it through freedom's door in a year," the prisoner had said. That had been five years ago. Today it was his turn.

He waited while the guard made one final check to verify that the inmate in front of him, Cleveland A. Spires, Private (E1) US Army, Retired, was entitled to his freedom today. When he was sure, the guard unlocked freedom's door and pulled it open. The grease on the steel hinges failed in Kansas's frigid winter air. The door groaned and the echo amplified it. The guard said something to him, but Spires didn't hear it. His attention was focused on the open door and the freedom that lay on the other side of it. Spires stepped past the guard and out of the US Military Disciplinary Barracks at Fort Leavenworth, Kansas. If what the guard said was important he would stop him and say it again, otherwise nothing was more important than getting through that open door.

He was free. He took a deep breath and held it. It was a harsh, cold, overcast Kansas winter day, but he thought it was beautiful. The air filling his lungs felt different; it was cleaner, crisper, and freer than the air on the inside of the prison's walls, or at least these first few breaths felt that way to him. He looked out over a grassy pasture that gave way to Fort Leavenworth's Air Field. He couldn't remember the last time he'd been able to see things that were far away. For the last ten years a wall, a door or bars had prevailed between him and things at a distance. He exhaled as a frigid prairie wind ruffled his trousers and served as a reminder of a long walk ahead.

At Fort Leavenworth's main entrance he passed through the iron gates that for over a century marked the installation's entrance. Now he was in the town of Leavenworth, Kansas and he headed for the bus station because a bus was what he could afford. He had $500 in his pocket; $200 generously given him by the US Government for the last ten years he'd spent in prison and $300 he'd earned as he learned to cut hair at the Disciplinary Barracks' Barber Shop.

Unquestionably, money was a problem, but something bigger than money was on his mind and as he walked he struggled with what his next move was going to be. His life was a shambles. His father had passed away while he was locked up, that message relayed by the prison chaplain nearly five years ago. His mother he assumed was still alive, at least no one had told him anything to the contrary. He wondered if she was still in Cleveland, Ohio. He wondered if his wife and son were there as well.

It had been his decision to cut off communication with all of them when he'd been sent to prison. He was ashamed of the way he'd ended up and he was sure they were ashamed of him. He tried to think of other options besides going to Cleveland, but $500 wasn't enough to inspire original thought. Tears came to his eyes. He dismissed them as caused by the wind. The sweetness of his freedom was quickly wearing off as reality washed over him like a tidal wave. He stopped and looked back at the iron gates fronting Fort Leavenworth and cursed himself. His prison term was over and so was thirty years with the US Army. He was leaving it just as he'd started out, as a Private. All he had to his name was a pittance of retired pay and a truckload of shame and guilt---shame and guilt over a ten-year prison sentence served for crimes he didn't commit.

From his fourth floor office window in Bell Hall Lieutenant Colonel Lucas Johnson watched Cleveland Spires walk down the middle of Fort Leavenworth. It was not coincidence that Lucas Johnson was at that window; he'd been there most of the day watching for him. He wanted to see Spires leave this place. As long as he was here at Fort Leavenworth he served as a reminder to Johnson of an unpleasant duty he'd had to perform ten years ago, a duty that had haunted him in these intervening years. Lucas Johnson was one of seven officers who'd sent Cleve Spires to prison ten years earlier. Seeing Spires leave Fort Leavenworth, Johnson hoped, would somehow be therapeutic.

The evidence had been compelling; finding him guilty took less than a day. But then the court martial board hit an impasse. It took them nearly a week to determine how Spires should pay for his crimes. Eventually they decided he should serve ten years in prison, that he should be reduced in rank to Private (E1) and that he should forfeit all of his pay and allowances during his time in prison. They could have given him more, but that was what the seven of them had decided fit the crime.

Johnson never forgot the experience even though Cleveland Spires wasn't his first court martial nor his last. Despite a preponderance of evidence, it just didn't make sense to Johnson that Spires could be such a bad egg. Until his conviction, Cleveland Spires was a poster-boy for how the Army can give you a chance, how you can become a success in the Army. Black, from parents of modest background who'd raised him in Cleveland, Ohio's inner city, Spires had risen through the ranks to become one of the Army's youngest Command Sergeants Major. To those who knew their meaning, the stack of ribbons above his left breast uniform pocket identified him as a courageous warrior and veteran of several wars. Even to the uninitiated, it was obvious Cleve Spires had done some things most soldiers had not. Indeed, only a few soldiers had service records that could compare to his. Certainly there was nothing about Spires' record that pointed to murder, smuggling and corruption.

For the first year or two after Spires' court martial, thoughts of it would interrupt Lucas Johnson's conscious thought and sometimes these thoughts would slip into his unconsciousness as well. He would dream, always the same scene, Spires standing ramrod straight as the military judge read the sentence they'd imposed, Spires' wife and son, clinging to one another as they grappled with the reality that their husband and father was being locked away from them for ten years.

As time went by, the thoughts and the dreams became less and less frequent until a year ago when Johnson was assigned to Fort Leavenworth's Command and General Staff College as Director of the Tactics Department. Before reporting in he'd gone to the Disciplinary Barracks' Barber Shop for a haircut. He'd been told haircuts there were inexpensive, waiting time was at a minimum and his type of high-and-tight hairstyle was pretty hard for the student barbers to screw up. When Johnson glanced down the two rows of barber chairs and saw Cleve Spires standing behind one of them his stomach knotted up so quickly he thought he might become ill. With that chance encounter, the thoughts and the dreams returned. There was hardly a day that went by that Johnson didn't think about the man who was locked up just on the other side of the installation.

Johnson watched Spires bend into the cold January wind. He had the sudden urge to bolt out of the building, chase after him and ask point blank if he'd killed that airman on Okinawa. But he didn't. Instead he wrestled with his emotions until the order and discipline that controlled his military mind took over.

It doesn't really matter. Cleveland Spires is leaving here and in six months you are too---back to command. Forget Spires. You'll never see him again.

At least that was what Lucas Johnson told himself on that blustery January day.

Chapter Two

Tetsu Agaki watched from his parked car as Cleve Spires stepped through freedom's door. Agaki was good at this line of work. He'd tailed people marked by the *Yakuza* for one reason or another for many years, but this was his first opportunity to apply his skill in the United States. As Spires walked toward Leavenworth's main gate, Agaki drove past him and parked the car on a side street adjacent to the post's main entrance and waited. When he saw Spires pass through the iron gates, Agaki left the safety of his car and followed his mark on foot. The most difficult part of his task lay ahead of him. Agaki was going to have to get dangerously close to Spires in order to know where he was heading from here.

Leavenworth's bus station was small but unusually busy. Two people were in line in front of Spires at the ticket window. Agaki was instantly self-conscious as the only Asian in sight but he stepped up and took a place in the line just behind Spires. Less than two feet of space separated him from his mark and his heart was beating so hard he thought Spires might hear it. When it was his turn, Spires stepped up to the ticket window. Agaki let the distance between them increase, but he made sure he was well within earshot. "One one-way ticket to Cleveland, Ohio, please."

The young lady behind the counter launched into her sales pitch. Efficiently and courteously, she outlined several special packages the bus line was offering that might provide him a better deal, all of which provided more travel than he wanted and cost more money than he could spend right now. Still he couldn't lose patience with her. She was much too attractive, pleasant and, after all, selling bus tickets was her job.

He allowed her to finish her spiel but told her, "Just the cheapest fare you have, one-way to Cleveland is all I need for right now, thanks."

The young woman deftly keyed his destination into the computer. "That will be sixty-five dollars. The bus is number 1402 leaving from gate 2 at six-thirty this evening."

As Cleve shelled out the money, she passed him the ticket with a cheery, "Thank you, sir. Have a good trip."

When Cleve stepped away from the counter, he noticed the oriental man, Japanese he thought, who had been behind him, was gone.

When Tetsu Agaki heard Cleve Spires ask for a ticket to Cleveland, Ohio, he'd turned on his heel and left Leavenworth's bus station. Now at Kansas City's airport, Agaki's flight to Cleveland was boarding. From a public phone near his gate he placed a call to Bangkok, Thailand. Now was a good time to call his employer because he wouldn't have a lot of time to chat if he was going to make his flight. Not having time to chat with Billy Driscoll was okay with Tetsu Agaki. It didn't matter how well Driscoll paid him, Agaki still didn't like the rude American.

Driscoll was in the middle of a "training session" with three new acquisitions when the phone rang in his suite in the Windsor Hotel in Bangkok, Thailand.

"Hold that thought, baby," he said to the naked Thai girl on her knees in front of him. He gruffly pushed her away, stood, and walked naked across the room. As he sat down on the edge of the bed to answer the ringing telephone, he nudged the two naked women who were erotically entwined there and motioned for them to get up.

"Hello." It was almost a snarl.

Tetsu Agaki was getting the sign from the gate attendant that he needed to board his Cleveland-bound flight so he spoke quickly. "As you said, Spires was released today. He bought a bus ticket to Cleveland. I'm flying there now and will resume my surveillance when he arrives. I have to go. The flight is leaving." Without waiting for a response, Agaki hung up and ran for the jet way.

Half a world away Driscoll flew into a rage. "Dammit, the little shit hung up on me."

The three women understood very little of what Billy Driscoll said. That didn't matter. It wasn't words that would hurt them; it was his rage. They'd seen that frequently since their arrival in Bangkok and it was never a good sign. They usually got hurt when he was like this. Driscoll ran a stable of whores. Violence and fear were his tools and he used them to make them compliant. None of the women who worked for him wanted to see "Beelee" get angry like this, even if they weren't the direct cause of it.

Command Sergeant Major Billy Driscoll was currently serving as the Command Sergeant Major of the First Battalion, First Special Forces Group. He'd been in Asia forever because he could speak Thai fluently, his Japanese was pretty good and he could hold his own in Tagalog, the language of the Philippines. He was also a decorated combat veteran. During a couple of tours in Vietnam he'd been awarded two Bronze Stars for valor and a couple of Purple Hearts. His file boasted a string of efficiency reports that were good enough to get him promoted to this highest rank that an Army non-commissioned officer could hold.

However, as good as he seemed, Billy Driscoll was living proof that the Army's system of enlisted promotions was not perfect. For the last ten years he'd built up a personal fortune by smuggling guns, ammunition, gold and drugs. For the last six years he'd operated a string of brothels in Bangkok. He was able to access his enterprises by using his position as the First Battalion's Command Sergeant Major to come and go from Thailand virtually at will. While he was there he rarely left Bangkok. He was little or no help to the soldiers of his Battalion who were spread throughout the country training different units of the Royal Thai Army and Marines. Instead he spent his time helping himself to his share of Bangkok's corruption In the final analysis, Command Sergeant Major Billy Driscoll was a scumbag.

Ten years ago, when he was just establishing his businesses in Thailand, he'd killed a kid on Okinawa. Willie Peterson was a military customs inspector assigned to the Security Police Detachment at Kadena Air Force Base. Peterson failed to do what Driscoll had paid him to do and that failure resulted in the detection of Driscoll's first shipment of stolen automatic weapons and ammunition into Japan. Driscoll became the prime suspect since he was the one who'd delivered the shipment of military gear with the contraband in it to the airport in Thailand. Billy Driscoll, however, proved to be remarkably and ruthlessly resourceful. All he had to do was divert attention away from himself. The authorities on Okinawa only had circumstantial evidence and not much of that. No one saw Driscoll put the contraband in the shipment. His Thai accomplices were completely anonymous. The only other person who could rat him out was Peterson, the military customs inspector who had let him down and Driscoll's business policy was that no one was afforded the luxury of letting him down.

Even Billy Driscoll was amazed at how easily his plan to exact revenge *and* divert attention away from himself had fallen into his lap. While walking down the hallway of his battalion's headquarters, he saw Command Sergeant Major Cleve Spires in the battalion's arms room meticulously inspecting a rack of 9mm Beretta automatic pistols. Driscoll bent down over a nearby drinking fountain stalling as the seed of an idea began to grow. Five minutes later, in the privacy of his office he thought his plan through.

He paid $5,000 to a friend of his, Sergeant Boz Williams, who sneaked a 9mm pistol out of the Battalion's arms room. Married three times and divorced as many, Boz Williams owed everyone. Five grand was incentive enough for him to be remarkably quick, efficient and quiet.

The weapon Williams took had been carefully chosen as one handled by the visiting Command Sergeant Major Spires. Williams passed the stolen weapon to Driscoll. Both were careful to preserve Spires' fingerprints, which were visible even to the naked eye on the pistol's grip and barrel.

Billy Driscoll took a lot of pleasure in what happened next. He told Peterson over the phone he wanted to meet with him, that he understood how things could go wrong. He told him he'd pay him the rest of what he owed him and that would be the end of it as long as Peterson kept quiet about their deal. Greed and naiveté lured Peterson to the meeting.

In the parking lot of the USO, near Kadena's Gate Two, Driscoll shoved the snub-barrel of a .38 caliber police special into the airman's belly and told him to cooperate or he'd waste him right then and there. Scared shitless, the airman let Driscoll lead him to a remote part of the sprawling American base like a lamb to slaughter. On a back road miles from the main part of the base, Billy Driscoll used the stolen weapon with Cleve Spires' fingerprints all over it to kill Peterson. By Driscoll's careful design, the execution took place just hours before Spires departed Okinawa returning to Fort Lewis, Washington.

Within hours of the body's discovery, the murder weapon was recovered from a shallow pond near the crime scene where Driscoll had thrown it. The gun oil preserved the prints even in the weapon's watery hiding place. The clear set of fingerprints led authorities to Command Sergeant Major Cleveland A. Spires.

Driscoll left nothing to chance. One more step was necessary to seal Spires' fate and the money was a good investment. Five days after Peterson's body was found, officials at Fort Lewis, Washington seized a package containing $10,000 in small denomination bills mailed to Command Sergeant Major Cleveland A. Spires from Okinawa. The next day he was officially charged with murder in the first degree.

The only glitch in Driscoll's plan was the pistol found tucked in the waistband of Willie Peterson's trousers. In his haste to waste him Driscoll had missed it. Spires' defense attorney argued that the presence of the other gun at the scene meant that whoever committed the murder had probably done so in self-defense. Thus if the Army insisted on charging Spires with this murder, the most he could be charged with was manslaughter barring the unexpected appearance of an eyewitness who would testify they saw Spires summarily execute the airman. This legal maneuver saved Cleve from the death sentence or life in prison. For Driscoll it meant Spires would be getting out of jail and that bothered Billy Driscoll.

In the ten years that Spires was out of circulation Driscoll had built his businesses in Thailand to the point that his Army salary was just pocket change. In a year he would retire from the Army and take up residency in Bangkok, but for now he used his suite at the Windsor Hotel as his corporate headquarters and from there he ran four bars. The bars made decent money from the sale of beer and liquor but the real profits came from the prostitutes who met their customers in the bars and serviced them in their back rooms. Driscoll once dabbled in drugs but got out of that business when the US turned up the heat on Thailand to stem the flow of drugs coming out of the Golden Triangle and from there to US cities. Though the profits from drugs could be huge, the risk was high, higher than even Driscoll cared to go up against. Instead he allowed the *Yakuza,* Japan's organized crime syndicate, to launder some of their drug money through his bars and he oversaw a smuggling operation for them that ran illegal guns and ammunition from Thailand into Okinawa, Japan where the *Yakuza* took them off his hands at a handsome profit.

Billy Driscoll thought he was a key player for the *Yakuza* in Thailand which is exactly what they wanted him to think. However, the truth of the matter was that Billy Driscoll, despite his Japanese language proficiency, was a *gaiging,* a foreigner. They didn't trust him. They viewed him as a rogue who took actions on his own without regard to their impact on the larger organization. The Peterson murder had infuriated them. Had US authorities bothered to look deeper than circumstantial evidence, they might have gotten into the *Yakuza's* organization. The *Yakuza* would have much preferred for Driscoll to take his lumps in prison for smuggling rather than risk their exposure. They would have seen that as a sign of his loyalty to them. He probably would have been rewarded handsomely for his silence and his time in jail.

Now, for the time being at least, the *Yakuza* tolerated Billy Driscoll. However, if they knew he'd hired Agaki to follow Spires they might have lost their tolerance. His decision to have Cleve Spires followed upon his release from prison was another grandstand play that Driscoll hadn't discussed with anyone.

Billy Driscoll stomped around the hotel room for a few minutes until the rage settled out of him. He glanced at the three naked women. He watched them until he could feel himself becoming erect. He sat down in a chair and motioned for the girl who had been in front of him to resume her duties. She did as she was told. Driscoll forgot about Agaki, the phone call and Cleveland Spires. A strange smile crossed his face and he said to no one in particular, "God, it's great to be the King of Thailand."

Chapter Three

At 4:30AM the bus pulled into the cramped parking area of the Greyhound Bus Station near the heart of Cleveland's downtown. Surrounded by high chain link with triple strand barbed wire across the top, Cleve thought it looked like some of the American base camps he'd lived in while in Vietnam. The driver honked the bus's air horn twice and an old man bundled in a heavy winter coat and wearing galoshes came out, unlocked the gate and swung it open. As Cleve got off he could see him fumbling with the chain, the lock and the key trying to relock the gate. It was cold and the wind swirled snow around the old man. Inside the station things were not much better. Two men, homeless he presumed, slouched asleep on the hard benches in the center of the otherwise barren room. Next to one was a grocery cart piled high with nothing that Cleve could discern was of any value or useful purpose. Each clutched a paper bag close to their chest, bottlenecks protruding from the open end of each bag. He caught the ammonia-stench of urine. This was his first time back in this bus station in thirty years. It was from here that he'd left for basic training. Nothing he could see had changed much. Urban decay was all around him, but he reckoned he had little right to judge either the poor condition of the station or the people occupying it.

Standing now in the cold bus station, guilt and frustration attacked him again. He asked himself why he'd come back here. Across the station, behind a thick wall of glass, probably bulletproof, he saw a lone ticket agent, propped on one elbow, watching television. He headed in that direction. He was half way there when he stopped in his tracks. He was here. It was never going to get any better until he faced them, until he told them how sorry he was. Maybe then he could go somewhere else and get on with his life. He reversed his course and headed out of the bus terminal, deciding to walk the five miles to his mother's house. It gave him more time to think about what he would say to her and to his wife and son whom he hoped he'd find there as well.

Through binoculars and from the safety of his rental car Tetsu Agaki watched Spires get off the bus. He respected his mark enough to know that it would be foolhardy to expose himself to Spires again as he'd done at the Fort Leavenworth bus station. Driscoll warned him not to take Spires too lightly.

He peered through the binoculars, through a plate glass window fronting the bus station. He could see Spires in there. Agaki's stomach cramped as he watched Spires move toward the ticket window. He breathed a sigh of relief when Spires turned and left.

Agaki knew where he was headed. Driscoll had given him Ida Spires' name. He had found the street address in the Cleveland phone directory and then spent some time during daylight driving around in the neighborhood. It made doing the same thing in the dark a lot easier. As soon as Spires left the bus station, Agaki drove to Ida Spires' house. He merely waited there for Cleve to show up.

Cleveland, Ohio in the winter is a bitterly cold place. Perched on the edge of Lake Erie, it is hit by cold Canadian north winds blowing off of the lake, driving the wind-chill to well below zero. Snowfall is regular and heavy. The weather this mid-January morning was no exception, but Spires was oblivious to the weather swirling around him. He was focused only on what he wanted to say to his family after all these years---after all of this guilt.

The house sat in the middle of the block, a typical row house built just after World War II to provide affordable housing to returning veterans. Lincoln Spires, Cleve's father, had been a part of that war. He had enlisted in the Navy. In fact he'd told Cleve to "join the Navy if you're going to join any damned one of 'em...at least you'll have a dry place to sleep and the food is decent." Cleve always thought it ironic his father believed only the Navy could provide a dry place for its people to sleep.

Cleve Spires stood for a moment in front of his mother's house. He looked up and down the street and shook his head. Fifty years ago when they were built, the houses were all identical. Two story brick with a basement, each house was fronted by a small yard bisected by a walk that led to four steps that gave way to a front porch. Hers was the only one that hadn't changed for the worse. Over half of the houses on the block were boarded up. Litter was strewn about the yards and up and down most of the street. Only half of the streetlights were working. Yet in her yard there was no litter. The sidewalks were shoveled clear and he could feel the crunch of salt under his shoes as he walked. The porch was empty of furniture now. The aluminum chairs would be neatly covered and stored in the basement, he was sure. Her house numbers were clearly illuminated by the only porch light visible on the block. Through the window he could see the blinds his mother always had at her windows, drawn at this time of night, every slat perfectly in place. The immaculate condition of the home in an otherwise ramshackle neighborhood was testimony to the iron will of Ida Spires. A remarkably strong woman, no matter how bad things got around her, she would not let what was hers fall apart.

As he stepped on the porch his stomach turned over. He knocked too lightly on the front door the first time. Upstairs, asleep in the back bedroom, she couldn't have possibly heard him out there barely tapping. Perhaps this was another way Cleve's psyche was delaying this reunion. He braced himself and knocked again, louder this time and in a minute he saw a light come on behind the drawn blinds covering the front door's glass. Seconds later a dagger of light crossed his face as Ida spread wider the narrow opening between two of the blind's slats. As quickly as the two slats had parted, they closed and from the other side of the door he heard faintly, "My God!" He heard fingers frantically sliding the chain lock free of its channel and he could hear her struggling with the dead bolt's mechanism that wasn't moving fast enough this one-hundred thousandth time she'd unlocked it. And then the door swung open and his mother stood backlit in the doorway.

Her voice cracked as she said his name. Tears filled her eyes and streamed down her dark cheeks. She stepped toward him to put her arms around her only son and the gulf he'd put between them over the past ten years closed as quickly and as surely as water closes around a hand dipped in a pool.

He tried to say something. He thought he should, but even the simplest of words, *"Mom"*, stuck in his throat and he couldn't get it out. The emotion of the moment was too profound. Her head lay against his chest and he could feel her gentle sobs as he stood there at the threshold. Neither of them could speak. Yet the comfort they took from one another equaled volumes. Cleve knew then and there that if his mother had ever harbored any hatred for him, it had long since gone away. He was glad now that he'd come here, that he'd come home.

She pulled him into the small foyer. Everything was as Cleve remembered it. "Cleveland," he couldn't remember the last time he'd been called that, but it is what she'd always called him, "you're home." She patted his chest with her hand as if reassuring herself that he was really there with her. "I'll bet you're hungry. I'll make us some coffee. Then I'll make you breakfast. I can't believe you're home." She led him down the hallway into the kitchen at the back of the house. He took a deep breath and smelled the same smells he'd smelled as a boy growing up here. It was as if everything inside this place had stood still while he and his mother had aged thirty years. He followed her down the hallway as he'd done as a little boy after being called in from play. There were so many things he wanted to say to her, so many things he wanted to know.

From his position across the street and two houses down, Tetsu Agaki witnessed Spires' reunion with his mother, its poignancy lost on him. Agaki correctly assumed Spires was inside the house to stay for the rest of the day. Now was as good a time as any for him to get to a phone, call Driscoll, and get further directions. Agaki's Thai was passable so, when the operator at the Windsor hotel in Bangkok answered the phone, Agaki replied in Thai, "Mister Driscoll's room please."

Just as he was about to hang up after a dozen or so rings, Driscoll answered the phone with another surly, "Hello."

"Driscoll-san, this is Agaki." Agaki braced for the stream of rudeness he knew he'd get.

"Listen to me you little son of a bitch, don't you ever hang up on me again. You don't do that with your buddy Fujiwara so don't think you can get away with it with me. I'm paying you just as much as Fujiwara ever did…"

Agaki had enough of this abuse, "Driscoll-san, I regret hanging up on you but I had to catch that flight to Cleveland. It was the last one from Kansas City yesterday and I wanted to arrive here well in advance of Spires. Are you interested in knowing what I have observed or do you still wish to chastise me over an unavoidable circumstance?

Driscoll seethed, but Agaki had information he wanted.

"All right, what have you found out?"

"It appears he has come home to Mother. I just observed a most touching reunion at her doorway."

"How sweet."

"I will continue to watch him for the next few days and try to determine if he intends to stay here, although I can't imagine why anyone would want to stay in this forsaken place."

Driscoll had the thought Agaki might be playing him for more time than was necessary. He was getting $5,000 per day plus expenses. "Listen Agaki, if I find out you're dragging this out just to get more money, I'll...

Agaki cut him off, "I will get on an airplane tomorrow morning for Japan, if you are satisfied with the information I have given you."

Driscoll was in a box. He hated paying out his hard-earned money to this little *Yakuza* snitch, but he wanted to be sure Spires was not going to come looking for him; he wanted to be sure Spires had not made some connection between him and the frame up during those ten long years in jail.

"All right, you little shit, here's what I want you to do. Watch this bastard for another week. Call me if he moves out of Cleveland. I want to know where this son of a bitch is, what he's doing, who he's talking to. No matter what, call me at the end of the week with your report. Got it?"

Agaki seethed at his employer's arrogance, but he took some consolation in knowing that he had Driscoll right where he wanted him. "Where shall I call you? At the Windsor?"

"Yeah."

Driscoll slammed the phone down smiling and thinking this time he'd hung up on Agaki.

Agaki, who anticipated Driscoll's childishness, had moved the receiver away from his ear and gently cradled it, glad the conversation was over. He'd been on the job for three days and had just been commissioned for seven additional days. He did the math in his head. He'd make fifty grand off of this deal.

Agaki did have one qualm about what he was doing. Agaki was surprised when Driscoll mentioned the name of Cato Fujiwara during their conversation. It made him wonder how much this *gaiging* knew about the *Yakuza*. It also served as a reminder that Cato Fujiwara didn't know that he was doing this small piece of surveillance work for Driscoll.

Tetsu Agaki and Cato Fujiwara were old friends. At the end of World War II they were teenagers scrapping on the streets of Tokyo for food and money to survive. From this humble beginning came the multi-billion dollar business that today was the *Yakuza* and Cato Fujiwara headed it all up. Tetsu Agaki could have been right up there next to his buddy, right at the top of this global criminal empire except that forty years ago he had to take a backseat and distance himself from his old friend. Agaki was busted for selling heroin and sentenced to jail for ten years. He'd served every day of that sentence. For his sacrifice he'd been well taken care of by Cato Fujiwara and the rapidly growing organization he was left alone to build.

After Agaki's release from prison Cato Fujiwara threw work his way whenever he could. Typically it was small stuff, like what he was doing now for Driscoll, but Fujiwara paid him well and that meant Driscoll would have to pay even more. It bothered Agaki the way Driscoll was throwing around his friend's name and he knew Fujiwara wouldn't like it but, when he did the math once more, he let it go. Tetsu Agaki had expenses and chief among these was a mistress in Tokyo that could be kept very happy on what Agaki was getting paid for this little job. The thought of Michiko's touch made even the American's extreme crudeness tolerable.

Ida Spires stood at the counter slicing some onions to mix with scrambled eggs she was preparing for her son.

"I haven't made scrambled eggs like this since your father…" She stopped her thought and mentally scolded herself for approaching a subject that might hurt him. There was an awkward silence.

"Mom, I'm sorry I wasn't here when Dad…"

She turned to him and held up her hand.

"Cleveland, don't be sorry. There's no need for you to be sorry. You couldn't have changed anything."

She turned back and continued preparing their breakfast. "He died in his sleep in the middle of the night. I was lying right there beside him. I didn't know anything was wrong until I tried to wake him up in the morning. It had to have been one of the most peaceful deaths God could ever grant a human being."

He hung his head and cried. She walked over and put her arms around his shoulders and patted him.

"It's OK Cleveland. He's in a good place now and he knew you loved him."

Her words and his tears left him speechless. When his tongue returned he blurted out, "How could he have loved a convicted murderer?"

Ida shot back a question of her own.

"Did you do it, son? Did you do those awful things they said you did?"

"No, mom, I didn't do any of it."

"Don't you think your father and I know that? Knowing that is what kept your father alive long after the doctors said he should have been gone. It's what keeps me alive today. If we believed any of it, it would have killed both of us long ago."

There was a silence while her words sank in and then she continued, "And someday everyone will know you didn't do it, Cleveland. I don't know how and I don't know when. I just know the truth will come out someday."

Now it was Cleve's turn to reach out to his mother and pull her close to him. Cleve Spires had badly underestimated his parents' love for him. That was a mistake he could never set right. However, he would never make that mistake again.

Ida broke the poignancy of the moment, "Now let me get this breakfast on the table."

She patted his shoulder again and returned to her cooking. The awkward silence returned. Both knew why. For the first few minutes he'd been in the house he held out some hope that she might have been asleep upstairs and that she hadn't heard his knock. Now he was sure that wasn't the case. He'd been home nearly an hour now. He and his mother were alone in the house. His wife and son were somewhere else. He needed to know where. He needed to know if they were OK. Ida knew the questions had to come out but she also knew her answers would hurt her son more than he'd been hurt already. He waited until she slid a heaping plate of eggs and bacon in front of him and set down at the table herself, then Cleve moved ahead.

"Mom, do you know where Liott and Daniel are? Are they OK?"

The old lady's eyes filled again and she nodded. She reached across the table and took his hand. Cleveland, Liott and Daniel returned to Thailand over nine years ago. I haven't spoken to either of them since they left."

The tears burst over the edges of her eyes and flowed down her face. Cleve felt sorry for her, but he had to dredge the information up from her despite its painfulness. "Its not your fault, Mom. I abandoned them. After that first phone call at prison," he paused to choose his words, "I couldn't talk to them after that. I felt completely helpless. I lost my family when they sent me to prison. Now that I'm out, I'd just like to know they are safe and happy."

He was blaming himself and before he got too far down that road she tried to reverse his course, "Cleveland, it wasn't your going to jail that made her leave." Ida was dredging up a bitter memory. "Liott was having trouble coping with life here. She's very proud. She wouldn't live here with your father and me. She insisted that she and Daniel have their own place. She got a job at the Airport Holiday Inn. They didn't pay very much and so she had to work a lot of hours but she found a place for her and Daniel. We'd see them once or twice a week. School didn't go well for Daniel. Kids made fun of him and when they started to make fun of Liott's accent he started fighting. He was sent home twice for fighting. The day after the second fight Liott called us from the airport and said she and Daniel were leaving for Thailand. She was taking him home where he could grow up without having to fight his way through life. Your father and I rushed to the airport to try and talk to her, but they'd already taken off by the time we got there. I'm so sorry Cleveland..."

He didn't really follow the rest of what she said. On the bus ride from Kansas he tried to imagine what she would look like after all this time; he tried to imagine what Daniel, as a young man, would look like. He'd prepared himself for them to be here, if not at his mother's, then at least in Cleveland. Instead they were on the other side of the world.

"We exchange gifts and cards at Christmas."

"What?"

"Daniel and I---I always manage a small gift and card at Christmas and on his birthday too. I don't know how they get to him. I just send them to 'Daniel Spires' 'Chuk Ra Met, Thailand'. I know he gets them. He always thanks me in his Christmas note. Somehow the system works."

She stood up from the table and walked over to a drawer under the telephone. She took a packet of cards tied with a red ribbon from the drawer and handed it to him. He held it as if they would break; they were that precious to him.

"Go ahead Cleveland, untie the ribbon and read them. They're all from Daniel. His English has gotten better from Christmas to Christmas, you'll see."

One of the cards contained a photo of the boy. The cards were in chronological order and the sixth card in the stack held a picture of a boy. He took it out and studied it.

"You should put that in your wallet Cleveland. Every father should have a picture of his son with him."

She told him to eat. His eggs would get cold. In between mouthfuls he told his mother about Chuk Ra Met, Thailand. He knew it well. He had met and courted Liott there while assigned to a Special Forces Training Mission in Korat twenty-five years earlier. Just talking about Liott, Daniel and Chuk Ra Met seemed to make him feel better.

While Cleve took a shower and cleaned up, Ida made up his room, the same room he'd slept in as a child. They spent the day catching up. Later that evening Ida cooked what she remembered as her son's favorite dinner; baked ham, sweet potatoes, and pumpkin pie for desert. Cleve didn't tell her she could have fixed him anything and it would have been his favorite meal. He didn't have to go through a cafeteria line to get it. There were no guards at her kitchen doors to keep him in there. She had prepared it especially for him. Cleve Spires was home and home he would stay for a good long time. At least that is what Ida Spires prayed for as she peacefully fell asleep with her son just down the hall in the room he'd slept in as a boy.

Chapter Four

Paul Stanley laid the passport on the counter at Narita's immigration checkpoint and hoped the agent couldn't read his nervousness. If they caught him he'd never be able to explain. This was his fourth time to do something like this and it would never become routine for him. The agent began thumbing through the passport as if he was looking for something in particular. Stanley's heart was pounding so hard he could feel the thud of it at the back of his head. He quickly did a gut-check. Above all things, Paul Stanley was a disciplined man. He choked down his anxiety and waited for the agent to complete the inspection of his travel document as if he were, in fact, who the passport said he was.

One last check as the immigration agent dutifully checked his face against the picture on the passport. They matched. He rolled the page over, hit the document with his stamp and handed it back to him. US Army Major General Paul Stanley, the Director for Logistics and Security Assistance, United States Pacific Command, stepped into Japan as Mark Amial, a citizen of Washington state who had died five years earlier. Amial's name had been resurrected especially for Stanley by a nameless, faceless source in San Diego who, with a referral from the right sources and five thousand dollars in small denomination bills, would provide a phony US passport.

Only eight people knew Paul Stanley was in Japan and Stanley's boss wasn't one of them. Admiral Chet McKeever thought he was on a hunting trip in the Canadian wilds. Instead Stanley was here in Hokkaido to meet with one of the strangest mixes of men he could imagine; a Japanese, a South Korean, a Thai, a Filipino, a Malaysian, a Vietnamese, a Chinese and, a North Korean. In the last ten years he'd met with them on three other occasions, about once every three years. This meeting was out of that cycle and naturally Stanley's curiosity had been aroused when they'd sent him a note asking him to join them on Hokkaido so soon after their last meeting just over a year ago.

If he was truthful with himself, he didn't know squat about them, about what they do. Despite his ten-year relationship with them, they had been very careful about what information they doled out to him. He thought they were businessmen and around him they simply referred to themselves as *the association.*

The Japanese associate, Saieto Yamamoto, was Stanley's handler, the one who dispensed information to him. In fact Yamamoto was the only one Stanley knew by name. Their strange carefulness, these clandestine meetings and Stanley's own lack of naiveté, told led him they were not exactly on the up-and up. At a minimum these guys were arms dealers, that was his value to them he thought. What they did with the shit he gave or sold to some of their countries he didn't know and he didn't really care. He suspected they might be smuggling weapons and ammunition in some rather large quantities and he was even OK with that. He hoped they weren't involved with drugs. While those were never mentioned, Stanley had not asked about them specifically either. One thing he knew for sure is that whatever the hell it was that this group did, they did it quite well because over the ten years of his involvement with them they'd paid him a staggering sum of money.

The first payment ten years ago had saved his ass. They had literally pulled him back from the brink of financial disaster. A US-based HMO was closing in on him for $150,000 in unpaid medical bills he owed for an estranged son's cancer treatment, but Stanley, a Lieutenant Colonel at the time, was tapped out. Alimony and child support payments for three failed marriages took almost all of his monthly salary. This medical bill would have taken the rest of it. Bankruptcy was looming as his only option and that would have ended his military career. His security clearance would have been pulled and that would have ended his otherwise successful career as an Army officer.

Stanley never could determine how they knew about his dilemma and, again, he frankly didn't care. All they had asked of him was to influence military sales to their countries if he were ever in a position to do so. As soon as he'd agreed he was given access to a foreign bank account with one million US dollars in it. He'd been very frugal with his new fortune. He'd paid off the HMO and a few other personal debts; other than that he'd not touched the money given him. He thought they liked that about him.

Six years after *the association's* million-dollar investment in him, it began to pay off. The Vice Chief of Staff of the Army, General Pete Rentz, an old friend of Stanley's had served as the President of the Major General Selection Board and in that capacity made sure

Paul Stanley was one of ten Brigadier Generals selected for promotion to Major General. Then he handpicked Stanley to be the Assistant Deputy Chief of Staff for Operations (ADCSOPS) on the Army staff in the Pentagon. Rentz needed someone in that position he could trust implicitly and Rentz's trust and respect for Paul Stanley went back to their days at West Point. Paul Stanley diverted a Tactical Officer on his way to Cadet Captain Rentz's room just at a time when Rentz had a bottle of whiskey and a woman in there with him. Had it not been for Stanley, Rentz would have been caught with his pants down and mustered out of West Point in disgrace. The secret had been theirs and theirs alone now for nearly thirty years. Pete Rentz trusted Paul Stanley as he trusted few others and now he needed him to handle some highly political sales of military equipment to foreign governments that the US hadn't traditionally supported.

At the Pentagon, Paul Stanley had limited success at steering some sales to his colleagues' countries but it hadn't been easy work. The Pacific Rim played second fiddle to the hotter spots in the world, like the Persian Gulf and the Middle East. To protect his cover he was forced to prioritize sales to those parts of the world at the expense of the Pacific Rim. Nonetheless, Japan and South Korea had gotten some important technology and for this he'd seen his offshore bank account grow by a couple of million dollars.

Two years ago, he gotten really lucky and managed to get himself reassigned from the Pentagon job to his current position as Director for Logistics and Security Assistance at Pacific Command. Of course, General Pete Rentz, now the Commander-in-Chief Special Operations Command had helped, but even without Rentz's help Stanley probably would have gotten the job. He had plenty of experience in the Pacific as a Brigade Commander in Korea and as an Assistant Division Commander for the 25th Infantry Division in Hawaii. Admiral Chet McKeever, Commander-in-Chief, United States Pacific Command, was nobody's patsy. He knew experience when he saw it, but there was another reason, beyond experience, why McKeever wanted to get Paul Stanley assigned to his command.

Stanley had credibility with the other generals and admirals that McKeever had to work with in his nearly one-third of the world. Stanley was a highly decorated infantry officer who could also speak logistics. The Silver Star at the top of the heap of ribbons above his left breast pocket was a highly visible testament to his courage. Stanley was the guy who could finagle the sale of missile technology to Japan; trucks to the Philippines and Thailand; old weapons systems to Vietnam and China and all the while watch over the reduction of US troops and bases in the vast Pacific and Indian Oceans. Whether he liked it or not, that's what McKeever's charter was. The current administration, just reelected to a second term, was slowly but surely dismantling the last of the US military's overseas presence and apparently Congress was going along with it. Despite their differences, President Glover, a Democrat, and the Congress, controlled by the Republicans, seemed to agree on two points: first, the US simply could not afford a large military and second, the smaller US military was even more affordable if it was located on US soil. McKeever had some delicate work to do in the Pacific Rim and he was going to need every ounce of Paul Stanley's experience to help him get it done. His credibility as a warrior could only help.

Stanley dug his spurs into his new job with an enthusiasm that made McKeever sure he'd picked the right guy for the task at hand. In a very short span of time Stanley engineered a sale of artillery and ammunition to China. In Vietnam Stanley had put together an aviation package that included repair parts, maintenance training, pilot training along with guns and ammunition for certain of the aircraft included in the package. Of course, these sales did not go unnoticed in the media. Editorials accused the US of arming its enemies and of becoming the world's most notorious arms dealer, but in the final analysis it didn't matter what the media said. The House and Senate Armed Services Committees had oversight responsibility for foreign military sales and as long as they concurred with what Stanley proposed nothing else mattered.

Of course, there was still some US firepower remaining in the Pacific Rim. Two brigades of the Second Infantry Division were still glued to the Demilitarized Zone separating the two Koreas. At Osan Air Force Base, just southeast of Seoul, there was still a US Air Force Fighter Wing. After that you had to go to fifteen hundred miles south to find any more combat troops in the Pacific Rim; Okinawa still held a Marine Corps Marine Expeditionary Brigade. It wasn't very much considering the vastness of the region.

Above the cries of the Commanding General, US Forces Korea, the Commanding General US Air Forces Pacific, and the Commanding General, Fleet Marine Force Pacific, Paul Stanley led the charge to strip all of the US logistical units out of the Pacific Rim. They weren't war-fighting units; they were support units, expensive to keep there. The generals argued that leaving combat forces without logistical back up is like having a fighter that can only deliver one punch. If that one punch doesn't end the fight, then look out. To quiet the brass he'd pissed off, Stanley negotiated some support agreements with the Koreans guaranteeing logistical support from them if the US was needed to help South Korea defend its borders, but McKeever and all of his fellow generals, including Paul Stanley, knew the political waters surrounding agreements like these were very murky. Nothing could make a foreign government do something it didn't want to do. Nonetheless, Washington seemed to be happy with the progress McKeever and the rest of the military brass were making toward force reductions in the Pacific Rim.

If any of this had ever made Paul Stanley's conscience twinge even a little bit, it didn't last very long and was not the least bit painful for him. He hated politicians, American or any other kind. That was why he saw absolutely nothing wrong with what he was doing. If it helped *the association* and if he got paid for it, then he wasn't going to worry about it. Stanley described his Army career as thirty years of twisted irony. He'd spent the Reagan years building American military power up. Then he'd spent most of the time since then taking it apart again. The current administration and Congress couldn't recognize a threat until it bit them in the ass. He was fed up with their shortsightedness. He'd do their bidding but he was going to make some money along the way. He'd convinced himself that he liked his colleagues in *the association* and he harbored some idea that he could continue to work for them even after retiring from the Army. He'd also convinced himself that they liked him as well. If pay were an indication of just how much they liked him, he would have to say they fucking loved him because by now his offshore account had grown to over four million dollars.

His single frustration was how little he really knew about them. He'd risked illegal entry into other countries on three other occasions to meet with them over the past ten years. He thought he'd demonstrated a certain loyalty to their cause, whatever the hell it was. He thought it was about time they confided in him. He wanted to know their names, what they did for a living, and how they'd come together, such a culturally and politically diverse group. He wanted to know exactly how they generated such profits that they could pay what they had. He resolved that as soon as he got to Hokkaido, his destination for this fourth rendezvous, he was going to press them to reveal more to him.

As he settled back in the taxi for the long ride from Narita Airport to Haneda Airport on the other side of Tokyo, Paul Stanley had an unnerving thought.

Maybe I'm better off not knowing what the hell these guys are up to.

As the cab gathered speed heading out of the Narita terminal area, he put this thought behind him.

No. You've already done too much on their behalf. Everything they've asked you to do; the sales to Vietnam, the missile technology to Japan, you've done it. You're a part of them and you can't stay in the Army forever. Find out as much as you can and see if you can be a part of it after you retire. You've gone this far for them, why stop now?

Chapter Five

Cleve Spires savored his first three days of freedom. He began and ended each with long walks to nowhere in particular with absolutely no purpose whatsoever. It didn't matter that the temperatures in Cleveland during this time of the year discouraged most other human life forms from outdoor activity. It was the pointlessness and purposelessness that he was enjoying. He was free now to go wherever he chose, whenever he wanted to go there.

However, three days was about as long as he could remain in this kind of free-limbo. His parents long ago had infused him with a work ethic that his military years had reinforced. He needed a job, a reason for being. It wasn't the size of what he might accomplish that was important to him. He merely wanted to feel like he was accomplishing something. He'd trained as a barber and he thought he'd give that his best shot.

The sign on the window read, "Speaks Barber Shop" so Cleve assumed Alonzo Speaks was still cutting hair here. This was where his father had gotten his haircut and where, as a boy, his father had brought him. Grayer and heavier than Spires remembered him, he still recognized the old barber as soon as he saw him. The recognition was not mutual. Speaks looked up when Cleve entered the shop but then went back to tinkering with some of his tools on the counter behind his chair. Cleve sat down in Alonzo's empty barber's chair and Speaks turned around to take care of his next customer.

"How are you Alonzo?"

"Do I know you, Mister?"

"Cleve Spires. It's been a long time."

The old man reached around and removed the sheet he had just placed over him.

"I think you need to find another place to get your haircut." His tone was flat and final and told Spires immediately there was no room for negotiation, no chance of the old man reconsidering. It was as if he'd been planning for years what he would say to Spires if he ever were to show up here.

The younger barber cutting hair in the next chair started to say something but the old man shot back, "Stay out of this Freddie. It's none of your concern."

Spires got up to leave and the old man unloaded both barrels on him.

“You gonna' walk out of here just like you walked out on your old man…”

Spires felt his fists clinch.

“You’re out of jail and your mother’s taken you back. But your father…”

Whatever the old man said after that Spires didn’t hear. The shop’s door closed behind him blocking any further insult. He was half a block from the shop when he heard someone behind him call out, "Sergeant Major Spires."

Hearing his name with his former rank in front of it shot a wave of further humiliation through him. He turned around to see the younger barber behind him.

"It's not Sergeant Major anymore.” It's...it's just Cleve."

"Sergeant Major," the young barber persisted, "my father doesn't understand. He wasn’t in the Army. He’s never served, but I did. I was in the 82d Airborne Division. I was at Fort Bragg when they sent you…" his voice trailed off.

Spires began to walk away.

“Lots of folks at Bragg said you got screwed. They said it was racial; that the Army wasn’t ready for a black Command Sergeant Major of the Army…”

Spires didn’t want to hear any of this. There was no point to it now. He kept walking away from Alonzo Speaks’ son.

“I'm sorry my father made such a big deal out of a haircut."

Spires didn’t look back. He didn’t say anything. He merely raised his arm and waved his hand. He meant it as a signal that it was OK; he meant it as a signal that he didn’t want to hear anymore about Fort Bragg, the Army, his father or the old barber's narrow-mindedness. He walked a couple of blocks and ducked into a corner restaurant, bought a *Cleveland Plain Dealer* and looked through the classifieds.

There might be something to the old adage that bad things happen in threes because he was rejected for two more jobs before the end of the afternoon. He was turned down for a position as a janitor and as a stockroom attendant because both applications had asked if he'd had any felony convictions. He'd answered honestly. Late that afternoon as he rode the bus toward home a mix of anger and self-doubt shaped his mood. Suddenly the crowded bus made him claustrophobic. He got off at the next stop and the walk helped to clear his mind. The anger subsided but the self-doubt nagged at him. The good thing was that he knew it. He didn't want to go home until he'd talked himself completely down from the psychological ledge he was perched on.

Ahead of him he saw a sign that read, "Blue Note Bar and Grill". He decided maybe a cold beer would help. It was a weeknight and it was early, but the Blue Note still had a pretty good crowd of about twenty people inside, most sitting at tables or booths. He took a seat at the bar.

"What can I get you?"

Her nametag read, "Wanda". Her eyes were as blue-green as the sea and he fell right into them. It took him a moment to answer her and when he did he was surprised by how pleasant his voice was considering what he'd gone through that day and the state of mind he'd brought in here with him.

"A beer would be great."

"OK, did you have a favorite or do you just want to trust me on this?" she asked with a smile.

Politely he returned the smile and said, "I'll trust you."

"Great, I've got a draft here that I think you'll like. I'll be right back."

As she walked away to the beer taps at the end of the bar he caught a whiff of her perfume. It was wonderful and unlike anything he could ever remember smelling. Then she was back with his beer and, to his surprise, more conversation.

"I haven't seen you in here before. Are you new in town?"

He hesitated to answer, afraid of where the conversation would go. His answer was a guarded, "Yes." He took a drink of beer and as he sat the glass down she asked him another question.

"Well, what do you think so far?"

"About the beer or about Cleveland?"

She laughed and smiled at him and said, "Both."

He liked her easiness but he continued to play it close to the vest.

"The beer's good and Cleveland's OK."

She broke away from him long enough to fill an order for a waitress but once that was done she came back to him.

"Where are you from?"

"Cleveland, born and raised, but I left a long time ago. I came back to visit my mother."

"That's nice. I was born and raised here, but, except for a couple of vacations, I've been right here---never left." Cleve nodded and she added, "Well, I bet you see a lot of change if you haven't been here for a while."

Having a conversation with an attractive woman was something that he hadn't done in a long time and he was tired of answering questions. Yet he wanted her to stay and talk to him. He decided to try asking questions rather than answering them.

"How long have you been working here?"

"I bought this place about a year ago. Decided I wasn't cut out to be the reclusive widow for the rest of my life. It's been good for me, doesn't take a lot of training to run a bar, just some common sense. I keep busy, get to meet people, and have some purpose to my life. Believe it or not, this place even manages to turn a little profit each month."

"Sorry about your husband."

Immediately she liked that he was considerate and had listened to what she had said. "Thanks. He was a good man. At least he didn't suffer---a cerebral hemorrhage. One minute he's fine and the next he's gone." Then she asked, "How about you? Your family here in Cleveland with you?"

He didn't want to answer this, but it was his turn and he'd have to answer if he wanted her to stay and talk to him. "No, other than my mother, I've no family," he told a half-lie, half-truth.

Then Wanda asked the question that cut right to the heart of the matter.

"Well you know what I do for a living. What do you do?"

I could just end this right now. 'Well I don't have a job. You see I used to be a Command Sergeant Major in the Army, but I got put in jail for ten years for murder and smuggling. Now I'm a retired Private, ex-con, out-of-work barber. Wanna' go steady?'

He actually surprised himself with what came out.

"Right now I don't have a job. I'd like to stay here in Cleveland for a while. It's been a long time since I've seen my mother, she's getting up there in years, and since I don't have anywhere else I have to be, Cleveland just kind of fits. Don't suppose you have a job here..."

To his surprise and perhaps to hers as well, she didn't hesitate, "Well, since you asked, I need a jack-of-all trades kind of a guy around here. I need someone who can clear a table and reset it, change a keg of draft which means hauling it up from the basement and hooking it up; maybe tending bar occasionally or helping out in the kitchen if we get real busy. Oh yeah, I almost forgot, I'd need you to stick around after we close and help me clean this place up for the next day's business. I can't pay much more than minimum wage, but I'll give you 50% of any bar tips I get in an evening which means you get about $20.00 a night from that. I can only provide about 30 hours or so a week. Got to keep you part-time so I don't have to pay all the stuff the government makes me pay a full-time employee. I'm the only full-time person on the payroll. If part-time's OK, I sure could use you. You don't look or act like a guy that's afraid of a little hard work. Damn, you know I just offered you a job and we don't even know one another's names. I'm Wanda---Wanda Cheevers. So how about it; you want to work here, just until you get something better?"

He hid his surprise well.

"My name is Cleve Spires and when do I start?" It wasn't leading soldiers. It wasn't cutting hair. It was, however, work and he felt like he should be honest and up front with her now rather than later. "Wanda, before you answer the 'when do I start' question, you should know..."

She cut him off in mid sentence by holding up her hand. "You're not a serial killer are you?" They laughed.

"No,"

"Well then, listen Cleve, I got an instinct about people. It never fails me. I think I can trust you to do a good day's work here at the Blue Note. I think I can trust you behind this bar with the cash drawer open. I think I can trust you to be courteous to our customers and polite to the others who work here. I'll trust that instinct."

"Thanks." He searched for more to say but was at a loss for words.

Wanda replied, "No thanks are necessary. Can you start now?"

He nodded, and then added, "This may sound silly, but I need to call my mother and let her know where I am." He waited for her to laugh. She didn't. "She's been having dinner ready about this time each night and she's expecting me. She'll be worried if I'm not there."

Wanda looked softly at him and said, "Cleve Spires that's one of the sweetest thing I've heard a grown man say in a long time. The phone is back in the kitchen on the wall just as you go through the double doors. There's an apron back there too. Make your call, grab an apron, and I'll show you around the place before it gets too busy."

It was 2:30 AM before Cleve Spires got home. He was tired but he felt better than he had felt in a long time. His world was beginning to rise from the ashes. He was home, free and now had found work. As he walked into his dark bedroom and over to the window to pull the blind before undressing for bed he looked outside at the snow that had begun to fall hard now. He saw a white Cavalier pull from the curb at the end of the block and drive away, passing in front of the house. It struck him as odd. There was no other traffic on the street at this time of night. The sight of it jogged a faint memory that a car like this had pulled in behind the bus this afternoon as he'd gotten off. Before he could give it too much more thought, a yawn overtook him. He was tired as he swung his legs onto the bed. In a moment he was sound asleep.

As Tetsu Agaki pulled the rental car away from the curb, he began to dread the call he needed to make. Today was the day he was to call Driscoll.

He got the usual terse, "Hello."

"Driscoll-san, this is Agaki."

"Where are you? Where's Spires?"

"Relax. There is little to report. I think he is trying to find work here in Cleveland, but he seems to be having trouble. Today he stopped at a school and a department store. He has just spent the night in a bar. He was there for hours. He continues to live with his mother. I do not know what his plans are and I do not feel comfortable making a prediction on what he will do at this point. I am sorry. What would you like for me to do?"

"Listen to me you little shit, if I find out your playing me for a fool---if I find out this son of a bitch has gone back to Mama and...

A smile spread across Agaki's face. He interrupted, "Driscoll-san, I will leave Cleveland today. It is your business. If you are happy with what I have told you, then I am satisfied as well. I am but your agent serving at your pleasure." There was a pause. Agaki delighted in Driscoll's predicament.

"All right you little prick, you got me over a barrel and you know it. I'm giving you another week, that's seven days from today, to get close to this guy and find out what he's going to do. Call me here one week from tonight, sooner if he makes a move. You'd better have it right, Agaki."

"I understand."

The smile broadened as he hung up the phone and realized that he'd just negotiated another $35,000 worth of work.

Agaki figured he could sleep until 7:00 or so. It was now 3:30 AM. He could get three hours of sleep anyway before he needed to pick Spires' trail back up again.

Getting undressed for bed, he had another thought.

Should I change rental cars? Perhaps tomorrow or the next day it would be a good idea. Not today, I'm too tired now.

Agaki went to bed.

Ida Spires hadn't waited up for her son. When Cleve phoned her from the Blue Note, he'd forewarned her he would be late. But the next morning, at breakfast, she wanted details. He told her about his two rejections before stopping at the Blue Note and she pitied him. How could the good Lord let a man like her son languish like this? She'd spoken with a minister years ago, when Cleve had first gone to prison, and he'd told her to trust in the Lord; that he has a plan. She'd bought that then because she had little choice but to believe. Now he was with her again and she wanted to believe in something less fatalistic. Ida Spires knew where the Blue Note Bar was. She'd passed by it many times, but she vowed she was going to stop in there someday to meet this woman, Wanda Cheevers, who had given her son back a small part of his dignity. Ida Spires felt she owed her a fair debt.

Chapter Six

It was just after midnight when Paul Stanley finally settled into his room at the Kilomanjaro Resort on Hokkaido, Japan's northernmost island. The trip had taken just over twenty-four hours. Add to this the time change between Japan and Honolulu and his body didn't know whether it was coming or going. He'd taken a brochure written in English from the front desk at check-in. Slumped on the edge of the bed, he quickly looked through it. Kilomanjaro's main attractions were its superb baths fed by natural hot springs, but the place was also close to several ski areas and that's when the oddity of the place struck him. Even at this late hour there should have been people up and about, but he'd seen no one except the clerk at the front desk. He wasn't about to complain, however. What he needed was sleep and the quiet would only help in that regard. The desk clerk had given him a package with a note attached to it. Breakfast was at 7:30 AM and he would be the first briefer tomorrow starting at 9:00 A.M.

He awoke to a spectacular sunrise, showered, shaved, dressed and left his room promptly at 7:30 A.M. looking for some breakfast. It was not until he passed through the lobby and turned down the corridor leading to the restaurant that he saw signs of other life. Seito Yamamoto greeted him at the restaurant's door, "General Stanley, you look well. Welcome to Hokkaido."

"Yamamoto-san, it's good to see you again. What have you done; leased the entire hotel?"

Stanley thought he'd made a trivial joke.

"The resort belongs completely to us for the next three days. There is a small housekeeping and kitchen staff that is here to tend to our needs. I hope you find everything to your liking."

"I am sure I will."

Small talk didn't last very long. Yamamoto took him by the arm and eased him into the restaurant's dining room. To the others Yamamoto said, "We are all here now if we could find seats we'll get breakfast started." He turned to Stanley, "General Stanley, your place is here," motioning for him to take a seat between the associates from North Korea and China. They didn't introduce themselves so neither did Stanley although he knew they knew who he was. It was awkward, the same awkwardness he'd felt in previous meetings, the same awkwardness that fueled his frustration with them. *Why the hell shouldn't I know who these guys are?* For now, however, he just kept his mouth shut and his ears open as he'd done in the past.

English was the common language among them and they all spoke it quite well. While breakfast was served he overheard some of them discussing the political climates in their countries. This was very different. He'd never heard them speak openly about their countries, their governments or their politics. As they began to eat, the associate from North Korea asked him, "General Stanley, what do you think my country is doing with the crude oil your government has recently given us?"

Stanley took the politically correct approach, "I hope you are distilling most of it into fuel oil for heating and cooking."

The North Korean shook his head, "General Stanley, is that what you really think?"

Stanley was on the spot now. He knew what the hell the North Koreans were doing with that fuel oil. He wondered how direct he should be, but then thought, *"What the hell, you're going to have to be direct with them at some point during this meeting. Might just as well get on with it here and now.* He answered the North Korean with a concise, "No," in return for which he got a broad smile. Then Stanley added, "You're refining it into gas, diesel and jet fuel to keep your military running."

"You are correct, General. While our tanks still run and our jets still fly, many of my countrymen starve and freeze. The idiot son of our now-dead-but-equally insane Dear Leader is to blame."

Stanley put down his knife and fork, looked at his North Korean colleague and said, "If you were to say those things in Pyongyang…"

"I would be publicly executed." The rest of the room had fallen silent and was eavesdropping on their conversation. "General Stanley the world has no idea what kind of a man rules North Korea today. He is a sexual deviant who dotes on young girls---not yet even women---only 13 or 14 years old. He smuggles them in using our Navy's ships and our Air Force's planes. The fuel it takes for these missions to satisfy his lust could be used to heat thousands of homes and cook food to feed tens of thousands of people. But it will not be long before Kim Jong Il is but a bad memory and there will be enough fuel for all people of a unified Korean to heat, cook and defend themselves."

Stanley looked around the room. He saw the associate from South Korea nodding and smiling.

"But how…?"

Seito Yamamoto stood up. "Gentlemen, we must step back a moment from such serious discussion or we will ruin General Stanley's breakfast." He paused briefly while everyone except Paul Stanley enjoyed a chuckle. Yamamoto turned and focused on Stanley who was still sitting stone-faced. Stanley was just about to tell them he was tired of being the butt of their jokes, the only one in the room who didn't know what was so fucking funny when Yamamoto spoke, his tone now very serious. "Paul, we intend to fully integrate you into our *association* over the next several days. You will become only the ninth person to know what it is we are trying to accomplish. What is about to happen is radical yet simple. It may at first hurt certain of our countries but the hurt will be short-lived. What we will do will impact your country. I cannot predict how severely. I have rarely been able to predict your country's reaction to world events."

Stanley seized on two words, "*world events*" and his mind raced.

Yamamoto continued with even greater solemnity, "Stanley-san, just by hearing the frankness of our discussion here at breakfast, you have crossed a line this morning. You are now on that side of the line where we must demand your absolute loyalty. You must never discuss what you will learn in this meeting with anyone who is not in this room. You must never so much as allude to our intentions with anyone outside of this group. To do so would make you a traitor to this brotherhood, which deeply values your membership and your contributions. Our plans depend on the element of surprise. If we lose that advantage, what we have worked so hard for over more years than you know will fail." He paused. All eyes were on Stanley. "Do you understand the line you have crossed and can we expect your absolute loyalty?"

Stanley's thoughts came so fast he wasn't able to sort them out. He tried to buy some time, "Yamamoto-san, I…I…"

Yamamoto's mood changed now from solemn to demanding. "Stanley-san, the question requires a simple "yes" or "no" answer."

For them it was that simple and he knew that they couldn't care less why it wasn't equally as simple for him. "*World events*" kept flashing in and out of his mind.

"General Stanley…"

He had to decide one way or the other and it had to be now. His mind flashed back to his desperate situation ten years ago. This group had bailed him out and made him a millionaire. Stanley put his hands on the table palms down, scanned around the room at his colleagues and then locked his eyes on Yamamoto and answered, "Yes."

Chapter Seven

Tetsu Agaki had it figured out. Spires was working at a bar named the Blue Note in Cleveland from 8:00 PM until 2:00 AM. He lived with his mother and he took the bus to work and walked home. For three nights he'd observed this routine as he followed Spires at a discrete distance. Unlike the nights, Spires' days didn't seem to have hit a routine yet, but there was nothing extraordinary going on there that made Agaki believe he was planning to go anywhere or do anything that would be of thc slightest interest to Driscoll. Today Spires went to a gym. That was a first. He was inside for about three hours and then he'd gone home. Agaki left him there, gone to his hotel for a nap and then, just to test his theory on Spires' nighttime routine, he headed for the bus stop he'd seen Spires get off at on the three previous nights.

At 7:30 PM he pulled along the curb about 100 yards short of the bus stop Spires got off at on his way to work. His mind was not on following his mark. Instead, he was hatching a plan to escape to a warmer climate for a few days when he happened to glance in the passenger side rearview mirror just as Cleve Spires was about to walk past the car. Agaki remained calm. His wasn't the only car parked along the street. As long as he didn't panic and draw some kind of attention to himself he'd be fine. He reached down and picked up a newspaper from the passenger seat and casually spread it open in front of him.

Spires' attention focused momentarily on the car. When Agaki reached for the paper his foot depressed the brake pedal enough to make the car's stop lights blink at Spires, but that attention was short-lived. What had Spires's attention now was the police cruiser he could see ahead of him that was parked behind Wanda's car in front of the Blue Note.

For a Thursday night the place was busy. All but three of the tables in the dining room were occupied and there were half a dozen patrons sitting at the bar. Wanda was there chatting up a cop.

"Cleve, come here a minute. There's someone I want you to meet."

He had no choice. He steered toward them.

"Officer Jess Whitehall meet Cleve Spires."

Whitehall extended his hand, "Pleased to meet you."

Spires took his hand. "You, too."

Wanda told Whitehall about Spires returning to Cleveland and how lucky she was to have found him before he took some other job. She told Cleve, "Jess patrols the neighborhood. If we ever need the police, he's probably the one who'd show up."

"Well, nice to meet you." Spires turned and headed for the kitchen doors.

Whitehall took his to-go meal from the bar and said goodbye while Wanda wondered what the hell was the matter with Cleve. She had introduced him to friends on several other occasions and he'd impressed her with his social manners. Whitehall was a friend and the cold shoulder Cleve had given him didn't sit well with her. She decided she'd ask him about it after they'd closed.

He sensed some irritation from Wanda, it didn't surprise him and he knew what he'd done to cause it. He stayed away from her most of the evening while he thought about what he needed to do to set things right. He decided he had to tell her what he'd started to tell her the night he'd taken the job, but he worried that she wouldn't understand.

At midnight Wanda locked the front door behind the last customer. The kitchen had closed an hour earlier so the cook and Cleve just about had it clean. Cleve had gone downstairs to get a new keg of draft beer for the bar. The Blue Note's back door opened into the kitchen from a rear service alley. The cook had just hauled out some trash to the dumpster and when he returned he closed that back door but didn't lock it. He was preoccupied stacking dishes and didn't hear either of the two men who'd just entered through that unlocked door as they approached him. The baseball bat caught the cook just above the left ear and knocked him unconscious. In the basement, Cleve heard the thump in the kitchen above him as the cook hit the floor and wondered what had happened.

The two were hyped up on some kind of drug and were looking for money and anything else they might come across. They were lucid enough to know that what they wanted wouldn't be found in the kitchen so they rushed through the kitchen doors and found Wanda behind the bar. The larger of the two approached her, while the other dashed into the dining room.

"No one in here. She's the only one."

The big one slammed the bat on the top of the bar and the crack rang out like a shot. Cleve, who had made his way to the top of the basement steps, heard the bat's crack and he now became very cautious. He eased the basement door open slightly.

"Well, baby, just so you know the cook's asleep on the kitchen floor for awhile," he tapped the thick end of the bat in the palm of his hand. "So I guess it's just you, me and my friend. Why don't I have him wait in the kitchen while you and I---," he motioned for his friend to go in the back and leave them alone. The smaller man obediently headed for the kitchen.

"I'll call you when she's through," he laughed. "You have a choice baby. You can take your clothes off or I'll rip them off, either way suits me just fine." He kept tapping the bat in his hand.

Her tormentor's back was to Spires. He looked for weapons but other than the bat there were none in sight and Spires watched him lay that on the bar as he began to loosen his belt.

Wanda was trapped. Her attacker stood between her and the only way into or out of the area behind the bar. She thought of trying to jump over the bar but he was too close to her. She couldn't possibly move fast enough to avoid his grasp. She got ready to resist him and he could sense a struggle ahead of him. He would have preferred her compliance but if that was how she wanted it that was OK, too.

"Now come on baby, it doesn't have to be this way. You can cooperate---."

Wanda's eyes shot past him as she saw Cleve step through the basement door about twenty feet behind the man. The man turned to find Cleve walking toward him.

"Where the fuck did you come from? Calvin, get in here," he hollered for his accomplice in the kitchen and grabbed the bat off the bar.

"The cook's in there with his head bashed in. You're next."

The second man came through the kitchen doors just in time to see his partner take two quick steps toward Spires and swing the bat at his head. Cleve ducked and the bat swished harmlessly past him. The momentum of the attacker's swing carried his upper body around so that his back was now exposed to Spires. Cleve had a split second to take advantage of his target and he used it well. He delivered a lightening blow with his balled fist to the soft right side of the assailant's lower back. The blow was so forceful and the energy from it was pinpointed so well that the attacker's lungs were immediately voided of air. When he tried to breathe he found he was completely unable to either inhale or exhale. Panic overtook him, but he could do nothing about it except fall to his knees and then onto his face gasping for air. The short, ineffective gasps weren't giving him what he needed and a deeper panic began to set in. The attacker thought he was going to suffocate as if someone had placed a plastic bag over his head. The gasps became shorter and his body writhed as if he were in some poison induced death-spasm.

Wanda took all of this in. For a moment she had been so frightened and then, in a matter of just a few seconds, she was safe; Cleve was safe. That roller coaster of emotion produced a kind of involuntary paralysis.

"Wanda, call 911."

She didn't move; she didn't acknowledge his command. Cleve ignored the second man for a moment who, when he saw how easily Spires had taken care of his partner, was thinking that maybe his best course of action was to haul ass.

"Wanda it's all right. He's not going to get up for a while. Call 911." He put a hand on each shoulder and stooped down to look her directly in the eye. "It's OK. Call 911."

He let go of her as she reached for the telephone behind the bar. Spires turned to take care of the second intruder but after two steps in his direction the intruder fled into the kitchen, past the cook who was trying to get to his feet, and out the back door. Cleve turned to Wanda who was on the phone talking to a 911 operator. "I'm going to check on Cookie. Tell them to send an ambulance."

On his way into the kitchen he grabbed the downed assailant by the coat collar and dragged him with him. He was slowly getting his breath back, only now Spires had the bat. "Don't fight me, or I'll wear this thing out on you and you better hope you didn't hurt anybody back here." He dragged him through the swinging kitchen doors and he could hear the assailant's head hit them none too softly.

In the kitchen the cook was up and staggering around. He had a bloody cut on his head but he was rapidly getting his wits back about him. Cleve found a dishtowel and pressed it into the wound and then wrapped a second one around the cook's head to hold the first towel in place.

Wanda's tormentor was coming to. Spires asked, "Can you tie this guy up, Cookie?"

Somewhat groggily the cook replied, "Yeah, sure." He found some twine on a shelf just behind him. "Is this the son-of-a-bitch that hit me?"

"It is."

The cook grabbed the twine off of the shelf. His recovery from the bash on his head was now progressing at a record pace. Cleve could hear the captured intruder yell as Cookie cinched him up tight, and tighter still, while Spires checked the alley for the one that got away.

By now they could hear the sirens and so could Tetsu Agaki. He'd seen a man emerge from the alley next to the Blue Note only moments earlier and run down the street. Now a police cruiser sped by him and came skidding to a stop in front of the Blue Note. He watched one of them approach the front door while the other went down the same alley he seen the man come from just minutes earlier. Both cops had their guns drawn. He could see the officer at the front door holster his weapon and go in through the just-opened front door. What the hell was going on? He wanted to get out of his car to investigate but decided against that. He'd just watch for now. Next came an ambulance. For thirty minutes he couldn't see anything else happening. Then a man with a bandage around his head was led out to the ambulance, which soon left, but without lights and siren. Then the two cops came out the bar's front door with a third man in handcuffs. They put him in the back seat of the patrol car and drove away. Agaki watched. At one point his hand was on the door handle. He toyed briefly with the idea of getting out and nosing around, but thought the better of it. Deductively he reasoned that since he hadn't seen Spires come out, he had to still be in the bar. Agaki trusted his logic; he watched and waited.

Cleve and Wanda sat down at a table, each with a cup of coffee. "Wanda, are you all right?"

"Yes, I'm fine now, thanks to you. Nothing like that has ever happened to me before and I hope it never happens again."

A silence fell between them. There was something she wanted to ask and there was something he wanted to say. It was a matter of who got up the gumption to go first.

"Cleve, where in the world did you learn to fight like that? What you did tonight wasn't just luck. You've had some training haven't you?"

He nodded and took a sip of his coffee. "Remember the night you hired me, I wanted to tell you something about me and you said it wasn't necessary?"

She nodded.

"Well now it's necessary. So here goes..."

For the next thirty minutes he told her everything; about his Army career, about his family, about his ten years at Leavenworth and how he came to be here, at the Blue Note, with her tonight. At some point in his storytelling she had started to cry.

"So that's why you were less than friendly with Jess Whitehall?"

He was ashamed of the way he'd acted. "Yeah, I suppose so. I'm not comfortable around police. The last ten years are all too fresh in my memory."

"I understand."

"Wanda, I know how it works. You know all that information Whitehall took from us tonight?" She nodded. "Well, tomorrow he or someone from the police department will be back to see you. They're going to tell you what kind of guy you've got working for you. I'm sorry..."

She interrupted him at that point, "Cleve, don't you be sorry about anything. You don't need to be. I do know what kind of a man I've got working for me and I only hope I can keep you around."

He felt good about what she'd just said. He liked being around her too.

"Thanks, Wanda. It's getting late. I'd better get on home."

"Well tonight I'm driving you home." He started to object but she cut him off, "And I won't take 'no' for an answer."

Agaki saw the bar's front door open and he slid down in the seat low enough to where he didn't think they could see he was in the car but not so low that he couldn't observe them. Down the street Cleve could see exhaust coming from the only car on the street besides Wanda's. Just then Wanda asked him something. He refocused his attention back on her as he opened the passenger-side door and slid into the car.

Agaki watched Cleve get in and the woman drive away in the direction of Spire's house but he couldn't be sure that was where they were going. The woman was a new addition to the routine so he followed them. Following at this time of night was risky because it was basically their two cars on the road. He hung way back. After a few short blocks he was sure they were headed to Spires' house. But who was the woman? What's her connection to Spires? He continued to follow.

Wanda pulled to a stop in front of Ida Spires' house. Cleve looked over at her, "Are you sure you're OK?"

"I'm fine Cleve. I got you home OK didn't I?"

"That you did."

She got serious as she turned to him, "Cleve, I owe you for tonight. I don't know what might have happened if you hadn't been there. Hiring you was one of the best things I've ever done. Want to know why?"

"Because I kicked that guy's butt tonight."

She laughed, "That---and because I've come to like your company very much."

Agaki, through binoculars, could see the woman lean over as if to kiss Spires. *So that's it. He's found himself a woman. My job is done.* He pulled out a notebook from his pocket and began to make some notes.

Wanda's kiss was the sweetest thing that had happened to him in years, but it surprised him and, at first, he only received her kiss. After a few seconds, however, the emotion of the moment drew him in and he returned it. As romantic kisses last it wasn't a record-setter, but it rekindled in both of them, for the brief moments that it lasted, a closeness that had been missing in both of their lives. When it was over he said to her, "See you tomorrow."

"You bet you will, hero. Count on it."

He got out of the car and headed up the walk. Behind him he could hear the crunch of her tires on the snow along the curb as she pulled away. He really felt good about his life, more in control of it than he'd been in years.

Chapter Eight

Paul Stanley couldn't finish his breakfast. He'd waited ten years to find out what these guys were all about. Now, on the verge of discovery, at Yamamoto's insistence, the conversation around the breakfast table had reverted to small talk. By 9:00 AM, a thirty-minute eternity for Paul Stanley, his imagination was running away with him. Whatever these guys were, they weren't ordinary businessmen. Yamamoto finally tapped the edge of his water glass and the room fell silent. "General Stanley, I believe you are the first briefer. You have our complete attention."

His presentation was a review of old news. When he'd been summoned here, there were no specific instructions on what they wanted to hear. There was little new to report, some old beat up trucks to the Philippines was about it and he didn't want to start out with that. Instead he chose what he considered to be his most recent and biggest success. "Very well, Yamamoto-san. I will begin with Vietnam."

His presentation was low tech. He laid his first slide on the overhead projector, a copy of the front page of the *Washington Post,* dated January 9th, of the previous year. The headline read, "Sale to Vietnam Approved". "This was the hardest thing we've done to date. Despite the trouble the press gave us, the Senate Armed Services Committee unanimously approved this sale."

The associate from Vietnam stood and introduced himself. "General Stanley, I am Nguyen Van Thuy…"

Yamamoto interrupted. "Mr. Thuy is Vietnam's Minister of Culture." Stanley now knew one other of this group by name besides Seito Yamamoto. Thuy's ministerial title wasn't lost on Stanley either.

Thuy continued, "I know how difficult this must have been for you given the past troubles between our countries. I congratulate you General Stanley." Thuy bowed deeply in the Eastern tradition. When he stood back up straight he smiled and asked, "Can you to do it again?"

Every eye in the room shifted to Stanley. He glanced at the clock in the back of the room, 9:01AM. He'd been briefing less than a minute and already he was on the spot. The room was suddenly very warm. *Do it again! The press crucified us for selling them this shit.* Stanley scanned the room. These guys wanted answers. Intuitively he was sure "no" was a wrong answer with this group, but if he said "yes" and failed, the consequences could be bleak. There was a deafening silence while he tried to formulate an answer.

Yamamoto pressed him. "Paul, this is an important question for us. Will this sale be approved? We have an operation coming up, Operation Light Switch, and there is some concern that our reserves of ammunition are not sufficient to sustain our initial successes."

Yamamoto's comments didn't help Stanley. He was trying to put the puzzle together but he didn't have anywhere near enough pieces.

Operation Light Switch? ...Sustain initial successes?... What the hell are these guys up to?

"Paul, I can see the wheels in your mind turning. There is much that you don't know, but we need you to concentrate now on the question. Will a second installment of the aircraft package have any chance of approval?"

Yamamoto's voice had an edge in it.

They wanted an answer from him and they wanted it now. An idea of outlandish proportion popped into his head. There was no time to think it through; he'd have to flesh it out as he proposed it to them.

"Do it again? A sale of exactly the same things in the same quantity?" Heads nodded around the room. "It won't be easy, but Congress has been in a selling mood. May I propose something to you that may sound crazy at first, but give it some consideration before you discount it."

Reassuringly Yamamoto said, "We consider you our expert on such matters. What is your suggestion?"

Stanley quipped, "There is no such thing as an "expert" when it comes to predicting what Congress will do."

He meant that as a joke, but his humor was lost on them. He wished they'd lighten up, but his experience with most Asians was that when they are focused on something there is little room for humor. Answers needed to be direct and on point.

He continued, "If we can show Congress that there is something in it for them, something that justifies their vote, then anything is possible." There were smiles all around. "For example, this aircraft package to Vietnam was approved because Admiral McKeever told Congress that this would give Vietnam an offensive air capability that counterbalances China's growing air power. Congress took this to mean the US could reduce its Air Force and Naval presence in the region. They could tell the voters back home that they *made* money by selling to Vietnam and *saved* money by reducing the numbers of US military stationed in the region."

They could be impatient as well as humorless and, impatiently, Yamamoto prodded him, "So what is it you are proposing?"

"Mr. Thuy's government requests more aircraft repair parts and ammunition. Tell Congress that your training program has increased requirements for these things. When the story breaks in the news---and the media will find out---China should file a loud protest with the U.S. over the political ramifications of the sale. However, China will suggest an alternative to cancellation. China will not oppose the sale to Vietnam if the U.S. will duplicate the sale of Howitzers and ammunition it made to China a year and a half ago. China can use the same rationale for the sale ---they used it up during training."

The associate from China asked, "If the sale to Vietnam was difficult, why would a simultaneous sale to both countries have a chance of success? Your free press will surely criticize one sale to say nothing of two."

"You are absolutely right. Backlash in the press is inevitable. Congress will watch what the press says but again it comes back to what's in it for them." It was his turn to ask a question. "Can China and Vietnam step up rhetoric about the Spratley Islands?"

Now they were silent. Thuy looked at his colleague from China who asked, "Why would we do that General Stanley?"

"If the oil cartels think that either China or Vietnam is going to make a play for the Spratleys they won't like it." He watched for their reaction to his bluntness. There was none so he continued. "They'll come running to Congress to do something. But Congress can't do anything---except sell you what you want. Why should they do that? Because selling guns, bullets and airplanes to each of you will keep your forces balanced. Congress can tell the oil cartel, 'See what we did for you, we armed China and Vietnam so they can fight one another.' Then while the two of you are wearing each other out, the oil cartel will go to Brunei, Malaysia, the Philippines, Taiwan or some combination of these countries and settle a deal to drill for oil in the Spratley Islands."

Again he watched as his answer sank in. Then it struck him.

"But what they're not counting on is that the two of you will use what we sell to you in some collaboration, won't you? That's it isn't it? That's what this Operation Light Switch is. China and Vietnam will cooperate to take over the Spratley Islands?" Stanley thought he'd put two and two together. He expected some sign that he'd guessed right or wrong.

What he got was another question from Yamamoto, "Can we get this through your Congress in time to take delivery by the end of June?"

The question was impossible to answer with certainty. There would be nothing to deliver if Congress didn't approve the sale and Stanley told them so. Yamamoto shook his head. Annoyed he shot back, "Answer my question General. How long will your Congress take with its decision?"

Stanley wasn't accustomed to being handled in this way. He started to get angry, but checked it. Something big was at stake here. Paul Stanley didn't know exactly what it was yet, but whatever it was, it was making everyone a little edgy. "Routine sales take about sixty days to get approved. This one is not routine. It will take ninety to one hundred and twenty days. So the worst case is Congress doesn't decide until the end of May. If you can have your ships immediately available to load, you might make an end of June delivery date, but it will be close."

His Vietnamese colleague offered, "I shall have four ships waiting by April First. Do you want them on the west or east coast, General Stanley?"

"How can you be so sure...?"

Yamamoto interrupted him, "Paul, I will explain much of this to you later. For now, where would you like the ships?"

It was clear he was to answer questions, not ask them. He thought for a moment and then suggested, "Put four off the East Coast, near Sunny Point, North Carolina and four more off the West Coast near San Francisco. We can cut shipping and loading time in the US if we use both the East and West Coast ammo ports."

He glanced back at the clock, 9:20AM, twenty minutes since he'd begun and his first slide was the only one he'd gotten to so far. At this rate he would be here all day. He had at least thirty slides remaining in the stack next to the projector. He was sifting through them to find the first slide on the Filipino truck sale when a kitchen door opened and a young Japanese man in a white kitchen jacket entered and walked toward a steam table on the other side of the room. Yamamoto flew into a rage. He jumped up from his chair shouting in Japanese. Stanley couldn't understand a word of it but it was obvious Yamamoto was becoming angrier with each step he took toward the young man. The young man said something back. Facial expression and body language told Stanley the young man's remark must have been argumentative. Then the young man made a tragic error. Like a matador who turns his back on the bull, he turned his back on Yamamoto and collected a stack of dishes from the steam table.

What happened next, happened so quickly that even if Stanley had the presence of mind to warn the kid, it wouldn't have come in time. Yamamoto grabbed a kitchen knife from among some other implements laying on the steam table, raised it high over his head and then plunged it into the young man's back.

Stanley was speechless. The crash of the dishes to the floor was deafening and added to the confusion Stanley was watching from across the room. The young man was struggling, flailing his arms to get to the knife. Yamamoto wasn't through. As quickly as he plunged the knife in, he pulled it back out and wrapped one arm around the young man's chest, steadied him, and then used the free arm---the one wielding the knife---to cut the young man's throat from side to side. Blood was suddenly everywhere. A large pool of it had already accumulated on the tile floor as Yamamoto released his victim who fell forward splashing into a pool of his own blood. Stanley watched. The geyser of blood gushing from the young man's neck dwindled with each dying beat of his heart. Finally it stopped, but not before the circle of blood was at least ten feet wide.

Everyone in the room, except Stanley, sat impassively and merely watched this murder take place. Though he'd done nothing to stop it, Stanley's gut reaction was far from impassive. The problem was that he was gripped by the shock of what he'd witnessed and, for the moment, he was without any power to say or do anything. Yamamoto stood over the young man mumbling something and then turned to face the group. "Would you please excuse me? I must find the manager and have him take care of this mess."

The associate from South Korea, apparently the second-in-command behind Yamamoto said, "General Stanley, would you continue please? The schedule is quite full and we will need to move on while Yamamoto takes care of this."

Stanley couldn't just go on. The corpse was still twitching occasionally as the last bit of electro-chemical life drained from it. This was not a time for business as usual and Stanley told them so.

"Continue? Move on? Do you realize what just happened here? That was murder. How can you just sit there? What did that kid do anyhow? You just can't fucking kill someone and then go on like it didn't happen. Besides aren't you all a little concerned? You are witnesses and potential accomplices. What happens when one of the other workers here tells the police what happened? What happens when this kid doesn't go home to his family?"

Paul Stanley was afraid of what he'd just seen. It was murder, clear and simple, and his just being there made him a part of it. He hated them right now for involving him in something so grotesque. Any pretension he'd given them that he was somehow not quite their equal, that he was loyal to their fucking cause, whatever the fuck it was, was gone from his voice now. He'd scolded these bastards.

The South Korean stood up and looked at Stanley. "Perhaps General Stanley you will permit me to explain a few things to you."

"Explain a few things? How are you going to explain cold-blooded murder?"

More firmly this time the South Korean spoke, "Sit down General Stanley."

Stanley stared at him and momentarily defied him by remaining on his feet. The South Korean gestured for Stanley to sit. He did. His knees were shaky, a combination of shock and anger. Stanley couldn't look at them. He turned his head and stared out the window into the cold Hokkaido day.

"This man was given explicit instructions not to come into this room when we are in session. All of the staff here at the resort were personally briefed by Yamamoto about this."

Stanley swiveled his head around, "Jesus H. Christ, you don't cut somebody's throat just because they wander into a fucking meeting room."

"Did you understand what the young man said to Yamamoto?"

"No, but did it deserve the death sentence?"

"The man was insubordinate. He told Yamamoto not to be so serious. He bragged he was present when Fujiwara and the leaders of the *Yakuza* had met here. He told Yamamoto he'd been in the room when Fujiwara himself was speaking. He said he did not think any of us were more important than Fujiwara."

Yakuza---Fujiwara---Stanley knew of the *Yakuza. What does the Yakuza have to do with any of this?* It was a fair question, but before he could ask it the South Korean continued, "General Stanley, the young man made himself a risk to our *association* at a time when we are not willing to risk anything that could compromise our hard work. You have been with us for nearly ten years now. But as an *association*, the eight of us have been working together for thirty years."

The South Korean paused briefly to judge how much he should reveal, and then gestured by sweeping his hand around the conference table, "We were all graduate students together in the United States at UC, Berkley. In the beginning the only thing we had in common was that we were Asian, but as we got to know one another during our studies we found out that we had much, much more in common than the color of our skin. Our views on politics, government, right, wrong, freedom and subservience were very much the same and we also discovered that none of us very much liked the way our governments were running our countries. At some point very early in our studies we decided that we would do something about it. During the years of our studies we formulated our Utopia and then we made a pact that each of us would aim our lives---our ambitions---at making it happen. We have done all of this General Stanley and we intend to put our Utopia into place after Operation Light Switch moves us into control."

"'Utopia'! What the hell are you talking…"

The South Korean held up his hand. "In due time, Yamamoto will explain all to you. For now please understand that while it is unfortunate we had to kill this man, when you consider his death in the light of what we have labored to accomplish over the last thirty years, you must see his death is of little consequence. If this man found it so easy to break a simple rule about entry into this briefing room; if this man was so free to brag about the meeting he observed with Fujiwara; then do you not think he might talk openly about our meeting today? What are the consequences if someone then decides to investigate why a South Korean, a North Korean, a Chinese, a Vietnamese, a Filipino, a Malaysian, a Thai, a Japanese, and an American were meeting in seclusion on Hokkaido? General Stanley, you must have observed that we are a most unlikely confederation. A reporter seeing us together or a politician finding out that this group had met on Hokkaido, would certainly start to ask questions. We have too much at stake---you and I---all of us---to allow this man to live. If Yamamoto had not killed him, I would have." The others nodded their agreement.

The South Korean continued, "You do not need to worry about the other staff here at the resort telling anyone about this. They all work for Fujiwara and are well compensated by him. All know to keep quiet about happenings here, and all know the consequences if they discuss anything about what they see or hear at Kilomanjaro. As for the young man's family, they will be appropriately compensated for his loss."

Stanley asked, "What if the family doesn't accept *'appropriate compensation'*?" He spat the words at them, contemptuous of the idea that a family would simply settle on money for the murder of a son.

"General Stanley that would be a most unfortunate decision for them to make." The implication was clear. While he did not yet fully understand the scope of Operation Light Switch he had witnessed a graphic demonstration of how important it was to this group of men to keep it under wraps. Paul Stanley sat somber faced. He was in the beginning phase of coming to grips with what he'd seen. Yamamoto returned to the meeting room with four white-coated men who began cleaning up the murder scene. "Gentlemen, may I suggest we adjourn to the garden while this is cleaned up."

Stanley was the first one out of the door. It was cold despite a clear blue sky and a bright sun. Yamamoto came over to him immediately. "Paul, I am deeply sorry you had to see that but I assure you it was necessary."

"I know. The associate from South Korea..."

Yamamoto interrupted, "Lee Pak Son is South Korea's Minister of Foreign Trade."

"Mr. Son has explained to me the reasons for your actions." He couldn't bring himself quite yet to say he understood, but he was getting his legs back underneath him. Stanley was moving back to the more formal English, the more stilted words and correct pronunciation he used when talking to Asians who spoke English as a second language. He was in fact recovering from what he witnessed and he would soon rationalize the murder in his own mind as the only course of action the *association* could take.

Before moving off to talk with Mr. Son, Yamamoto asked, "Paul, have you taken the baths here at Kilomanjaro yet?"

"No, I arrived late last night and went directly to bed."

"In that case, I invite you to take them with me tonight after we dine. The mineral baths here are among the best in the world. Their mineral content and the temperature to which Mother Earth heats the water combine to make them therapeutically perfect."

"I look forward to joining you." In western tradition, Yamamoto extended his hand and Stanley shook it. When they returned to the meeting room in the restaurant area, there was no sign of what had happened there. The clean-up crew was very thorough as if they had practiced that sort of thing before.

Stanley resumed his briefing, which lasted the remainder of the morning. Throughout he was interrupted many times by questions. Before each associate asked a question for the first time, each told Stanley his name and the position he held in his country's government. All of the associates, except Yamamoto, were cabinet-level officers in their respective governments.

Over lunch Stanley pondered the questions asked of him during the morning session. All, except Yamamoto, pressed him on the details of the military capability brought by the arms sales Stanley had engineered. Yamamoto didn't ask a single question even though some of the technology sold to Japan was the most sophisticated weapons technology in the world. Stanley checked the urge to ask Yamamoto about his apparent lack of concern. He decided he'd wait and see if the afternoon's briefings didn't shed more light on Operation Light Switch.

At 1:00 PM the associate from China led off. "The Chief of Staff of the Army and Air Force are loyal to me. In turn they have delivered nearly all of their generals. However, both men are greedy for money and power and will bear watching after the revolution."

There it was for the first time out in the open. One of them had actually said it---*Revolution.* The word sent shock waves through Stanley. *A coup in China---My God, it's unbelievable.* Whatever he might have imagined they were up to paled in significance. This one word, *revolution,* and this one moment suddenly defined for him his value to them. Armed revolution was their agenda and over the years he'd been helping to arm them. Throughout the afternoon Stanley sat and listened as the associates from Vietnam, the Philippines, and Malaysia all laid out their plans for *coups d' etat* in each of their countries. They named names of men who would lead their Armies, Air Forces, Marines, Naval forces; they assessed who was loyal to their cause and who was not. Stanley knew some of the men they talked about; some of them he considered friends. In a question directed at no one in particular, he asked, "Do any of these people know I am one of you?"

The response was like a dentist drilling on a tooth that both the dentist and the patient thought was anesthetized. Stanley knew immediately he'd touched something very sensitive. The other associates looked at Yamamoto. Stanley's eyes shifted to him as well only to find that Yamamoto was already locked on to him with an icy stare. Yamamoto barked his response, "No, they do not and you will not talk with any of them about your involvement until after Operation Light Switch has moved to Phase II."

It was as if Yamamoto was the Pope and Stanley was an unruly schoolboy who'd just farted in the Sistine Chapel. Yamamoto stood and walked over until he was directly in front of Paul Stanley. His tone was more reasonable now but still firm. "Suffice it to say these men whose names have been revealed to you, know only that a *coup* is to take place in *their* country. They do not know anything about our plans for *coups* elsewhere. They do not know of the existence of this *association.* Their loyalty lies with the associate in this room. Later they will find out about our affiliation with one another---that's Phase II. You must be sure you do not betray the existence of the *association* as you deal with any of these men in the upcoming months."

Now was not the time for analysis or questions Stanley judged, but he tried to take everything that had just transpired and freeze-frame it in his memory. Each of these guys was playing a slight of hand game with the people who would actually do the fighting. They hadn't been totally honest with their co-conspirators and in the revolution-game that could be a deadly mistake. If their plan, as he knew it to this point, had a flaw, this might be it. Still now was not the time to point this out to them. For now he merely nodded and said, "I will be careful."

At 5:00 PM Yamamoto called the day's briefings to an end and dinner was announced for 6:30. Stanley excused himself indicating he wanted to freshen up before dinner but this was really the alone-time he was looking for. In the solitude of his hotel room, he sat on the edge of the bed, leaned forward and cradled his forehead in his hands and thought.

Each country represented here is planning a coup. But with the exception of these eight men---and now me---none of their accomplices know anything about the other coups. These guys are trying to take over Asia. Why? What the hell have I gotten myself into?

It astounded him that all of this had been kept so secret for so many years. So many people in each country were involved. It was inconceivable to him that no one had slipped in a drunken stupor or on the pillow of some mistress or in any other of a hundred ways that secrets have been compromised over the ages and some scrap of information given away that eventually led to discovery. Yet, here they were, on Hokkaido, with their secret apparently secure and in what Stanley judged to be the final stages of planning. *This will make the surprise at Pearl Harbor and the World Trade Center seem trivial.* He tried to think of an event in history that was similar to Operation Light Switch. He couldn't. In fact the more he thought about it the more he thought the comparison to Pearl Harbor or the terrorist attacks on 9/11 were poor ones. *These guys aren't attacking us. They won't fire a shot at the US. This will be just a series of civil wars. And we won't intervene---hell we can't intervene.*

As he thought one nagging question kept coming to him. He was still missing a key piece to the puzzle and without it he couldn't even begin to see the picture the completed puzzle would reveal. *Why? Why are they doing this?* He couldn't begin to guess. By 6:00PM, he'd thought himself into a world-class headache. He took two aspirin and lay down on the bed. *What the hell, let 'em revolt. Who the hell cares?* He closed his eyes, but couldn't sleep.

Chapter Nine

The excitement at the Blue Note made him two hours later than normal. If he woke Ida, she'd notice the time and want to know what made him so late. He was tired and didn't feel like talking more tonight, so he was careful not to make too much noise as he climbed the stairs to his room. He closed the door slowly behind him; the room was bathed in soft light filtering in through the open slats of the window blind. As he unbuttoned his shirt he could still taste Wanda's lipstick. He walked over to the window as he pulled his arms from his shirtsleeves and looked out onto the street below. It was deserted except for one car parked at the curb with its engine running. He could see the exhaust in the cold night air and he could see someone sitting in the driver's seat. He flashed back to the car he'd walked past that night on his way to work, the one that had blinked its stoplights just as he approached. A second flash back took him to the car that had been down the street from the Blue Note just as they were leaving tonight. He looked again at the car sitting outside his house. It was the same car. He was sure of it.

Someone was following him and it made him furious that someone would invade his newfound personal freedom like this. He went downstairs through the darkened house, retrieved the jacket he'd hung in the hall closet only a few minutes earlier, and left through the back door.

Tetsu Agaki was finalizing some notes when he stopped writing and looked out the windshield at the snow plowed against the curb. It was miserably cold. He felt a gust of wind rock the compact car and watched the snow blow in swirls across the street in front of him and off the top of the piles along the curb. Driscoll had given him a week. Three days of that were gone and he'd made the decision that Spires wasn't going to go anywhere else. Now was his chance to stick it to that fat-ass Driscoll to the tune of twenty thousand dollars. For his last four days in America he was going to go to Disney World. Agaki closed his eyes for a second to imagine how much different Orlando would be than this place when Cleve Spires, who'd circled the block so he could approach the car from the rear, tapped on the passenger window.

When Agaki turned toward him Spires instantly recalled the oriental that had been behind him in line at the Leavenworth bus station. He'd been there one minute and gone the next. *What the hell?* Spires wanted answers.

Agaki panicked. He floored the gas pedal and the four-cylinder engine suddenly screamed like two tomcats fighting in the quiet of early morning. He struggled with the automatic gear selector but it wouldn't move out of "Park". Spires tapped on the window again, harder this time. Agaki struggled some more and then remembered the safety feature that had confounded him on previous occasions. He had to push on the brake pedal before the car would go into gear. With one foot he kept the gas pedal to the floor and with the other he tromped the brake and snatched the gear selector from "park" to "drive". The little car bolted from its parking spot.

Spires was bent over and his attention focused on the narrow area looking through the passenger door window. As the car sprang from the curb he instinctively jumped back and when he did the range of his peripheral vision broadened dramatically. Out of it he caught a flash of light. He yelled something at the car's driver but it was drowned by the tinny noise of the cheap motor whining at high revs. It wouldn't have mattered anyway. What happened next took only a split second.

Vic Celles was finishing six hours behind the wheel of his Cleveland Metropolitan Transit Authority Bus. He was tired, hungry, and ready for his day to end. His signboard read, "Out of Service". For a change it wasn't snowing, the streets were clear and, at this early hour, traffic was nonexistent. There was in fact only one car in sight; parked along the curb about one hundred yards in front of him. Confident he could safely boost the big bus to a faster speed, he eased his foot down on the accelerator and watched the speedometer until the needle moved to the short mark between forty and fifty. When he looked back to the street it was just in time to see the one car parked along the curb lurch directly in front of him.

Celles jerked the wheel left and tromped the huge bus's air brakes but the distance between him and the car was too small for either of these actions to make a difference. The right front half of the bus impacted Agaki at about forty miles per hour, enough speed to carry the bus to a position on top of the little car. Tetsu Agaki never knew what hit him. As the driver's-side door caved in he was mercifully knocked unconscious and could not feel what happened next as the right front wheel of the bus rolled onto the car's roof and crushed the driver between the floor of the car and the roof that had folded down on him. He was literally cut in two at the waist.

Celles, who wasn't wearing a seat belt, was thrown forward smashing his head on the windshield of the bus. For the moment he was unconscious. Spires took all of this horror in from his position on the sidewalk next to where the car had been parked.

Get to the guy in the car. Move the bus. Get it off the car.

He ran to the door of the bus where he could see the driver slumped over the wheel. The bus's front door was crumpled and would not yield to Spires' best efforts to pry it open. He tried the back door of the bus but the hydraulic piston holding it in the closed position would not let him pass. Looking around for anything he could find, Cleve grabbed a piece of cement block and finished breaking out the front windshield already shattered by the impact of the driver's head. He climbed in over the crumpled bumper, pulled the driver from his seat and laid him in the aisle. Spires knew the driver needed help, but he was still alive. He didn't know about Agaki. Static from the bus's radio caught his attention.

He picked up the mike, keyed the switch on the side, and said, "Anyone on this frequency, do you read me, over?"

In a second came the response, "This is Cleveland Metro Dispatch. Who's this?"

"There's been an accident on the 900 block of Marcus Avenue. There are two people hurt including your driver. Please send an ambulance now. Get some help now."

Cleve was relieved there was no debate by the dispatcher. The bus's engine was still running. He managed to find reverse, get the air brakes holding the bus on top of the car released and back the bus clear of the car. He pulled the handle that opened the bus's doors but only the back door swung open. He raced back through the bus, jumped to the ground and ran to the crumpled heap that once was Agaki's car.

"Damn," he spoke the oath to no one in particular; a one-word summation of a hopeless opportunity to save the man he'd wanted to confront. Agaki's head and upper torso were visible through the opening that used to hold the driver's-side window. His eyes were open but unseeing. Though horrible, death had been quick for this man.

Who is he?

Cleve cleared the broken glass from around the window opening and reached in trying to feel something that might yield some identification. He felt the pockets. There was a billfold. It contained some US dollars, some Japanese Yen, an American Express Card, and an international drive's license. The name on the credit card and the license was *Tetsu Agaki.* The address on the driver's license was a Tokyo address.

OK, now you know who he is. Why the hell is a Japanese guy following me?

Then he noticed a notebook lying amidst shards of broken safety glass on the seat next to the dead man. Spires reached for it and began to thumb through the pages. It was an address book. Much of the information was written in hieroglyphic-like Japanese. But some of the names and addresses were in English. Those in English appeared to be Westerners. There was a "Steve Armstrong" with a San Francisco address. As he turned the page to a "Frank Brooks" who lived somewhere in Los Angeles he heard the first siren. Next was a "Steve Cowper" with no address, just simply the entry "Honolulu". The next page yielded a "Michael Cooper" of Detroit. The sirens were much louder now; they were coming directly to him. Flipping to the next page, Spires found "Billy Driscoll", Windsor Hotel, Bangkok. His eyes froze on that page. He blinked back tears from the bitter cold. He could see the flashing lights now from the emergency vehicle approaching. Help and probably the police would be here soon.

Billy Driscoll. The name brought back stark memories of a courtroom at Fort Lewis, Washington.

He could see the emergency vehicle coming down the street past his mother's house. He tucked the notebook in his hip pocket and returned to the bus to check on the accident's single survivor. He was elevating the driver's feet and covering him with his coat when the paramedic entered the bus. Cleve told him, "This one's still alive. The one out there is dead."

The paramedic began to look after Celles just as Spires saw the first police cruiser pull up behind the ambulance. Cleve thought momentarily about just walking home. *Can't do it. The paramedics have already seen me. Don't know what the bus driver saw. Maybe he even saw me next to the car. Maybe he'll tell the police I was trying to carjack the poor son of a bitch.* He felt a rush of adrenaline. *Come on. Get a grip. You've done nothing wrong. Tell them the truth.* He watched the two cops get out of the car and walk toward the bus, its front door now open and hanging off to the side after the second paramedic pried it open. Cleve almost instinctively moved to the back of the bus as if to avoid them as the police entered through the front door. The cops and the docs spoke among themselves for a moment and then one of the paramedics pointed at Spires. The officers moved down the aisle toward him.

"Are you the one who called the dispatcher?" the younger of the two patrolmen asked.

"Yes," Cleve answered guardedly.

"Well, that was some quick thinking. There's not a lot of activity around here this time of the morning. Paramedic says if it hadn't been for you, the driver might have gone into a shock-induced coma."

Cleve swallowed and told a lie, "I was on my way home from work. I live right over there at 914. The car was parked at the curb. I was right beside it when the guy all of a sudden tromps the gas and pulls right out in front of the bus." He was nervous. After a brief pause he continued, "I don't know, maybe I scared the poor devil when he saw me on the sidewalk next to his car. Don't know what a Japanese guy would be doing in this part of town anyhow."

The officer stopped his note taking and looked up at Spires. "How do you know he's Japanese?"

He'd gone too far. *Dammit!* "After I checked the driver and saw he was still breathing, I had to back the bus off of the car. As soon as I saw him I knew he was dead. I felt in his pockets for ID. He's got a billfold with some money, a credit card, and a driver's license. His name's 'Agaki', he's got a Tokyo address on the license, and Japanese Yen. So I figured he's Japanese."

Back to his note taking, the officer next asked, "You got first aid training?"

"Yeah, I got quite a bit of it in the Army."

"Were you a medic?"

"No. I was an infantryman, but they taught us."

"Ok, sir, can I have your name, please?"

"It's Spires...Cleveland Spires."

Again the young patrolman stopped writing.

"You the same guy that dropped Cletus Phipps tonight in some bar around here?"

"Yes."

"Well, that was some nice work. That son of a bitch has been just asking to be locked up for a long time and tonight you made that happen." The officer returned to his note taking. Spires just stood there. He heard the second police officer call for a wrecker to remove Agaki's car and he saw him use the bus's radio to notify the Transit Authority dispatcher to send a second wrecker for the bus. Then the note-taker said, "OK, Mr. Spires. Thanks. I think that will do it for tonight. You can go on home. We'll handle it from here."

"That'll do it---for tonight." They'll be back.

As Cleve walked up the steps of his mother's house, she opened the front door. "Cleveland, what's going on down there? I heard the sirens. Was anybody hurt?"

He sat down on a dining room chair, looked at his mother and said, "A man was killed, another hurt, and the police will be around here asking questions soon---count on it, Mom." He explained to her how he happened to be at the accident scene and produced the notebook he had taken from Agaki. "Mom, something's going on here. It just isn't coincidence that a Japanese guy with Driscoll's name in his notebook is parked in front of our house. This guy's been following me from the day I left Leavenworth; a Japanese guy followed me into the bus station when I bought my ticket home. I think the guy that died out there tonight is the same guy."

She looked at him and knew he was going back in time---back ten years to the court martial. She didn't want him to do this. She didn't want him to ever leave her house again. She also knew she couldn't prevent him from doing either.

"Mom, I've got to go to Thailand and talk to Driscoll. He's a key to the court martial. The stuff they say I smuggled was found in his team's equipment. I think Driscoll had a hand in that and somehow got the blame shifted to me. He may even be the guy who killed that airman on Kadena. I might have Driscoll to thank for everything that happened to me. If that's right then I *really* want to thank him, the bastard."

He rarely swore in front of his mother. Usually she took him to task when he did. This time she didn't. "Cleveland, it's late, let's sleep on all of this and we'll talk about it in the morning." She knew his decision to go to Thailand would be no different then, but she didn't want to think of him going there, she didn't want him talking about it.

The next day was Sunday and he was restless. His mind kept mapping out all the things he needed to do to get to Bangkok, to Driscoll. However, planning was all he could do; nothing was open, except his imagination, and it was running away with him. He did manage to kill some time by scouring the Sunday paper for any mention of the break-in or the accident, but both events had happened too late to make the Sunday *Plain Dealer.* He called Wanda and told her about the accident. He warned her the police would probably be around asking questions. When an ex-con winds up talking to the police twice in the same night, they will be suspicious. He asked her not to tell them she'd driven him home that night. He said he'd explain on Monday when he saw her. He apologized for getting her involved but it was very important.

On Monday morning Cleve Spires probably made his biggest mistake although it was unavoidable if he was going to confront Driscoll. He applied for a US passport. By noon he had completed the application, gotten the prerequisite photo and delivered all of it to the courthouse where they advised him processing would take three weeks. He booked a flight on Northwest to Bangkok and then began to worry. *Three weeks---what if Driscoll figures out I'm coming after him and goes into hiding. For sure he'll know something is up when Agaki doesn't contact him.*

Monday night he went to work with all of this working in his head. He was going to have to tell Wanda and, while he hadn't had the time to explore fully why, he wasn't looking forward to having to do that. They were busy so that made it easy for him to put off talking to her.

At 11:00PM, Wanda was behind the bar and he was helping her tidy up when the news came on. Midway through the late night news they carried a feature on the break-in, the accident and Cleve Spires. They called him a hero with a past and the report finished with a picture of him in his uniform, ten years earlier, being led from the court-martial room in handcuffs on his way to prison. Stunned at the visual, the audio was lost on him. The half a dozen or so people at the bar who'd been congratulating him fell into an awkward silence as well.

Wanda watched him. Torn in two directions, in her heart she felt sorry for him while her mind told her to be cautious. She had driven him home that night. He'd apparently told the police that he'd walked home. He'd told her the police would be around asking questions and he'd been right. He'd asked her not to tell them she'd driven him home that night. She didn't; instead she'd told the police she didn't know how he'd gotten home, but that he usually walked since the buses didn't run that late. Now she wanted to know why she'd had to lie for him.

At midnight the Blue Note closed for the night. She asked him straightforward. He answered her honestly. She believed him. Then he added, "I'm leaving for Thailand as soon as my passport comes through."

That said, things changed between them. The prospect that their relationship would grow beyond friendship faded. "You'll see your family, then."

"No."

His answer was too quick, too emphatic; Wanda didn't believe him this time.

He continued to work at the Blue Note and they remained friends. Cleve Spires knew he'd hurt her, but as many times as he'd gone back over that Monday night, there was no other way he could have handled it. There was unfinished business in Thailand and he had to make that his priority. Two weeks after the break-in at the Blue Note, one week before he was to leave, the police visited Cleveland Spires at his mother's home. It wasn't a Patrolman or a Sergeant; this time it was a plainclothes Detective. "Mr. Spires, I'm Detective Bergstrom. I want to ask you some questions about the accident you witnessed recently and your current travel plans."

Cleve knew better than to get pissed at the cops, but apparently they'd been checking up on him. It was the same feeling he'd had the night he looked out his bedroom window and seen Agaki's car. People were checking on him without his knowledge, without his consent and it pissed him off. "What's the problem?" he asked curtly

Bergstrom was there to ask questions, not answer them. "Mr. Spires, do you know Victor Celles?"

"No."

"Mr. Celles was the bus driver you provided first aid to that night."

"I never knew his name. I hope he's all right."

"He is, but he told us he didn't see you walking down the sidewalk as you indicated to the officer that night. He told us that he recalls seeing you or someone alongside the car as if you were talking to or trying to get the attention of the driver. Did you know Tetsu Agaki, Mr. Spires? Were you out there that night talking to Agaki?"

"Detective Bergstrom, I did not know the gentleman. I don't know how many more ways I can tell you that. He repeated the lie, "I was on my way home from work. I was right next to the car when he ran in front of that bus. Maybe I scared him and I'm sorry for that, but I wasn't doing anything wrong. Tell me detective, would it make sense for me to do what I did that night if I was there doing something wrong?"

Bergstrom offered no answer. "Well, does it?"

He shrugged off Spires' question and asked, "Did you know where Mr. Agaki was staying?"

Now in complete frustration Spires threw his hands up in the air. Bergstrom took that as a "no". " There is a phone record that Mr.

Agaki placed two calls to Bangkok, to the Windsor Hotel. You are familiar with Bangkok I believe?"

Spires didn't like this smart-ass, but he'd just proven helpful. *That bastard was connected to Driscoll.* Cleve did not say what he'd just thought. Perhaps the notebook he'd taken from Agaki would be helpful to their investigation and perhaps, if he turned it over to them, what they might uncover would help him prove his innocence. However, they might just as easily use it as evidence against him in some insidious way. He'd cooperated ten years ago and gone to jail. He wasn't going to be so naive this time. Cleve looked squarely at Bergstrom and said, "So, that's what this is about. The dead man called Thailand and because I was convicted of a murder there, I'm now a suspect. Well, I don't know Agaki and I don't know what connection he has in Thailand. I do know the Windsor Hotel. In fact, I've stayed there, but that was many years ago. Now what specifically is it that you suspect I have done?"

Bergstrom, with an air of confidence that really pissed Spires off, replied, "We're not sure, but we don't believe in coincidence. We've put a hold on your passport application with the State Department. You should cancel your travel plans to Thailand. We'll let you know when we're finished. Until then I suggest that if you leave Cleveland you check with me first." Bergstrom handed him his business card.

There was nothing Spires could do. He let Bergstrom get out of the house and into his car before he let go and when he did the curse brought his mother out of the kitchen. This time she got after him. He explained, she told him it was OK, but it wasn't. For the time being, Cleve Spires was stuck in Cleveland and could do no more to clear his name until the police had finished their games.

Cato Fujiwara became physically ill when news of his old friend's death finally made its way to him. When he did find out, it was well after Agaki's body had been returned to Japan and cremated in the Shinto tradition. He raged at everyone around him, he should have been told immediately. They scurried around to find out what had happened. The death had occurred in the US, the family had been informed of Agaki's death and they had handled all the necessary arrangements. Tetsu Agaki's family had always been shielded from his connection with the *Yakuza.* No one in the family knew to tell him, so Cato Fujiwara simply had not been informed. When he found out, Fujiwara cancelled a complicated schedule so that he might make a personal visit to his old friend's wife. One of the cancelled meetings was with his chief counsel who went to him to advise against his going. "You are a respected businessman. He's a…" he searched for the right words, "a convicted drug dealer, a nobody. Think of your reputation…"

The young lawyers advice incensed Fujiwara and he interrupted him with a warning, "You should be more careful when you judge others. Tetsu Agaki and I started this business years ago. I deserted him in life for caution's sake. In death I will take a chance and honor my old friend."

An hour later the armored limousine pulled in front of Agaki's apartment building and Fujiwara, with two bodyguards, took the elevator to the top floor. What he found when he reached Agaki's apartment was more tragedy than he'd expected. Not only was the family in mourning over the loss of a father, Agaki's wife, who had been ill for many years, had passed away almost as soon as she'd been given the news of her husband's death. The grieving son and daughter touched Fujiwara in a place he'd seldom been touched, his heart.

However, Cato Fujiwara's heart didn't function the way other people's hearts did. Money was a salve he could spread liberally over his emotions. On the drive back, he picked up the mobile phone, punched in a number and directed that generous bank accounts be established for each of Agaki's children and his grandchildren. What he did next was very rare for him. Not an introspective man, time and human emotion were both in short supply for him, on the ride back to his office, he allowed himself to reflect. He knew many people, tens of thousands he supposed, but Agaki was one of only a handful he considered to be friends. All of the others were merely business acquaintances and he was to them what they were to him, simply means to achieve very profitable, albeit illegal, ends. Agaki, one of his few true friends, was gone, and that was like a milestone passed. Cato Fujiwara put his head back on the headrest, closed his eyes, and remembered with some fondness the less complicated days when the two of them scrounged on the streets of Post-World War II Tokyo for their next meal.

When he arrived back at his office he punched the intercom button for his chief counsel who was not in his office. His secretary picked up.

"Where is he?" it was a demand as much as a question.

"He is in a meeting with…"

"Get him to my office now."

"Yes Fujiwara-san," she said into a connection gone dead on the other end.

Five minutes later the chief counsel knocked on his door and entered, "I was in a meeting…"

"I don't care." Introspection had been replaced by what normally drove Cato Fujiwara, a strange combination of impatience and caution, "I want to know what Tetsu Agaki was doing in the United States. Find out."

"But Fujiwara-san…"

Fujiwara looked up from his desk, "Did I ask for your opinion?"

Retreating, the chief counsel bowed and excused himself.

Chapter Ten

The evening meal prepared at the Kilomanjaro was superb. It began with an exquisite sushi arrangement served on an elaborate tray garnished with wasabi, fresh ginger root and cocktail sauce if the diners should prefer the more western method of spicing up the succulent shrimp served as part of the tray's main offering. Following the sushi and shrimp cocktail, they moved on to more western fare; each associate was served a wonderfully tender filet mignon drenched in garlic butter. Though long out of season, fresh asparagus, each stalk of like size, was served with their filets. The hollandaise sauce, served on the side, was some of the best he'd ever tasted, yet Paul Stanley did little more than pick at his food. Small talk buzzed around him; he listened politely, but his mind was on more serious matters. After dinner they adjourned to the bar for cognac and cigars. Stanley took a snifter, initially declining the cigar until he noticed he was the only one not smoking. To fit in better he reconsidered and selected a Macanudo from the humidor. The strong cognac and nicotine started to give him some relief from the day's strain. He was almost starting to enjoy himself when a man he thought was probably the manager of the resort walked up to Yamamoto, whispered something and left. In a moment Yamamoto announced that they should move to the baths.

Stanley had been in Japanese bathhouses before. He knew the ritual of the bath in Japan, but he thought this group, as diverse and unique as it was, might have their own rituals. He decided he'd follow their lead. Stripped naked, their clothes hung on a wooden peg on a wall outside the shower area, they filed past an attendant who gave each a pair of wooden sandals, a short wooden stool and a pail containing a long-handled brush, a wash cloth and a bar of soap. They proceeded then into a white tiled shower area where each man took a position in front of a low showerhead and sat on their stools. The cloth was used to work up a good lather and the brush was to wash the back. The social conversation of the bar followed them into the shower room and the hot water from the shower and the steam worked to relieve his headache. As he scrubbed he looked around for where they would go next, but the only other door he saw, besides the one they'd just come in, was one he was sure led outside where the temperature was near zero. The scrubbing ritual took about 10 minutes. When Yamamoto stood up from his stool, the others did too.

"Gentlemen shall we. Stanley-san, would you follow me please." Stanley obediently fell in behind Yamamoto who headed for the door Stanley thought led outside. When Yamamoto swung it open a Japanese garden with delicately pruned evergreens on either side of a stone path unfolded in front of them. In the summer time it would have been breathtaking, but the blast of frigid air that blew past Yamamoto and washed over Stanley took his breath away. The pine clumps on the ends of the branches were capped with six to eight inches of snow. When the door to the shower room closed behind them there was no light to be seen yet they could see clearly the path in front of them as the unblemished snow reflected even the smallest amount of ambient light. The path's stones crunched under their wooden sandals as the weight of their footsteps broke the ice that bound them together in winter's icy grip.

It was all lost on Paul Stanley. *Is he shitting me? Maybe he's got brass balls but mine aren't and I sure as hell don't want to freeze them off.* Within seconds of stepping onto the garden path, his wet, naked ass was quivering from the cold. He scuttled along behind Yamamoto who seemed perfectly at ease in the freezing temperatures. After about fifty yards the path forked. Yamamoto was in the lead; Stanley was behind him, his shivering growing worse by the second. At the fork, Yamamoto went left and Stanley dutifully followed him. The others behind Stanley peeled off and took the right fork. In that direction Stanley could hear the voices and laughter of women. While seven of his colleagues were about to end their day in the pleasures of the flesh, Paul Stanley was on his way to school. His education on the *association* was about to start again.

The water steamed in the cold night Hokkaido air. Yamamoto slipped into the natural stone pool easily. As cold as Stanley was from running around dripping wet and buck-ass naked in the snow, the hot water in the pool burned like hell as he eased his body off the rock ledge. It started to snow. Stanley stood waist deep in the hot water, his nether region on fire while everything above the waterline was freezing. Yamamoto was smiling at him from across the pool, only his head visible above the water. He'd neatly folded his washcloth and draped it over his skull. Stanley eased his way down into the pool as his lower half adjusted to the intensity of the water's heat. Yamamoto first offered a lesson in the bath. "Stanley-san, do you have the wash cloth?"

"Yes. Yamamoto-san." Stanley held it up.

"Good, then I suggest two things. First, we are in the bath now, a most informal place for Japanese, especially when the men sharing the bath are good friends. I suggest we dispense with formality and you call me "Saieto". If I may, I shall call you "Paul". Secondly, if you will fold the washcloth in half and then in half again and place it over your head as I have, it will help to insulate your scalp and prevent heat loss. I suggest about every three or four minutes that you rewet it in the hot water. Otherwise it will soon freeze up there."

They both laughed. "Saieto, you have given me wise counsel now as you have throughout the years of our friendship."

"Thank you, Paul. In a way, that is why we are here. I want to complete your education tonight, but to save time and avoid repetition, tell me what it is you think you have learned today."

Stanley thought for a moment before he spoke. "Until today I thought you were businessmen who traded in arms, some of it legal, some of it not. Today I have learned you are revolutionaries. I am amazed at how you've kept your existence and your plans so secret for so long." He thought for a moment to see if there was more. Yamamoto allowed him time to think. "But I have no idea why you are doing this. Why are you planning to overthrow these governments when we have been able to prosper so well under them?" Stanley paused again, "And you, Saieto, are a true puzzle to me. Our colleagues are well placed in each of their governments, but you are not part of Japan's government. The others ask me about the military capability of what my country sells to theirs, but you have not asked me a single question about the military technology sold to your country, even though it is some of the world's most advanced." Stanley realized he was asking questions rather than telling what he thought he already knew. "I'm sorry, you might expect me to know more and ask less, but…"

Yamamoto poked a hand out of the water as if to reassure him, "No, no. It's all right Paul. We have teased you with limited information; we have made you fit it together as if it were pieces to a puzzle, especially today. All of it was purposeful. Today was a final test of your loyalty. I watched you carefully---your movements---what I think you Americans call 'body language'. I listened to you. The man's death today was unplanned and unfortunate, a truly harsh test that you passed well. With everything I observed today I am confident that you are one of us."

"So let me begin by telling you more about Operation Light Switch. There will be *coups* in each of our countries; you already know that. What you don't know is that all of them will occur at precisely the same time. Some may take longer than others to successfully complete, but at the end of two days, perhaps three at the outside, we expect to have full control of the governments, key businesses, media centers, airports and seaports in each of our countries."

Stanley was amazed.

"When will these things happen?"

"That will be something I shall not disclose to you." He paused for a moment and then added, "You can't divulge, either accidentally or under duress, what you don't know. I will tell you, however, that it won't be long. Two of our colleagues have been diagnosed with cancer. We must act before the worst might occur. That is why we pressed you so hard on another sale to China and Vietnam today. In all likelihood these sales are the last you shall ever have to negotiate for us."

"OK, then tell me why. What do you get out of shaking up the political structure of the entire Far East?"

Yamamoto paused. "Not just the Far East, my friend, the entire world. Once we have seized control we will cease all trade, all relations with countries that are outside of the *association.* There will be no importing, no exporting, no embassies, nothing between us and the rest of the world."

Stanley squatted, suspended by the water, with only his head sticking out above its steamy surface. He had to take a moment to comprehend what he'd just heard. *No trade with anyone outside the association. That's ludicrous. The US is Japan's largest trading partner---Japan will lose everything in this deal---who will she export to that will pay what the US pays for her goods? Where will the imports come from? What about oil, iron, other minerals needed for industrial production? Where will it all come from?* Finally he found his voice.

"Saieto, this is crazy. It can't possibly work. You will ruin these countries. Look at how much just Japan will give up in trade with my country alone. Your industries will need natural resources. Where will these come from?"

"Paul, those of us in the *association* are very aware of what Japan and to a certain extent, South Korea will give up. Japan and South Korea will show the other countries of the *association* what it means to sacrifice for the good of all, but before you say it won't work, please consider that the natural resources you mention are in untapped reserves in our eight countries. They are untapped because the terrain of the country is hostile; the distances within countries and between countries is great; the industrial infrastructure in every country except Japan and South Korea is lacking; and, until now, governments haven't cooperated and petty cultural differences have divided us. But the days of insurmountable obstacles and petty differences are about to end. Japan and South Korea bring with them the industrial knowledge to build the roads, bridges, railroads, and ships to tap these resources. Nearly two-thirds of the world's population lives in Asia and most of that majority live in the eight nations comprising the *association.* This affords us a vast and willing work force which at the same time is a vast and willing market for products, products that we will produce for our people."

"Paul, there is a parallel if you can see it. We are going to create our own Industrial Revolution, much like what your country did a hundred years ago. Only we are now at a tremendously greater level of technical proficiency than your country was at the turn of the last century. We don't have to discover the power of the steam engine---we have nuclear power. Our railroads can move at over 200 miles per hour. Our ships, which are many, move thousands of containers, millions of gallons of oil, relying on powerful engines rather than the wind. Industries in Japan and Korea can build the equipment to build roads, bridges and the like. Computers can simulate any number of engineering functions that a hundred years ago had to be accomplished through trial and error. Our industrial revolution will take five years---ten at the most. How long did it take your country?"

It was a rhetorical question and not important for Stanley to answer.

"Seito, you call them 'petty cultural differences'. I don't want to seem harsh, but there is out-and-out hatred among many of these countries that has been going on for decades if not centuries. The Vietnamese have always hated the Chinese. Thais distrust anyone who is not Thai. And forgive me Seito, but Japan is hated by nearly all of these countries. You can't possibly expect their populations to just swallow the pill you will feed them in the days following Operation Light Switch."

"We are prepared to handle that portion of each country's population that won't adapt to our new way of doing business. Dissenters will be isolated from what we are sure will be the majority and given a chance at re-education."

"And for those who choose not to be re-educated?"

"They will be eliminated."

He said it so matter-of-factly, *"They will be eliminated."* Stanley had a different term, "That's not re-education Saieto; that's genocide." Stanley surprised himself with his bluntness, but what would be the point in trying to sugarcoat something so hideous. "The Khmer Rouge tried it and look where it got them."

Yamamoto stared hard at him. Stanley thought he'd really pissed him off, but then, quite matter-of-factly again, Yamamoto gave Paul Stanley something to think about. "Paul what you are thinking is what I would expect of an American. You are a country that has gone around the world on various crusades claiming your desire to see other countries of the world become less savage. What would the world do without you Americans to be its conscience? But tell me Paul, who was the watchdog for your American Indians during the peak of your country's much-acclaimed industrial revolution? Who watched out for their interests as your pioneers moved west and discovered Indians on the best farm lands, on the best mineral deposits, or in the way of your railroads?"

Stanley didn't answer.

"Your silence tells me you see my point."

He did. "So the military will be the enforcer?" He said it with a certain tone of disdain as if that was not a fair role for the military.

"You Americans and your biases. You have such a strong military yet your government wouldn't think of using it on American citizens. Your constitution that you are so proud of, with its checks and balances, prevents such a thing and you look down your noses at any country that isn't structured the same way. Things in this part of the world *are* different and what we will do with the military after Operation Light Switch is no different than the way things are today in the Pacific Rim? In every country of the *association* except my own, the military is the institution that gives the government true credibility. Don't you think that the current governments in China, Vietnam, North Korea, South Korea, the Philippines, Malaysia and Thailand would use their military to enforce their ability to rule, to stay in power if they had to?"

Stanley didn't answer. Yamamoto was leading him in circles probably to conclusions that proved his points well and Stanley was following along like a little boy, but Paul Stanley was a soldier not a statesman, not a student of international governments. In this battle of wits he was outgunned. Instead of answering he asked a question, "What about Japan? You can't pull this off with her and the Self-Defense Forces will never go against the people. Those days ended when you surrendered at the end of World War II."

"You are right, Paul. The *coup* in Japan must be successful and Japan is unique. It is the only country in the *association*---in the world, perhaps---where government derives its power from purely economic forces, where government and business are so tied to one another. Have you heard the term *Zaibatsu*?"

Stanley shook his head.

"It refers to Japan's most influential business leaders. These men, fewer than thirty, control my country's government. There is not a politician in Japan that will cast a vote until they have determined what the *Zaibatsu* think. Thirty years ago I tried to gain influence with some of them but I had little to offer. My competition was American wealth that drew the *Zaibatsu* to the west." Yamamoto shrugged his shoulders. "These men will regret turning their backs on me, Paul. There will be no place for any of them after Operation Light Switch. None of them will survive."

"You haven't answered my question Seito. How will you take them down? The others are using their Armies, but you don't seem to be very interested in that approach."

"Well, I don't want you to think that I am not grateful for the things you have sold to Japan. They have their purpose. We can use the aircraft, the missiles, the ships and all of the associated technology to defend our shores. You have made Japan nearly impenetrable from outside forces---what you might call a perimeter defense. However, fifteen of the thirty *Zaibatsu* have their corporate offices in Tokyo and the city is the seat of Japan's government. The airports and seaports that are in Tokyo are among the most important in the world. These are the targets we must hit and we can't hit them with aircraft, missiles and ships."

"So you *will* use the Ground Self Defense Force?"

"Japan's Army?" He laughed. "The Army is the weakest of the Self Defense Forces. The most challenging task the Japanese Army has faced since the end of World War II was the clean up of the Kobe/Osaka Earthquake in 1995. They are good custodians armed with brooms and shovels."

"Seito, if they aren't for you, they will certainly be against you."

"Undoubtedly, they would if the existing government had the time to alert them, but they won't. As a military man I shouldn't need to point out to you that even if the existing government should manage to muster a sense of urgency, the military is not ready to react immediately to the situation we will confront them with. The Air Force will not fly missions into the heart of Tokyo and the Navy will not launch missiles in that direction either. So that leaves only the Ground Self Defense Force and you know Japan's Army as well as I, they lack training in tactics. They are woefully incapable of moving with any agility and, for the most part, their weapons are the least sophisticated."

"So how will you do it, Saieto?"

"The *Yakuza.*"

"Organized crime...you're going to turn your country over to organized crime?" *This is fucking nuts.*

"How much do you know of them?"

"They're crooks. If it's illegal they're into it. How can you…?

He raised his hand above the surface of the water, "Again you judge much too quickly, much too morally. Your American is showing Paul, and in this part of the world it's not as attractive as it is in New York City, or Chicago or Los Angeles. Make no mistake; Cato Fujiwara is a Commanding General as loyal to me and as ruthless to the cause of taking control of the government of Japan as I am. His organization is our Army for this operation and they are well disbursed throughout the country and well armed in a country where the police aren't. Small teams will simply walk in and take over on the appointed day. One minute the current government will be in charge of an economy that trades globally. The next minute we will be in charge, participating in an exclusive partnership of seven other Asian nations. Resistance won't be tolerated and Fujiwara's people will deal quite expeditiously with anyone who stands in their way. After the *coups* we will rebuild Japan's military under our careful guidance, but for now we don't need them."

"What about US reaction?"

"Do you remember what I said about my inability to predict how your government reacts to economic, political, or military situations?"

"Yes."

"I wasn't joking. I also don't know how the states of the former Soviet Union, Middle Eastern countries or other Asian nations will react either, except to say that no country, except the US, is in much of a position to do anything and thanks to you, the US is not nearly as capable today as it was several years ago. The weapons you have sold us will be used to defend against any country foolish enough to oppose us. You Americans won't attack us; it is our considered opinion that your country's current administration wouldn't react militarily even if it had the ability to do so. Not even the United States can make a nation or group of nations trade with it if those nations choose not to. Then there is the fact that you have hardly any military capability remaining in this part of the world thanks in large part to your efforts on behalf of the *association.* I would be interested in knowing if you see this differently."

The place fell quiet while Stanley tried to think. The wind had come up now and it rustled through the pine boughs. "I don't know. A lot of companies will lose a lot when you close your markets. I still don't know why you insist on doing that. Isn't there a lot of money to be made by broadening markets rather than reducing them?"

"Paul, it is this very perception among westerners that dictates our decision to close our markets. You think we can't survive without you. You think we need your multi-national companies to come here, pay our children next-to-nothing to produce goods to supply your markets where those same goods are then sold at unconscionable margins of profit. Your western companies take these profits and re-invest next to nothing in Asia. Then, when you find you can produce something cheaper elsewhere, you leave, you move on to greater profits, while the workers you leave behind wonder where their next meal will come from. Yes, your politicians and business leaders will cry 'foul', but frankly we won't care."

"And me?"

"That is up to you, my friend. You have been instrumental in getting us to where we are. You may chose to live among us, but it is likely you will be the only westerner remaining in our eight countries. Among us it may be awkward for you at times and for that I will apologize in advance. The rest of the world will want to know, 'Why you?' Your own kind will brand you as a traitor."

The word plunged into him like a dagger---*traitor*. His stomach rolled over.

"On the other hand, the money in the account is yours. You may stay in America, such as it will be when we are finished, and you have my word that none of us will ever expose you. As long as that information is protected, you can live in the US. I suspect you will be among America's richest men, Paul. Many will lose everything when our markets are suddenly closed to them."

The two men were silent for a long time, looking at one another, only their heads above the hot mineral water. Stanley had to ask; "Saieto, this morning you asked me if I was prepared to cross the line. What would you have done if I had been unwilling to take the step?"

Yamamoto stood up and moved toward the edge of the pool. "Paul, as a military professional you surely recognize surprise is the essence of Operation Light Switch. You witnessed the measures we will take to preserve our advantage of surprise." Reaching the edge of the pool, he raised himself out of the water and onto the ledge. Yamamoto stood in the freezing night air, turned and looked down at Stanley. His entire body was shrouded now in a cloud of steam as the cold night Hokkaido air collided with the heat coming off of him. He looked supernatural.

"Had you not crossed the line, Paul, there would have been two deaths here today." He headed for the door to the shower room without looking back, leaving Stanley alone.

Chapter Eleven

Two weeks after the Cleveland police told him not to leave town, Cleve Spires called Detective Bergstrom. The call didn't go well. Despite his patience and tact, none of it had worked. The phone call ended with Bergstrom saying, "These things take time Mr. Spires. You should know that by now." Bergstrom hung up on him.

Cleve Spires was still pissed when he got to work that night. At about 10:30P.M. Wanda told a customer setting at the bar that she wasn't going to serve him any more. She was polite as she always was when performing this delicate task, which she had to do about twice a week. Like many of the customers she'd had to cut off, this one tried to negotiate. "Aw, c'mon baby, I'm OK. Make me another one and one for yourself while you're at it. Anything, anything you want baby, just put it on my tab."

She was about to politely refuse both the request and the offer when Cleve, who'd just finished changing a keg of draft, grabbed the guy by the necktie and pulled him nearly across the top of the bar. "Exactly what part of 'no' don't you understand?"

Wanda stood there for a moment surprised, searching for something to diffuse what had just happened so unexpectedly. She'd not seen him this way since the night of the break-in, but this wasn't a criminal as it had been that night, this was just some guy who'd had too much to drink. Spires started to say, "Now get your ass..."

She put a hand on his shoulder and told him, "I can handle this. Thanks." At her touch his fist clinched tighter and that drew the tie's knot tighter around the patron's neck. "Let him go, Cleve."

He did. The patron started to say something but Wanda wheeled on him, pointed to the door and screamed, "Go!" The guy picked up his change, muttered something about no tip, never coming back here and then he left after bouncing off the doorframe on his way out. When she was sure one of her problems was gone, she turned to confront the other, but Cleve was gone as well. He retreated to the kitchen and stayed there.

At midnight Wanda let the last customer out the front door, turned the bolt on the lock and headed for the kitchen. "Would you like to tell me what the hell that was all about tonight?"

The kitchen was suddenly smaller than he'd ever known it to be. "I'm sorry."

She shot back at him, "Don't tell me you're sorry. You haven't been yourself for the last two weeks, not since the cops put the stop to your travel plans, but that doesn't allow you to rough up the customers, Cleve. This is a bar. People come here to drink. When I think they've had enough, I cut them off. I did that long before you got here and I'll do that long after you leave. Do we understand each other?"

"Yes."

"OK. Now would you like to talk about it?"

He explained. She listened. What made perfect sense to him, didn't to Wanda. When he was finished she said, "You know this Driscoll-guy could kill you. He's done that before hasn't he? He killed that kid that you went to jail for so what makes you think he won't do the same thing to you."

"He won't."

She laid her heart on the table, "You know I care a great deal about you."

"Don't say that."

"Not saying it won't make it any the less true. I don't want you to go. I want you to stay here. So does your mother. We both want to know you're safe. We both want you with us."

The idea of just forgetting about Driscoll, about Thailand, had been on his mind almost from the beginning. He was happy here. Life for him was getting to be very comfortable and, with Wanda in it, it could become even more so, but every time he allowed himself to think how happy he might be, the prison at Leavenworth would flash him back. "Wanda, I have to do this. When I was in prison, I tried to think of how I wound up there, of who would do this kind of thing to me. I was never able to piece it together. Now I've been given a scrap of information that could unlock the whole puzzle. If I don't go to Thailand, there will always be a wedge between us, something that I should have done, but didn't."

She wasn't crying, but he could see the tears welling up. He was being so stubborn, so unreasonable. He went to put his arms around her and she pushed him away. "Leave me alone. I have to try and make some sense of all of this."

He did as she asked.

The next morning she hesitated in front of her telephone, but eventually made the call she didn't want to make. Then she called

Cleve at home. "Can you come over to the Blue Note right now? I've got someone coming who can help you with your passport. He's an attorney."

"Wanda, I can't afford a lawyer."

"Dammit, Cleve," she swore at him for the first time, "he'll be here in an hour. If you want his help, be here, if you don't, stay home. He's a friend, my husband's college roommate. He wants to talk to you. Take it or leave it."

"OK, OK. I'm sorry. I know it wasn't easy for you to arrange this meeting. I'll be there---and Wanda---thanks."

She almost said, "You're welcome", but caught herself. She was still frustrated and angry with him and politeness didn't match her mood. Yet she gently set the phone back in its cradle as if she were saying goodbye to him for the last time.

The man sitting in the gray pinstriped suit at the table talking with Wanda was white; that surprised Spires. He wasn't sure why, he just assumed Wanda's attorney would be black, like them. The attorney stood as Cleve walked up to the table. Wanda made the introductions and then left.

Lee Shaw said, "Sit down and tell me your story, Mr. Spires."

Cleve began at the bedroom window the night he looked out and saw Agaki parked at the curb near his house.

Shaw interrupted, "Ah, Mr. Spires, I'd like to hear it all. Go all the way back. Start with your military service, I'd like to hear about that."

Cleve looked at him as if he was some kind of voyeur and then asked the lawyer, "Why?"

Shaw put his hands on the table and leaned toward him, "Because Wanda is an old and dear friend. On top of that she is one of the best judges of character that I've ever met. You've made quite an impression on her, Mr. Spires. I'd like to find out what she sees in you."

"Are you doing this for me or for her?"

"That's a fair question. Right now it's for her."

Spires looked at him and smiled. He liked his honesty. "All right, that's a fair answer." Cleve took him through the last thirty years of his life. Along the way the lawyer asked quite a few questions, especially when they got to the court-martial.

When they were through Lee Shaw simply said, "Well, the police can't do this to you, Mr. Spires. Give me a day, two at the most, and the travel restriction will be lifted. You can be on your way, if that's what you're sure you want to do. I assume you've thought through what might happen when you and Driscoll meet. I assume you don't expect him to drop down on his knees, confess and beg your forgiveness."

"Yes, I have and no, I don't."

"I also assume you know that even though you are a US citizen, any laws you violate in Thailand are subject to Thai courts," he paused and then added, "and Thai prisons."

"Mr. Shaw, you don't need to try and scare me. Remember, I served in Thailand. I know it better than you, better than most. It's a risk I'm willing to take."

"All right, Cleve, I was just trying to…"

"…talk me out of it," he finished the lawyer's sentence. "For Wanda's sake, I know."

Shaw stood, nodded and said, "I'll be in touch, Mr. Spires.

When he arrived at the Blue Note for work that evening one of the waitresses handed him a note. It was from Wanda. In it she told him Lee Shaw had called and said the restriction on his travel had been lifted. His passport application would be expedited and he should have it in about a week, ten days at the most. She signed it, "God's speed, Wanda." He was thrilled at the news. "Where is she?"

"I don't know. She called me this afternoon and asked if I'd fill in and manage the place for a while. Said she needed to get away for a while. It's her first vacation…"

Spires walked away, not listening to anything else she had to say. Her absence struck him like a slap in the face.

Chapter Twelve

Paul Stanley knew how to sleep on airplanes. It was an art form developed over his many years of military service. He'd spent interminable hours strapped uncomfortably into the red nylon seats of C-130s or C-141s as the guest of the US Air Force. So he should have found blissful rest while wrapped in the luxurious arms of Japan Airlines' first class cabin. Yet, even with his seat fully reclined, soothing music flowing into his over-padded earphones and enjoying a slight buzz from the alcohol he'd consumed, sleep would not come and the flight between Tokyo and Honolulu had never seemed longer. The word "traitor" kept returning to the forefront of his thoughts. *You should have known the payback for the kind of money they were giving you would be more than just peddling a few rusty trucks and guns. Before now you might have gotten out. You didn't know very much until now. But now you know; now you're either in or you're dead.*

Within a week of his return to Hawaii, news reports started to appear. One had to look to find them. They were confined to the print media; *Time* and *Newsweek* both did reports on the growing tensions between China and Vietnam over the Spratley Islands. Within two weeks he'd gotten a call from the head of the Defense Security Assistance Agency (DSSA) in Washington D.C., telling him Vietnam had formally requested a second aircraft package identical to the sale concluded only nine months earlier. When Stanley got the official notification of the request, it was labeled "Secret". Two days later he read about it in *The Washington Post.* Three days later China lodged its protest, demanding that the US either forget the sale to Vietnam or strike some kind of deal to sell them arms as well.

Stanley took some measure of pride as he saw his idea coming to fruition. Things were happening just as they'd discussed on Hokkaido. Next steps were, however, clearly his to take and his alone. His boss, the Deputy Commander-in-Chief, US Pacific Command, Lieutenant General Lynn Kinney and Admiral McKeever, the Commander-in-Chief, US Pacific Command, would have to endorse the sales to the Department of Defense. Stanley's job was to convince them it was the right thing to do.

On 15 February, he was standing in front of Kinney ready to brief. They were alone, just the two of them, which was a bit unusual, but Stanley had told him, "You aren't going to like some of this. Maybe you'd just like to hear it first and think about it, without a lot of other people giving you their two-cents worth." Kinney had agreed.

"Sir, the US should sell the aircraft package to Vietnam and the artillery package to China as requested."

Kinney liked the way Paul Stanley put the bottom line up front; he didn't fuck around with stuff. But this bullshit made his stomach turn. Kinney had been a Platoon Leader and Company Commander in the course of two tours in Vietnam. He'd struggled with his feelings the first time the US sold this shit to the Vietnamese. Now the bastards were back again wanting more. To make matter worse the Chinese were asking, almost demanding the same deal. It just didn't seem natural to sell things that go boom to your enemies. "Why? Why the fuck should we sell them anything, Paul?"

"Three reasons, sir: the Spratleys, economics and Sun Tzu."

Kinney laughed and then said, "OK, convince me."

Stanley went through some slides on what had already been sold to Vietnam, what they'd done with it and concluded, "Sir, their Air Force is now one of the best in the region and as long as the Vietnamese Air Force can defend Vietnam's claim to the Spratley Islands, the Chinese will never occupy them without a fight, a fight that we don't have to fight."

Kinney, expressionless, nodded in moderate agreement, "Keeps the oil-boys happy, I suppose."

Stanley shifted to the China sale. "This is the economics lesson, sir and it's an easy one. We have a lot of old artillery pieces and ammunition that we can't use. We can sell them now, while they're still worth something, or we can hang on to them until they're no good to anybody and then we can pay a lot of money to have the ammunition demilitarized." He held up a stack of at least a dozen overhead slides, "I can go through these and show you the cost detail to taking this stuff apart and rendering it useless, but the bottom line is it will cost us a helluva lot more to do that than what we will make from the sale."

He waved his hand at Stanley, "Save it for the staffers on the Hill that have got the time for that kind of shit. I've got the economics. How does Sun Tzu fit into this?"

"Sun Tzu said the best way to know your enemy is to lie down with him. Sir, both countries are going to get this stuff from somewhere." He put a slide up, a satellite photo, and across the bottom it was marked, "Top Secret—NOFORN". "This is a Chinese production facility that intel says will be operational in two years. My point is as long as we're selling them stuff, we have some idea of what they're getting and how much they have."

Stanley turned off the overhead projector, "Questions?"

"I have one I'd like to ask Sun Tzu."

Stanley laughed, "What's that, sir?"

"Did he ever sell anything to his enemy and then have it stuffed back up his ass?" Kinney didn't laugh so Stanley didn't either. "OK, Paul, schedule this brief with Admiral McKeever. I'll go along with your recommendation. These are crazy times we are living in, I don't give a good goddamn what Sun Tzu says."

A week later Admiral McKeever gave his approval, which was forwarded to the Defense Security Assistance Agency. By the end of February, the proposed sales to Vietnam and China were forwarded to Congress for their consideration.

By the end of March, neither the House nor Senate Foreign Relations Committees voiced an objection to the sale. The press had laid off the story, preoccupied for the time being with more pressing domestic issues. By April 15th, the House Armed Services Committee had passed the request to the Senate Armed Services Committee (SASC) with a recommendation to approve.

On 5 May, the SASC, the last hurdle the sales had to clear, took up the matter in open committee. CSPAN was providing live TV coverage of the SASC hearings on the sales, more because that was their routine than because they expected anything would happen in the hearing room. There were some reporters present, the usual ones, from AP, UPI, World News, Reuters, etc. who were always present when the SASC met, again, more from routine than anticipation of any breaking news story. But a Senator from Texas was about to insure that the Senate Armed Services Committee's hearing on the sale of arms and munitions to Vietnam and China would be anything but routine.

Senator John McClint (R-TX) had been elected to Congress ten years earlier. He was a veteran of political battles on the Hill, and in his ten years had built an excellent reputation in the Senate. It was that reputation for doggedness and fairness that had earned him a seat on one of the most powerful committees in Congress, the SASC. McClint had abstained when the Committee voted on the last sale to Vietnam. He was the only Republican on the committee who had not voted as the party had expected and it hadn't mattered. Now the Vietnamese were back, wanting to buy more, and the US, in McClint's view, was going to compound its mistake by selling to the Chinese as well. He would not be so easily persuaded this time to be silent. In fact, he was prepared to take some rather drastic measures if this sale was approved.

McClint was not a friend of the Vietnamese. He had been their guest from 1966 until 1973 in an awful place called the Hanoi Hilton, which, for those who had the misfortune to live there, was more like living in Hell. In the seven years he was imprisoned in North Vietnam, he'd endured torture by his captors, which included virtually no medical care following sessions in which his arms and legs were broken. He still bore the signs of this physical abuse nearly three decades later. He couldn't fully straighten out either of his arms and he walked with a marked limp because his right leg was shorter than the left one. At night, his teeth soaked in a cup next to the bathroom sink, all of his natural teeth either knocked out by his tormentors or lost as a result of his improper diet for those seven years.

But John McClint's deepest scars were on the inside, so well hidden that even his most loyal and long-time staffers didn't know they were there. Though it had been over thirty years since his release, he would still wake up in a pool of sweat at least three nights a week when his dreams would dredge up a memory of some event from his days as a prisoner of war. He didn't trust Asians in general and he most assuredly did not trust the Vietnamese and the Chinese. He would have happily given them all of the ammunition they needed to kill one another.

However, what was bothering Senator McClint was a *really* bad feeling that the ammunition was for some purpose other than the mutually assured destruction of Vietnam and China. He'd been inside the Beltway long enough, however, to know he would need more than just a bad feeling in his gut if he were to get the SASC to kill this sale, either through its inaction or its disapproval. He'd gone through some elaborate preparations for this hearing and now he was ready. He was sure he could influence enough of his colleagues on the SASC that he could at least create a stalemate in the committee. If he could do that much---just create a stalemate in his committee---the sale could not go through.

McClint was the third Senator to speak during the hearing's opening session. The first two Senators, both Republicans like himself, had endorsed the sale. Now it was McClint's turn, and he motioned for his staffers to bring in his evidence. Three Asians, two men and a woman, entered the hearing room. Neither of the two men were whole. One was missing both arms; the other was missing a leg that appeared to have been severed near the hip.

The man with the missing leg was Laotian. As he sat down, he placed an object wrapped in cloth on the table in front of him. He spoke no English, so the woman was there to translate. McClint wasted little time and his first question was straightforward, "Sir, how did you lose your leg?"

Through the interpreter, he answered, "My village lies in Northern Laos about two kilometers from the border with Vietnam. One night last November, we were all asleep, it was late, and the bombs began going off all around us. We did not know why or even how the bombs were coming in. We only knew we were dying. Only a few of us survived. We were a village of almost 75 people. Four men from the village were hunting when the bombs came. When they returned they found my neighbor and me alive. Everyone else---all of my family---" he began to cry, "all of my family are dead."

"You said there were 'bombs' falling on your village. How do you know that?"

The press had moved in by now, expecting that whatever was under the cloth would answer McClint's question. They weren't disappointed.

"I have a piece of one here."

He removed the cloth revealing an olive green fragment with writing on it, "US MK-4…" there had been more at one time, before the bomb had detonated in this man's peaceful village, but it didn't matter at this point. The committee chairman had to bang his gavel several times to get the room back to order.

"Mr. Chairman, I would like to stipulate for the record: 'I have had experts certify this bomb fragment is from a US made aerial bomb of the type sold to Vietnam as part of the last sale of aircraft and weaponry. Apparently some of the stocks we sold last November, for some inexplicable reason, have been used to kill most of this man's village.'"

Reporters from Reuters, AP, and UPI were on mobile phones to their editors. The Committee Chairman ordered them to leave the room or terminate their calls. They were disrupting the committee's work.

McClint moved to the Chinese man who was able to speak some English.

"Sir, tell this committee how you lost your arms?"

CSPAN cameras focused on the Chinese man, and now the images they were carrying outside the committee room were starting to get some attention. Every member of Congress has at least one TV somewhere in his or her office. Most have two. One is always tuned to CSPAN; the other usually has CNN or MSNBC or some other twenty-four hour news service on the dial. The word spread like wildfire throughout the Congressional Office Building that John McClint was performing some theatrics in the SASC hearing that were worth watching.

In Hawaii, Paul Stanley stood in front of the TV in his bedroom. He'd been brushing his teeth when McClint took the podium. Now he sat down on the foot of the bed, stared into the TV and said, "Oh shit!"

The Chinese man leaned awkwardly toward the microphone on the table in front of him. "I lost when gun exploded. Bad round. I only one alive. Three killed."

"Tell the committee, sir, what type of artillery piece it was and what you might know of its origin."

"105mm Howitzer. China bought from US."

"And the ammunition you were using that day, do you know where it came from?"

"US."

McClint had not wanted the man to have a translator. He thought the short, clipped answers would be more effective. They would allow his colleagues and the press to fill in the blanks and they could only be filled with reasons to cancel this sale based on the two examples he'd brought them today. A hush fell over the Committee chamber. McClint excused the two men and the translator. As they opened the door to leave the blinding, there was a blinding flash of cameras, lights, and a flurry of questions shouted at them from a covey of fifteen to twenty reporters. That commotion spilled briefly into the Committee chamber until the door closed behind them.

Senator McClint was not through. "My fellow committee members, I did you a disservice a year ago when the first sale of weapons and ammunition to Vietnam was presented to us. I abstained in that vote. The sale was made and today you have witnessed the effects of our decision to sell implements of war to these two nations. First, we have sold defective equipment; equipment that is too old to be reliable for our soldier's use but is good enough to sell to other nations of the world so it will kill and maim their soldiers. Can we dismiss this as 'buyer beware?' I think every member in this room has a deeper conscience than that. Today you also saw proof that a customer of ours is using the weaponry we have sold them to kill innocents without any reason or provocation. To the citizens of the US, I implore you to write, phone, visit, or in some way communicate to your representatives in Congress to stop the insanity of selling our old stocks of weapons and ammunition. Certainly, the United States, the leader of the world, has more marketable commodities than its outdated guns, bullets, and bombs."

McClint's eyes were misty with tears. He stared straight into the CSPAN camera in front of the podium and his face was somber. "For my part, my fellow citizens and fellow committee members, I cannot in good conscience advocate this sale to either country, much less both. I failed you the last time." He looked at his fellow committee members and told them, "I will not be a part of your failure if you choose to approve this sale." Then he returned his stare to the camera, "I will resign my seat in this Senate if we approve this sale."

He turned and left the chamber, through a back door, away from the media. Later that day he would meet the press, but for now he avoided them. John McClint wasn't grandstanding for them or for anyone else; he was deadly serious about what he'd just said. John McClint truly believed they had made a terrible mistake.

In Hawaii Paul Stanley struggled with what he should do. McClint's actions were devastating. Stanley cursed him and he thought McClint must have worked around the clock to scrounge up these two guys. He wondered if anyone was going to investigate to see if their stories were credible. He tried to think if there was anyone he could call to suggest that, but he decided it wouldn't be smart to do that. His job was to get CINCPAC to recommend the sale. He'd done that. People might ask too many questions if he started recommending what should be done about the stink McClint was raising. He thought about contacting Yamamoto, but he didn't have a clue as to how to do that. Yamamoto had never given him any phone number, address, email, website, nothing that might allow Stanley to make contact. Besides this was world news. Yamamoto would see it soon enough for himself. All Paul Stanley could do was watch all of this from Hawaii and worry.

That evening the CSPAN footage of the testimony of the men from Laos and China were played in part on every network's evening news. McClint's dramatic closing remarks and his sudden departure from the committee chamber were played in their entirety. Over the next two weeks, his face appeared in every newsmagazine, every major newspaper, and he was on every major television news show airing in the morning, in prime time, and late night.

The Vietnam-China arms sales became *the* issue and the parties quickly began to get their members in line. Democrats opposed the sale, if, for no other reason, than the Republicans favored it. The Republicans controlled the majority on the fifteen member SASC. If party lines held true the Democrats would cast seven “no” votes and the Republicans would cast eight “Yes” votes. But McClint, a Republican, had already made it clear which direction he was going to go. Anticipating McClint's swing to a “no” vote, this sale to the Vietnamese and Chinese was in trouble. The committee decided its final vote on the issue would be on 20 May, giving each committee member time to turn their staffers loose on researching the issues surrounding this sale. The debate, spurred by McClint's performance, would be heated and public, and it would continue right up to the date of the final vote.

Chapter Thirteen

Cato Fujiwara's patience, not his long suit anyway, was at its end just about the time the chief counsel knocked on his door and strolled into his office. "I have the information you wanted on this man," he fumbled awkwardly through the folder in his hand, "this man, Agaki."

There was no reply. The chief counsel paused for a moment as if he expected to be thanked for the quick work he'd done to ferret out the information, but Fujiwara didn't even look up from the paper he was reading. "He was killed in a automobile accident in Cleveland, Ohio. A man named Spires was a witness and is apparently a suspect in Agaki's death."

Fujiwara slammed both fists down on the desk. His move was so sudden, so violent that it caught the young attorney by surprise and he stepped back a step. Fujiwara sprang out of his chair and glared at him as he spat the first question at him, "How do you know this?"

"We have a contact in the New York City Police Department. He got the information from the Cleveland Police. I have their police report here." He held up the file.

"Go on."

"I...I don't know what..."

"Tell me about Spires you fool."

"Spires was there; apparently he saw the whole thing happen."

"Was he responsible for it?" Fujiwara screamed this question.

"At this point it is not possible to tell. The driver of the bus involved in the accident says he saw Spires standing on the sidewalk next to Agaki's car just before it pulled from the curb in front of the bus. Spires claims he was merely walking home from work and observed the car pull from the curb into the bus's path. The police suspect a connection between Spires, Agaki, and Thailand. Apparently Agaki called the Windsor Hotel on two occasions from his hotel room in Cleveland."

"Who did he call?"

"I do not know, Fujiwara-san."

"Find out."

"But Fujiwara-san..."

He shot him a glance and the chief counsel knew not to argue. "Where is Spires now?"

"In this city, Cleveland, I presume."

"Don't presume. I want to know for sure where he is. Is there anything else?"

"No Fujiwara-san"

"Two hours."

"Excuse me."

"I want you back here in two hours with the information you have failed to get for me."

The chief counsel fumed on the way back to his office. He had many more pressing matters lying on his desk, matters that the organization depended upon him to complete. Why Fujiwara was wasting his time on such trivial matters as Agaki's death remained a complete mystery to him.

The Japanese-American police captain in New York City verified Spires' whereabouts and one other piece of information that the Chief Counsel thought Fujiwara might find of interest. Finding out who Agaki called in Thailand was more difficult and time consuming. Just before his two hours was up, a *Yakuza* agent in Bangkok came through for him.

"Agaki called Billy Driscoll at the Windsor Hotel."

Fujiwara, who'd been shuffling through some papers, dropped them onto the desktop and looked up.

"The man Spires is still in Cleveland, but this is interesting; he has applied for a passport and travel to Thailand."

Fujiwara gave an instant precise direction.

"Call our agent at Japan Air Lines. Tell him to search all airline bookings for any travel arrangements made by Cleveland Spires. I want to know precisely when and where he may be planning to travel."

The chief counsel pulled his notebook telephone directory from an inside coat pocket and dialed the number. He held while the contact searched the computer. Within a minute the chief counsel said, "Hai. Domo," and disconnected the caller. He turned to Fujiwara, "Cleveland A. Spires has booked a reservation to Bangkok for two weeks from today. It is the second booking he has made."

Fujiwara considered this last bit of information for a moment. "Good. Call our agent back and tell him he is to call you immediately if Spires boards any international flights or if his travel plans change in any way. You and he are not to discuss this with anyone unless I ask you to. Get my chauffeur and tell him to bring the car around."

Billy Driscoll had just returned to Thailand after a month tending to his duties as Command Sergeant Major at his battalion's headquarters on Okinawa. These trips to Okinawa were distractions for Driscoll. It took time away from his businesses in Bangkok and in his absence he was sure his managers were ripping him off. Now he was back, he had six weeks of uninterrupted time he could devote to his enterprises and to finding out what the hell had happened to his snitch, Tetsu Agaki. He called the mid-level *Yakuza* punk who'd put him in contact with Agaki to see what he could tell him and that hadn't been much. "Well, there's five grand and pick of my stable if you can find out where the little son-of-a-bitch is."

Two days later, Inamu Inamine showed up at The Exotica, Driscoll's flagship bar on Soi Cowboy in Bangkok. "Agaki is dead."

"What?" The news shocked Driscoll. "How?"

"Car accident in someplace called Cleveland."

"When?"

"I'm not sure, but I think about a month ago, maybe not quite that long."

Driscoll ran a time line in his head and, based on when he expected to hear from Agaki and didn't, a month was probably a good guess.

Inamine stepped close to him and whispered in his ear, "Be careful Billy-san. Fujiwara is asking questions. Agaki was an old friend of his apparently. If he thought you had something to do with it…" He let Driscoll fill in the blank.

He got Inamine settled in with two of his best girls, took a beer from behind the bar and went into his office. He told the madam, "Don't let anyone bother me." He needed time to think this through.

A car accident in Cleveland... He tried to think of ways that Spires could connect Agaki to him. *Even if Spires saw it happen he wouldn't know who the fuck he was; he couldn't make a connection to me. I'm OK. Spires is still in Cleveland. How do I know that? Because Agaki was in Cleveland when he bought it. So Spires is still there---in Cleveland with Mommy.*

He trained his thinking on Fujiwara. *Can Fujiwara link me to Agaki? Only if Inamine tells him he gave me Agaki's name. Inamine wouldn't do that, not if he wants to keep coming down here and banging my girls.*

He thought some more about his risk with Inamine. He even gave some thought to having him eliminated, but thought better of that idea as it might draw even more attention his way. The hit would have to happen here in Thailand and that would spark the question what was Inamine doing there.

Shit. Even if Fujiwara figures it out, there's a good goddamn reason for making sure Spires hasn't put two and two together while he was cooling his heels in jail. If Spires rolls me over, he rolls over the Yakuza too. It's in Fujiwara's best interest to know what that dumbshit is doing. He'd want to know if he's headed our way.

He thought for a moment more and then decided, *No, I'm OK. Too bad about Agaki but that's life---or death.* He chuckled at his ironic little joke. Then he went back out into the bar to have one more conversation with Inamine about how important his silence was. Driscoll found him in a back room with the two girls he had assigned to him. Driscoll talked, Inamine listened and the girls performed. "Inamu, keep your mouth shut and this kind of stuff is yours whenever you're in town, on the house."

Chapter Fourteen

When Cato Fujiwara found out Cleve Spires saw Agaki die and that Agaki had called Billy Driscoll, he knew exactly what Agaki had been doing in Cleveland and who had put him up to it. He was furious with Driscoll and it had nothing to do with Agaki's death. Fujiwara was outraged that he was acting alone, again, as he had ten years ago. What if he hadn't found out about this? What if Spires had gotten to Driscoll? Now was not a time he wanted either the Thai police or the cops in Japan looking into his organization, and that could have happened if they had pressured that coward Driscoll. Billy Driscoll didn't know it, but he was as good as dead. The only question was 'how' and Cato Fujiwara had an idea.

His limousine swung into the driveway of Seito Yamamoto's estate on Tokyo's extreme western fringe. The trip had taken an hour and a half, slightly longer than usual, but far from the three hours it sometimes took if traffic was snarled. He'd been making this same trip every other day for the last six months. This trip was out of that every-other-day sequence. He'd phoned ahead to let him know he was on his way.

Yamamoto met him at the front door. "I sensed in your phone call some concern."

"A small problem, but one I want you to know about. Do you remember an American by the name of Driscoll? The time would be about ten years ago?"

As they walked back to his office Yamamoto thought and then replied, "Um...yes, vaguely. He worked for you, out of Thailand as I recall."

"Your memory is excellent. He still works for us."

Yamamoto replied, "Cato, it's not like you to keep people who displease you, and as I recall you were unhappy with Driscoll then."

"It was a business decision, now in light of what he has done, perhaps a bad one, but we chose to keep him on our payroll as a means of keeping an eye on him."

"I understand. So what is it he's done now that brings you here."

"Ten years ago, Driscoll killed a man on Okinawa and then placed the blame on a man by the name of Cleveland Spires. Spires went to prison for ten years. Apparently, he is now out and there is every likelihood that he is on his way to Thailand to confront Driscoll. If he gets to him, Driscoll will tell what he knows to save himself. I cannot let that happen."

"How far into your organization could an investigation reach if Driscoll were to tell everything he knew?"

"He could give up information and names that could lead the police to me."

Yamamoto winced, "Well, it should be easy to solve the problem in Bangkok."

"It will not be difficult, but I have an idea that I would like you to consider." Fujiwara took him through it step-by-step.

"It is ingenious, my friend," Yamamoto told him, "but timing is everything. You are sure such a thing can be timed so well?"

"I am."

They bowed to one another and Yamamoto said, "Then I look forward to hearing that Mr. Spires is in a Thai jail."

Fujiwara wasted little time. From the car phone he called an agent in Bangkok. "A man by the name of Cleveland Spires will arrive in Bangkok on 12 March. Here is what I want you to do." He quickly laid it out for him, not an overly complicated plan, but there was one tricky detail. When he was finished he warned his agent, "You must not fail. Call me when you have finished it."

Cleve's passport arrived on March 5th, well ahead of his scheduled flight to Bangkok. Ida was less than thrilled at this newfound government efficiency. Wanda had dropped out of sight. For two weeks he'd tried to find out where she was. He'd been to her house nearly every day, looking for her or some sign that she'd been there. He'd called and called, but there was no answer. If anyone at the Blue Note knew where she was, they weren't telling him. He'd asked everyone about her. He hated leaving like this, without talking to her, but it was obvious that she didn't want to talk to him.

On March 7th, Cleve confirmed his airline reservation.

On the morning of March 10th, Cleve Spires called a cab, kissed his mother good bye, asked her to let Wanda know he'd be back as soon as he'd finished his business with Driscoll. He also asked Ida to try and make Wanda understand. She resented him asking her to do that; it implied somehow that *she* understood why he was doing this.

The weather outside matched her mood perfectly as she watched the cab pull from the curb in front of her house. It was raining. The temperature hovered just above freezing and the Cleveland, Ohio sky was a cold, steel gray. Ida didn't have a good feeling about this. She feared she'd never see her son again.

Chapter Fifteen

Each night that he was in Bangkok, it was Billy Driscoll's habit to visit each of his bars in random order. He thought this was a good way to keep his managers on their toes. He owned two bars in Pattpong and two bars on Soi Cowboy, two of Bangkok's most notorious and well-known sex districts.

Though he would never admit it, Driscoll had his favorites. At the Club Exotica her name was Nha. As Driscoll arrived there on the evening of 12 March, Nha was with a customer. The Madam offered to interrupt her and send in another girl, but Driscoll waved her off. "Let her finish, Mama-san, I'll have a beer while you show me the books from last night." Driscoll was first and foremost a businessman. She rushed off to get both the beer and the books.

Cleve Spires should have been exhausted after traveling through half of the world's time zones. Instead he was pumped with energy as he looked around the lobby of the Windsor Hotel. It had been ten years since he'd spoken Thai, but he'd started to use it at the airport and was surprised at how easily it was coming back to him. He stepped to the desk and, in passable Thai, asked for Mr. Driscoll's room.

The young Thai woman at the front desk responded in Thai, "I am sorry, sir, but hotel policy does not permit me to give out the room numbers of our guests. You may use the house phone over there and ask the operator to connect you with your party's room."

There was no answer when the operator connected him, but the fact that she had routed his call to a room told him Driscoll was registered here. His first thought was to just have a seat and wait for him to come in, but the lobby was crowded. He wasn't sure he would see him and if Driscoll happened to see him first then it would be a long trip for nothing. He wasn't sure he would recognize him either; it had been ten years. When a tour bus pulled up and unloaded about 50 Japanese men, the lobby became even busier. This was not the place to get to Driscoll; there were too many people and he couldn't predict what Driscoll would do when he saw him. With Agaki he'd learned a lesson about surprising people.

He went back to the front desk and the same young woman whom he'd spoken to earlier. "Mr. Driscoll doesn't answer his phone. Could you tell me where I might find him?"

From her response, he could tell his question made her uncomfortable. She wouldn't look at him as she busied herself at a computer keyboard and stammered, "No, sir...I...I do not know where he goes." When the men from the Japanese tour group swarmed the counter she ignored him, glad for the work that pulled her away from him. He decided to have a seat and wait her out, but as he turned to walk away from the reception area, he saw something that gave him another idea. Most of the larger hotels in Bangkok have a pool of taxicabs that line up at their entrances waiting for fares. The Windsor was no exception.

Most of the drivers were outside their cabs and talking among themselves. The first three he talked to either didn't know Driscoll or didn't want to help him. The fourth driver, however, proved to be more forthcoming. "You have US dollar? You pay US dollar?" the man said in difficult-to-understand English.

In Thai, Cleve responded, "Yes, I have US dollars. You can speak in Thai. I understand Thai. How much?" He'd learned long ago you never agree to anything in Thailand without establishing the price up front.

"No. No. We speak English," the driver insisted. "I not want others understand what we say." He pointed to the other drivers. "Twenty dollar, I take you Driscoll's bar on Soi Cowboy. If he not at bar...you wait...he come...he go every bar at night."

Cleve nodded and the driver held the door open for him, smiling from ear to ear. After Cleve settled in the back of the cab, the diminutive little driver crawled in the driver's seat, flipped down his visor sunglasses and roared from the taxi stand. The taxi's meter was winking at Cleve, blinking "0.00 Baht" as they slowly made their way in Bangkok's miserable traffic. There was a reason why the driver hadn't turned it on. Cleve figured it was because the "regular" fare to where he was being taken was far less than twenty US dollars. As they sat in traffic Cleve asked him in Thai, "Do you know Driscoll?"

Now speaking in his native language the man said, "Oh, yes. Beelee owns many bars in Bangkok and has many women working for him. I will drop you at the closest one. If he isn't there, just wait on him. He will come. He goes to each of his bars every night, but never in the same order." He laughed. "Beelee is a good businessman.

He keeps girls guessing. While you're waiting on Beelee maybe one of his girls can make you happy." He winked and smiled at Spires.

Three minutes later, the cab driver pulled onto a narrow street not four blocks from where they'd started. He pointed down the street to a sign reading "Club Exotica", and held his hand out for his twenty dollars. He'd made good money for such a short trip. In Bangkok, a Thai could live on twenty US dollars for a week very comfortably. Cleve didn't complain. He knew the fee was for the information and not for the transportation. Spires could sense he was close to coming face-to-face with the scum who cost him his family, ten years of his life, his career and his pride. He got out and headed for the Club Exotica.

The assassin was an Amerasian man, a boy really, only sixteen. He'd come to Bangkok from Chunburri, a city about 60 kilometers to the south, because there was more opportunity in Bangkok for someone like him. His Thai mother died of AIDS when he was thirteen. His father, a westerner, had no idea the boy existed. His mixed blood made him an outcast in Thailand, but the hardscrabble life he'd led since birth made him a survivor as well. He'd found something he could do; kill people, and he'd made good money at it. His victim tonight was his twenty-fifth contract.

His instructions were to follow his target, Driscoll, at a discreet distance and at some point a black man would approach his victim. The hit was to occur precisely at that point of meeting. The price was 1000 US dollars; payment was all up front. He was warned that the black man might be skilled in martial arts so he was to avoid contact with him at all costs. If he were to get caught, he should use the pistol to kill himself. If he fucked this up the *Yakuza* would kill him, but he would beg for death if they had to do it. The boy wasn't threatened. His job was easy. All he had to do was pull the trigger and get the hell out.

He'd picked Driscoll up as he'd left the Windsor Hotel that evening. Driscoll, completely oblivious to the tail, went first to the Kangaroo Club and then here, to the Club Exotica. If there was a tricky part to this job, it was now. He needed to keep track of where Driscoll was inside the club, yet he wanted to have as much warning about the black man's arrival as possible. He was waiting outside the Club Exotica, when he saw the taxi turn on to the street and stop just up the street. A black man got out and headed straight for the Club Exotica. The boy ducked into the bar and saw Driscoll was still seated in the same place he'd been five minutes earlier. He took a seat at the bar about ten feet behind his target and simply waited.

Nha's customer walked past the madam adjusting his shirttail down into his trousers. Nha followed just behind him. The madam caught her by the arm and whispered, "Beelee's waiting for you."

Nha, naked as the minute she was born, with mischief in her eye, placed her finger over her lips as a signal for the madam to remain silent. The old woman nodded with a wry smile. Nha crept to the edge of the bar, got down on all fours and crawled under the table where Driscoll sat absorbed in the ledger in front of him. The assassin saw her and was sure she'd just made herself as much of a target as Driscoll, but that was her hard luck.

Cleve Spires felt a little light-headed as he stepped through the open door and into the darkness of the Club Exotica. It was the pure adrenaline rush he'd experienced plenty of times before in combat. It would subside. He took a deep breath and that helped.

The only lights in the place were over the stage, in the middle of the circular bar, where a half a dozen naked dancers gyrated to an American country and western tune. The music was cranked up to headache-level and the place smelled of stale beer and smoke. Spires gave his eyes a minute to adjust. Two customers sat at the bar. Girls in bikinis sat in groups of three or four at tables along a wall behind the bar. To his left, along the wall that ran parallel to the street, were booths, and there, sitting in one of them, looking down at something, was Billy Driscoll, not twenty feet away from him.

In the booth closest to the door, Fujiwara's agent watched Spires walk in. He reached over and fondled one of the two girls sitting with him. She giggled and nuzzled his neck while her hand reached for his groin. The plan, to this point, was coming together perfectly. He mentally braced himself for what was to come next, while the girl continued to play.

The assassin fixed on Spires from the moment he entered. He waited for him to pick Driscoll out and move toward him. When he did, the boy stood up with his back to Spires and Driscoll for a split second, as he pulled the 9mm pistol from the waist of his pants. Spires saw him out of the corner of his eye. Then, in a ballet-like movement, the boy spun and moved toward Driscoll, closing the distance between them to just a few feet.

Under the table, Nha was ready to make her move to surprise "Beelee". She reached up and began to unzip his trousers. Driscoll, completely caught by surprise, reacted to her unexpected touch by jumping nearly six inches from his seat, just as the assassin squeezed the pistol's trigger.

The noise was deafening even over the din of the music. The bullet entered Driscoll's neck traveling on a downward trajectory. Driscoll's death would be slower now as the bullet severed his spinal cord and tore out the right side of his heart before exiting his body still at a deadly speed. It hit Nha directly in the face. She died as Driscoll was supposed to---instantly.

The Club Exotica was thrown into utter chaos. No one saw the assassin flee out the back door and fade into the back alleys of Bangkok. Fujiwara's agent looked at the chaos around him and smiled as he moved out of his booth. The two girls sitting with him had run screaming to the bar's back rooms. He casually strolled out the front door and began looking for a policeman. Cleve Spires stood over the slumped body of Billy Driscoll, unable to believe what he'd witnessed.

He grabbed him by the shoulders, moved him off the bench he had been sitting on and laid him on the floor. Then he reached under the table and pulled Nha next to Driscoll. She had no pulse. Her once pretty face was now pulp. Blood was everywhere. Spires immediately moved back to Driscoll whose body twitched spasmodically. Cleve Spires had seen soldiers fighting off death before, but he also knew when the battle was lost. This was Driscoll's last battle, but maybe before the final breath was gone, he could get the bastard to give him the truth.

"Driscoll, you son of a bitch, do you know who I am?"

There was no answer. His eyes were open, but Spires suspected he couldn't see. He hoped he could hear, maybe even talk but there was a lot of blood pouring out of him onto the bar's floor.

"Driscoll, it's Cleve Spires."

No reaction.

Then it came---Driscoll's last-gasp effort to communicate with a world he was about to leave. Cleve put his ear close to his mouth and heard faintly, but clearly, "Fujiwara" and then "Yakuza". He kept his ear close, hoping for more but that was it. Driscoll was dead.

"Fujiwara" meant nothing to Spires, but he knew from his time in the Far East what the *Yakuza* was. Remembering his luck with Agaki, he searched Driscoll's body. There was no notebook, no wallet, but there was a roll of bills, US dollars.

As he started to stand, a bottle crashed over his left shoulder. It hurt mildly and luckily the breaking glass didn't cut him. He wheeled around and found a petrified Madam standing behind him. She had aimed for his head and missed, as Spires had moved to stand up.

In her best English she was screaming at him, "You kill Beelee...you kill Beelee."

In Thai he responded, "I didn't do this."

She looked at the roll of dollars in his hand and repeated, "You kill Beelee."

Spires headed for the door he'd come in, not sure what he should do next. He didn't like the way this was shaping up. As he stepped through the door, he saw a policeman walking with another man toward the Club Exotica. As soon as they saw Spires, they broke into a run. The man with the policeman shouted in Thai, "There he is. That's the man."

It was happening to him all over again. His next decision was an easy one. He reentered the Club Exotica, and exited this time out the back through the same door used by the real assassin. He headed down the alley looking for the darkest cranny he could find. He could hear them behind him shouting and running, but he couldn't see them. That was a good thing; it meant they couldn't see him either. This was an advantage he'd need to capitalize on quickly. Fifty meters further down the alley he found what he was looking for; there was a small passage way between two buildings not two feet wide. It was pitch black as he entered and went into the darkness as far as he could---about 50 feet he estimated---until he reached a wall. Essentially, he was trapped now. If they saw him duck down the passageway or randomly happened to check it, they would find him.

Cleve watched them run past the entrance to his hiding place. The policeman was using a radio. Cleve heard him calling for reinforcements and he heard an acknowledgement that they were on the way. Spires needed to get as far away from here as he could. He waited for their footsteps and voices to fade, and then decided to leave the darkness and go back in the opposite direction toward the Windsor Hotel.

Though he'd spent three years in Thailand when he was in the Army, he had little experience in Bangkok. Essentially, he knew how to get back to the Windsor Hotel and not much else. As he moved out of the darkness and into the shadows of the alley, he became conscious of something grasped in his hand. It was the roll of money he'd removed from Driscoll's body.

Great! Now they can add robbery on top of the murder charge. What have you gotten yourself into? He remembered Lee Shaw's warning. If he were caught he'd face charges in a Thai court and he was a *farang,* a foreigner.

He ran to the main road leading back to the Windsor Hotel. Sukumvit Road is a busy thoroughfare and when he got to it, he slowed to a brisk walk. A large black man is easily spotted in Thailand, continuing to run would only make him stand out more. He needed to blend in as best he could. The Windsor Hotel was a half a block off Sukumvit Road. As he turned on the side street leading to the hotel, he looked over his shoulder and counted at least four police cars heading in the direction he'd just come from. He could hear more sirens in the distance.

Think...Think...What are your options? Go to the airport, get on an airplane, and go back home. Can I be identified? Can I be extradited back to Thailand for murder? Can I be tried in the US for killing Driscoll? He is an American citizen, the son of a bitch. There were so many questions and, when he filled in the answers he thought might be true, they chilled him. He remembered Agaki. *Could the Cleveland police charge him with that one, too?* For a moment, panic overtook him. Nothing was making sense. He was smart enough, however, to realize his mind was racing and he needed to focus.

What are my options? C'mon Cleve. Think.

What did Driscoll say?..."Fujiwara"... "Yakuza". Think about what just happened. That guy with the Thai policeman...Was he Fujiwara? I sure as hell can't hang around here to find out, but I could go to Japan. That's where the Yakuza is. Maybe there I can get a line on this guy Fujiwara.

Another police car passed somewhere nearby him and momentarily broke his concentration.

Think about this now. They knew I was coming here tonight. This whole thing is a set up. How did they know? Why hit Driscoll?

His mind was racing again.

Whoever this guy Fujiwara is, he must have the answers. If I can get to Fujiwara maybe I can get myself out of this fix. Get to the airport. Japan, that's where the Yakuza lives. That's where I'll find out about this guy Fujiwara. More sirens reminded him he needed to get on with whatever he was going to do.

He was nearly back to the Windsor Hotel, and as he approached the line of cabs near the hotel's entrance, he saw the driver who had taken him to the Club Exotica, "I need you to get me to the airport fast---can do?

"Can do," the driver replied as he opened the rear door for Cleve.

The driver weaved in and out of traffic, dodged down side streets and sped up to outrageous speeds when he was able. Spires tried not to look outside, figuring he was better off not seeing how fast things were going by. He remembered the roll of money he'd found on Driscoll and retrieved it from his pocket. Careful to conceal it from the driver, he found it contained nothing smaller than a fifty, mostly hundreds, totaling $4,950.00 US dollars.

The Club Exotica was still in an uproar. Most of the girls had gotten dressed, but few had left. The police were systematically questioning everyone who'd been there at the time of the shooting. The Japanese man who'd first summoned them was talking with several Thai police and occasionally would glance over at an adjoining table where the old madam was talking with a couple of cops. He was sure she'd corroborate his story that a black man was the shooter. He'd given her $100 US and told her there was more where that came from if she would tell the cops she'd seen the black man shoot Driscoll. The Madam didn't know who he was; neither did she know why he was willing to give her money for something she was already going to tell the police anyway. She didn't see the trigger pulled, but that didn't make any difference to her. She would just say that she did. A small lie didn't matter. She'd seen the black man rush up to "Beelee" and Nha. She saw him talking to Beelee as he laid on the floor dying. She saw the money in his hand. He was the murderer even though she didn't see the actual shooting. Now she was getting paid by this other man to tell her story. She didn't complain. The $100.00 went into her pocket.

No one knew Spires' name. That's what they all told the police and it was almost true. Fujiwara's agent damn well knew his name, but he couldn't give it to them without raising too many questions about how he knew Spires. He listened to the radio traffic over their walkie-talkies and worried that these bumbling jackboots were going to let Spires slip through their fingers. He knew the price of failure, and he was not looking forward to his required call to Fujiwara as long as Spires remained free.

He offered the police a suggestion; perhaps they might want to seal off the airport in case the assassin decides to flee the country. He helpfully provided them the logic behind his suggestion. This was obviously an execution. The assassin was not a Thai. He would not linger in a country where he was so easily recognized. The airport was the most likely avenue of escape. To make sure the detective took his advice seriously he pulled him aside, took a roll of 1000 Baht notes from his pocket and peeled off five. "The dead man is a friend of mine. I want you to catch the bastard that did this. There will be twenty more of these coming your way if you catch the black man---dead or alive."

As Cleve's taxi pulled onto the ramp leading to the departing passenger's unloading zone at Bangkok's international airport, the driver was forced to pull over to make way for a police car approaching from the rear with its siren blaring. That car went screaming by them followed closely by two more. Cleve did not like this at all. He slouched his six feet three inch frame down as much as the small back seat of the old Toyota would allow. By the time they got into the area where cars, vans, and busses were permitted to discharge departing passengers, there were at least a dozen police cars pulled haphazardly to the curb, and the police were attempting to organize themselves to begin a search. Cleve gave the cab driver directions in Thai, "Roll your window down, please. I want to hear what's going on."

Through the open window he heard the police shouting to one another the description of who they were looking for. The driver looked over his shoulder at Spires slumped in his back seat and realized he had who they were looking for in the back seat of his cab.

Cleve said in Thai, "I know what you're thinking, but I didn't do it. It's a big mistake. I'll pay you $100.00 if you get me out of here." He held the roll of money up so the driver could see he had the cash.

The driver said, "Two hundred dollars and I'll get you out."

Cleve was not in a position to barter. "OK."

The driver smiled and said, "Good, do not worry. Lay down on the back seat. You must trust me. Think of it this way, I'll get no money if they capture you---they will take it all for themselves and arrest both of us. I will get you out of here."

He turned back around and began to move from the curb lane into the faster moving outside lane. A passenger on the sidewalk, not seeing a fare in the cab, motioned for him to pull over. A policeman was standing next to the passenger and was baffled by the driver's lack of response. He made a move to get the driver's attention, when a call on his radio diverted him away from the cab, allowing Cleve's driver to merge into the faster moving traffic and exit the departure area of the airport. As they drove further away from the airport, Cleve remained prone on the backseat. He could hear sirens heading towards the airport.

The driver asked, "Where do you want to go? If it's too far we'll renegotiate the price."

Cleve did not immediately answer. He was reformulating his options. The cab driver pulled to the curb and stopped. Spires didn't like standing still. Somehow he felt if he could keep on the move, he'd be harder to find.

Without turning around the driver said, "Mr. Spires," he'd heard his name from the police at the airport, "you are in much trouble…"

"What's your name?" Spires asked the driver.

"Tradip."

"Well, Tradip, how much to take me to the village of Chuk Ra Met?"

"Where is it?"

"Just north of Korat, maybe ten kilometers."

"The driver stopped looking in the rearview mirror and turned to look at Cleve. "Korat is two hundred, maybe three hundred kilometers from here."

"Yes, I know. I'll make it worth your while."

The driver knew he had the money. He was actually starting to like this black man who spoke his language better than any American he'd ever met, but business was business.

Tradip flipped his visor sunglasses up and said very seriously, "You know my risk is great. If we are caught, we will both go to jail. You will be the lucky one. They will hang you. I will have to survive there. Do you know what a Thai jail is like?" Tradip was a good businessman; he'd made a good case for why he was going to demand a large fee, and after an appropriately long pause he told Spires, " I will need five hundred US dollars."

"I will pay you six hundred dollars if you can have me there by morning."

Cleve knew he was asking a lot of the driver and even more of the old Toyota. They couldn't use the good roads leading into and out of Bangkok because the police would surely have these blocked. The roads outside of Bangkok that they could use would quickly deteriorate into two-lane gravel and, eventually, single lane trails with dirt surfaces. The driver would need to push his old car hard, avoid the deep ruts, and have luck on his side to make Korat by tomorrow morning. The driver smiled and promised to try his best.

Four hours after Driscoll's assassination, it was painfully obvious to the *Yakuza's* agent that Spires, for the moment, had made good his escape, so he punched in the number to Cato Fujiwara's personal line slowly. The phone rang once before he picked up, as if Fujiwara had been sitting there waiting on it to ring.

"Fujiwara-san, I am sorry to report the task is only half complete. Driscoll is dead. Spires is the suspect, but has not yet been captured. I have not provided the authorities his name but the police believe me and an old woman at Driscoll's bar were eye-witnesses to the double murder..."

"Double murder?" Fujiwara interrupted.

"Yes, Fujiwara-san, one of Driscoll's girls was under the table where he was sitting at the time of the assassination. She was directly in the line of fire and died quicker than Driscoll."

"Quicker than Driscoll?" It was a question and the timbre in Fujiwara's voice was rising now. "And Driscoll...tell me of his death. Did he say anything before he died?"

"I don't think so. He was mortally wounded through the neck and chest. Judging by the bleeding, the bullet must have ripped out a large part of his heart. I departed nearly immediately to find the police so they could arrest Spires. When I returned Driscoll was dead. No one I spoke to at the bar recalls Driscoll saying anything to anyone before he died. They have a massive manhunt underway in Bangkok. If he is in this city, he will be found. The airport and the seaport are blanketed. There is not a policeman in Bangkok who is not looking for him. He will be caught soon, Fujiwara-san. I guarantee it."

"I know you guarantee it," was Fujiwara's cold reply. "You guarantee it with your life."

He hung up the phone.

Chapter-Sixteen

Spires finally gave into sleep during the long trip north out of Bangkok. On the outskirts or Korat, the driver woke him for directions to Chuk Ra Met. Cleve blinked away the sleep and surveyed his surroundings. It had been nearly twenty-five years ago that he'd worked as a military advisor in this area, but fortunately nothing in rural Thailand changes very much. He knew exactly where he was. An hour later the driver stopped the old cab on a two-rut dirt path next to a rice paddy. As Spires peeled off the money he said, "Tradip, you won't tell the police…?"

Before he could finish, the driver turned and gave him a pained expression. "My American friend, you hurt me. On the way here, while you were asleep, we passed at least four National Police cars. It would have been easy to betray you. Instead I have delivered you here as you asked."

Spires held up his hand and nodded. He knew this little man was a scoundrel. In Bangkok he would take anyone, anywhere, in search of anything, for a fee, but Spires trusted him. He'd passed two serious tests, the first at Bangkok's airport and the second was the trip northward to Korat. The driver extended his hand. Cleve took it and then gave him seven hundred dollars as extra insurance for his silence.

From where he was, it was about two miles to Chuk Ra Met, and as he walked along the top of the narrow dikes that separated one water-filled rice paddy from another, he could smell the mustiness of the wetlands in the morning's stillness. All around him was the emerald green of tropical Thailand. Ahead of him he heard a rooster crow, calling the villagers to their day's work. The corral where the villagers kept their water buffalo was exactly where it had been twenty-five years ago, and the pungent smell of ammonia mixed with manure assaulted him. Ahead he caught his first glimpse of villagers who were at work in the banana grove. As he got closer, they stopped working and stared at him. At least a hundred meters separated them, so it was difficult for him to recognize any of them. He wasn't sure if they were staring at him because they recognized him or they were just surprised to see a black man walking into their village. He trudged on, his mind centered on seeing Liott and Daniel. He didn't notice the villagers from the banana grove fall in behind him at some distance.

He stopped at the edge of the huts that formed the village's heart. Women huddled about the well drawing water for their morning chores. He looked, but Liott wasn't among them. One hundred meters from where he stood, he could see the hut of Liott's father and a pang of conscience froze him for the moment. He took a deep breath, looked around and, for the first time, noticed the workers from the banana grove who'd followed him. It was as if they were there to block any retreat he might consider and it was then that he decided he was well past any point-of-no-return. If he were to leave, now the villagers would tell Liott and Daniel they'd seen him, they'd start searching, maybe go to the police---he stopped thinking beyond that point. He had to go on.

As he passed each hut, others joined the parade that was forming well behind him. When he reached the hut of Liott's father, he stood in the doorway. Her back was to him as she prepared breakfast on a low table in the hut's center. Her father saw him first, stretched out a thin left arm and bony index finger and began to wail unintelligible things as he pointed to Spires. Liott spun around to see her husband for the first time in over ten years.

In perfect English she screamed, "Cleve, my darling." She ran to him, threw her arms around his neck and pulled his face to hers. She smothered him in a deep, long kiss and when their lips broke apart she whispered in his ear, again in perfect English, "I have missed you so, my darling."

Behind her the crippled old man continued to wail.

"What's the matter with your father?"

"He had a stroke, Cleve. His right side is paralyzed. He can't talk, but he's glad to see you. I know he is."

They walked over to the old man and Cleve knelt beside him. Her father's eyes were lit up and sparkled behind a veil of tears and, though the stroke had severely contorted his face, Cleve recognized a smile smeared across it. He put his arms around the old man and in perfect Thai said, "Thuripp, it's good to see you again. Thanks for taking such good care of my wife." The old man's head rested against Cleve's cheek and he could feel the old man patting him on the back with his good left hand. Liott stood there looking at her father and her husband and had just begun to cry herself when applause and shouts of joy broke out from behind them, from the hut's doorway. Liott turned and Cleve and Thuripp looked up to see nearly all of the people of Chuk Ra Met gathered around their doorway to share in the joy of this long-awaited reunion.

Spires was overwhelmed. Liott had stepped to his side and put her arm around him. Her father, with the help of a crude crutch, struggled to his feet and hobbled over to them. The villagers were still cheering and applauding. Cleve bent down and whispered to Liott, "I'm so sorry..."

She placed a gentle finger over his lips. "There's no need to be. It's all right now. We're back together. Come and sit down. I must get Father off his feet. You can tell us about your trip. Daniel will be home soon for breakfast. He won't believe it when he finds you here. He has kept a calendar you know. This last year has been very long for him. He's counted the days since your release from..." She stopped short; she didn't want to talk about prison, she didn't even want to say the word. "He's been asking about you every day since your release."

They helped the old man into a chair fashioned out of a tree trunk and made comfortable with palm fronds. Then Cleve turned to Liott and said, "Everything here is the same as it was, including you. You haven't changed, still as beautiful as I remembered."

"I'm sorry we were not there when you got out."

"It's OK. I can't believe you have waited for me all of these years."

She turned to him with a puzzled look on her face. "Of course I've waited, but I had to wait here."

"My mother told me about the trouble in Cleveland."

"Is she angry with me, Cleve?"

"No, Liott, she isn't. You did the right thing."

Daniel burst through the doorway, "Papa..." The sound of it---*Papa*---what he'd always called his father, fell on Cleve's ear like a song. He stood and turned to see the man his boy had become. Much taller than the average Thai, he towered above the other Thai men who, with their wives and children, still milled around outside Liott's father's hut. Cleve guessed he was 6 feet, 1or 2 inches tall. Broad muscular shoulders tapered to a narrow waist, and below that stretched long, well-muscled legs. It was obvious the life Liott and her family had carved out here in Chuk Ra Met had agreed with their son.

For the moment, his troubles in Bangkok faded from his thoughts. He couldn't spoil the perfection of the moment with bad news. There would be time enough for that later. Cleve looked at his wife and son and beamed with pride.

———

Wanda Cheevers called Ida Spires when she returned to Cleveland. Ida was glad to hear from her even if the news she had to tell her wasn't good.

"How is he?"

There was a sigh and then Ida told her, "I don't know, Wanda. He hasn't called."

"I have a feeling---a bad feeling..."

Ida interrupted, "Wanda, I've worried about him since he was born. Cleve can take care of himself. He knows what he's doing. He also knows we're waiting to hear from him and he'll call as soon as he can. I know he will."

When the call from Wanda was finished, Ida hung up the telephone and stood there staring at it. If a stare could have made the damn thing ring, this one surely contained the telepathic power to make it happen. But Ida Spires, despite an iron-strong will, wasn't a Stephen King character. The phone didn't ring. So she picked up the receiver and dialed the operator for assistance in placing a call to the Windsor Hotel in Bangkok, Thailand, "No, I don't have the number operator. I'm sorry."

It took what seemed like forever before she finally heard, "Go ahead, the Windsor Hotel is on the line."

"Hello, you have a guest there, Cleveland A. Spires. Can you connect me please?"

"Thank you, just a minute," was the courteous reply.

Ida waited.

"I am sorry we do not anyone by that name registered here."

Ida suddenly felt helpless. Her mind was spinning as she tried to think of other ways she could contact her son. After a long pause, the operator said, "Hello, are you still there."

The voice on the other end of the line pulled Ida out of her thoughts. "Yes, I'm still here. Would you please check one more time to be sure? He's supposed to be there by now."

"Yes, ma'am."

Ida knew she was grasping at straws. The pause was shorter this time, but produced the same response. "I'm sorry, ma'am, we have no one by that name registered at the Windsor."

Ida, who had put up a good front for Wanda Cheevers, was now desperately worried about her son.

Liott led him to a grove of palm trees where four rice paddies came together. It was a wonderfully cool night. The only sounds were those of palm fronds bumping against each other as a gentle breeze rippled through them.

Chuk Ra Met had celebrated Cleve's return. Villagers had been in and out of the hut of Liott's father all day long. This was the first time they'd been completely alone since he'd walked back into their lives that morning. The village was quiet now, its people were going to sleep. Hardly a speck of light came from any of the huts, and for as far as the eye could see there was nothing but rice paddies with soft moonlight shimmering off their watery surface.

On a grassy knoll at the grove's center they talked first about Daniel. He was her salvation in the years Cleve was in prison. Without him she would not have wanted to survive even the first month alone. Cleve sat with his head down. He couldn't look at her as she talked. Tears streaked his face.

"Don't cry, my darling."

"Liott, I'm so sorry I wasn't there for you. I wasn't there for Daniel."

Liott gently brushed away his tears. "What happened wasn't your fault. Daniel and I know that. As for the ten years, well, it's time gone by my love. All we can do is go forward from this moment on." She leaned over and kissed his cheek.

He turned to face her and kissed her lips. The day-old events of Bangkok seemed ages ago. He put his arms around her and pulled her close to him. As they kissed, more passionately now, he put the ten years at the Disciplinary Barracks behind him, finally. She was right; it was time-gone by. He longed to touch her and to be touched. He undressed her, slowly, as if he were discovering every inch of her for the first time. When she was completely naked, it was her turn to rediscover him. They made love there in the palm grove. Liott never wanted them to be apart again. Cleve didn't want the sun to come up.

Chapter Seventeen

Lucas Johnson's secretary showed up at his office door with a furrowed brow and urgency in her voice, "Colonel Johnson, it's General Will for you. It's not his secretary, sir. It's General Will, himself, holding on line 47 for you."

Lieutenant General John Will, the Commanding General of the US Army's Combined Arms Center and School at Fort Leavenworth, Kansas, rarely placed his own phone calls and when he did, it was to other generals. She was right to be concerned.

Johnson pulled his head out of the report he was reading. "Thank you, Alice." Then he reached across his desk, punched the light that was blinking on the phone and said, "Lieutenant Colonel Johnson, sir."

"Lucas, this is General Will, I just got off the phone with the Chief of Staff of the Army and I've got some bad news and some good news for you. Do you know Bull Howard?"

Cerebral flares immediately began popping in Lucas's mind. Colonel Bull Howard was the Commander of the First Special Forces Group at Fort Lewis, Washington. Lucas was supposed to replace Howard this summer as Commander of the First Special Forces Group. He hoped nothing was going to change that. "Yes, sir, I know him."

"Lucas, Bull Howard has been relieved of his command today and the Chief of Staff has asked him to submit his retirement papers. He's lucky. The Chief is spitting mad and could just as easily have court-martialed him."

"Bull Howard is one of the best…"

"Yeah, I know. Surprises me too, but it's messy and involves a cover up of an investigation that was supposed to be done on the Command Sergeant Major who was murdered in Bangkok a few weeks ago. You'll take command without ceremony on Monday. The Chief wants this transition between you and Howard to be low-key if possible. Lucas, the Chief is looking for answers on the Command Sergeant Major. He wants to know before the press does, so your priority is preset for you. Barbara and the kids will have to make this move by themselves."

Lucas was quiet. Will didn't expect a reply. Both knew there were no options. This was as direct an order as you could get from the Chief of Staff of the Army.

"Welcome to command, Colonel. This won't be easy, but the Chief and I have every confidence in you. We'll do everything here that we possibly can to make your family's move as painless as possible. I'll have my exec call the Transportation Office and give them a heads-up."

A million thoughts crowded into his mind, but Lucas managed to say, "Yes, sir. Thank you for calling." He called home and told his wife what was going to happen. She'd been with him since his first duty assignment nearly sixteen years ago, and since then there had been twelve or fifteen moves; she'd lost track of exactly how many. She took this one in stride.

Then he called Command Sergeant Major Dave Goodmon. The phone rang twice and a booming voice answered, "Headquarters First Special Forces Group, Sergeant Major Goodmon."

Johnson and Goodmon knew one another well. Their bond had been forged in combat. Goodmon had been the Team Sergeant Major for a mission Lucas led into Baghdad. It was that mission that had won him and Goodmon the Silver Star.

"Sergeant Major, This is Lucas Johnson."

There was a delay and then a muted, "Hello, sir."

Johnson sensed dejection in Goodmon's voice and it bothered him. He was going to need help when he got to Fort Lewis and, since General Will's call, he'd been counting on much of that help to come from Goodmon, someone he knew, someone he could trust. "What's the matter, Top?"

"It's bad sir, very bad. This shouldn't have happened. I tried...really tried...but I couldn't get Colonel Howard to take me seriously."

"What happened Sergeant Major?"

Uncharacteristically, Goodmon answered Lucas' question with a question. "Do you know Colonel Howard?"

It was the second time in an hour that he'd been asked that question and Lucas wasn't sure how his answering would produce an answer to his question, but he respected Goodmon enough to go with him on this. "Never served with him, but I know him by reputation."

"Well then you know he's loyal like a dog to soldiers. But probably something you didn't know is that Command Sergeant Major Driscoll saved his life in 'Nam. Have you read about Driscoll's death?"

"Oh, yeah." The murder had been well covered in the *Army Times,* with front-page stories appearing several weeks in a row.

"Well, there's more to it than Driscoll just getting murdered. Right after his death a DOD IG (Department of Defense Inspector General) Hotline complaint was passed to the Group Headquarters here. I saw it first. The complaint alleged Driscoll was running a string of bars and whorehouses in Bangkok. The lady complaining was the wife of a sergeant assigned to the First Battalion. She said her husband went to Thailand for training and when he came home, he gave her the clap. When she found out he'd infected her, she unloaded on him. He told her he got it from a girl at a bar in Bangkok and the rumor was the battalion's Command Sergeant Major operated the bar. The sergeant asked her not to make a big deal out of it. He didn't want to hurt his chances for promotion by pissing off the Sergeant Major, but when she found out Driscoll was murdered, she decided she had to tell what she knew. She told the IG that she didn't think it was right for a command sergeant major to even *be in* a whorehouse---much less *own* one."

"You're right, Top---pretty ugly stuff."

"Yeah, well, it gets even worse, sir. Colonel Howard wouldn't investigate. He kept saying the sergeant's wife was fabricating all of this to get revenge on her husband."

"You're kidding?"

"No, sir. While all this is going on, the Battalion Commander of the First Battalion appoints a Summary Court Officer to settle Driscoll's estate. You know the drill, SOP when a soldier dies on active duty. When the Summary Court Officer went to Driscoll's quarters to inventory his personal effects, he found a slew of pornographic pictures of Driscoll with a bunch of different Thai women and ten grand in cash. Then he went to the Military Banking Facility on Kadena to see if Driscoll had any accounts there. Want to guess how much?"

"Not a clue."

"Driscoll had an account with over a quarter of a million dollars in it."

Lucas whistled into the phone.

Then Goodmon's voice took on a tone of disgust, "Sir, when the Battalion Commander called Colonel Howard and told him what they found in Driscoll's room and about the bank account, Colonel Howard blew him off. The Colonel told him Driscoll was single so he didn't have anything to spend his paycheck on. Then he told the Battalion Commander he needed to deal with the sergeant who needed to deal with his wife."

"I tried to tell Colonel Howard, he needed to pursue an investigation no matter how much he was in Driscoll's debt for saving his life in Vietnam. The cash, the pictures, and the huge bank account---it's too suspicious. You know what I mean, sir---where there's smoke, there's fire. He didn't listen. He thought he was being loyal to an old friend who'd saved his life. Colonel Howard sent forward something that said an investigation wasn't necessary. Sergeant Major Driscoll is deceased. The Army Staff didn't buy that and he was told to investigate and report. They gave him a week."

"The Colonel dummied up a second report---didn't let anybody see it---just sent it in. He said he'd personally investigated and questioned the sergeant, the sergeant's wife, and some others. The whole thing came apart when one of the DOD IG people sent a copy of the Colonel's report to the sergeant's wife since she'd been the one who lodged the original complaint. She went to the Battalion Commander; both of them knew Colonel Howard hadn't conducted any investigation; there were no interviews conducted like the report said. The Battalion Commander registered his own Hotline complaint. After that sir, it took about a nanosecond for the DOD IG to report the lie to the Chief of Staff of the Army."

"Colonel Howard's already gone. The XO is acting commander until you get here and take over. Our guidance is to have your assumption of command order ready. The minute you arrive, you sign it and you've got it. I was really looking forward to seeing you again sir, but not like this, this isn't..."

Lucas interrupted him. There was no point in Goodmon beating himself up over this. "Well, it's rarely a perfect world, Sergeant Major. Bull Howard was a good man who made a mistake and put his loyalty in the wrong place. It'll be good working with you again, Top. I'll see you on Monday." It was 3 April and Lucas Johnson was taking command three months earlier than he'd anticipated.

Chapter Eighteen

They had lingered in the palm grove after making love. They didn't talk. Instead they held each other, stroked the others cheek and hair like lovers do and they would kiss, tenderly, again and again, like lovers do after lovemaking. Sometime after midnight Liott led him back to her father's hut. The countryside around the village was very quiet now and the village was swallowed by the darkness. They fell asleep in one another's arms. Sometime between leaving the palm grove and falling to sleep, Cleve's thoughts turned back to the events in Bangkok.

He woke before Liott. His thoughts picked up where they'd left off the night before. The day he didn't want to see come was bearing down on him. Behind him he could hear the labored breathing of the old man whose bed was tucked along the back wall of the hut. Next to him he could feel Liott's gentle, rhythmic breaths as she slept. These were simple people, with uncomplicated lives and, while he longed to live among them, his life was full of troubles right now, troubles that were not Chuk Ra Met's troubles.

"How long have you been awake?" She'd awakened, and he was so far into his thoughts that he hadn't noticed.

"Oh, not very long, " he said unconvincingly.

She rolled over, put her back against his and pulled the light coverlet that was over them to her chin. "I was afraid you'd find this bed too small," she said expecting him to say that it wasn't, that he didn't ever want to sleep again without feeling her next to him.

He didn't answer, still grappling with how he was going to tell them about his troubles. Liott rolled back to face him, "Is something wrong, Cleve?" When he still didn't answer, she asked the question again this time with something in her voice that told him she was becoming frightened.

"I have to tell you something."

Now she was afraid, but she desperately wanted him to talk to her. so she tried to be encouraging, "Whatever it is, it can't be as difficult as what we have already been through."

"Liott, do you remember a man named Driscoll at the court martial?"

"No, I don't think so."

Cleve refreshed her memory about Driscoll's testimony. Then he brought her up to date, "I went to see him two nights ago. While I was with him, he was murdered---Driscoll and one of his girls."

"Cleve…" she was shaking her head as if she were able to read his mind.

"Liott, it gets worse. The police think I killed them. I had to get out of Bangkok. I didn't want to come here. I didn't want to bring this kind of trouble to you and Daniel again. I didn't want to bring this trouble to Chuk Ra Met, but I had no other choice. It was come here to Chuk Ra Met or go to jail again for something I didn't do."

She jumped up from their bed and stood for a moment with her back to him. He was ashamed he'd ever come here. He followed her out of bed, but once he was on his feet he didn't know what else to do or say. He was afraid to touch her, afraid that his touch might be revolting to her. When she did turn toward him, her eyes were riveted on his. She had the same frightened look he saw during the court martial and he couldn't bear that look. There was a minute of deafening silence and then she asked, "So you weren't coming back to see Daniel and me?"

The question was a dagger in his heart, but he didn't want to compound his sins against them by adding a lie to the list. "No. I didn't think you or Daniel ever wanted to see me again."

She turned away. He watched her shoulders heave and fall to the rhythm of her sobs. If the joy of yesterday had ever occurred, it was so far behind him now it had faded from his memory. He'd hurt her yet again and for that he'd wished he were in a Thai jail awaiting trial rather than be here in Chuk Ra Met. All he could say was, "I was wrong, Liott. I am so sorry, but I am sorrier to have brought you this new trouble."

They stood there like that, her back to him, for a long time. She resented his lack of faith in her, in Daniel. He should have known they were waiting, that they still loved him. Yet she understood him as well. She knew what a proud man he was and she tried to put herself in his place, to imagine what it must have been like for him during those years in prison and now it was happening all over again. When Liott Spires turned back to her husband, she had found an inner strength that pushed her resentment to the side and replaced it with righteous indignation and determination. "I will not let them do this to us again. We are going to see someone who can help."

"Who?"

"Pram Saraveet."

"Where is he?"

"In Korat" She grabbed his hand and said, "Let's go."

Pramrashorn Saraveet, Colonel of Infantry, Royal Thai Army, and currently the Commanding Officer of the Tiger Brigade, was an old friend. Twenty-five years earlier, Staff Sergeant Cleve Spires and Lieutenant Pramrashorn Saraveet, "Pram" to his friends, had trained Royal Thai Army and Royal Thai Marines in special operations tactics. Saraveet had been the best man at their wedding twenty-three years ago. Today, as the highest-ranking military officer in the region, Colonel Saraveet was a powerful and influential man.

Liott led Cleve down Korat's back roads and alleys to Saraveet's residence rather than his office. The maid made them comfortable until Pram showed up for lunch. While they waited, Liott filled Cleve in. It was Saraveet who had insisted that Daniel continue to use his English. Saraveet had tutored him until he started high school, and Daniel would practice his English lessons with Liott. That accounted for her marked improvement in English. Saraveet had seen to it that Daniel was accepted into one of Korat's best private schools, and when Liott's very meager income couldn't afford the tuition, books or fees, he'd paid them.

"He never replaced you Cleve, but he helped Daniel in so many ways. I don't know how to explain their relationship..." Her hands were balled into fists. She didn't want him to get the wrong idea, but she wanted him to know the size of the debt they owed this old friend.

Cleve helped her out. "Liott, every boy needs a father and I couldn't be around for a large part of Daniel's growing up. There's no one better you could have picked to take my place than Pram Saraveet. He's as good a man as I know."

If Saraveet knew about the trouble Spires had gotten himself in, it didn't show when he arrived home for lunch and found Liott and Cleve waiting on him. It was a warm reunion between two old friends.

Cleve, however, knew enough about Thailand that he didn't jump to the conclusion that the hunt for him was over. Even though Korat is a big city, this was still Thailand, and information didn't move around here as fast as it did in the States. If Saraveet didn't know about the trouble his old friend was in, it was simply because news of the manhunt hadn't migrated this far north yet. If it had, Saraveet would have been one of the first to know that Cleve Spires was a fugitive. In Thailand, the military, the Royal Thai Army in particular, has a civil defense role that occasionally crosses over into law enforcement. If the National Police want somebody badly enough, they won't hesitate to contact the Army and request their assistance in tracking down the suspect.

They sat on a porch shaded by a huge tree and ceiling fans kept the humid air of mid-day Korat moving. They ate a wonderful lunch of spicy hot soup and fruit and reminisced about old times and talked of Daniel's growing up. Cleve relished the stories of Daniel. Then Saraveet offered, "Cleve, here in Korat there are Thai businessmen who would pay handsomely for a westerner who can speak Thai as well as you."

Saraveet's offer to help was an easy segue to the point of their visit. "Pram, I do need your help." He told Saraveet the trouble that had driven him out of Bangkok and now to Korat. Then he went back to everything that had happened to him since his release from prison.

When Spires was finished, Saraveet thought for a moment and then offered, "They will search for a few more days in Bangkok and when they are unsuccessful one of two things will happen. Either the deaths of Driscoll and the woman will go into an inactive case file, or they will expand the search and ask the Army for help. If they do that I will be notified. For now, you are safe in Chuk Ra Met. Go back there, keep a low profile..." He paused as he had another thought then asked, "Does Daniel know about this?"

Liott answered, "No."

Saraveet offered, "Well, then I suggest you tell him along with the rest of the villagers in Chuk Ra Met what you have told me. We don't want Daniel talking about his father's return or a villager boasting to the wrong people about the American they have living in their village. We need to limit the number of people who know you are in Chuk Ra Met until we see which way this is going to go."

Liott asked him, "What do you think they will do, Pram?"

He shrugged, "I don't know," and then added, "but the three of you should enjoy your time together after all of these years of being apart. I will keep a watchful eye on things here in the district. I'll let you know as I am able to find things out."

Ida Spires and Wanda were having lunch. They talked of nothing but Cleve. It had been two weeks since he'd left and there had been no word. Both women were sure something was wrong, and both wanted to help. Wanda thought of the idea, but it was Ida who went to police headquarters with a picture of her son. Why not file a missing persons report with the Cleveland Police Department? What could possibly be wrong with that idea? The Cleveland Police could contact the police in Thailand and they could search for Cleve.

Sometimes, not often, and never when it is appropriate, big bureaucracies can be remarkably efficient and this was, unfortunately, one of those times. When the Cleveland Police Department passed the missing persons report and the picture on to Thai authorities, a Thai cop screened the information and he just happened to know about the shootings on Soi Cowboy. He knew they were searching for a black, American male. He passed the photo to a Thai homicide detective who took the picture to the old woman at the Club Exotica. Bingo! The Thai homicide detective, who could speak some English, called the Cleveland Police Department and was connected to Detective Bergstrom in that department's homicide division. Bingo, again! From that point on it was only a matter of minutes before Ida's missing person report turned into an open homicide investigation and Cleve Spires was the primary suspect.

The next day Saraveet received an official communication requesting the assistance of his Brigade to help the Thai National Police find Cleveland A. Spires, an American, wanted on three counts of murder: two in Thailand and one in Cleveland, Ohio. A picture, a copy of the one given the Cleveland Police Department by Ida Spires, accompanied the request.

Pram Saraveet waited until dark and then set out for Chuk Ra Met. The village's population was fewer than twenty-five. Everyone knew he was there before he got to the hut of Liott's father. When Cleve and Liott saw him they could read the look on his face. Liott began to cry and Cleve's stomach turned over.

"It's not good, my friend. They have identified you and I received instructions today to have my soldiers look for you. You are suspected of three murders, two in Bangkok and one in Cleveland. I am sorry; I wish I had better news."

Cleve Spires had never felt more trapped in his life. This was even worse than when they arrested him at Fort Lewis. Now he was endangering the life of his wife, his son and an old friend, not to mention the lives of the villagers of Chuk Ra Met.

"Well, I can't stay here any longer. It's too dangerous for all of you."

Liott shot back, "Don't be silly Cleve. There is no place more safe than here."

"But..."

Saraveet interrupted him, "She's right Cleve. You wouldn't last an hour anywhere else in Thailand right now. I've thought about this all day today. If the villagers here are loyal, I think your best bet is to lay low, right here in Chuk Ra Met, until the manhunt winds down. When that happens, I can get you out of the country. What I don't know is where you should go."

Saraveet asked Liott, "Can the villagers be trusted?"

She nodded. Spires missed the question and her answer. He was deep in thought. Saraveet and Liott continued to talk but Cleve was not listening.

"I need to go to Japan."

Liott, panic on the edge of her voice, said, "What?"

"I need to go to Japan." He went over to a bag, rummaged around in it and came up with the notebook he'd taken from Agaki's body. The *Yakuza's* there and I'll bet this guy Fujiwara…"

"No! You can't leave us. You can't go there alone." Liott was practically screaming at him.

Saraveet tried to be a voice of reason. "Cleve, she's right. You need more proof that this Fujiwara is connected…"

"C'mon Pram. What reason would Driscoll have to lie? He was dying for Christ's sake. This guy Fujiwara is a link somehow. Spires held up Agaki's notebook and asked, "Do you know anyone who can read Japanese?"

Saraveet took the book from Spires and began thumbing through it. After flipping through five or six pages, Saraveet stopped and looked at him.

"He's in here! *Cato Fujiwara* and there is an address and phone number as well."

Cleve asked, "When did you learn to read Japanese?"

Saraveet smiled at him. "I have not let the years slow my brain down as much as they have slowed my body." He shrugged his shoulders. "It was not so hard for me to learn it. Asian languages, for an Asian, are a bit simpler than for a Westerner."

By now Liott was beside herself. She could see Cleve was going to leave her again. "You can't leave. You are safe here. There is nothing that we need outside of this village. As long as you stay…"

Liott couldn't talk anymore; she put her back to them and slumped down on edge of their bed as tears overtook her. Cleve put his arms around her, but she took little comfort from it. Saraveet could see there was little else he could do, but he offered some advice. "There is nothing more we can do tonight, my friend. Liott is right. You are safe here for at least the next day or so. My soldiers will come to look in the village. You will know when that is to happen. You should find a good hiding spot away from the village. Later we can talk about the future."

Cleve did not let go of Liott. She was limp in his arms. "Thank you Pram. You are a true friend. We'll wait to hear from you."

A week later he returned, at night, to tell them his soldiers would be in Chuk Ra Met in the morning as part of their search responsibility. "They won't talk to everyone, but I can't control who they will talk to, so you must let all of the villagers, even the children, know that they can't mention Cleve."

When he left, Cleve walked with him to the village's edge. "We've decided I must go to Japan and try to find Cato Fujiwara." Spires didn't bore him with the details of the decision, and Saraveet wasn't surprised by it. He didn't see his old friend as a guy who would sit back and let someone stick it to him like this.

"I will look into ways of helping you get out of the country and into Japan. Please understand that nothing will happen for at least a month. This manhunt for you is massive, but you're safe here. I have agreed with the National Police that they will concentrate on searching inside the city of Korat, and my soldiers will search the outlying villages of the District. After tomorrow, Chuk Ra Met will be checked off our list and there will be no more for you to worry about as long as you stay right here. If you don't hear from me, don't worry. I will stay away from Chuk Ra Met so as not to draw attention to the village. Be ready to go at a moment's notice. If I have a window of opportunity to get you out of Thailand, it may only be a narrow one, so we will need to move quickly."

"I have good news Fujiwara-san. The Thai police have Spires' name and a photo. They have expanded the search for him to nationwide."

Fujiwara spoke calmly into the phone, "But the fact is, he is still a free man isn't he?"

"Correct, Fujiwara-san but..."

Fujiwara hung up on his caller and called for his chief counsel.

The agent was no longer of any consequence. The madam could positively identify Spires when he was caught. The man had failed, and then he'd tried to put a better face on the situation than was, in fact, the case. He gave the chief counsel a note with the agent's name on it.

"See that he is eliminated."

This was more the way the chief counsel preferred to have it. Fujiwara's disdain was focused on someone other than himself. It was an easy matter to arrange. The bungling agent was kidnapped coming out of his Bangkok hotel. From Bangkok, he was driven to Pattaya and put on a fishing boat and taken some miles off shore. Two buckets were filled with wet concrete. When the doomed man saw what his tormentors intended, he struggled to pull his feet from the buckets of freshly mixed cement. Two sledgehammer blows smashed his kneecaps, and after that he couldn't move his feet at all. When the concrete had hardened enough that it wouldn't dissolve in the corrosive salt water, they moved him to the side of the fishing boat and laughed at his screams as they pushed him over the side.

Fujiwara dialed Yamamoto's private number.

"Saieto, I wanted to let you know Driscoll is dead."

"Good, Cato, I am glad that is finished."

"Well, it is not exactly finished. Spires has not been taken into custody. The Bangkok police appear to be inept. I am told a massive manhunt is underway for him. The police believe he is definitely the murderer. I suspect it is only a matter of time before he is either caught or killed. I will keep you advised."

On 17 April, Colonel Pram Saraveet returned to Chuk Ra Met late in the morning and found Cleve and Daniel working in the rice paddies. "It's time my friend. I have arranged passage for you to Japan but we must be at the docks in Bangkok tonight. Are you ready to go?"

Cleve nodded. Daniel's eyes filled with tears but he managed to be strong, "Go to mother, Papa. I'll finish things here. Always remember I love you." Father and son hugged one another and Saraveet followed Spires back to the village.

It wasn't necessary for them to explain things to Liott. She knew what Saraveet's presence meant; it was time for Cleve to leave her---again. Pram Saraveet's heart broke for this family. Cleve quickly gathered his few belongings and gave Liott's father a hug and asked him once again to take good care of his family. Then he went to Liott.

Saraveet waited outside the hut. Daniel joined him and the two men waited together. Cleve joined them in a minute. Liott remained in her father's hut. When they were gone, Daniel went inside and tried to comfort her as best he could.

It was well after midnight when Saraveet's sedan pulled along the vessel's berth at the Port of Bangkok. Even at this late hour the ships on either side of theirs had crews working to load and unload them. The place was a chaotic scene of men, trucks, containers and cargo all moving in every direction. Amidst all of this organized confusion, they arrived virtually unnoticed. The ship's master, a friend of Pram's, met both of them at the freighter's gangway. When he was sure he had done as much as he could to guarantee safe passage for his friend to Japan, Pram headed back to Korat. The freighter departed on its scheduled tide. It was going to take a month to get to Yokohama, with scheduled port calls along the way in Malaysia, Singapore, Indonesia, Taiwan, The Philippines and Okinawa. It certainly wasn't the most direct route to where he wanted to go, but it was the best that Pram Saraveet was able to come up with given the fact that Cleve Spires was still very much a wanted man in Thailand.

Chapter-Nineteen

On the trip from Seattle-Tacoma International Airport to Fort Lewis, Washington, Lucas Johnson and Dave Goodmon caught one another up on personal matters, family, mutual friends and the like. Both knew that once they started to dig into the mess that had brought Johnson to command three months early, there might not be time for conversation like this and both considered it important, a matter of respect between them. Since Desert Storm, when they'd last seen one another, Goodmon had become a grandfather for the second time, and Johnson's daughter was born. Now Johnson was plopped in an easy chair in the corner of his new office. Lieutenant Colonel Dave Ellison, his executive officer, and Goodmon flanked him. Each held a fresh cup of the mud Goodmon called "coffee" retrieved from the terminally stained pot that was constantly at the side of his desk. Anyone in the Group Headquarters was welcome to partake and most did---once. Johnson took a sip of the coffee and screwed up his face. "Shit! Sergeant Major, you're still passing this horse piss off as coffee. After all these years I thought you'd learn…"

"You don't like it? It's special, sir. I brewed it just for you. After PT this morning, I put my sweat socks in there during the brew cycle. I think they give the stuff a certain woody flavor."

They chuckled, Lucas sat the coffee mug on the floor beside his chair and then they got down to business. Lucas asked Ellison, "What's your impression of the First Battalion?"

"Top notch outfit, sir. Huge mission---strung out all over the southwestern Pacific. On any given day they have soldiers in Indonesia, the Philippines, Australia, Malaysia; you name it in that part of the world and the First Battalion has had troops there in the past year. Thailand is their heaviest commitment. They've got people there year round."

"Tell me about the Battalion Commander."

"He feels badly about Colonel Howard, but he believes he did the right thing by alerting the IG."

It wasn't the answer Johnson was looking for, so he worded the question more directly. "How could Driscoll be so dirty and the Battalion Commander not know it?"

Goodmon said, "He *was* the *Battalion Command Sergeant Major,* and he'd been there for nearly seven years. He spoke three languages. Hell, right or wrong, people in that unit looked up to the guy because he'd been there for so long. No one was looking for him to be dirty. Sir, I had a couple of NCO's tell me they'd gone to a couple of bars with Driscoll in Bangkok. They said all the girls there seemed to know him, but they didn't think that was unusual. He was single, he'd throw money around and the girls would come around. You know how those bars in Bangkok are. If you court-martialed every GI that went in one of those places there wouldn't be anyone left in the damn Army, Colonel."

Ellison's opinion differed, "Sir, what the Sergeant Major says is true, but I think that Battalion is spread too thin. The Battalion Commander is literally never on Okinawa. Lieutenant Colonel Greene told me he had an arrangement with Driscoll. The Sergeant Major would take care of everything in Thailand, and Lieutenant Colonel Greene would handle things everywhere else the Battalion had troops deployed. Greene's been there six months and Driscoll has been there six years. Greene was Driscoll's third battalion commander. Greene didn't want to screw with something that didn't appear broken, so he went along with it. It wasn't until the Summary Court Officer turned up the stuff in Driscoll's room that anybody began to suspect something was wrong."

"Have the police figured out who the shooter was?"

Goodmon answered the question with a question.

"Have you ever heard of Command Sergeant Major Cleveland Spires?"

Lucas Johnson leaned forward and slammed both hands down on his knees. "I was a member of his court martial board. Driscoll was a witness for the prosecution during the trial." It all came back to him in a flood.

Goodmon continued, "Spires is still loose. Thai police, INTERPOL, damned near everybody's looking for him. An eyewitness ID'd him from a photo---a mama-san at the bar where Driscoll was killed."

Lucas was only half listening to him. He was remembering the last time he saw Spires when he was leaving Fort Leavenworth.

Goodmon asked, "So you think this is some kind of revenge killing. Spires hit him because Driscoll fingered him?"

"I don't know, and I'm damn glad I don't have to answer that question. My job is to figure out what Driscoll was up to. I don't think we can do that from here. Sergeant Major, how's your Thai?"

"Goodmon responded in Thai, "Good."

"OK, then. See if we can get out of here tomorrow. Let's talk about who we should visit in Bangkok."

The long flight from Seattle to Bangkok was exhausting, but Lucas didn't want to waste any time. Goodmon told the cab driver in Thai to take them directly to the Windsor Hotel. The young woman at the reception desk got the manager for them. He pretended not to understand English when Lucas introduced himself. But when Goodmon provided a Thai translation of Johnson's introduction, the manager knew he was going to have to talk with the Americans. He invited both into his office and closed the door.

In pretty good English now, the manager confessed, "I assume you want to discuss Mr. Driscoll. I apologize for my deception just now, but you caught me off guard."

Lucas interrupted, "Why do you feel you need to have your guard up?"

"Mr. Driscoll was a regular customer here, but he was killed elsewhere. Mr. Driscoll was involved," he paused searching for the right word or phrase, "in some unseemly businesses here in Bangkok. I hope you do not suspect foul play here at the hotel. The Windsor is a respected hotel. We wouldn't want our reputation..." his voice trailed off. "I'm sure you can understand my...I mean the hotel's position."

Lucas was wary. *He lied once; he'll do it again.* On top of that, he just plain didn't like this guy. He didn't think this guy was concerned about the reputation of the Windsor Hotel at all, but he was vitally concerned that he be removed from suspicion. Johnson pressed him, "How *regular* is regular. Do you have receipts of his room bills or anything substantiating he stayed here and how often?" Lucas had copies of Driscoll's travel vouchers for the past year in his briefcase, but this was a test.

"I had an arrangement with Mr. Driscoll. It was not illegal but it facilitated his requirement and permitted us to get paid the correct amount for the suite he occupied during his stays with us."

"I'm not sure I understand."

"Mr. Driscoll stayed in the Hibiscus Suite whenever he was with us. The suite costs about $200.00 a night. Mr. Driscoll came to me and explained he did not want everyone to know he was spending nearly twice as much as he would be reimbursed when he filed his travel claim. He said it was none of their business and he could afford to pay the extra money. I would give him a receipt for $100.00 per night. He would pay me $200.00 a night for the suite."

Lucas thought, *...and you put the other hundred dollars in your pocket, didn't you?* Johnson restrained himself; there was nothing he could do about the manager and, though it might raise an auditor's eyebrows, there was nothing illegal about this arrangement Driscoll had with him, from a US government point of view. On the vouchers Lucas had with him, Driscoll had only claimed reimbursement for $100.00 per night. The government would have reimbursed him up to $120.00 a night. Technically Driscoll had saved the government $20.00 a night by staying at the Windsor.

Lucas changed the line of questioning.

"You say Driscoll was a regular customer. We know he was here at least six of the last twelve months. Tell me, what did he have in his room at the time of his death?"

The manager shifted in his chair and then shifted again. The fact was, for the last three years, the suite had been Driscoll's exclusively. When the manager read in the Bangkok newspapers about the killing, he went to the Hibiscus Suite and took his pick of Driscoll's worldly possessions. Driscoll's gold jewelry and about $20,000.00 cash was his share. The hotel's two assistant managers split Driscoll's wardrobe evenly between them. They also took their choice of several thousand pornographic photos Driscoll had taken of some of his girls. These were very marketable among the hundreds of thousands of male tourists visiting Bangkok each year. About all that was remaining after these three vultures finished picking through the room was a shoebox full of various papers. The manager took it from a desk drawer and gave it to Lucas.

"Thank you." Lucas took the box and bluffed a little, "This is all that he had with him?" Lucas shook the box and could tell there wasn't much inside. "Driscoll spent a lot of time at this hotel. He obviously had a good working relationship with you. What can you tell me about what Driscoll did here in Bangkok? Specifically I want to know about his involvement with any bars here in Bangkok."

The manager was rushing to respond, but Lucas warned him, "I expect you to be very honest with me, sir. If you are, I will not pursue why a man who was in Thailand as much as Driscoll only has a shoe box full of effects remaining in his hotel room after his death. Do I make myself clear?"

The little chiseler was really squirming now, "You must understand, I do not know anything directly. It is only what I have heard, sometimes second and third hand. Mr. Driscoll was the money behind four bars, two in Pattpong and two on Soi Cowboy. He probably employed 200 to 300 people in these places. Many people were saddened by what happened to Mr. Driscoll."

"What kind of work do these *employees* perform in these bars?" Again, Johnson knew the answer, but he wanted to hear it from this man.

"Most of them are hostesses."

Lucas put his steely eyes right on the manager's, "Sir, you're not the genteel type. Stop trying to be. What do these hostesses do?"

The manager knew it was useless to drag the game of cat and mouse out any longer. He didn't know for sure how much these two Americans knew, but if he kept trying to evade their questions, he would only piss them off and that would lead to further questioning. "They're prostitutes and they made Mr. Driscoll very wealthy."

Johnson shot Goodmon a glance and asked, "Did he have any partners in these businesses?"

"I…I don't…I mean, I wouldn't know."

"Are there any other American servicemen who stay here as much as Driscoll?"

"No."

"Well, then did you ever see him with Thais."

"Mr. Driscoll always had women in his…"

"No. I mean Thais who might be his business partners."

The manager thought for a minute and then responded, "I can't recall seeing him with anyone, but I suspect he must have had some partners who were Thai. As a foreigner, he couldn't own property here. I also don't think the government would give him a business license." Hoping that this little bit of information, this tad of cooperation, might get him off the hook, his eyes darted quickly back and forth between Johnson and Goodmon. "That is what I know, gentlemen. I hope it is of some assistance in getting to the bottom of this terrible matter."

Goodmon asked, "Do you know the names of the bars?"

As the manager gave the names and locations, Goodmon copied them down. It was five o'clock in the afternoon. Johnson said, "It's too early to go bar-hopping."

The manager asked, "Where are you staying?"

Goodmon gave him the name of the hotel and the manager said, "I'll arrange a car to take you there."

Goodmon looked at Johnson who nodded. When they were in the car Goodmon asked, "You think he's telling the truth?"

"About Driscoll, yes; about himself, not on your life. He had something going with Driscoll. Now he's got something going with whoever inherited those four bars, but it's not him we're after, just Driscoll."

They arrived that evening at the Club Rose at 8:00PM and by 8:05 both concluded Lucas had been right about the manager at the Windsor Hotel. They were expected at the Club Rose and no one would wait on them. One of two Aussies sitting at the bar told a hostess they wanted to buy the "two American blokes" a couple of beers. Lucas overheard them give her the order. She refused without an explanation. When he persisted the girl proceeded to distract the two Australians by removing her Bikini top and bottom and squeezing herself in between the two of them. They forgot about the Americans.

Events at the Club Majestic were much the same. No one even spoke to them, yet as other men entered the bar, at least two girls would approach the newcomer and escort him to a table. While one would take an order for drinks, the other would sit down and move enticingly close. Johnson and Goodmon were lepers.

They took a cab from Pattpong to Soi Cowboy and when things at the Kangaroo Club played out exactly the same way, they left and headed down the street to their last stop, Club Exotica, where Driscoll had bought it.

A rather fat, scowling Thai woman met them inside the door. She neither prevented their entry nor did she invite them in, so Lucas brushed past her looking for the restrooms. He heard her mutter something but didn't look back because the call he was answering was more urgent than whatever the old woman had said. Sergeant Major Goodmon took a seat at the bar and waited. As Lucas walked through the club, crowded with at least forty girls, they moved out of his way like he had the plague.

The men's room stank. The urinal was a tile wall with a trough along its bottom that led out under the rear wall of the room. Lucas was sure the trough didn't lead to a sewer but instead merely drained the urine onto the surface of the alley behind the bar. On his way out of the toilet he noticed the poster next to the dirty, scratched mirror above the sink. He couldn't read the words because they were in Thai but he recognized the picture, Cleveland A. Spires. He pulled the poster off of the bathroom's wall and took it back to the bar where Goodmon was waiting, unserved.

"Can you read this?"

The Sergeant Major apologized, "Sir, I'm doing good to speak this language. I can't even guess what that says. Is that Spires?"

Johnson shook his head yes. "Yeah, that's him. How much do you know about him?"

"I doubt there's a Sergeant Major in the Army today that hasn't heard about the trouble he got into. I don't know a lot of details, just that he did ten years at Leavenworth for murder and smuggling---that's about it."

As the bartender busied himself with other customers, ignoring them, Lucas gave him some more information including the doubts that had haunted him all these years. When he was finished, Goodmon gestured in the direction of the madam who'd met them at the door. She sat scowling at them from a booth across the bar. "I'll bet that ugly old Mama-san over there is the eye-witness to Driscoll's demise. She might be able to give us some answers, sir."

The old woman's booth was strategically located; girls and their customers had to pass by her as they came and went from the back rooms. Goodmon and Johnson sat down, uninvited, across from her. Goodmon spoke in Thai and that made the Mama-san visibly uncomfortable. "Mama-san, what does this poster say?"

A girl and her customer walked up and handed the old woman some money, which the girl had previously collected from the customer. In exchange, the old woman fished around in a box sitting next to her and handed the girl two towels and a key. Then she wrote something in a journal she had on the table in front of her. Goodmon waited until she completed her administrative duties and then repeated the question.

For some reason she answered in English. Johnson figured she was trying to avoid saying too much. Goodmon started to interrupt and tell her to speak Thai, he'd translate, but Lucas put his hand on Goodmon's arm. "No, it's OK, she can tell me in English or Thai." He was trying to gain her confidence.

She was angry, "That," she was pointing at Spires' picture, "son of bitch kill Beelee...here." She pointed to the floor. They followed her finger and could see a dark stain on the floor. "One month---him kill Beelee and number-one girl---Nha. Business no good now. Police catch, soon."

Goodmon asked in Thai, "How do you know it was this man?"

Now she reverted to Thai, but she spoke too fast and Goodmon had to ask her to slow down. He translated for Johnson, "She says she saw it happen. She says Spires came in here, walked over to Driscoll, pulled a gun and shot him in the back of the head. The girl was under the table---you figure what she was doing there---and the bullet went through Driscoll and hit her in the face. She says the girl died quicker than Driscoll did. The police are still hunting for Spires."

"Let's go Sergeant Major. I've had enough *fun* for one night."

Goodmon negotiated a cab to their hotel. During the ride there

Lucas was lost in thought. *Spires came back here and killed Driscoll. Revenge? For what? Because Driscoll set Spires up to go to jail for ten years? Or maybe Driscoll and Spires were working together and Spires got caught and Driscoll didn't. Spires comes back here after he gets out to collect his share and Driscoll doesn't want to play fair. Anyway you play this out it looks like we were right ten years ago.*

When they entered the lobby of their hotel, Lucas suggested, "Top, there's a couple of cold beers in the refrigerator in my room. Let's have a look through that box of stuff Driscoll left behind."

There were a lot of receipts, most written in Thai, so neither of them had a clue what Driscoll had bought. There were some pin-on military insignia, which caused Lucas to comment, "That asshole at the Windsor left this because it wasn't made of gold." The last item out of the box was a small hardbound book. There was nothing on the outside indicating its title or its purpose. Lucas opened it up and found it appeared to be an address book, with all of its entries hand-written. They went through each page. Both Johnson and Goodmon had a surreal feeling as they thumbed through the pages of the dead man's book. Driscoll was a panderer and maybe worse, but the book contained the names and addresses of Special Forces officers and noncommissioned officers that they knew. Mentally they reminded themselves that just because someone's name appeared in Driscoll's book, it didn't make them criminals.

When they'd gone "A" to "Z" Lucas asked his Sergeant Major, "Did you notice anything unusual?"

"No, sir. Looks like an address book to me. Hell, I knew the son-of-a-bitch for two years, you could have found my name in here just as easily as any of these other guys' names we found."

"Yeah, but I'm not talking about people. I'm talking about banks. Look here," and he flipped back to the "C's" and pointed to an entry marked, "The International Bank of Costa Rica". Under "P" they found "The Bank of Panama" and under "S", the National Bank of Switzerland". With each entry, there was a number listed, like an account number. "Except for these three banks, there's nothing except people listed in here."

"You think our Sergeant Major Driscoll was into some international banking?"

"I do, and I'd hate to guess how much he might have stashed in these three accounts if he had a quarter of a million dollars in the military banking facility on Okinawa." They finished their beers and Lucas said, "I think we've learned as much about Driscoll as we're going to learn here in Thailand. He picked up the phone and while he waited for the hotel operator to answer he said, "Let's see if we can get booked on a flight back to Seattle tomorrow."

Lucas Johnson didn't sleep that night. He couldn't get Cleve Spires out of his mind. He tried to understand the bitterness that must have been festering in him during those ten years in jail. He tried to understand how the Army could have been so wrong about men like Spires and Driscoll. Both of them had been at the top of their profession, yet both of them were really nothing more than criminals. He wondered where Spires was now, how he'd managed to avoid capture and what else he might do. As he lay there restless in his bed he had no way of knowing that just a few miles from his hotel, at the Port of Bangkok, Cleve Spires was boarding an old freighter headed eventually for Japan.

Two days after arriving back at Fort Lewis, Lucas sent his report on the improper business affairs of Command Sergeant Major Billy Driscoll to the Chief of Staff of the Army, who in turn passed it on to the DOD IG exactly as Lucas had written it. The report asked the IG's assistance in following up on Johnson's theory of offshore bank accounts.

Chapter Twenty

The trip from Bangkok to Yokohama took nearly the month he'd been told it would. He hadn't been off the ship since boarding it in Bangkok. He'd kept track of time with a calendar, carefully crossing out each day as it passed. It hadn't made time pass any faster; the month had been an incredibly long one.

On 15 May, he crawled from his hiding spot, a gear locker accessed through a trap door on the deck of the engine room. He'd been in there about two hours this time and it was a miserable place, pitch black and reeking of oil and diesel, but this spot had allowed him to avoid detection by immigration and customs officials at five different ports. On the captain's advice, he waited another hour after the Japanese authorities left the freighter, then Cleve grabbed his backpack and headed down the gangway. Utterly alone, all he had going for him was a little over four thousand dollars he'd taken off Driscoll's body the night he was shot and the notebook he'd removed from Agaki's shirt pocket the night he'd bought it in Cleveland. In the negative column he lacked even the most rudimentary ability to speak Japanese, no one to teach him, no one here he could trust, no one to lead him around this megalopolis known as Tokyo. He ran head long into the language barrier after hailing a cab a few blocks from the port. "Do you speak English?"

The driver didn't.

"OK, let's try this." Spires produced Agaki's notebook, handed it to him and pointed to the Kanji lettering giving Fujiwara's name and address.

Cleve held his thumb up and questioned, "OK?"

The driver knew where Spires wanted to go, but there was another problem. Could this guy afford the fare? Where he wanted to go was a long way away. He said something to Spires in Japanese.

Cleve shrugged his shoulders and shook his head, "I'm sorry, I don't understand."

The driver reverted to sign language. He pulled his billfold out and removed a 1000 Yen note, pointed to it and pointed to Cleve, and said something again in Japanese.

OK, what's this guy telling me? It will cost 1000 Yen? Maybe he wants to know if I have Yen. Hell, I'll just show him the roll and see what happens. He produced Driscoll's roll of money and the driver's eye's got as big as hubcaps. Motioning for Cleve to get in, he handed back Agaki's notebook.

Though it was 9:00P.M., the traffic from Yokohama west into the heart of Tokyo was absurd. Along the way, the driver pulled over to a money-changing booth. He said, "dollar" and pointed to Cleve and then "yen" pointing to the booth. Cleve got the message. He got out of the cab and changed $2000.00 of Driscoll's money into Yen.

At 11:00PM, the driver pulled to a stop in front of an immense skyscraper. Cleve was sure they'd failed to communicate somehow. He pointed to the skyscraper and then to the address in the notebook. "Are you sure this is the place?"

The driver didn't understand. He pointed to the notebook in Spires' hand and then again to the building and nodded.

"OK, if you say so." Spires had watched the fare accumulate on the cab's meter as they had gone along. The reading on the meter was just under 10,000 Yen, so Cleve gave him one of the notes he'd just gotten from the moneychanger. This was his first exposure to how expensive things were in Japan, especially in Tokyo. That cab ride came to just under a hundred bucks. He got out of the cab, craned his neck back to look up to the top of the building, and scratched his head. Things were not getting any easier. The lobby entrance was open so he went in. He checked the building directory, which fortunately was in western script as well as in Japanese. There must have been two hundred businesses in the building, spread between floor one and floor seventy. The name "Fujiwara" was nowhere to be found. He glanced at his watch. It was nearly 11:30PM and the security guard at the desk in the lobby was giving him the eye. He decided it would be best to leave.

Once outside, he crossed the street to a small park adjacent to the skyscraper's entrance, took a seat on a park bench and, for a moment, let his mind wander. It was obvious he would make no further progress tonight. He'd have to wait until the morning, when he could get into the building less conspicuously. The late spring air made even Tokyo's overcrowded conditions and pollution seem pleasant. He was daydreaming when a black limousine stopped in front of the building's entrance and snapped him back to reality. Amidst the hundreds of small cars whizzing up and down the busy street, the limo stood out like---well, like Spires thought he stood out among all of the small, yellow-skinned, and silky-black-haired Japanese. When no one got out of the limo, he assumed it was picking someone up. A minute later, the skyscraper's front door opened. One man came out looking around him as he walked toward the car. He opened the rear door on the passenger side, gave a quick motion in the direction of the building's door, and resumed his scanning. When the building's door opened a second time, two men emerged. The younger of these two appeared to be protecting an immaculately dressed older man. The pair moved directly to the limo's open rear door and got in. The first man who'd come out the door, closed the limo's rear door, took a front seat and the limo moved from the curb into traffic. Cleve Spires had no way of knowing it at the time, but he had just caught his first glimpse of Cato Fujiwara.

He awoke to someone tapping on the sole of his shoe. A beautiful spring evening had turned into an even more beautiful morning and the park bench had proved to be an inexpensive and very nice hotel room, until now. The policeman, who'd thumped his shoe with his nightstick, wasn't pleased. Vagrancy isn't a crime in Japan. In a country where hard work is the expectation, most Japanese simply ignored vagrants, homeless people. The police, on the other hand, were less accepting of them, but since there was no law against it there were only certain things they could do. One of their tricks was to keep them moving. If vagrants moved, then they somehow weren't vagrants anymore.

"I'm sorry. I don't speak Japanese."

The cop raised his voice and waved his nightstick. Cleve didn't have to understand the cop to know he was pissed and he certainly didn't want any trouble with the Tokyo police so he quickly collected his backpack and moved off in the direction the cop had indicated. The cop's problem was solved and Cleve was relieved to see his departure apparently satisfied the officer. Though he had slept reasonably well on the stone bench, he decided he'd not do that again.

He found a subway station, cleaned up in its well-kept public restroom and then headed for the skyscraper. The huge lobby was a busy place during the morning rush hour, and despite his physical differences, he felt less conspicuous simply because the place was so busy. He headed for the elevators and got on board one that was packed. When the doors rolled smoothly closed, he suddenly felt very conspicuous; everyone was staring at him. He avoided eye contact, which wasn't hard to do since he stuck out head and shoulders above the next tallest person around him. He decided he would ride to the highest floor currently illuminated on the control panel and get off.

On the 65th floor he walked around the hallways to get a feel for how the floors were laid out. He assumed each floor's basic plan, at least for the common areas like hallways, rest rooms, and stairways, would be identical from floor to floor. He found a stairwell and started up. Each floor was marked with its number.

When he got to the 70th Floor he found two doors exactly as he had found on the floors underneath. One door opened on to the 70th Floor offices and was unlocked. The door leading to the higher floors, however, was different from the ones he'd encountered on the floors below. This one had some Japanese writing on it that was, of course, unintelligible to him. This door also had a cipher pad with the card-swipe channel along one side and a blinking red light located just above the door's handle. Just for the hell of it, he pushed and then pulled on the door. Nothing moved. *The directory only lists 70 floors. I wonder what's up there that requires extra security.* The thought came to him that perhaps *the Yakuza* would want extra security.

He'd been standing in the stairwell for a minute trying to decide what he should do next, when he noticed the other difference about the 70th floor. Security cameras were one of the first things he'd looked for in the lobby, in the elevator and in the stairwell. Until now, there had been none. This one was trained on the locked door and anyone receiving the camera's images could observe him standing there. Quickly, he stepped through the unlocked door, out onto the 70th floor, and well out of the camera's range. *Well, you just gave someone a TV close up. What's your next brilliant move?*

He roamed the hallway of the 70th floor for the next 15 minutes. He found three other stairways. Each contained a camera and a locked door leading to the floors above him. Reluctantly, he resigned himself to the fact that he was not going to go any higher by way of the stairs. He headed back to the elevators and pushed the "down" button because there was no "up" button. When the elevator doors opened, they revealed an empty compartment and this gave him an opportunity to study the control panel. There were numbers 1 through 70 covering a huge panel that was nearly as tall as the elevator's door. Under the button marked "70" were five other buttons but these were unnumbered. He pushed the fifth unnumbered button to see what would happen. Nothing---and then the doors rolled smoothly shut. He wasn't sure if the elevator was responding to his command or someone else's until he noticed the descending numbers on the control panel's digital display. The elevator stopped at 62 and an attractive Japanese lady got on. She smiled at him and pointed down. Cleve nodded. She punched 59 and the doors closed. Cleve continued to study the control panel. On the short ride between floors 62 and 59, he discovered why he could not get to the top five floors of the building by way of the elevator. On the right side of the control panel was another keypad like the one on the stairwell. This one had a red blinking light, like the stairwell door, but instead of a swipe channel for a magnetic strip, this had a slot into which a card with a magnetic strip was inserted. Instinctively, he rechecked the elevator for TV cameras. If there were any they were very well concealed.

OK, what do you know now? Wonder what would happen if you got on with someone headed to one the top floors and you just rode with them. It's risky. For the moment, he judged trying something like that might be too risky. He retreated to the lobby and a small coffee shop located near the elevators. He bought a coffee and sat down to watch and think. He'd been here all morning. He knew if he persisted, he'd draw unwanted attention. The elevators weren't the way to Cato Fujiwara and neither were the stairs. He pulled out Agaki's notebook and began to leaf through it. Before he left Thailand, he'd had the good sense to ask Pram Saraveet to translate into English all of the names and addresses that Agaki had entered in Kanji. Since it didn't appear he was going to be able to use the direct approach, maybe an indirect approach might produce something. Maybe one of the other people in the address book could be persuaded to give him information on Fujiwara.

Cleve did a quick scrub of Agaki's notebook and that produced four names with addresses in Tokyo. "Fujiwara" was one. There was one "Agaki". *Probably a brother or a son,* he reasoned. There was a "Mio Miyasato", a woman he presumed only because the name had a feminine ring to it. The final Tokyo address was for a "Michiko Tomichi" whom he was certain was a woman. He thought going after the "Agaki" would be imprudent based on the assumption that, if one Agaki is associated with the *Yakuza,* then all Agaki's---at least the one's in this address book---are part of the same organization. While this might be the most direct route to Fujiwara, it was also the route that would tip the *Yakuza* off that he was here in Tokyo. *Not that they don't already know that after your performance in front of the camera this morning.*

He left the skyscraper and hailed a cab, showing the cab driver Mio Miyasato's address in Agaki's notebook. Before Spires could sit back in the seat, the cab roared from the curb. The address was not far from the skyscraper. The cabby pulled over in front of what looked to be about a fifteen-story apartment building. The fare was 2000 Yen. Shaking his head, Spires paid the nearly twenty-dollar fare, pointed to the building and then to the notebook. The cabby nodded and Cleve got out. Pram Saraveet had carefully translated everything in Agaki's notebook from Japanese to English for Cleve. He was looking for apartment 715. He found the elevator and punched the button for the seventh floor. When the door opened, he found apartment 715 directly across the hall. He rang the doorbell. Mio Miyasato, daughter of Tetsu and Fumiko Agaki, was home enjoying a week long vacation from her job as an accountant with a large Tokyo-based manufacturing firm. She was reading when the doorbell rang.

Cleve introduced himself and asked if she knew a man by the name of Tetsu Agaki.

She hadn't used her English in years. She understood his name, *Cleveland Spires*, and her father's name, *Tetsu Agaki. Who is this man? Why would he come here and ask me if I know my father?* "Tetsu Agaki my father. He no live," she responded in halting, difficult-to-understand English, but Spires understood the word, *father* and immediately regretted coming to this address for the same reasons he had decided to avoid the "Agaki" in Agaki's address book.

He had to be cautious now. This was Agaki's daughter, and his safest assumption was that she was *Yakuza* herself. Spires delivered an academy award performance, "What do you mean your father 'no live'? You don't mean…Oh, no…I'm so sorry."

"My English...long time...University...no good. My father no live."

"I had no idea. Your father is an old friend of many years ago. I'm visiting Tokyo. When I stopped at the address I had for him, a man there gave me your name and address. I could not understand what he was saying, but he wrote down it down for me. A cab brought me here. I am sorry to have bothered you." He bowed awkwardly and moved toward the elevators to leave.

She hadn't understood any of what he'd said. She was happy to see him go. The memory of her father's death was painful for Mio primarily because it reminded her of her mother's recent death. She was the one who had raised her brother and her. She was the one who had always been there for them when they were growing up. Whatever this man wanted with her father, he was too late. Mio forgot about Cleve Spires, her father, and tried to forget, though it was considerably harder, her mother.

Once he got back to the street, he walked at a brisk clip for five or six blocks before stepping to the curb to hail a cab. He showed the driver the notebook, this time opened to the name "Michiko Tomichi". The cabby nodded but then in fair English said, "You pay?"

Cleve asked, "How much to go here?" and pointed to the address in the book.

"Maybe 10,000 Yen...maybe more."

Cab fare was going to eat up all of his money, but he needed these cabbies and their knowledge of the city to get around. He had no choice. He pulled the roll of yen from his pocket. The driver smiled, flicked the switch on his meter and eased into traffic. The trip took nearly an hour, but wound up in a very nice residential neighborhood in front of a building with only five floors. Cleve forked over 7,000 yen to the grinning driver and got out of the cab.

The mailboxes in the entrance way were all in Japanese and Agaki's address book did not have an apartment number for Michiko Tomichi so Cleve had no choice but to ring some door bells in an attempt to find her. There was no answer at the first two he tried. At the third apartment the lady closed the door in his face when it became apparent his English and her Japanese were never going to come to terms with one another. The fourth door produced a usable result.

"Hello. I am looking for Michiko Tomichi. Can you tell me if she lives in this building?"

The attractive young Japanese woman in the door spoke passable English and seemed to understand nearly all of what Cleve said. "Michiko live here...no more," she said shaking her head. "She go."

"I see. Do you know where she lives now, or how I might get in touch with her? It is important that I speak with her."

"No where she lives." The woman continued to shake her head, so he took her rough English to mean, "No, she didn't know where Tomichi lived now." Then she helpfully added, "She work Lions Den Disco---Rapungi---do you know?"

"No."

The young woman looked out in the hallway both ways and motioned for him to come in. Cleve thought this strange but he stepped into the apartment's foyer. The place was lavish. *Whatever she does for a living, she must do it very well to afford a place like this in this city.*

"I write for you. Michiko at Lion's Den tonight 9:00." As she bent down over the table in the foyer to write, the front of her robe gapped open, exposing her breasts fully to Cleve's view. He didn't mean to be rude but it was difficult not to stare and the young woman caught him at it. Smiling coyly at him and making no effort to cover up what she was showing him, she went back to her writing.

Well, she certainly isn't shy. He put two and two together; works in a bar, lives in a place that must cost thousands each month and she's OK with men looking at her. He figured she did a lot more at the Lion's Den than just serve drinks.

She handed him the paper with the address on it in both western letters and Japanese. “Any cab take you. Lion's Den Disco and Rapungi both easy. Maybe I see you tonight."

“You and Michiko work here together?" he asked, holding up the piece of paper she’d handed him.

"Hai."

"What is your name?

"Sanji."

"Sanji, I hope I see you tonight," Spires said with a coy smile on his face, “but don’t tell Michiko I am coming. It has been many years since I’ve seen her and she doesn’t know I am here. I want to surprise her.” He hoped Sanji bought the story about an old friend who’d just arrived. If she warned Tomichi about his coming to the Lion’s Den tonight, and if Tomichi knew what Agaki had been doing in Cleveland, he could be walking into a trap. This time, however, he judged it was worth the risk.

He was tired and the night was shaping up to be a long one. He needed a place to stay. Years ago he’d spent a night at Hardy Barracks, a small US military installation in downtown Tokyo, not far from Rapungi as he faintly recalled; it was the Pacific Headquarters of the *Stars and Stripes,* a daily English-language newspaper sold almost exclusively to US military personnel living overseas. He caught a cab, and at the end of another nearly 10,000 Yen-ride the cabby dropped him off at the entrance to Hardy Barracks. His retired ID card got him past the Japanese security guard at the front gate.

There was some risk to stopping here. He was an American...an ex-serviceman...wanted for killing a Command Sergeant Major. He half expected to find a "wanted" poster with his picture on it hanging on the bulletin board in the Hardy Barracks Billeting Office, but his paranoia went away when his blue, retired military ID got him a room for $10 per night. He could stay there for up to five days and then he could stay another five days on a space-available basis. Finally he’d found something affordable in Tokyo. He got directions to the area called "Rapungi", rested, showered, put on his best clothes and at 9:00 headed for the Lion's Den Disco.

Rapungi is full of trendy bars, some of which cater to Tokyo’s youth, others to the city’s businessmen. It is lavish, crowded, and, more than anything, expensive. The cover charge at the Lion's Den was 5,000 Yen. Spires coughed it up. He could only imagine what the hell a beer would cost in this place. As he stepped into the crowded main bar area, he made several quick observations. First, he was the only person in the bar who was not Japanese. Some of the customers were staring at him. Second, the ratio of men to women in this place was about one to four. Finally, the women were absolute knockouts and dressed in revealing outfits that left just enough to the imagination to keep well-heeled Japanese businessmen buying them overpriced, watered-down drinks. There was no sign of Sanji, who he hoped might steer him toward Michiko. He could still feel the stares of some customers as he found his way to an empty table in the back of the room. He'd no sooner sat down than one of the hostesses came over to take his order. Her English was pretty good.

"I'd like a beer please and if Michiko Tomichi is here would you tell her I'd like to see her."

She smiled seductively at him and responded simply, "Hai."

She was gone less than a minute, returning with a beer and a check for 1000 yen.

"Michiko come soon."

Spires gave her 1500 yen for her trouble and decided to nurse this beer for as long as he could at these prices.

As Michiko Tomichi approached, he had to give Agaki credit. She was beautiful. As for Michiko, she didn't know whom this man was who wanted to see her, or how he had gotten her name. But her job was to respond to a customer's demand, and this customer, whoever he was, had asked to see her. She hoped he had enough money to make her time worthwhile.

Michiko Tomichi hadn't been a prostitute for very long, but since Agaki's death she had come to grips with the fact that that was what she was. She had been Sanji's neighbor until the money from Agaki stopped paying the rent. When he died, Sanji took her under her wing and along the way introduced her to Inamu Inamine who liked what he saw, gave her a salary she couldn't refuse, but told her she'd better not fail to satisfy any customer who was willing to pay for her time. Now, partly out of necessity, partly out of fear, she was starting her third month at the Lion's Den Disco. She was building a bank account and her plans were to one day just disappear to her own private paradise, leaving this filth behind her.

"Michiko, my name is Cleve Spires. I'm trying to locate someone and I think you might be able to help me."

Her English was OK. Some she'd learned in school. Some Agaki had helped her with. While Americans were rare at the Lion's

Den; this one wasn't the first she'd entertained here. The others had paid her well for her time, and she had learned early in this job that business always came first.

"You buy me drink."

It wasn't a question; it was a demand, a precondition of her spending any time at all with him. Cleve nodded, she motioned a waitress over and gave her drink order in Japanese.

"Michiko, I need to ask you about Tetsu Agaki and another man that I think you might know, Cato Fujiwara."

She had sat down on a chair next to him, so close that their knees touched but now she stood back up. "Who are you?"

"My name is Cleve Spires, I'm an American..."

"Agaki dead. Fujiwara, I no can talk."

From her clipped English, Cleve wasn't sure if she knew Fujiwara, but didn't want to talk about him or if she just simply didn't know him. Michiko Tomichi, on the other hand, knew very well that answering questions about Fujiwara would mean trouble, trouble that she didn't want any part of.

Cato Fujiwara had been to the Lion's Den once in the three months she'd worked here. There'd been a wild party in one of the bar's back rooms. One of the girls had overdosed on something and died. Fujiwara was hustled out of the place, and the rest of the group had "cleaned up". Michiko had watched the papers. There was never a hint that anything had happened. She and the other girls talked. It was an open secret that this place belonged to the *Yakuza.* It was also well understood that the less you knew and the less you said, especially when it came to Cato Fujiwara and his organization, the better off you'd be. Michiko didn't know what the connection was between Tetsu Agaki, Fujiwara, and this man, nor did she want to know. Her drink came and Cleve paid the waitress 2000 Yen.

"I have to talk to Cato Fujiwara and I was hoping..."

"I no help."

"But..."

"Thanks for drink," and she walked away leaving him sitting there.

The girl who'd taken his drink order strolled past and he caught her attention. "Is Sanji here?" She nodded. "Could you ask her to come over?" he slid a 500 Yen coin in her direction.

Two minutes later, Sanji approached the table and sat down next to him. He felt her foot rubbing against his leg. "I see you with Michiko. What's wrong? Maybe you like what you see at Sanji's house today?" She winked at him. "You buy me a drink."

"I'll buy you a drink if you tell me about Cato Fujiwara."

This time it was Sanji who stood up. “This bad place to ask about Fujiwara. No one here tell you anything. You better go---best for you, Michiko and me. Best for you, not ask about Fujiwara." She walked away as Michiko had, not ten minutes earlier.

There was little point in hanging around. He hadn’t been in Tokyo for forty-eight hours yet and he’d struck out with what he thought were his best leads. He went outside to clear his head and decide what his next move should be.

Chapter Twenty-one

Michiko Tomichi's evening at the Lion's Den Disco was ruined. She was poor company after Spires' visit, and when your job is to sit, make small talk and half-heartedly fend off the advances of drunk, horny businessmen, being poor company just doesn't cut it. She'd spilled two drinks already, one on her, and the second right in some guy's lap. She smelled of gin, her head throbbed, and at midnight she decided to go home. Just about the time she was walking out the front door of the Lion's Den Disco, Inamu Inamine walked into his club through the back door and was pleased to find the place full of customers, too many in his view without female companionship. He took a headcount and came up one girl short. By process of elimination, he quickly figured out Michiko wasn't there, one of his newest and prettiest ponies. He started asking the other girls if they knew where she was. Taking a john home wasn't permitted until after 1:00AM. That way the club reaped big profits from cheap liquor sold at exorbitant prices for a maximum length of time. By the time he'd gone through three girls and gotten nowhere, he was starting to get pissed. He looked for Sanji; she was the one who'd brought her in.

"Where is Michiko?"

Sanji was lining up a customer for the night. Without looking up, she waved her hand and shrugged. That was the last straw for Inamine. He wanted to hit her for her insolence, but instead he politely excused himself to Sanji's prospective customer before he grabbed her arm and yanked her from behind the table. He led her to his office telling one of the hostesses to give Sanji's customer a bottle of their best scotch on the house, and to tell the gentleman he was sorry, Sanji might be back and she might not. When they reached his office door, he threw her into the room like a rag doll and slammed the door behind him. The noise reverberated through the club like a gunshot.

"One more time, Where is Michiko?" He had her attention now.

"She went home. She was upset. There was a man here tonight who upset her."

"Who was this man?"

"I don't know..." He stepped toward her menacingly; she shrank away and screamed.

"Who was this man?" He shouted it this time.

"An American. He was at my apartment building this afternoon looking for her. He said his name was Spires or something like that. I don't know. I can't remember. I told him Michiko worked here. He came here tonight. He was asking questions about Fujiwara-san."

Now she had his attention. "What did she say to this man?"

"I don't know. I wasn't there when they were talking, but I don't think it was very much if anything."

"And what is it that makes you think that?"

She swallowed hard and answered, "Because he asked me about..." she paused and it infuriated him.

He screamed at her, "About what?"

"He wanted to know about Fujiwara-san."

"And what did you tell him, Sanji?"

She began to cry, "Nothing Inamine-san. I told him nothing except that this was a bad place for him to be asking those kind of questions."

"Where is this man now?"

"I don't know, Inamine-san. He left when I wouldn't talk to him."

"How long ago?"

She looked at her watch, at him and back to her watch, "I, uh, I..."

He grabbed her and shook her hard, "How long ago, you stupid bitch?"

"Maybe two hours. He left maybe two hours ago."

"When did Michiko leave?"

"Just as you arrived."

He pulled her to him. She could feel he was erect. Inamine was enjoying his domination of her. He put his face within an inch of hers. "I should kill you right here and now. Fujiwara would want me to do that," he reached down, unbuttoned her blouse and fondled her breasts, "but I'm going to let you live. I have some business first, Sanji, but tonight you will serve me." He pushed her away hard and she fell. He walked over and put his foot down on her chest, "Wait here for me. Do not leave or you will regret it." He leered at her and pressed down harder with his foot. "There is one other thing---the next time I ask you a question, answer me. You will save both of us embarrassment."

Cleve Spires was sitting on a bench about a half block from the entrance to the Lion's Den Disco. He saw her come out, and since nothing else had come to him as to what to do next, it just seemed natural to follow her. Michiko Tomichi led him to a modest three-story apartment building that was rather old looking on the outside. He lingered across the street from the entrance and waited. About a minute later, a light came on in a front apartment on the top floor. Ten minutes later, the lights went out in Michiko's apartment. Spires thought he could go up and get the apartment number from the door, but just before he stepped from the shadow concealing him, a car pulled to a stop on the deserted street in front of the apartment building. A man got out and went inside.

Inamu Inamine was a loyal soldier of the *Yakuza* and he was also an opportunist. Inamine knew Driscoll was dead. He knew that Agaki was also dead. He knew that Cato Fujiwara had an interest in the black American that Driscoll had hired Agaki to follow. He would gain great favor with the chief counsel and Fujiwara, himself, if he could deliver information on the black man. He searched his files, found Michiko Tomichi's home address and then headed there.

He knocked on her apartment door loudly. She wasn't asleep yet. She got up, turned on the light, pulled on a robe and made her way to the door.

"Who is it?"

"Inamine, Michiko. Open up."

"It's late and I'm not feeling…"

"Open this door or I will kick it in. If I have to do that it will go much worse for you."

She was scared to death. She ran to the kitchen and grabbed a paring knife, then threw it in the sink and began rummaging through a drawer looking for something more menacing. As she was searching, Inamine kicked in the front door.

Spires saw the light in her apartment come on a second time. He thought maybe the man who'd gotten out of the car was the reason. Then he had the thought that maybe that was Fujiwara; maybe she'd called him to let him know there was a man tonight asking questions about him. Spires sprinted across the street and into the apartment building.

Tomichi tried to dash into the bathroom and lock the door, but Inamine was too close. He grabbed her first by the robe, which ripped cleanly away leaving her naked. Then he spun her around to face him and slapped her soundly across the face. The blow was so powerful it sent her reeling back across the little apartment until she tumbled over a knee-high table. He towered over her. He had a long stiletto in his hand. "Where is Spires?" She was barely conscious. He picked her up and shook her so hard she could feel her neck snapping.

Cleve Spires stepped into the lighted doorway from the dark hallway to see Inamine with his back to him. He was whipping Michiko back and forth like she was made of paper.

Spires hollered, "Let her go!"

Inamine did as Spires asked, not out of obedience but out of surprise that someone was interfering. He spun around to face Cleve, drew back his arm and launched the stiletto at Spires, who dove for the floor. The stiletto passed well over him and imbedded itself in the door's frame. For a split second Cleve was defenseless, laying face down on the floor. That was all the time it took for Inamine to step over and give him a quick, solid kick in the back of the head. Inamine's kick stunned him. *If he does that again, I'm dead.* Even though his brain was working, his reflexes weren't. As much as he wanted to get up and fight, he couldn't make his body respond to what he knew he needed to do. He lay there and waited, but the next blow never did come. Instead he heard a man scream. Quickly he was regaining the control of his reflexes; he got to his feet and saw what had saved him.

Michiko found the knife she was looking for, a long carving knife with a blade at least six inches long and, while Inamine was focusing on Spires, she buried it in Inamine's back. She'd let go of it and it now stuck out grotesquely between his shoulder blades. Inamine was like a wounded animal. He was cursing at the top of his lungs, flailing his arms around trying to get at the knife but it was out of his reach. Inamine hit Tomichi with his forearm and sent her crashing into an adjacent wall. Spires staggered toward him and it was then that Inamine decided to retreat. He ran out the door with the knife still protruding absurdly from his back.

Spires let him go and went to look after the girl. He got something to cover her, cleaned her split lip and put a cold towel on the side of her face where Inamine's last blow had struck. "You can't stay here. They will think you know a lot more than you do. Someone will be back here very soon and they can't find you here."

She understood most of what he'd said but was too dazed to answer him in English. Cleve found a suitcase and began to pack a few things in it. When she began helping him, he knew she'd understood the urgency of getting away from where they were. When the suitcase was full he closed it, grabbed her by the hand, and led her to the street where they hailed a cab. They made their way back to his room at Hardy Barracks. The Japanese security guard allowed her in after Cleve put her name on a sign-in roster and then signed his name as her escort while she was on the installation.

While she showered, he fell asleep on the couch in the room. He heard her come out of the bathroom. "Feel better?"

She didn't look at him but bashfully replied, "Hai."

"Good. You take the bed, Michiko. I'll sleep here."

This wasn't at all what she expected, what she'd come to expect from the men in her life. She still couldn't look at him but she managed to say, "Thank you, Mr. Spires."

"Cleve, Michiko---please call me Cleve."

"Hai."

"Good. We can talk about all of this in the morning. For now you should get some sleep."

She crawled into bed and lay there for a few minutes while he showered. She had never allowed herself to trust a man completely. Agaki had been the first that she'd ever allowed herself to trust even a little, and look where that had gotten her. Now she was in a situation where the *Yakuza* was after her and the man who'd saved her from them was apparently the very reason they were looking for her. Yet, inexplicably she felt very safe here with him, whoever he was, whatever they wanted him for. A yawn overtook her; she pulled the covers up around her neck and fell asleep.

Inamu Inamine made his way back to the Lion's Den Disco, fighting off blacking out the entire way. When he got there, the place was closed and the back door locked. He fumbled with his keys, managed to unlock the door and staggered into the bar. Sanji was waiting there for him just as he'd told her to be.

"Help me."

She could see the knife, still protruding from his back."

"Who did this?" The tone of her voice was all curiosity and zero concern.

"That bitch Michiko. I'll kill her..."

Sanji laughed at him. "How will you do that Inamu? You need help and from the looks of the blood you are losing, you need it soon."

"I have a doctor's name. You will drive me to him."

"Who are you talking to, Inamu?"

He lunged at her but he was too slow and too awkward and as she dodged him she grabbed a chair and hit him in the legs with it. He crashed to the floor and screamed in agony.

"Just lay there and die quietly, you miserable excuse for a man."

He struggled to get up, but couldn't. An hour later, Sanji checked his pulse and found none. She left by the back door and didn't lock it behind her.

Chapter Twenty-two

Michiko woke first. She sat up in the bed and saw him, asleep, on the couch, his head cocked at what look like a particularly uncomfortable angle. She got up and quietly headed for the bathroom. She flicked on the light and the exhaust fan, wired to the same switch as the light, rattled noisily spoiling her attempt to be quiet. She closed the door hoping that the racket wouldn't waken him. She gazed into the mirror to see her swollen lip and bruised cheek. She splashed cold water on her face and it burned in those places where she'd been hit. She looked like hell, but it could have been much worse. If it weren't for the man in the other room, she'd probably be dead. When she came out of the bathroom she found Cleve up and moving around, rubbing his neck.

"It hurts?" she asked patting her neck.

"Naw. It'll be all right." He rubbed some more.

"Tonight..." she nervously searched for her English and couldn't find it. She pointed to him and then to the bed. Then she lay down on the couch and smiled at him, "Better for me."

He liked that she was smiling, that she was animated and that she seemed to want to please him. He needed someone like her who knew her way around the city, someone who could speak Japanese, someone who was on his side in Tokyo. He went into the bathroom and came out with a Q-tip and some peroxide. He gently dabbed it on her lip. She didn't ask him what it was, she didn't flinch, she just let him minister to her. She was beginning to trust him more and more.

"Hungry?" He made a motion like he was eating.

"Hungry---yes," she said smiling at her success with a new word and recall of an old one.

On their way out of the building to search for breakfast, Cleve spotted a *Stars and Stripes* tucked away in a magazine rack next to the front desk; he grabbed it and they went on. Two blocks away they found a coffee shop that also served a selection of pastries and muffins.

While they'd waited for their food, he pulled out the newspaper. Scanning the masthead, he was disappointed to discover it was a month old. He read it anyway. The front page carried a story on the sale of weapons and ammunition to China and Vietnam. He shook his head at the irony of the US supplying such things to either of these two countries. On Page 2, in a section headed "Military News" a small picture caught his eye. The caption under the picture read, "Colonel Lucas Johnson, Commander First Special Forces Group." He recognized Johnson as the same Johnson who'd served on his court martial board. They ate their breakfast in silence while he studied the article and the picture. Both carried him back ten years.

After breakfast they walked aimlessly for a few blocks. Spires' mind was elsewhere and Michiko was unsure of herself. Finally she screwed up her courage and said, "Thank you, Spires-san…my life over if you not come."

"Call me Cleve."

"OK, Cleve," she smiled.

Her smile brought him back to the present. He smiled back and asked her, "Michiko, are you OK with talking about last night?"

"Hai, it's all right."

"Do you know the man who attacked you?"

"Inamine---Inamu Inamine…" he started to say something, but she put her hand on his arm, "boss---Lion's Den Disco---bad man---*Yakuza.* He…" she searched for words, "he say I know you. He want to know where you go."

Spires' heart was hammering in his chest. She'd just confirmed what until now he'd only suspected, that the *Yakuza* was looking for him. He choked back his panic and asked her, "Michiko, do you remember me asking you about Cato Fujiwara last night?"

"Yes, I remember."

"Who is he?"

She gave him a puzzled look. It had never occurred to her that Cleve Spires wasn't in some way connected to them. Why else would he be looking for Fujiwara? She blurted out, "You not know?" There was a pause and then she asked him, "Why Inamine look for you? Why *Yakuza* look for you?"

There was a sidewalk bench ahead of them and he steered her to it. They sat down and he started with ten years ago, stopping frequently to ask if she understood. She said she did. He showed her Agaki's notebook with her name and old address in it. He told her Sanji led him to her at the Lion's Den.

"All I know is that Billy Driscoll is dead and just before he died he said two words, 'Fujiwara' and '*Yakuza'*. I think the *Yakuza* killed Driscoll and put the blame on me. I think this guy, Fujiwara, believes Driscoll told me something, something about the *Yakuza,* something about him. They think I'm some kind of a threat to them and that's why Inamine came looking for you last night. He saw us together or someone told him I was at the Lion's Den last night to see you. They're trying to get to me through you."

She nodded as if she understood. "Cato Fujiwara, bad man. He boss of all *Yakuza.* Inamine work for him." Then she clarified something for him, "Inamine not see us together. He not come Lion's Den until after midnight. You---me---we both go before Inamine come Lion's Den last night."

"Then how did Inamine know to come looking for you?"

She thought before answering, "Maybe one of the girls tell him you come see me."

They were communicating much better than he'd hoped. "Maybe you're right." He thought for a moment and then suggested, "Why don't we go see Sanji? Maybe she can tell us how Inamine wound up at your apartment."

She smiled at him and said, "OK."

At 9:30 AM the cleaning crew that cleans the Lion's Den Disco arrived as they usually do, but this morning they found the back door unlocked. They let themselves in. At 9:45 the ambulance arrived and by 10:00 the police were on the scene. By 10:30 the Chief Counsel was told of Inamu Inamine's death. The police were calling it murder.

Cleve knocked on Sanji's apartment door. There was no answer but Cleve knew she was in there. He'd watched the peephole and seen the light through it change when Sanji put her eye up to see who was at her door. Michiko was about to knock again when Spires stopped her and said through the door, "Sanji, let us in. We're not going to leave. We know you're in there." Nothing. Michiko translated what Cleve had said into Japanese. Cleve saw the light at the peephole change again and then the doorknob turned and she let them in.

The women spoke in Japanese. Michiko told her what had happened last night and how she'd stabbed Inamine.

Sanji, in Japanese, said to Michiko, " So it was you who did all of us a favor."

"Hai"

Sanji reverted back to her English and told both of them what had happened between her and Inamine last night. She ended by telling them he was dead; she'd made sure of that before leaving the

Lion's Den last night. While Sanji seemed to take great satisfaction in what she'd done, the news of Inamine's death wasn't as satisfying for Spires. He'd hoped Inamine might be a way to get to Fujiwara. He looked at his watch. It was eleven o'clock in the morning.

He told both of the women, "Someone must have found his body by now. The *Yakuza* will know he's dead." He asked Sanji, "Who else knew you were supposed to wait for Inamine last night?"

"All of the girls saw what he do to me. I not want to wait on him, but they tell me to wait. If I not do what Inamine say he kill me for sure the other girls say to me. I wait." She was smiling now. She looked at Michiko and in Japanese said, "Look what he did to you. We are all better off now that that pig is dead."

Michiko didn't respond at all. For certain there was no love lost between her and Inamine, but she knew the news of his death bothered Cleve, though she wasn't sure why.

Spires became very serious. He turned to Sanji, "You are not safe here any longer. The police will talk with the other girls and so will the *Yakuza.*"

Sanji brushed his concern off and told him he didn't need to worry. She'd already called all the girls and told them what had happened. All of them were glad Inamine was dead. "No one tell police anything."

Cleve shook his head, "That might keep the police away, but it won't keep the *Yakuza* from finding out how he died, especially if they manage to find out I was at the Lion's Den last night." He turned to Michiko. "She's not safe here, Michiko. You've got to make her understand."

Sanji wasn't smiling now. She asked Michiko in Japanese, "Where can I go? The *Yakuza* is everywhere in Japan. You can't hide from them." Michiko translated her concern to Cleve.

Spires thought for a moment and then told the two women, "I have an idea, but we must go now. If you wait you will be caught and I won't be able to help. Will you go right now? You don't need to pack anything. Where you are going everything will be provided."

Sanji looked puzzled, "Where is such a place?"

"Thailand. My family is there now. I won't tell you exactly where until we are at the airport and you are boarding the airplane. If the *Yakuza* should capture us before then I wouldn't want either of you to be able to tell them where my family is."

The two women talked in Japanese and then Michiko told him, "She will go."

"Good, then let's get out of here."

At 11:45 they crawled into a cab, made a quick stop at Sanji's bank and then headed for Narita Airport. Along the way Spires told her that once she landed in Bangkok she should go to the Windsor Hotel and find a cab driver by the name of Tradip. "He has funny sunglasses that flip up and down over his glasses. Tell him I sent you to him. Tell him I want him to take you to the same place that he took me and for that you will pay him what I paid him, seven hundred dollars. When you reach the village of my wife and son, let them know what has happened and let them know I am safe."

Cleve offered her the money to get from Bangkok to Chuk Ra Met, but she refused it.

At 4:00PM Sanji boarded a Cathay Pacific flight to Bangkok by way of Hong Kong.

While the police were not making any headway, by 4:00 PM the chief counsel knew that a black man had been at the Lion's Den the night before with an interest in Michiko Tomichi. When they'd gone to Michiko's apartment they found the front door open and most of her clothes gone. They assumed Michiko was on the run. They went back to the same girls who'd told them about Michiko. It wasn't long before they told them about Sanji; she was the one who had more information. She wasn't at her apartment when they got there, so several of the chief counsel's best men remained there, waiting for her.

At 5:00PM the chief counsel went to see Fujiwara. "Fujiwara-san, Cleveland Spires was at the Lion's Den Disco last night and he may have killed Inamu Inamine. They found Inamine with a knife in his back at the Lion's Den this morning."

"Who is 'they'?"

"The company that cleans the place; their men found him. They called the police. A policeman on our payroll called me. I put several of our men on it, to find out what happened. They tell me that several of the girls who work at the club saw a tall, black American there last night. None of the girls know his name, but who else could it be? He apparently spoke to two of Inamine's girls." He looked at his notebook, "Michiko Tomichi and Sanji Onoro. We think they know where Spires is."

"You have finally done some good work. Find these two women. Find Spires. I will pay two million yen to anyone who can lead us to either of the two women and five million yen if they lead us to Spires." He paused, then added, "We need the women for information, so the reward is only payable if we find them alive. The five million for Spires will be paid regardless if he is dead or alive."

"Yes, Fujiwara-san."

"I want you to see me personally each day and update me. I expect results and I expect them fast. Do not fail in this mission. Do you understand?"

They'd fixed Spires in Tokyo, with two of their whores. There was no way they could fail to get him now. He confidently told Fujiwara, "We will have all three of them soon."

On the trip back from Narita Airport they'd worked out a plan, a risky one, but everything now was risky. In an effort to try and get to know his enemy, he'd asked her every question he could think of about Cato Fujiwara and the *Yakuza.* She had told him everything she knew.

It was nearly 7:00PM when their cab dropped them at Hardy Barracks. Once in their room, Michiko showered first. Cleve thought of at least a dozen more questions as he showered, but, when he came out of the shower, he found her asleep on the sofa. They were both tired and tomorrow was going to be an even busier day than today. The questions would wait. He didn't wake her.

At 7:00AM the next morning, the 9th of May, Michiko sat alone in the park across from the main entrance of the same skyscraper Spires had staked out on his first day in Tokyo. Cleve had gone to get them a bite to eat. On his way back with their food he saw her at the curb holding a cab door open and waving frantically at him to hurry. He broke into a run.

Once in the cab, Michiko gave the driver instructions in Japanese. Within a matter of a few minutes, the cab came up behind a black limousine that Cleve was sure was the same one he'd seen his first night in Japan. Michiko gave the driver some other instructions, and the driver let his cab fall back to a safe distance as they continued to follow the limo for about two hours. When the limo swung into the driveway of an estate outside the western limits of Tokyo, Michiko told the cab driver to pull over and let them out. The bill was 15,000 yen. Cleve paid, shaking his head while he counted out the money. The two walked down the sidewalk toward the driveway where the limo had turned in. A high wall surrounded the property. They couldn't see in, but neither could anyone on the other side of the wall see them. They used that to their advantage until they reached the driveway entrance. From that vantage point Cleve peeked into the estate. He recognized the two bodyguards and then the same impeccably dressed man he'd seen coming out of the skyscraper his first night in Tokyo. Michiko grabbed his hand and whispered, "Fujiwara".

His stomach rolled and he could literally feel the hair on the back of his neck stand on end. One hundred yards separated them. Spires fought back the urge to do something stupid. He grabbed her hand and led her away from the driveway, away from the estate. When they were several blocks away he found a street-side bench. His stomach was still in a knot from finally seeing the man he'd been stalking. As they sat down and began to talk about where they were and what they should do next, he became aware that Michiko was still holding his hand.

Chapter Twenty-three

The morning of 20 May broke dismally over Washington, D.C. A gray mist shrouded the Capital and the forecast was that it would be that way all day. The Washington *Post's* headline read, **McClint Vows Resignation**. The vote on the arms sale had become partisan politics at its best. The Democrats opposed the sale, each giving his own reason, but implicit in each Democrat's explanation was that they had to oppose it simply because the Republicans favored it. There was, however, one notable Republican exception: Senator John McClint, R, TX. News analysts had all done the math. The Republican Party held a scant one member majority on the Senate Armed Services Committee and McClint, despite tremendous pressure from his party, had made his opposition abundantly clear and that meant the sale would fail to pass the SASC.

The phone rang in Paul Stanley's quarters on Palm Circle at Fort Shafter, Hawaii at 2:00AM. He had been drop-dead tired and was in a deep sleep, so it took him a moment to realize the phone was trying to wake him up and then another one to find the damned thing. When he found it he barked a rather abrupt, "Stanley" into the receiver.

"Paul, it is Saieto Yamamoto, I must ask you to do something for us."

This was the first time Yamamoto had ever called him. Stanley knew instinctively that this call was about the ammunition sale. "If it is within my power, Saieto, you may consider it done. How can I help?"

Yamamoto moved right to his point, "We need for you to expedite the movement of the ammunition. The ships are already in position; they have been there for over a month now. The delay between approval and movement of the munitions must be minimal. Time is of the essence."

"I can influence that Saieto, but how can you be so sure about the vote. This thing is in real trouble. McClint..."

"Paul, there are details you are better off not knowing. The *association* has been hard at work on this since the media turned it into such an issue. It has been very expensive for us, but the sale will be approved."

"I understand, Saieto." He didn't, but Stanley had learned that if Yamamoto warned him off then there was nothing he could do to drag it out of him. Besides, Yamamoto was probably right, in the long run he was much better off not knowing the details.

"Paul, we are counting on you. This is the one area where we are powerless. Drop me a note and let me know what you are able to do."

"Wouldn't a phone call be better?"

"Only quicker. And if you can't help, I have no other recourse. I'm only calling you now because of the urgency of my request. If I had the luxury of time I would have sent you a note. These days the mail, snail mail I think you American's call it, is more secure than the telephone."

"I will let you know what I am able to arrange."

Yamamoto gave him an address.

The *association,* in particular Yamamoto, had followed the events in the SASC closely after McClint's theatrics. The bombing of the Laotian village was a huge bumbling error that they thought they had covered up completely. It had been a simple night training mission, but a faulty radio receiver had led the pilot well off course. A payoff of several million dollars to the Laotian government by the Vietnamese associate had kept the incident out of the Asian press, out, that is, until McClint brought it to the attention of the world press. It was a tip of their hand at a critical time and the *association* should have been more careful. Yamamoto needed to do damage control.

By the 7th of May, Yamamoto gave Cato Fujiwara the mission to insure the sale cleared the US Congress. Cost was not an object. Fujiwara had been curious as to why Yamamoto had such an interest in what happened in China and Vietnam. Yamamoto told him he had some very close business connections in both countries that profited immensely from the last sale, and they were looking to add to their bank accounts. "They are paying me, Cato, and I am paying you. It is a good business arrangement for all of us."

The *Yakuza* had a well-developed network of agents in the US. Fujiwara picked Akito Namura as his principal agent for this particular assignment. By May 9th, Namura and his team were on the job. He assumed the Republicans, except for McClint, would all vote for the sale. McClint was looked at by Namura's researchers, but considered very quickly to be "incorruptible". Namura focused his efforts on the Democratic members of the SASC.

By May 11, Namura had hit pay dirt, the junior Democratic Senator from Ohio. An accountant, well paid by Namura, and using some corrupt contacts within the IRS and the State Income Tax office in Columbus, Ohio, made the discovery. The Senator was playing it by the numbers on his Federal Income Tax returns, but had been overly innovative in his state income tax reporting.

It took longer for him to find his second target. Ironically it was the senior Democratic senator on the SASC who became his prey. The senator departed his office in the Congressional Office Building at about 10:00PM completely oblivious to the car following him. This was the third night the Senator had worked late this week. On the other two nights he had uneventfully led Namura's man to his home in Fairfax, Virginia. Tonight, however, the Senator seemed to be taking a detour. He headed into the District instead of out into the suburbs. Namura's man followed him up 14th Street, turning right onto M. This was a rather seedy section of downtown Washington D.C. that most people would avoid this time of night. Namura's man remained diligently close.

The girl stepped out from between two parked cars; teased, bleached blond hair, a dress so short that as she bent down to look in the window of the Senator's car, it rode over her butt, and she did not appear to be wearing anything underneath. When she got in the car, Namura's man knew he'd struck gold. The expensive Nikon camera with the telephoto lens and the high-speed film worked well in the low light of the empty parking lot. The 8X10 glossies were pornographic perfection. Namura bagged his second Democrat with virtually no time to spare.

On May 19th, the day before the committee vote on the ammunition sale, Namura sprang his trap. The junior Democrat from Ohio was enjoying a lunch on the steps of the Capital Building when Namura's messenger gave him the envelope, suggested that he might want to open it immediately and then quickly scuttled off. The senior Democrat was handed his package with the same suggestion, as he strolled down the hallway of the Senate Office Building with several of his staffers. Each package provided a number that the senators were to call. Namura was waiting. The calls came back-to-back.

Bluffing, each one tried to tell Namura that he didn't know whom he was dealing with, and that a U.S. senator couldn't be blackmailed. They were children playing an adult game. Namura was very experienced in the art of blackmail, and this was the part of the hunt that he liked best---springing the trap and watching the mark try to wriggle free. "Very well Senator, then I assume you will be able to explain the contents of the package you have received when it is given to the press tomorrow morning."

Each tried to argue his way out of the jam, but Namura had them and they knew it. Eventually both Senators got around to asking what it would take to keep these packages out of the hands of the press.

"A simple abstention or "Yes" vote on the upcoming sale to Vietnam and China is the price to keep all of this quiet." Then Namura sweetened the pot, "And for your abstention or "Yes" vote, one million dollars will be placed in an overseas account. The day after the sale is approved, you will be given the name of the bank, the account number and the access code."

Each had the balls to ask him for some assurance of the deposit. Namura sneered into the phone, "Listen to me, the only assurance you need is that those packages will be delivered to the media as promised if you fail to vote as I have suggested. Do I make myself clear?"

The Senate Armed Services Committee had moved the final vote to the largest hearing room available in the Capitol Building. The media had practically demanded this and, of course, the politicians had no choice but to oblige. The meeting came to order exactly on time and, after a few introductory remarks, the Committee's Chairman began, "The People's Republics of China and Vietnam seek approval to purchase a specified amount of military equipment, including weapons and ammunition from the Government of the United States. On the matter of this sale, I ask each member of this committee how do you vote?"

The vote started with the majority party, so every camera in the room scanned in the direction of the junior Republican Senator who sat at the far left of the committee chair.

"Yes," was the one word reply.

Each Republican replied in the same way in turn---all except Senator John McClint.

At the conclusion of the Republican vote the count was seven "Yes" and one "Opposed."

Now it was the Democrats turn. The junior Democratic Senator felt the lights and the cameras boring in on him. He stared into the end of the microphone and voted.

"Abstain."

The Chairman looked at him quizzically and then interrupted the vote.

"Did I hear correctly? You abstain?" His voice now full of derision, he asked the junior Democratic Senator, "You have no opinion on this matter?"

There was no verbal response, only a nodding of his head.

"For the record Senator, please answer my question aloud."

The junior Democrat glared at the Republican chairman, "I abstain."

Smiling at the junior Democrat, the senior Republican said, "Well, Senator, that is an interesting, albeit indefensible, position for you to take."

The committee room buzzed momentarily as the surprise sank in. The Chairman banged his gavel and order was quickly restored. This one abstention, though surprising, did not make anyone in the hearing room change their mind about the anticipated outcome of the vote. All the abstention meant was the final vote would be seven "Yes", seven "Opposed", and one "Abstain." The sale would be stalemated.

The next five votes went quickly and by the party line. The tally stood at seven "Yes", six "Opposed", and one "Abstain". It was now the senior Democrat's turn and he began to offer a rationalization for his vote before he'd even cast it. The Republican chairman would have none of it.

"Senator, it's time to vote, not give speeches. Please dispense with the rhetoric. How do you vote on the issue at hand?"

"I abstain."

The room went dead still for only a moment. No one was prepared for this. Everyone was going back over the vote count one more time in their head to be sure if what they thought had just happened, had happened. Once that moment passed and everyone realized the sale was approved, the room fell into chaos. The Chairman was banging his gavel to no effect. The press was out of control. The two Democrats who had abstained were deluged with reporters. Senator McClint was surrounded as well.

The two Senators tried to explain their abstentions. They could have more easily justified a "Yes" vote than an abstention. In the weeks that followed, they were crucified by the liberal press and mocked by the conservatives as two of the most indecisive, ineffectual lawmakers to ever sit in either house of Congress.

In Honolulu, Paul Stanley watched the proceedings on CSPAN. It was early in the morning in Honolulu, 4:00AM, but he called the Deputy Commander-in-Chief Pacific Command, General Kinney anyway.

"Sir, it's Paul Stanley. Sorry to bother you so early but I thought you'd want to know the SASC just approved the ammo sale to Vietnam and China." Stanley let that sink in.

There was a pause and then Kinney said, "How the hell did that happen? McClint change his mind?"

"No, sir. McClint voted just like he said he would but two democrats abstained." Paul Stanley moved immediately to the reason he'd called, "Sir, I'm going to get on the phone to United States Transportation Command and push them to get the ammunition moving as soon as possible. We need to get this done before the goddamned protestors and terrorists have a chance to get themselves organized."

"Do it, Paul. And let me know if you need my help to make it happen."

Stanley didn't need to take his boss up on his offer of help. He got complete cooperation from TRANSCOM, and by May 25th trainloads of ammunition were flowing into the military ammunition ports at Sunny Point, North Carolina and Concord Naval Weapons Station, California. Ship loading began on May 30th on both coasts and was expected to take at least two weeks. TRANSCOM promised Stanley that by June 15 eight shiploads would be on their way to the Far East.

John McClint became a tragic hero of epic proportions though that was never his intent. He was simply looking for an escape from his tortured emotions, when he took a .38 Caliber pistol on May 21st, put the barrel in his mouth, and pulled the trigger.

He left a note behind asking his ex-wife to forgive him. She had remarried in 1969, three years after his shoot down over North Vietnam, when she thought he was never going to come home. McClint had never remarried. He asked her to help their daughter, who was grown, through college, and off on her own, to deal with what her father had done.

And then McClint offered an explanation for taking his own life. He wrote,

"I cannot deal with the dreams any longer. They will become more intense now that we are helping China and Vietnam to rearm. I think constantly while I am awake about their use of the things we sell them. When I am asleep I remember my life with them from 1966 to 1973. I am never at peace with myself; I am still at war and death seems my only way out. I love you both."

He'd signed it simply *"John."*

By June 1st Paul Stanley was sure he had done as much as he could to get the weapons and ammo moving to China and Vietnam. He sat down at his desk at home and penned a note to Seito Yamamoto as he'd been asked to do. There was one other piece of news, not as critical as the transportation, but important enough that Stanley thought Yamamoto would want to know as well so he included it in the note. When he'd finished writing he read the note aloud to himself. He made some changes, read it aloud again and, when he was satisfied that it said all he wanted it to, he licked the seal on the envelope and mailed the letter the next morning from the Aiea Post Office on Oahu.

Chapter Twenty-four

Cato Fujiwara turned his back on his chief counsel and stared out the window behind his desk at the city that sprawled below him. "We have informants all over Tokyo---all over Japan." He said it as a matter of fact, and between the two of them it was. Both of them knew precisely how many were on the organization's payroll, something that only one or two others inside the *Yakuza* knew, and a bit of information that was pure speculation among Japan's various police forces. The chief counsel didn't say anything. Fujiwara wheeled around, slammed his fist down on his desk, "Then how is it possible a black man, who towers over everyone around him and is traveling with two of our whores cannot be located?" Fujiwara's eyes bored into him like a chisel.

He needed to produce an answer, but Fujiwara's anger was so well aimed directly at the young attorney that he engaged his mouth before putting his mind in gear. "The women are protecting him..."

Fujiwara bent over and opened his center desk drawer, pulled out a revolver and leveled it at his head. "If you insult me with the obvious again I will shoot you where you stand. I will not wait forever for you to find them. I want to know that Spires and the two women are dead within the week or I will be in need of a new chief counsel. As long as they are alive, you have much to worry about. Is that clear?"

Fujiwara waved his hand toward the door. The chief counsel's time today had not been wisely used.

Spires was running out of money. He'd paid hundreds of dollars in taxi fares over the past five days shadowing Fujiwara's limousine to and from the estate on Tokyo's western edge. He also worried that he and Michiko had become predictable and Spires knew that was not a good thing. It was a simple rule, one that Vietnam had indelibly etched into his memory; never return to base camp by the same trail you used to leave it. They had spent seven nights now at Hardy Barracks; Michiko had been with him five of those.

To make matters worse, he was getting impatient. They had little to show for the time and money invested to this point. They had gotten no closer to Cato Fujiwara than they had on the first day they'd followed him to the estate. Though the time of day appeared random, Fujiwara's trips to the estate weren't. He had gone there every day for the last four days. They had speculated that it was a second home, that it was a work site, but they didn't know for sure and they didn't have a plan to find out.

Their cab was a safe distance behind the limo and both he and Michiko were all too familiar with the route heading to the estate for the fifth consecutive day. Cleve asked, "Any ideas? He pointed to his temple as he asked the question.

"I look for apartment today. You watch Fujiwara."

The quickness of her response surprised him. He sat there for a moment and then shook his head, "Michiko, I don't have money…"

"OK. I have."

"No."

"Yes." She was firm with him. "Safe there. Not so many people. He come there every day. Save money. No taxi. We watch him better."

They rode in silence for a long time. He tried to think of a reason why her plan didn't make sense and couldn't. She said, "No worry. Good idea. I want to do." She took his hand and smiled at him.

When the cab pulled to a stop near the estate, she scrambled out and waited while he paid the fare. It was about 11:00 AM. She took him by the hand and said, "Come." He obeyed and she led him to a coffee shop about three blocks from where the cab had dropped them. "I go now." She pointed to him, "You come back here at 5:00," she pointed to the five on his watch. "I find us place." He could tell she thought she was really helping him, helping them. He smiled at her, nodded and they went their separate ways.

The estate that lay inside the high stone wall occupied the entire block and by Japanese standards was huge. He was sure there were places in the heart of Tokyo where ten thousand or more people would live and work in the same amount of ground and the air above it. Cleve wanted to get inside and see the estate from the ground level, but he knew that was risky. There had to be more to security here than simply the stonewall. There could be surveillance cameras, dogs or even guards he'd not been able to see from the driveway entrance or from the roof top four blocks away that had been his only vantage points until now. Impatience overshadowed risk.

He turned a corner and the wall stretched out at least three hundred yards in front of him. Ahead of him, about half way down this side of the estate, he could see a large tree growing in the narrow strip of earth between the street and the sidewalk. Traffic down this side street was nonexistent, there were only a few cars parked along it and they all appeared to be empty and as he stood behind the tree on the sidewalk he couldn't see any neighboring houses. Someone, however, had been careful to trim the tree's branches so that they did not extend over the wall. If he climbed the tree he could be seen from the estate, so that left him with the wall as an option. He jumped up being careful to grab only the edge of it. It took all of his strength to literally chin himself up high enough to see. He'd anticipated the first security measure; he'd seen it used before in this part of the world. It was the reason for his careful handhold and he was glad that he had remembered. His middle finger was no more than an inch away from a razor sharp piece of glass embedded in the top of the wall. Pieces of glass like it were randomly placed every few inches all the way around. It was a passive but effective security measure. He would not be able to raise himself any higher than he was and even though Cleve had tremendous upper body strength, he couldn't hang there with the slim handhold for very long.

He pulled himself up until his eyes were just peering over the top of the wall. Off in a distance he could see the main house where Fujiwara came daily, but he couldn't pick out any details about the place through the tall trees that shrouded it under an umbrella of green. There was open ground between the trees surrounding the house and the wall except for areas, randomly spaced along the entire wall, where shrubbery filled in. While the grass in the open area was cut, the shrubbery patches weren't so well maintained. They were wild and thick and came directly up against the wall. His muscles in his arms and chest began to twitch as they did just before they failed. In one last gasp of energy he boosted himself just a few inches higher and was able to see that he was exactly opposite one of these shrubbery patches. He dropped from the wall. An idea began to form and he thought that if he were going to try and enter the grounds, this would be as good a place as any to do it from.

Michiko was late. At 5:30 he started to get really worried. He moved to a recently vacated table near the coffee shop's front window and began to diligently scan every person who passed. Finally, at six-thirty he saw her coming down the street and he darted out on the sidewalk. When she saw him she broke into a broad smile that told him she was OK. Relieved to see her, he couldn't be angry.

"I was worried," he said gently.

She took his hand without saying anything, and led him off in the direction she'd come from. They were heading back towards the estate. He didn't like the idea of the two of them casually strolling down the street this close to the fox's lair. Two blocks ahead of them he could see the cross street that Fujiwara's limo would roll down on his way back to the skyscraper. If he happened to look in the right direction he might see them.

"Michiko, I..."

Just then she led him across the street and down a cross street that Spires estimated was two blocks from the estate. It was much narrower than the road they'd been on and there was no traffic. In fact, Spires wasn't at all sure that Fujiwara's limo would fit down this street. The doors of the buildings literally opened onto the sidewalk. There were no shops that he could see. He assumed that this was a strictly residential area. Midway down the block she stopped in front of a doorway and pointed to Japanese lettering above the door and said something he couldn't understand. Then she pointed to the number "42" on the wall next to the door. Michiko produced a key and smiled at him, "We live on fifth level. Wait---you see---you like." She seemed as excited as a schoolgirl as she spoke in Japanese and clipped English all the way up five flights of stairs.

He looked around the small but tidy apartment. "Michiko, this is very nice." He was smiling at her and she delighted in his approval. He could smell food. She'd been cooking. He stepped up to a large window in the living area of the apartment. He could feel her come beside him and she put her hand on his shoulder. In the fading daylight he could discern the outline of the wall around the estate and the patch of trees that hid the house, but he thought that when the sun came up in the morning, they'd have a bird's eye view of the place. He was thrilled.

She pointed to the blackness outside the window. "Why I get this place. Tomorrow you see. See good Fujiwara." She ran into the kitchen and returned with a wrapped package.

"What's this?"

"You open."

He did and found a pair of binoculars. He turned, reached out his arms and she fell into them. She pressed herself against him and moved in a way that suggested he could do more if he wanted. He held her close for a moment more and then took his arms from around her and put his hands on her shoulders, "Michiko, thank you very much. You have really helped me today."

She understood him. Her English was getting better by the day. For her his smile was like warm sunshine. "I make you food," and she ran off to the kitchen to get their dinner.

That night, after they'd eaten, Cleve stood at the window for hours staring into the darkness. She fell asleep and he carried her into the bedroom. She felt him pick her up but she pretended to be asleep. He was so very gentle with her, unlike any man she'd ever known before. She wasn't sure what love was supposed to feel like. She only knew that she'd never felt this way about any man that had ever been in her life until now, and, if this wasn't love, she doubted love could make her feel any better. She lay in the bed with the covers pulled over her and listened for him in the other room until sleep overtook her.

When she awoke in the morning she opened the bedroom door to find him where she'd left him, standing in front of the window staring into the estate. Only now it was daylight and Cleve had this day to pull his plan together. He'd need as much of the ten hours of daylight as possible to get to know the estate and its terrain.

Chapter Twenty-five

Cleve moved a table and chair close to the window so that he could sketch a map of the estate. The binoculars she'd given him were helpful and he used them to examine as many identifiable terrain features as he could on the estate's grounds. He would estimate their size, shape and location relative to his target, the house, and then place them on his sketch. Michiko didn't bother him; instead she busied herself in the kitchen cleaning up from their dinner the night before and preparing a light breakfast for the two of them. At about 9:30 AM on the morning of their first full day in their new apartment, Cleve turned to her and said, " Michiko, I need you to go shopping for me." He went to his backpack and pulled out a black shirt. "I need black pants, like this shirt." She nodded. "I need a black hat," he tugged his hands over his ears to help her understand. "Get some black shoe polish," he held up a shoe, pointed to the black shirt and made a brushing motion.

She nodded, but he saw confusion on her face.

"Do you understand?"

"Hai."

"Good. I'll also need a thick blanket." He went into the bedroom and brought a blanket out. "But very thick."

She didn't understand.

He held the edge of the blanket up and put it between his thumb and forefinger and raised his forefinger about a half an inch. "Thick, much thicker. Understand?"

"Hai"

They stood there awkwardly for a moment; she had a question and in Japanese she knew exactly how to word it. In English all she could do is blurt it out, "What you do Cleve?"

It was a question he didn't want to answer, but knew he couldn't avoid. "Tonight, after dark, I'm going to look around," and he pointed out the window towards the estate. He knew she understood him because he could see the panic in her eyes.

"No. You not do."

He looked at her and said gently, "Michiko, I must do something."

That afternoon she went to get the things he'd asked for, while Cleve spent the rest of the day studying the estate. He wanted to know where he was every inch of the way after he crossed the wall and to do that he needed to commit his sketch to memory. He wouldn't take it with him. It would be too dark for him to use at night.

A concern for him was security, or rather the estate's apparent lack of it. From a security standpoint the estate was the exact opposite of the fortress on the top five floors of the downtown skyscraper. He could see no guards, no dogs, no surveillance cameras---nothing in the way of security. Of course, there could be surveillance devices he couldn't see like motion detectors, sound detectors, but he'd never be able to see those types of things at this distance, even with his binoculars. He'd just have to keep a sharp eye out once he got across the wall.

The shroud of trees kept the estate's main house well concealed from view. However, every now and then, as the wind moved the tree branches around, he got a glimpse of some antennas on the roof. He thought he'd counted four whip-type antennas and one small satellite dish. The satellite dish could be for television but the whip antennas were probably linked to some type of radio set-up. He thought this might be some kind of communication center for the *Yakuza,* but dismissed that idea quickly. If that were the case, why wouldn't Fujiwara just establish a communications link between here and the skyscraper and save himself the trip out here every day?

He waited until midnight and then got dressed. He smeared the shoe polish over his forehead, cheekbones, hands---anyplace he thought might reflect light. At 12:30AM he hugged Michiko, grabbed the thick tarp she'd bought, rolled it as tight as he could, tucked it under his arm and headed for the estate. She turned off the lights in the apartment and went to the window. To her frustration and yet to her relief, she couldn't see any sign of him.

He'd gotten lucky. The cloud cover was mostly solid and when a few breaks did occur, the fingernail moon did not provide a lot of light. When he got to the spot where the tree overhung the sidewalk, the same place he'd hoisted himself up earlier, he unrolled the tarp, doubled it and then doubled it again and threw it so that it draped over the top of the wall. As he pulled himself up onto the tarp he could hear the glass crunching under his weight, but the tarp did its job well. Cleve swung his feet over and dropped into the bushes.

From where he was, he plotted a course across the two hundred meter open area to a particularly large tree near the house. If he was going to be spotted, now is when it would happen. He broke out of the shrubbery and hit a dead run within seconds. He wanted to look around him to see if he could see anything coming at him from the rear or the side, but if he did that it would slow him down. He kept his eyes fixed on the tree that was his target. When he got to it he hunkered down near its trunk and looked around. Nothing. He waited to see if perhaps there was some hidden detector that had seen or heard him and sent a silent signal to the house or to some security guard somewhere. After fifteen minutes had passed there was still nothing. He moved toward the house.

He could see the outline of windows on the side of the house nearest him but they were all dark. As he got to the house, he decided to move first to the back and see what was there. For him that was the dark side of the moon. It had been concealed from his view at the apartment by the trees and the house itself. What he saw when he got there startled him. Looming out of the darkness he could see four large satellite dishes---each aimed in a different direction. Cleve was not enough of a communications expert to know what these dishes were capable of, but he judged from their size, that Fujiwara wasn't using them to get ESPN. He also assumed their directional alignment had some importance. This was a discovery of some kind. He didn't know why or how at this point, but these dishes were important. He took out paper and pencil and began to sketch the layout of the dishes. He estimated their diameter at ten to twelve feet.

When he had completed his sketch, he moved back around to the side of the house he'd come from. He was at a point midway between the house and the line of trees surrounding the house when someone inside turned on a light. He was suddenly bathed in a shaft of light coming through a window directly behind and slightly above him. He dove to the ground under the window and hugged the foundation of the house. The noise he'd made seemed deafening to him but he'd gotten out of the blaze of light quickly. He lay there making no further sound for a full five minutes. This was another opportunity he thought, fraught with danger, but nonetheless an opportunity.

Slowly he raised up to a point where he could peer in. Inside, seated at a huge desk, covered with papers, some of which he could distinguish as maps, sat a Japanese man who appeared to be totally engrossed in the information in front of him. The man's head was down and he wanted to see his face, but Spires was smart enough not to focus his attention on the man at the desk until he'd scanned the entire room. At the room's doorway, he saw a shadow first and then another man appeared carrying a tray with a teapot. He ducked down momentarily and then slowly rose back up. Spires watched him pour the tea for the man sitting at the desk and then leave the room. The man at the desk never looked up from his work.

Maybe this place doesn't belong to Fujiwara at all. Maybe it belongs to this guy and he and Fujiwara are business partners. Maybe I can get to Fujiwara through this guy. His security sure seems to be pretty lax. Wonder who the hell he is?

His mind was on a different plane. For the moment he'd lost his focus on what was happening around him and that was just long enough for the dog to go unnoticed. The sudden bark, not ten feet behind him, jangled his every nerve. He stood dead still. The dog was close---very close. Then he felt it nuzzle its nose against the back of his shoe-polish blackened hand. His knees nearly buckled from the surprise. It barked again.

He'd seen guard dogs work. This wasn't a guard dog. If it were, he'd be fighting it off right now. No, this was a pet and it probably lived here with these two guys, whoever they were. He dropped to one knee and whispered, "Good boy, come here. Good boy."

It was a Doberman pinscher of some good breeding Spires judged by its disposition, sleek coat and solid conformation. The question was, now that he'd made friends with it, could he just head out across the open area, back to the wall and off the estate without the dog raising a ruckus?

It was a question he didn't have to answer. Cleve and the dog heard the voice at the same time. It was in Japanese so he couldn't understand, but he knew that someone from the house was calling the dog because whistles followed each of the calls.

"Well it's been nice meetin' ya'," he whispered, "but if you don't go in, we're all goin' to be in big trouble."

Cleve shut up. Another call followed by a whistle. The dog turned and bolted toward the caller. Spires heard a door close and then figured it was time to get the hell out of there. He'd pushed his luck hard enough for one night. He made his way to the wall, over it and back to the apartment.

Inside the house the man who'd delivered tea was affectionately scolding the beautiful animal. He didn't know what it was the dog had gotten into, but he had gotten into something black and greasy in the short time he'd been outside. There was also some trace of it on the dog's tongue as if the dog had licked at something with this black greasy substance on it. He cleaned the wonderful creature up, patted him on the head and both went to bed. Yamamoto remained hard at work in the study, planning the final stages of Operation Light Switch.

When Cleve returned to the apartment, Michiko was waiting for him. As soon as the door was closed she was in his arms. She gently kissed him on the cheek. She didn't know how to ask him what he'd found and he didn't know how to tell her. She could, however, sense his excitement. Even though it was nearly 2:00 AM, they sat down and he tried to tell her what he'd seen. By 4:00 AM, he thought he'd gotten her to understand. Both were exhausted. Cleve sat back into a corner of the couch and fell asleep. Michiko snuggled next to him, put her head on his chest and fell asleep to the gentle rise and fall of his breathing.

They awoke at 9:00 AM and Cleve went to the shower. He'd fallen asleep with the black shoe polish all over him. He'd no sooner gotten out of the shower than Michiko broke in on him. "Come." She motioned for him and repeated, "Come. I show you. I have idea."

He cinched the towel around his waist tighter and followed her into the living room and the window looking into the estate. She pointed at a lone figure walking away from the gate of the estate. The satchel over his shoulder told Cleve he was a mailman. Michiko said, "I go look at," and she pointed to the front gate.

"What?"

"I go see who live there," and she grabbed a stack of papers from the table by the window and began shuffling through them.

"You want to check his mail?" He didn't think about it, he just responded, "No, it's out of the question. That's getting too close…"

He didn't finish his thought because what she was thinking was a good idea. It would tell them who the guy in the house is. He said to her, "I'll do it. I'll check the mail. You shouldn't have to…"

She shook her head, laughed and said, "No." Then she grabbed a pencil and wrote something in Kanji on one of the sheets of paper. She held it up for him. "What this say?"

He stood there stupidly. She was right. He couldn't do it, but she could. He was forced to relent but not after getting some ground rules in place. First, they would watch the estate for mail delivery patterns. When is it delivered? When does someone from the estate come to get it out of the mailbox? And then she is at the box for no more than one minute---sixty seconds---no longer---no matter how much mail is in there. Michiko's smile was back to full beam. She agreed to his rules but grew impatient with his new-found patience.

At Cleve's insistence, they observed the mail delivery for three days. While the postman delivered at different times daily, the consistent pattern over the three days was that no one came to get it out of the mailbox until after 5:00PM each day.

On the fourth day, Michiko learned the name of the owner of the property from a utility bill, "Seito Yamamoto". On the fifth day, she found an envelope that she couldn't read because it was in English. She didn't know what to do, so she put all the other mail back in the mailbox and stuck the English envelope in her pocket and returned to the apartment to show it to Cleve. There would be plenty of time for her to return it to the mailbox before 5:00PM.

The *Yakuza* was an omnipresent organization in Japan---in the world for that matter---but still there had been no leads on Spires or either of the two women. The chief counsel was out of options. His survival at this point hinged on his ability to lie to his boss.

"There is good news today, Fujiwara-san. One of our men has seen Spires and the woman in the Shinyaku train station. We will get them."

He raged, "Why didn't he get them. How long is this going to take?" The tirade went on and on.

The chief counsel let it run its course and responded, "There were too many people around, Fujiwara-san. It was the busy hour and they managed to get on a train. We have the station and the surrounding stations blanketed. We will get them. We have a trail to follow now."

The chief counsel knew he'd only bought himself a day, two at the most. He hoped that would be sufficient and that he wouldn't have to lie again, but even as he left Fujiwara's office he was fabricating the next story he would tell his boss.

Michiko handed Cleve the envelope. The address was written in English to Seito Yamamoto. There was no return address but the postmark was Aiea, Hawaii. He heated some water and slowly steamed the seal on the envelope. The steam loosened the glue enough to allow him to slip the edge of his jackknife's blade under the seal and gently lift it open. He removed the letter inside and read it. Michiko stood at his side and looked at it and looked at him for some sign that this was important. It was.

1 June

Dear Saieto,

I am happy to report that your shipments to both China and Vietnam are on schedule and should depart the US in time to reach their destinations by month's end. I am assuming the ship's Captains also share our sense of urgency and that their ships will remain seaworthy. I trust this meets your operational time line.

There is some news regarding me personally. I have been asked to retire by 30 September. This was not unexpected, but it does mean that I will no longer be able to serve the association in my present capacity. My future plans are undecided and I remain flexible. I seek your counsel as to any thoughts you may have about how the association might use me after my retirement.

Very Respectfully,
Paul

Spires knew they had stumbled on to something. After reading about the sale to China and Vietnam in that old copy of the *Stars and Stripes* he'd followed the sale closely in the English language newspaper, *The Tokyo Shimbun.* Now some guy who is visited every day by Cato Fujiwara is getting a letter from Hawaii about shipments to China and Vietnam. Coincidence? Those satellite dishes across the way make this some kind of major communications hub. "Operational time line" has a distinctly military ring to it. Was this letter written by someone in the US military in Hawaii, tipping these guys off about these shipments? What operation's timeline is being met? "What association? Retiring from what?" He read the brief note over and over. Each reading spawned another question; each reading made him think the *Yakuza* was up to something involving the weapons and ammunition on its way to China and Vietnam.

He wasn't good company for her the rest of the day. He tried to make her understand the contents of the note but the conversation quickly got too technical for both of them. She took pride in the fact that she'd brought him this note that seemed to be important. He ruminated over what he should do now. By dark he thought he'd decided, but it was a drastic change of course. He moved a chair close to the window and stared into the night's blackness. Michiko went to bed.

When she came out of the bedroom the next morning she found him slumped awkwardly in the chair. She gently woke him. Over a cup of coffee he told her, "Michiko, I must go to Okinawa?"

Again she understood his words but not his motivation, "Okinawa?"

"There are US Forces there, Special Forces, and I have to give them this note." He held it up.

She didn't need further explanation. What he was doing was crazy in her view, "No. American police put you," she didn't know the English word for prison. "No good, Cleve." Her voice was rising and fear had her on the edge of panic.

"Shh," he put his finger to her lips. "It's OK. This is important, Michiko. I think the *Yakuza* may try to hijack this stuff the US just sold to China and Vietnam. I have to warn them of what's going to happen."

She got angry, "You don't know. What about me? *Yakuza* not stop look. I go with you?"

"No. I can do what I need to do in Okinawa without you. Tokyo and Okinawa are not safe places for you now. I want you to go to Thailand, where Sanji went and wait there for me. You will be safe there. OK?

She turned her back to him. He could see her shoulders rising and falling. She was crying. He went to her and put his hands on her shoulders, "Michiko, you have helped me very much, but you have done as much as you can. I can do what I need to do if I know you are safe in Thailand. Please do as I ask."

She stood there with her back to him for the longest time before she turned and looked at him, "No airplane. Haneda Airport small. *Yakuza* there for sure. They catch you."

OK. How?

She didn't know the words so she put her fingers together in a point and made a wavy motion with them and said, "*Maru,*" the Japanese word for "sea".

"A ship? There's a ship that goes to Okinawa?"

"Hai. I buy ticket." She held up three fingers. "Three days, then Okinawa."

In Cleveland, Ohio, Ida Spires was beside herself with grief. Lee Shaw told her the Cleveland Police Department had reopened the case against her son in light of information received by the National Police in Thailand. Ida had realized too late that she had played into their hands when she provided them with a picture of Cleve. At Ida's request, Shaw had done what he could to keep his fingers on what the police were doing. The latest news was not entirely good, but there was an upside. The Thai Police had moved the case to an inactive status. They believe Cleve is no longer in Thailand.

"Where is there an upside to any of this? she asked.

"Ida, if he's not in Thailand, then he's still alive; he's free and trying to clear his name." He tried to be convincing. He closed his conversation with some advice. "Ida, I think we need to keep quiet. That way we won't give the police anything else to work with. If Cleve happens to call, tell him Cleveland is the last place he should be right now. As an attorney, I guess I shouldn't give you that kind of advice, but he'd be arrested immediately if he showed up here. Once that happens he can't work to clear his name. I don't think any of us are capable of taking that chore over for him. Our approach ought to be as long as we hear nothing to the contrary, we should assume he is alive and kicking somewhere in the world, trying to establish his innocence."

There was no disguising him. He was too big, too black and couldn't speak the language. They would just have to get him onto the ferry as quickly as possible and hope the *Yakuza* wasn't watching the ferry terminal.

Cleve waited in a nearby coffee shop while Michiko went to RKK Line's ticket office and purchased the ticket on the ferry to Okinawa. She managed to get him the last private accommodation available on this sailing, scheduled to depart in less than two hours. They spent an hour in the coffee shop talking quietly about her trip to Thailand. They went over the same details he'd given Sanji about the cab driver, Tradip, at the Windsor Hotel, how to recognize him, what to say to him so that he would know Spires had sent her. Finally he'd told her what to pay him and made sure she had the money to get to where she was going. They used a pay phone at the coffee shop to book her flight to Bangkok. Michiko didn't like not knowing the name of where she was to finally end up, but she understood his reason for not telling her and, more than anyone else, she trusted him. She couldn't get out until 6:00 A.M. the next morning and Cleve didn't like the idea of her spending the night in the apartment alone. She assured him it would be all right.

Thirty minutes before his scheduled departure time, they walked hand-in-hand to the entrance to the terminal building. He held her tightly and whispered into her ear, "Thank you, Michiko." He kissed her lightly on the cheek, turned and headed to the gangway.

Okinawa is a prefecture of Japan so this was a domestic voyage. He didn't need to worry about customs or immigration. He went directly to his compartment and stayed there. Michiko had packed some provisions for him to snack on during the three-day voyage.

She didn't leave the port immediately. Instead she went to the ladies room to clear her eyes and regain her composure before starting the long train ride back to the apartment. When she came out of the ladies room she scanned around the terminal building and then walked out. It was a short walk from the ferry terminal to the subway entrance. For the first block, she turned and looked behind her frequently just to be sure no one had spotted her. Once she'd satisfied herself that no one was following her, she thought of Cleve. One block from the subway station she walked past a pachinko parlor with its garish neon lights flashing and changing colors in constant, gaudy crescendos. Even in daylight, the bright colors bounced off her jet-black hair and made it look strange shades of red, green, blue and yellow. She was oblivious to it all and didn't even notice the man slouched in the arcade's doorway smoking.

But he noticed her. He was first attracted by her figure, even though she was dressed casually in slacks and a loose fitting blouse. When he got to her face there was a glimmer of recognition, but he didn't react immediately. He waited for her to pass and then reached in his pocket and removed the picture of Michiko Tomichi he'd been given. He was sure it was her. He looked quickly around for the other woman and the American black man. They were all supposed to be together. He didn't see the other two, but he was sure he'd just seen Michiko Tomichi and there was a price on her head, paid only if she was turned over to the *Yakuza* alive. He decided he'd follow her and maybe she would lead him to the other two. Michiko, lost in her memories of Cleve, hadn't the slightest inkling she was being followed.

Chapter Twenty-six

"We have the woman, Fujiwara-san."

"And Spires?"

"Not yet, but..."

"Get it out of her. I trust you know how to do that. You have twenty-four hours---no more," he wagged his finger at his chief counsel, "to find him." He stood there awkwardly wanting to ask Cato Fujiwara what was so damned important about Spires. Their entire organization, nearly all of his time, had been consumed with trying to find this man. Why? But he knew better than to ask. After a moment of this awkwardness, Fujiwara waved his hand toward the door. The chief counsel turned and left. The news he'd brought, while informative, wasn't apparently good enough. His stomach rolled as the pressure of having to find Spires in the next twenty-four hours settled in on top of him.

Michiko Tomichi lay strapped to a stainless steel table, naked and heavily drugged. This wasn't part of the plan. By now everyone expected her to be dead, but to have told her torturers where Cleve Spires was before she died. That was going to have to wait a while.

Her kidnapping began quite efficiently. The *Yakuza's* agent from the pachinko parlor followed her to the apartment she and Cleve had shared. When it appeared she wasn't going to move from the apartment, he'd phoned the number he'd been given. Two minutes after that the chief counsel was informed one of the women was under observation. He'd given precise instructions to two of his men, handpicked because they'd killed successfully for him before on several occasions, to go there, to give it some time and watch for Spires and the other whore to show up. If the pair of assassins was lucky enough to find all three together, they were to kill all of them and dispose of their bodies. If, however, Spires didn't turn up, they were to take one or both of the whores to the *Yakuza's* technicians in Sagamihara. The technicians would handle matters from there.

The two watched the apartment until nightfall and when Spires and the other whore hadn't shown up, they made their move. Michiko was in the shower when they picked the lock on the apartment and entered. It was at this point that things began to go awry, terribly so, from Michiko's standpoint. Both men raped her before shooting her up with an injection of heroin to keep her quiet during the drive to Sagamihara. The trip took nearly three hours in heavy traffic so they each took turns alternately driving and raping her again in the back of the panel truck.

When the van pulled into the driveway at the house in Sagamihara, the technicians heard it. They were expecting a delivery, a female subject, who would be the focus of their night's work. Their task was simple; make the woman tell them where a man by the name of Cleveland Spires was hiding. They were assured the woman knew, it was just a matter of applying the right amount of pain in order to get at the information they wanted.

Inside the house the technicians waited for the delivery to be brought to them, but after five minutes had passed and no one had gotten out of the van, they went out to see what was the delay. They found the two thugs struggling to get Michiko back into her clothes. While she wasn't fighting them, the heroin had taken her to the edge of unconsciousness. Arms weren't going easily into sleeves and legs were proving difficult to get into pant's legs.

"You fools," one of the technicians growled, "what have you done to her? You were supposed to bring her straight to us." He put his fingers on Michiko's wrist and felt her pulse and as he did so he saw the syringe they'd used to inject her lying on the floor of the truck. "What did you give her?"

"Heroin."

"How much?"

"The syringe was full."

"How long ago?"

"The last injection was two hours ago…"

The technician screamed at the younger of the two assassins who'd just answered his questions, "The *last* injection! How many times did you… You dumb fucking bastards…"

"Fuck you. You didn't have to move her around the city. You sit here and wait for us to deliver her to you. We have to take all the risks. Without the heroin she was unpredictable. With it, she was cooperative. What fucking difference does it make to you? You're just going to kill here anyway."

The older of the two assassins had delivered people here before. He'd also removed a few who'd survived, but that number was much smaller than the number of his deliveries. He'd never asked what happened to the others he hadn't been asked to remove. It was enough that he'd seen what these two could do, so he placed a hand on the shoulder of his young colleague.

The technician said, "Your young friend hasn't been here before has he?

The older assassin shook his head.

The technician said to the younger man, "This woman has information that is of some importance to Cato Fujiwara. Shall we tell him that our task was made more difficult because you couldn't keep your pants on."

"You can tell him anything…"

The older assassin lost patience with his younger partner and he slapped him soundly on the back of his head. "Shut up, you idiot. You will get us both killed."

The older assassin turned to the technicians, "We apologize if we have made your job harder. The woman was in the shower when we took her. Look at her. She is beautiful," there was a pause, "and we are men, so…" He didn't finish; he didn't need to. What was done was done.

"Get her dressed and get her inside and down the basement. We are wasting time."

Both assassins did as they were told.

The stale air in the basement carried a horrible stink. Very little effort was made to clean up; blood stains covered the floor. Chains and ropes were suspended from the ceiling. Several car batteries with jumper cables were along one wall. Thick blankets of soundproofing material lined the walls and the ceilings. Victims could scream their lungs out down here and not a whisper could be heard on the main floor of the house.

Michiko knew she was going to die. Though she was in and out, she'd heard enough of the exchange between the four men to know what was in the works. When they got her into the basement, they'd stripped off the same clothes they'd just struggled to get her into, bound her hands and feet and then hoisted her by her hand shackles until she could not touch the floor.

The two assassins had left. Now it was the technicians' turn. "Michiko, we are going to have to hurt you very badly unless you tell us where the man Spires is." She heard them but she did not respond.

Torturing a person was not something that could be rushed. The pain had to be taken to its very peak, to a point just short of unconsciousness and then allowed to subside. As it does, full consciousness returns, and brings with it the fear of more pain. The weak ones give up quickly, not wanting the pain to return. The stronger ones are slowly and methodically worn down, each time consciousness returns the fear is stronger and the pain is more intense.

The problem facing the two technicians now was the heroin. They couldn't judge how much pain she might be feeling and they didn't want to kill her before she told them what they wanted to know.

One of the technicians threw ice water on her face. "Michiko, do you know where you are?"

She'd focused her eyes momentarily on her tormentor.

"Michiko, you are going to die here. You can die quickly or you can die slowly. The choice is up to you." He hit her across the stomach with a section of rubber tubing causing her to swing back and forth. Her head rolled around loosely.

He turned to his partner, "Those damn fools have her too doped up. Call the chief counsel and tell him we can do little until the effects of the heroin wear off. Tell him we will phone when we have any information of value," the one technician paused for a minute and then added, "and be sure you tell him who gave her the drugs."

While one of them had gone off to make the call, the other lowered her down and then placed her on a stainless steel table with a trough running around all four sides. The trough was slanted so that liquids running off the table into the trough would flow to a drain located at one corner. A bucket stood ready under the drain to catch anything that fell from the drain. He shackled her hands and feet to the table and went upstairs, with his partner, to wait for the drugs to wear off.

Cleve Spires did not come out of his cabin during the three-day voyage to Okinawa. He was hungry and tired. Sleep, when he allowed it to overtake him, led to dreams of Michiko. He dreamed the *Yakuza* had caught her. He woke up in a sweat and tried to reassure himself that it was just a dream. It helped if he tried to imagine where she would be in her journey to Chuk Ra Met.

It took the entire night for the drugs to wear off. The technicians checked her hourly, dousing her with cold water and checking the reaction of her pupils to bright light. Near dawn on 8 June, the technicians determined Michiko was alert enough to feel pain. They began the process.

"Michiko, you're going to die. We'll make it quick if you will tell us where Spires is. If you don't tell us what we want to know, we'll make dying longer and slower than you ever thought possible."

One of the technicians released her right hand from its manacle and held it in front of her eyes. While she awkwardly struggled, he used a pair of pliers and with a sudden violent jerk snatched the fingernail from her index finger. The pain was excruciating. Michiko's screams bounced harmlessly off of the dense soundproofing.

Holding the fingernail in front of her tear-filled eyes he asked, "Where is Spires?" She revealed nothing. "Very well, Michiko, there are nine more where this one came from. If you think this hurts---well, this is just a warm-up exercise."

By noon she was near death. Her heart had stopped once and the bastards revived her. Still she had given them nothing about Spires. One of them called the chief counsel. "It's been six hours since we started. She doesn't have much life remaining in her. We have a last resort but I don't know how long she will endure it."

"I'm on my way over. Don't do anything until I get there."

The technicians were waiting upstairs when he arrived two hours later. "Where is she?" There was more than a hint of impatience in the chief counsel's voice.

"Downstairs."

"Take me to her."

"As you wish, but I must warn you, it's not pretty. She has endured much more than I imagined she could.

Ignoring the technician's warning, he headed down the basement steps. The smell of burnt flesh was his first sensory perception. When he saw Michiko Tomichi lying on the table, he vomited. The technicians offered him a glass of cold water.

Michiko was regaining consciousness and she tried to fight it off. She'd learn quickly that that was when the pain came. She wished she could just die. One of the technicians stood close to the stainless steel table looking at her. He opened one of her eyes with his thumb. Michiko registered recognition and fear.

"Let me talk to her." The chief counsel pushed the technician aside.

The two technicians exchanged glances. *Who the hell does this bastard think he is? We've spent all day trying to drag it out of her and he thinks he can come in here and just talk to her.*

"Tomichi, where is Spires?" The two technicians smiled at one another. "Tell me where he is and I will tell them to kill you. There will be no more pain."

Michiko had virtually no energy remaining. Where she found it she had no idea, but it came from somewhere deep within her. She spit a vile combination of saliva, mucous and blood on the chief counsel, forever ruining his expensive suit jacket, the white silk shirt underneath it and the designer tie sandwiched in between. The technicians laughed at her monumentally outrageous act of insubordination and at the chief counsel as he tried to wipe the stain only to make it worse.

The chief counsel flared like a match, enraged as much at the technicians as at Michiko. He raised his fist high over his head and brought it crashing down on her stomach. She felt her spleen rupture at impact. It hurt as badly as anything they had done to her up to that point. She could feel her pupils dilating. She was losing consciousness.

The chief counsel was furious. He swore at her again and again. He was frantically looking for something, anything he could hurt her with. He wanted her killed. He wanted to be the one that did it. The technicians talked him down from the height of his rage.

One of the technicians grabbed a pitcher of water and threw it on Michiko's face. It did not revive her. The technicians asked the chief counsel to go upstairs and calm down while they proceeded with the last resort. The ruptured spleen was now dumping blood into her abdominal cavity rapidly. The two worked frantically to revive her. Michiko regained consciousness one last time.

A technician took a knife and held it in front of her eyes. "I'm going to cut you, Michiko and then I'm going to skin you alive. Tell me where Spires is and I'll end this right now. You can be in peace. Just tell me where Spires is."

No response.

He cut an incision along her collarbone to the tip of her right shoulder. As he cut he used her collarbone as his guide. She could feel the edge of the knife riding against the bone. She could hear the not-so-sharp edge scraping its way along. Michiko couldn't muster even enough energy to scream but her nerves sent the pain signals to her brain. Her once beautiful eyes hid now behind loose flaps of skin that once were her eyelids. It was as if her eyes were sinking into her head as her life's blood now flowed out onto the stainless steel table. With his fingers the technician slowly, peeled the skin down to a point just above her right breast. She went blank, into a deep oblivion and the pain began to subside.

A minute later they could detect no pulse. The technicians attributed her death to the skinning, but her abdomen was full of blood from the ruptured spleen. The chief counsel had been the one who killed Michiko Tomichi.

"She's dead," the technician reported to the chief counsel, who was sitting in the living room still trying unsuccessfully to wipe Michiko's stain from his clothes.

The technician who'd performed the last act said, "I don't know what happened. She didn't have much remaining in her but I at least thought I'd get her torso skinned before she bled to death."

"She revealed nothing?" the chief counsel asked with a hint of desperation in his voice.

"Nothing," replied the other technician.

"Then you have failed and I will have to pass this on to Fujiwara-san."

His threat pissed them off. One of them sneered at him, "You may tell Fujiwara-san anything you want to tell him. Do you know why we have been doing this for as long as we have?"

"Why?" The chief counsel was growing impatient with these two ghouls and he did not like their insubordination.

The technician told him, "Because no matter how big the *Yakuza may* get---no matter how many people it may employ---no matter how much money it may pay them---we are the only two who will do *this* kind of work. Your threats do not bother us, but we do have some advice for you. You had better think of your next move because Fujiwara will ask and you'd better have an answer. Otherwise we might have the pleasure of seeing you here again under different circumstances."

They laughed at his predicament.

"Fujiwara-san, the woman Tomichi has died after many hours of torture. Unfortunately she did not reveal the whereabouts of Spires."

Fujiwara looked at him with a cold stare. "And now what is your plan to find him?"

The chief counsel remembered the warning the two ghouls had given him. There were really no innovative solutions remaining. All of the *Yakuza's* resources had been put on alert and produced only the woman. Fujiwara grumbled and waved him out of the room.

Cato Fujiwara knew he'd been lied to. There was no sighting at the Shinyaku train station. The two had been under his nose all of the time. The apartment the woman was taken from was just a few blocks from Yamamoto's estate. He had to assume that they had been watching him, that Driscoll must have told Spires something about him before he died. Fujiwara picked up the phone and dialed a number.

"Take the chief counsel to Sagamihara tonight. Tell the technicians to take their time with him."

He disconnected the phone and dialed his secretary's number.

"Have the car brought around. I'll be gone the remainder of the day."

"Yamamoto-san, Spires has eluded us. We caught the woman who has been helping him but she died without revealing anything." He waited for Yamamoto to explode. He didn't. Fujiwara began to grasp at straws. "I think he may try to escape to South Korea. He might think he can blend in easier because there are still quite a few US troops there. I have a working relationship with Korean organized crime, although the forces of competition occasionally strain it. I can ask them to watch for him..."

Yamamoto interrupted, "Cato, tell me how serious can it be if Spires remains on the loose? He's a fugitive. How can he hurt you?"

"I think Spires may have followed me here. I think he and the woman may have been watching us..."

"And why do you think that?"

"The woman was taken from an apartment just several blocks from here."

"And what do you think they might have learned?"

Cato Fujiwara was never questioned; he was always the questioner. He didn't like the role reversal at all. Impatiently he replied, "I don't know. How can I know that? That is why we must catch this man Spires and kill him."

Seito Yamamoto could see his colleague coming apart and it angered Yamamoto that Fujiwara's vaunted organization allowed Spires to slip through their net, but Spires was not the issue for him that he was for Fujiwara. What Yamamoto needed was Cato Fujiwara and his organization to concentrate on Operation Light Switch in Japan. Yamamoto controlled his anger and made a decision that he did not reveal to Fujiwara.

Fujiwara said, "I will of course need to offer an explanation to the Koreans. I intend to tell them I want Spires for the death of a good friend."

Yamamoto wasn't paying attention. He was thinking through his own plan.

"Yamamoto-san..."

"Ah, yes, the Koreans. Cato, if you think that is where Spires is, then by all means use your contacts there to catch him. I remain confident in your organization's ability to find Spires." He lied. "Please keep me posted on your progress."

Spires waited until he thought most of the passengers had departed the ferry and then he walked off the ship, through the passenger terminal and onto the street.

He hailed a cab and told the driver, "Torii Station, please."

The thirty-mile drive from Naha Port to Torii Station, home of the First Special Forces Battalion, took 90 minutes. He put his head back and tried to sleep. He couldn't. All he could think of was Michiko. The feeling that he had abandoned her haunted him.

Seito Yamamoto phoned Paul Stanley for only the second time in their near-decade long partnership. Yamamoto was a meticulous planner and did not like making phone calls asking for help. The necessity of this phone call meant that there was a flaw in his planning process. Nonetheless, he needed Paul Stanley and the mail was too slow.

"Paul, this is Saieto. I must ask another favor."

Stanley, who had been sound asleep, was fully awake now. Yamamoto didn't call unless it was something important and urgent. He swung his feet around and sat on the edge of the bed. "How may I help, Saieto?"

"Have you heard of a man named Spires---Cleveland Spires? He is wanted in Thailand for the murder of one of your soldiers."

Despite the hour and the fog of sleep that still addled his brain, he remembered the incident. "Yes, I read about it. I only know what I've read in the newspapers though, Seito."

"Spires' presence in the Pacific Rim threatens the security of Operation Light Switch. Cato Fujiwara's organization has tried to catch him, but even the sizeable resources of the *Yakuza* have not been up to the task. Either Spires is very lucky, very good, or both. I know the US military has some intelligence capability remaining in the region. I need that capability focused now on locating Spires. Operation Light Switch is imminent Paul. After it has occurred, Spires is of little consequence to us, but for now he is more than just an annoyance."

Stanley wasn't sure how to respond. His field was logistics and Yamamoto was now asking for assistance in the intelligence field. J-2 handles intelligence; J-4 handles logistics.

"I'll try, Saieto, but you understand that the intelligence business is not exactly my line of work."

"I know, Paul. I trust your ability and judgment implicitly." What other choice did Yamamoto have?

Stanley was about to hang up when he had a sudden second thought.

"Saieto, did you receive my note about the ammunition shipments?"

"No, it hasn't come yet. When did you send it?"

Stanley had a queasy feeling in his stomach.

"I sent it air mail. I mailed it on the first or second of the month. It should have been to you by now."

Yamamoto did not seem to share his concern. "It will come in the next day or so I am certain, but since I have you on the phone, tell me what it said."

Stanley recapped the information contained in the note.

"The news of your retirement saddens me. You've been a valuable source of information and your efforts have put the *association* in a position to execute Operation Light Switch sooner than any of us expected. As I mentioned to you on Hokkaido, it will be your decision to remain in your country or come to ours, Paul. If you choose to join us, you will be well placed in our government, even though you are Western. Your loyalty to us has been amply demonstrated." There was a pause. Yamamoto had other work he wanted to get to. "Paul, it's not necessary for you to decide now. Think about it and let me know."

"I will Saieto. Thank you."

Yamamoto turned to the stack of maps and the pile of notes beside the maps, forgot about Paul Stanley's letter and went back to work on the more important business of finalizing plans for Operation Light Switch.

Kidnapped while on his way to his car in the skyscraper's underground parking garage, his abductor had knocked him unconscious. He awoke naked and chained to the stainless steel table that had held Michiko only the night before. A smiling technician bent over his still dilated pupils and said to him, "Mr. Chief Counsel, welcome back. We've arranged a few surprises for you."

Chapter Twenty-seven

Marine Corps Lieutenant Colonel Jim Rouse grabbed the phone between the first and second ring and thought, *The shit is starting early this morning.* Usually he could get some things done without interruption at this early hour, but this call might be a harbinger of a busier day than normal. Rouse hated his job. He hadn't sought it; he'd been nominated and handpicked for it. As one of the Marine Corps' brightest and best Lieutenant Colonels this kind of duty was necessary for him to endure. As Executive Officer to the Deputy Commander-in-Chief, US Pacific Command, Jim Rouse was really a timekeeper. It was his job to keep Lieutenant General Lynn Kinney on schedule. Some days that was easier than others.

"General Stanley, General Kinney has just one opening this morning and that's from 0630 to 0645. He's wall-to-wall meetings after that."

"I'll take it, Jim."

"Fine, sir. The subject?"

Stanley didn't want to say. "Uh, it's a personal matter, Jim."

Rouse grew cautious. Kinney didn't like surprises. These were the kinds of things that made Rouse good at what he did. He had to walk a fine line between not pissing off a two-star general who worked for his boss and not pissing off his boss. His boss always took priority.

"Uh, sir, no offense, but I'll need to be a little more specific. The General wanted to use that time to catch up on some paperwork. If he's going to see you, he'll want to know what it's about." Then he added, "I hope you understand, General Stanley."

Stanley did. It was the way of the world in the front office at CINCPAC. "Jim, it's an intelligence matter involving the murder of that Sergeant Major in Bangkok a month ago."

That was good enough. "Sir, the General just walked in. I'll let him know you're on the way up."

"Thanks."

Three minutes later Stanley was in front of Kinney's desk. "Sir, this is about the Driscoll murder. You recall it?"

He looked at Stanley, "Not likely to forget it Paul. The good Sergeant Major it seems, was running quite a few enterprises in Bangkok. What about him?

Stanley began with the truth. "Well, I received a call last evening from a friend of mine in Tokyo." The truth ended there. "He's an Inspector with INTERPOL. They would like our help." Kinney looked at his watch. Stanley needed to get on with it. "Bottom line---he was wondering if we could assist them in locating the person who shot Sergeant Major Driscoll, a guy by the name of Cleveland Spires. He thought since Driscoll was a serviceman and Spires is an ex-serviceman, we might be willing to give them a hand."

"That's not exactly the bottom line, Paul. The bottom line is, 'what exactly is it INTERPOL is asking?' Do they want our troops actually searching for Spires? If that's what they're asking for, they'll have to be a helluva lot more formal about their request than some guy making a phone call."

Stanley needed to be not only quick, but cautious as well. Kinney was known for two things, quick decisions and sticking by them. If Kinney said "no" there would be no revisiting the issue.

"Sir, he just wants us to be INTERPOL's eyes and ears. He knows we can't apprehend anybody. He doesn't want us to do their job, but he asked if we could help them pinpoint this guy's location."

Stanley pressed his case further. "Sir, there's a compelling reason for us to want Spires caught. We simply can't afford to have this guy out there running around killing anyone else. He's a renegade. What's worse, he's a renegade who's out there carrying around a US military ID card. He creates trouble someplace and it's a bad reflection on us. You know how much we've got going on right now. We sure don't need him muddling things up."

"Paul, we're not a police force---we're a military force. There is a difference, you know."

"Yes, sir. You're right, but we do have forces in a lot of places and INTERPOL thinks Spires might turn up at some of our installations. So, all I'm suggesting is that we simply circulate his profile and ask our components to notify the nearest INTERPOL office if Spires is seen."

Kinney nodded agreeably. It seemed a good solution that didn't require a lot of resources, and Stanley was right about avoiding any black eyes. "OK, Paul, but the instructions will be very specific; we don't attempt to apprehend or arrest. I'll let the J-2 know. Who's your friend at INTERPOL? The J-2 folks will contact him."

"Uh, well sir, he said he'd be on the road for the next several weeks."

Kinney looked annoyed.

Stanley pulled one out of his ass. “He said to contact their operations center in Tokyo if we were able to help.” He’d visited there once on a visit to Japan. It was a hole-in-the-wall place compared to military operations centers, but he was glad now he’d wasted the time to see it.

“Dammit, Paul. This sure seems like a half-ass way for INTERPOL to do business.”

“You know sir, I told my friend that same thing last night when he called me about this. He gave me some bullshit about how pressed they are for people…”

“Yeah, like they’re the only ones with that problem.”

Stanley nodded knowingly.

“All right. I’ll tell JICPAC (Joint Intelligence Center, Pacific) to get on it.”

Stanley went back to his office pleased with his ability to manipulate his three-star overseer.

Spires got out of the cab at Torii Station’s front gate. Okinawan cab fares were no cheaper. The fare was 5,000 Yen. The blue retired military ID got him past the Japanese guard at the front gate. It had been ten years since he’d been here last, but Torii Station wasn’t that big compared to most military installations. He remembered the way to the First Special Forces Battalion Headquarters, but when he got there he found things very different. The wave of international terrorism that culminated in the horrible events of 9/11 had been taken very seriously. The First Special Forces Battalion compound on Torii Station carried a very high rating as a potential terrorist target; not much had been left to chance. The entire Headquarters was a controlled area surrounded by 12 foot-high chain link fence with concertina wire strung menacingly across the top. The main entrance required a special identification card to be swiped through a channel and then a keypad required a PIN number to be entered. None of this is what he’d expected. Just getting into this place was going to be a challenge. At what he thought was the main entrance to the compound, he found a speaker box with a button underneath it. He pushed the button.

Almost immediately a tinny voice answered, "Yes." He had not been prepared for such a quick response. He started to say something, but an irritated voice said, "You have to push the button to talk. Who do you want to see?"

Cleve pushed down the button he'd pushed earlier and said, "The Battalion Commander."

"He's TDY."

"Is the Battalion Command Sergeant Major here?"

"Yeah, just a minute."

The irritation in the voice was even more apparent. Spires wondered who the smart-ass was on the other end of this connection. How did he know he wasn't talking to an officer? Then a quick scan around provided him the answer to his question. About twenty-five feet inside the chain link and just to his left he spotted a TV camera mounted on a post and trained on the gate.

Momentarily the voice was back, "I'm sorry Mister, the Sergeant Major is busy today. He said if you come back tomorrow maybe he could talk to you then."

"But it's important."

"Listen Mister, I'm sure it is important, but if I go back in there and bother the Sergeant Major again, he'll just get ticked off. He's real busy. Your best shot at getting to see him is to wait and come back tomorrow like he's asked."

Cleve asked the voice, "When will the Battalion Commander be back?

"He's due back tomorrow. That's why the Sergeant Major's so busy. He's getting his shit together for the old man tomorrow."

There was little he could do except relent. He found the billeting office and was lucky enough to get a room for the night. He hated wasting this time. Each day that passed put the ammunition shipments to Vietnam and China closer to somehow getting into the *Yakuza's* hands.

The Marine Corps Colonel on duty as the watch officer in the JICPAC Operations Center on Hickam Air Force Base took the call from the DCINC, General Kinney. He understood exactly what the DCINC wanted and how to go about getting it done.

The Colonel's call to the INTERPOL operations center in Tokyo was a bit more complex. His counterpart was unfamiliar with any INTERPOL request to PACOM for assistance in the Spires case. However, after some discussion both men dismissed this as a typical lack of communication that occurs between large, bureaucratic organizations. INTERPOL and PACOM had cooperated before, and this was simply another case of one hand washing the other. Within minutes the Marine Colonel had a digital photo of Spires pulled from an email sent to him by INTERPOL. The same email produced the latest wanted bulletin on Cleveland A. Spires. From there he jumped into the NCIC Data Base, typed in "SPIRES, CLEVELAND A." and within two minutes had a hard copy print out of Cleve's record of conviction ten years ago. Finally, on a separate computer, loaded with the latest encryption software, he banged out a message:

Cleveland A. Spires, an American citizen, is wanted in Thailand for the murder of CSM (USA) William Driscoll. Spires was last seen in Tokyo, Japan. Spires' photograph is forwarded as attachment one to this E-mail. Attachment two is the current INTERPOL Bulletin concerning Spires. Attachment three is a record of Spires' previous conviction for murder and smuggling.

US CINCPAC considers Spires a threat to American interests in the region. Your assistance in locating Spires is desired. In the event Spires is seen in your location you should notify the nearest INTERPOL office. A current list of INTERPOL offices, their addresses, and phone numbers is Attachment four.

PACOM UNITS ARE ADVISED NOT TO ATTEMPT APPREHENSION OR DETENTION OF SPIRES. HE SHOULD BE CONSIDERED ARMED AND DANGEROUS.

Signed
WHITWORTH
COL, USMC
JICPAC WATCH OFFICER

He clicked his computer's mouse on the "send mail" icon and seconds later got a message on his screen indicating his email had been successfully sent to Intel Network Group A which meant that every J-2, G-2, and S-2 in the entire Pacific including Alaska just got Spires' information.

———

Spires slept fitfully, worrying about his delay at the First Battalion and Michiko's safety, although he told himself she should be in Chuk Ra Met by now. After a long night he got out of bed at 5:30 AM, showered, dressed and was at the First Battalion's Headquarters by 6:00 on the morning of 10 June.

He'd pushed the button on the speaker box.

"Yeah."

He asked to see either the Battalion Commander or the Battalion Command Sergeant Major.

"Neither one of 'em's here. They're at PT. They won't get here until around eight." Spires went back to his room. The two hours dragged by.

At 7:00 AM the First Special Forces Battalion S-2 dialed the combination to the vault that was, in fact, his office. Once inside, he turned on the desktop computer sitting on the credenza behind his desk and went to make a pot of coffee. When he returned, the screen contained a message notifying him of electronic mail waiting. He printed a copy of the message and the four attachments on the laser printer next to the computer.

As he took his first sip of coffee he read the e- mail from JICPAC. Determining that the Sergeant Major, Executive Officer, and Battalion Commander should see this e-mail, he put a routing slip on the top with the blocks "CSM", "XO" and "Bn Cdr" checked. He walked down the hall to the Sergeant Major's office and placed the printed e-mail with all of its attachments in the box on the Sergeant Major's desk marked "In".

The Sergeant Major arrived at the battalion's headquarters at 7:50 AM and retrieved a cup of coffee before diving into his "In" box. The Battalion Commander got there five minutes later. It had been two weeks since they'd seen one another and there was a fair amount of information each had to share with the other. The Sergeant Major grabbed the stuff in his in-box and went to the door of the Battalion Commander's office, "Sir, I'll be right in. Let me look through this stuff and make sure something hot didn't come in between last night and this morning."

"Sounds like a plan, Sergeant Major."

At 8:00 AM promptly, Spires was back on the speaker at the entrance gate to the battalion's headquarters.

"Yes."

"I'd like to see the Battalion Commander or the Sergeant Major. I was here yesterday and told to come back today."

"Just a minute."

The Corporal---the same Corporal who'd been the middleman between Spires and the Sergeant Major the day before---walked into the Sergeant Major's office and said, "Sergeant Major, that guy is back again."

"Are you shittin' me?"

The kid hated this part of his job. No matter what he did, it wasn't right. He'd been yelled at so many times for not letting someone in who should have been allowed in, and so many times for letting someone in who should have been kept out, that he didn't know what was right and what was wrong anymore.

"Who is this guy? What's his name?"

"I don't know Sergeant Major."

"Well, Corporal that would be useful information."

"Yes Sergeant Major." He turned to go get the guy's name, while the Sergeant Major took out the email that the J-2 had put in his mailbox fifteen minutes earlier.

"He says his name is Spires and he needs to see either you or the Battalion Commander."

The Sergeant Major was reading the INTERPOL circular on Spires at that moment and he nearly spit a mouthful of coffee all over the desktop.

He looked up at the Corporal and commanded, "Stay right here. Don't do nothin' until I come back."

The Sergeant Major turned and headed into the Battalion Commander's office.

"Sir, we got a problem." He handed Lieutenant Colonel Darrell Greene the email from the JICPAC. Greene read it.

"What's the problem Sergeant Major?"

"A guy who says he's Spires is at the front gate and wants to see either you or me."

"You're shitting me."

"Sir, I wish I was."

Greene quickly scanned the message again. "Wonder what the hell he wants here?"

The Sergeant Major shrugged. "Sir, this guy has been trying to see me since yesterday. I just blew him off, but he's back. He must be serious about wanting to see us. Maybe he's just tired of being on the run and he came to us because he figured he'd get better treatment."

"Well, he's here and I'm not about to let a killer get away, even if Driscoll was a scumbag. I don't give a shit what this message says. Go to the arms room and get a 9mm for yourself and one for me. If he tries something we'll be ready. When you bring the pistols back we'll have the Corporal let him in and escort him to my office just like he would any other visitor to the headquarters. Hell, he can't take both of us."

Five minutes later the box told Cleve, "The Sergeant Major can see you now." There was an electric buzzing, Cleve pushed on the gate, and it gave way. He walked up the sidewalk to the doorway where the corporal met him.

"I'll take you to Lieutenant Colonel Greene's office." Cleve thanked him.

Greene knew his career would be over if something went wrong. He quickly assessed Spires who seemed calm enough, but Greene was ready for anything. He hoped his Sergeant Major was as well. Things moved quickly from this point on, thanks to Cleve.

"Colonel Greene, do you know who I am?"

"Yes, Mr. Spires, I do. It is my duty to inform you that you are under arrest. It is my intention to detain you here until proper authorities are notified and come for you."

"Colonel Greene, I know you think I killed Billy Driscoll. But Billy Driscoll isn't the reason I've come here. I have information---information that I think is relevant to the sale of military supplies the US just made to Vietnam and China. I think the *Yakuza* may somehow be planning to get their hands on it. I've come here today to pass that information on to Colonel Johnson."

"Colonel Johnson? What does he have to do with this?"

"No offense, sir, but I trust Colonel Johnson with the information I have. He'll give it serious consideration. This information can't get lost because you think you've captured a killer."

Greene asked him, "What makes you think Colonel Johnson will give it consideration?"

"Because he gave me fair consideration ten years ago. He was probably the only member of my court-martial board that did."

Greene thought, *That's sour grapes.* Then he demanded, "Show me what you have, Mr. Spires."

"No Sir. I don't want to be rude or insubordinate, but I will give what I have only to Colonel Johnson."

"Why shouldn't I just call INTERPOL right now and tell them to come get you?"

"That's your prerogative, Colonel, but I urge you not to be so hasty. They'll take me away and the information I have will go with me. It's good information, Colonel. I'm not sure what it all means. It requires further investigation, but there's something going on with those weapons and ammunition and the *Yakuza.*"

"Why should I believe you? You killed Driscoll. You killed that kid here ten years ago. Give me one good reason I should believe you."

"First of all, don't believe everything you read, Colonel. I didn't kill anybody, but Billy Driscoll did, ten years ago right here on Okinawa and the *Yakuza* killed Driscoll because of what he knew. Yeah, I was in Bangkok. I was there to see Driscoll because I was trying to find out why he framed me ten years ago."

There was silence for a moment and then Spires tried some logic. "Colonel Greene, if I were Driscoll's murderer, why would I have come here today?"

It was a rhetorical question. Spires continued, "Because I suddenly repented my sins? Because I want to be arrested and sent to Thailand to stand trial? Think about it. I was on the loose. No one knew where I was. Hell, I avoided the *Yakuza* and I was right in their back yard following their top guy for nearly a month in Tokyo. Why would I come here and turn myself in? Unless I have something that I think is important---even more important than saving my own neck."

Greene leaned back in his chair and looked at his Sergeant Major who shrugged his shoulders. He thought for a moment and then looked at Spires, "All right. You've bought yourself some time, but not much. Colonel Johnson is due here this afternoon for a visit. You'll be the first person on his itinerary, Mr. Spires."

"Thank you." Spires hung his head and breathed a sigh of relief.

"Yeah, well, don't get too comfortable. You will remain here in this office. An armed guard will be posted here to keep an eye on you. If you try anything---anything at all---his instructions will be to shoot. Do I make myself clear, Mr. Spires."

"Perfectly."

The Military Airlift Command flight carrying Lucas Johnson to Okinawa arrived at Kadena Air Force Base pretty much on time. This was Johnson's first visit to the First Battalion since taking command of the First Special Forces Group. He was looking forward to meeting Darrell Greene and getting a first hand look at this Battalion, one of six that fell under Lucas' Group command.

Greene met his boss in the VIP Lounge at the MAC Terminal and told him what awaited him once they got to Greene's office. On the twenty minute trip from Kadena Air Base to Torii Station, Greene tried to fill Johnson in on the details of how Spires had just shown up on his doorstep that morning. Johnson listened to some of what Greene was saying, but he missed a lot of it. He was flashing back ten years to the court-martial; six months ago to Fort Leavenworth; and two months ago to Bangkok. *Why does Cleveland Spires keep turning up in my life?* By the time they arrived at the First Battalion's headquarters, all that Lucas knew for sure was that he was going to see Spires---beyond that, he had no idea what would happen next.

When Lucas Johnson entered the Battalion Commander's office, Spires was sitting on a sofa. Cleve stood up, assumed the position of attention, and said simply, "Good afternoon, sir."

"Good afternoon, Sergeant Major." Johnson couldn't believe he had just been so incredibly stupid. "I'm sorry---Mr. Spires."

"Its OK, sir. I've made the adjustment. You don't need to apologize."

"Lieutenant Colonel Greene tells me you have some information on some arms shipments you want to tell me about."

"Yes, sir. I do." He pulled out the note he'd intercepted and handed it to Johnson. As Johnson read, Cleve supplied details of what had happened to him since arriving in Bangkok to confront Driscoll.

Lucas read the note twice. There was no direct reference to the arms shipments or to the military. "OK, so tell me what you think this is telling us."

"It's not just the note sir. It's who I've been following, his organization, this note and these arms shipments. If you add them all together, something strange is going on. I don't know what it is exactly, except I know it's no good."

Lucas asked, "Who do you think 'Paul' is?"

"I think he's someone in the military, stationed in Hawaii, who had something to do with these shipments."

Lucas turned to Lieutenant Colonel Greene.

"Darrell, do you have a CINCPAC organization chart."

"Yes, sir."

It was a long shot, but Johnson thought that the "Paul" they were looking for just might be stationed at Pacific Command. PACOM would manage foreign military sales in this part of the world. Greene produced a folded piece of paper after rummaging through the middle drawer of his desk and handed it to Johnson.

Johnson unfolded the chart and spread it out in front of him. Organized by staff directorate, the chart contained the names of all key staff personnel, nearly 500 people, assigned to United States Pacific Command. Methodically, Johnson started with J-1 and worked his way through all eight staff directorates ending with the J-8.

His search produced half a dozen "Pauls" but only one seemed to be in a position to have impacted the arms sales. *"Paul Stanley"*, the J-4/Director for Logistics and Security Assistance himself, was certainly in the right position to know all about these shipments.

Cleve thought they were really on to something. Johnson had another question.

"How do I know you're telling me the truth? How do I know you didn't write this note yourself and make up this story just to avoid extradition to Thailand?"

"Sir, that's not my handwriting on that note, but we don't have time to get my handwriting analyzed. We need to start checking out Fujiwara, this guy Yamamoto at the estate in Tokyo, and this two-star general at PACOM. Start doing that now and while you're doing that you can have someone analyze my handwriting. You'll see I didn't write that note. Don't assume I'm lying. It would be a big mistake, sir."

Lucas knew if Spires was right, time was crucial. He decided to take a chance on him.

"Darrell, I need to use your STU III."

Greene found the key for the secure telephone. Lucas inserted it and punched in the numbers for SOCPAC. After three rings, Lucas got the man he needed to talk to on the line.

"Hurley."

Brigadier General Mike Hurley, Commander, Special Operations Command, Pacific, was Lucas Johnson's operational boss when Lucas or any of his soldiers were operating anywhere in the Pacific Command Area of Responsibility.

"Sir, Lucas Johnson. I'm on Okinawa. I need to go secure on this phone call and get some guidance. I'll initiate the switch to secure if you've got your key in and turned on."

Hurley quickly checked.

"OK Lucas, I'm ready. Go ahead and initiate."

Lucas pressed the button marked "secure". Fifteen seconds later both callers had a message on the LED window at the top of their phones that said, "Secret". For Hurley and Johnson there was an echo caused by the short delay while the phones scrambled and then unscrambled their words, but it wasn't bad. All an unauthorized eavesdropper would hear is garbled noise.

Lucas told Hurley what was going on. He closed this part of the phone call with, "Sir, I have a gut feeling he's telling the truth---that he's on to something. We don't have a lot of time to play with this. If this note involves those ammo ships, they are due to arrive out here between now and the end of the month."

"OK Lucas, you've made me a believer for the moment. I want you and Spires on the next available flight back here to Hawaii, either military or commercial, whichever is quicker. Have someone call me on this line and tell me your travel plans when you know what they are. I want to ask this guy a few questions first. If I'm satisfied after that, then we'll go to the DCINC."

"Roger, sir. We'll be there as soon as we can. Out, here."

Johnson hung up the telephone. The word "Secret" faded from the LED on the phone's window. Johnson turned the key, removed it from the phone, and handed it to Greene.

He'd flown nearly half way around the world, and now he needed to go back almost to where he'd started, and he hadn't been on Okinawa for an hour. "Darrell, I need to get out of here and back to Hawaii---the sooner the better. You and your Sergeant Major did the right thing with this. Make sure that any of your people who know that Sergeant Major Spires was here get the word that they aren't permitted to discuss having seen him or to speculate in any way as to his whereabouts. We need to keep all of this pretty quiet until we see where we stand. I'm sorry the visit was so short. I'll be back."

Spires broke in, "Sir, there's a woman…" He told them about Michiko. "She should be in Thailand by now. I'd just like to know that she got there safely. Can one of Colonel Greene's troops on the ground in Thailand go to Chuk Ra Met and check it out for me?"

Johnson turned to Greene who was nodding. "Yes, sir. We'll take care of it. Where's Chuk Ra Met?"

Spires answered, "Ten miles north of Korat. If your guy has trouble finding it, have him go to the Tiger Brigade headquarters in Korat and ask for Colonel Pramrashorn Saraveet, no one else. Pram will get your guy to Chuk Ra Met."

Greene nodded again. Spires said, "Thanks. I owe you for this." He offered his hand and Greene took it. Cleve's concern for the woman added to his credibility in everyone's mind.

The flight time from Okinawa to Hawaii was nearly eleven hours. There was lots of time for them to talk. It was awkward at first; neither was sure how personal they should get with the other. Spires opened up first, telling Johnson about his time in prison, and how wrong he'd been about his father, his mother, his wife and son.

Lucas Johnson remembered that day he'd watched Spires walking out of Fort Leavenworth. He remembered the urge he'd had to ask him one question. He thought he'd never have a better opportunity than now to ask it.

"Did you do it? Did you kill that kid at Kadena?"

Immediately, but somewhat dispassionately Spires said, "No."

They fell silent for a long while. Johnson felt sick to his stomach. Cleve just sat there. Not sure if Johnson believed him or not. Finally he said to Lucas, "It's OK. You know that, don't you, Colonel. If I'd been in your shoes at that court martial, I would have found me guilty too. The evidence was pretty well stacked up against me---Driscoll had seen to that."

The silence between them returned as the huge jet engines on the C-5 pushed them toward the Hawaiian Islands. When he finally did talk, Johnson told Spires about seeing him at the prison barbershop that day. He laughed when he told him how quickly he'd gotten the hell out of there and that got a smile out of Spires. Johnson began to talk about his family, about Barbara and their two children. What Cleve learned about Lucas Johnson confirmed what he'd thought all along; he was a good, fair man. So, too, did Lucas Johnson learn things about Cleve Spires he didn't know, and what he learned caused him to rethink some of the conclusions he'd reached. Before they landed in Hawaii, a bond of respect had begun to form between them.

Chapter Twenty-eight

The C5 lumbered down out of a clear, warm Hawaiian night sky the same day it left Okinawa, but barely; it was near midnight as Spires and Johnson deplaned at Hickam Air Force Base in Honolulu. Brigadier General Mike Hurley was waiting for them planeside with a sedan, customs and immigration had already been seen to.

"Throw your bags in the trunk. I've got a safe house set up here on base." Hurley drove. Lucas sat in the front and Cleve slid in the rear seat on the passenger's side. As they pulled away from the huge airlifter, Hurley looked at Spires by way of the rearview mirror, "A lot of people are looking for you."

"Yes, sir, but they're looking for the wrong man."

"So you say."

Cleve Spires had spent a professional lifetime in the rigors of military courtesy, but it was late, the trip long and Hurley's tone didn't sit well with him. While he knew better than to lose his temper with superiors, especially superiors wearing stars on their shoulder boards, he wasn't in the Army anymore and he didn't like the way this conversation was heading.

"General, I didn't sneak into Okinawa, turn myself in and then fly all the way back here just so you can accuse me of something I didn't do. I'll defend myself when the time comes for that. Right now I'm here because I think I've stumbled into something much larger than the murder of Billy Driscoll, who, by the way, was no saint. I think that shipment of weapons and ammunition that's on its way to Vietnam and China is in some kind of jeopardy. Could we talk about that?"

Hurley turned into a semi-circular driveway and pulled to a stop. Maybe Spires had earned a little respect with him or maybe not. At any rate the tone was gone while Hurley explained where they were. "This dormitory is still under construction. You're on the first floor. During the day workmen will be on the floors above you so you'll have to keep a low profile."

Lucas asked, "Who got the message from JICPAC?"

"Oh, just about everybody. Between the police and us there's a lot of people that have his picture." Hurley looked into the rearview mirror and turned his attention to Spires. "And we're the good guys, Spires. If the bad guys want you as badly as you say they do, the *Yakuza* can get to you as easily here, in Hawaii, as they can on mainland Japan. So don't think for one minute that just because you're back in the States that you're suddenly safe. That will get you killed. At least here on Hickam, access to the base is somewhat controlled. You're as safe here as anywhere until we can figure out what the hell is going on. Let's get your gear inside."

Hurley's tone was back. Spires felt like Hurley was scolding him, like a schoolboy. Johnson caught the tone and Spires reaction to it. He shot Spires a look that told him to hang on. Without saying a word, Spires opened the door and was the first to climb out of the sedan. He waited for Hurley to pop the trunk open, grabbed his stuff after Johnson took his and they followed Hurley into the darkened dormitory complex.

Once inside Hurley took off the gloves. "Look Spires, I'm your judge and jury now. I'm not here to be your friend. If I'm not convinced that what you got jeopardizes the shipments, then it ends here and you go to jail. Got it?"

Spires went through it all for Hurley and answered a million questions along the way. The note and the sketch of the satellite dishes at Yamamoto's estate were most compelling for Hurley. At 3:30AM Hurley looked at Johnson and said, "I'll get us in with the DCINC as soon as I can. In the meantime you're bunking here. I'll call you on your cell phone and let you know when the General can see us." Mike Hurley wasn't ready to completely trust Cleve Spires, but he understood the political sensitivity of the arms sale and he sure as hell didn't trust the *Yakuza.* In the meantime it was Lucas Johnson's job to keep an eye on Spires.

A scant two hours later, Cleve heard Lucas' cell phone ring. Their meeting was in one hour with General Kinney in his office at Camp H.M. Smith. Hurley would pick them up in 30 minutes. Traffic at that time of the morning wouldn't be bad, but they didn't want to be late for this meeting.

They were waiting when the DCINC walked in. Hurley made the introductions, saving Cleve Spires for last.

"I suppose there is a good reason why I have a fugitive in my office." Kinney was glaring at Spires. This wasn't the start either Johnson or Spires had hoped for.

Hurley pressed forward, "There is sir, but it takes some explaining. I'm going to let Mr. Spires start."

Cleve began and it was going pretty well. When they got to the note, Mike Hurley interrupted Spires and interjected the possibility that the note might have come from Major General Paul Stanley.

Kinney turned to Spires and demanded, "Let me see it." He snatched it from Spires' hand and quickly read it. Then his attention shifted to a stack of papers on the corner of his desk. He began sifting through them and didn't stop until he was three-fourths of the way through the six-inch stack. He pulled out a paper-clipped bundle of papers and laid it in the center of his desk and then placed the note next to it.

"Damn."

The others couldn't see what he was looking at. Hurley stepped to the desk and after a moment commented, "Looks the same to me, sir."

"Damn if it doesn't," said Kinney, who was comparing the signature on the note to Paul Stanley's signature on a staffing sheet on top of the paper-clipped bundle Kinney had removed from the stack. The "P" and the "l" were particularly distinctive and appeared to their untrained eyes to be the same on each of the two signatures.

Spires added, "If you check the postmark, you'll see it was mailed from here, in Hawaii, General."

Kinney nodded, "OK. Go ahead."

Spires finished his story. They were ready for questions. Instead, Kinney leaned back in his chair, put his hands together, formed a steeple with his two index fingers and laid them against his chin. He thought for several minutes. The others stood by quietly letting him process all that he'd just been given. Finally he reached for a phone and punched four digits. The CINC's Executive Officer picked up.

"I need to see the CINC right now. Who's he got with him?"

There was silence while he got his answer, then, "Well, listen I got a no-shit real-live problem I need to see the CINC about and I need to see him right now. Get him the hell out of there and let me know as soon as he's cleared. I'm bringing some people with me and I don't want him to see them." He hung up.

Kinney looked up at them. "Stanley was in there briefing the CINC on something. Does Stanley know you Mr. Spires?"

Cleve answered, "Not that I'm aware of, sir. But my photo..."

Kinney held up his hand, "Yeah, I know. Who do you think authorized the circulation of your information to units in Pacific Command? Stanley asked me to do that. Seemed odd at the time, seems even odder now. Why do you suppose he'd do that?"

The question went unanswered as the phone rang, and a minute later they were being escorted into Admiral Chet McKeever's office. This time General Kinney handled introductions.

"What the hell has got your bowels in such an uproar this morning Lynn?"

"Sir, we may have a problem with the arms shipments to Vietnam and China."

McKeever leaned forward in his chair.

"I'm going to let Mr. Spires start."

When Spires was done, the Admiral asked a single question. "Do the four of you really think that Paul Stanley is involved in some kind of a plot with the *Yakuza* to steal these arms shipments?"

Hurley spoke first. "Sir, I know this isn't easy to swallow, but we have too much here to just turn our backs on it. Can I suggest we get CID (US Army's Criminal Investigation Division) to do a handwriting analysis to see if the handwriting is a match? While they're doing that, get the J-2 to take some satellite shots of this place in Japan that Spires has been watching. Depending on what we get, we go from there."

McKeever liked it. It was a measured response in proportion to what they knew at this point. "OK, Mike. You get the CID to give the handwriting analysis a priority. I'll get some pictures ordered up of the estate. In the meantime, Mr. Spires, thanks for bringing this to our attention, but I want you to consider yourself under house arrest. Do you understand?

"Yes, sir."

"Colonel Johnson, you will keep this man in your sight at all times while we sift through this. Do you understand?

"Yes, sir."

While Hurley initiated the handwriting analysis investigation with the commander of the Criminal Investigation Division, Johnson and Spires waited in a conference room. Spires asked Johnson, "Can we check with Colonel Greene. I'd like to know that Michiko's safe in Thailand. I'd just like to know that she's OK."

Lucas found Kinney's Executive Officer and asked for a secure phone line. The exec gave him a key and told him the phone in the conference room was secure. The conference room door was closed, so Lucas pushed the speaker button so Cleve could hear the conversation for himself.

"Darrell, it's Lucas Johnson. Any news on Michiko Tomichi?"

"Nothing good, sir. She wasn't in Chuk Ra Met. My soldier spoke with Spires' wife and with a woman named Sanji; neither of them had seen her. Mrs. Spires really pushed him for information about her husband, but all he told her was that he was safe and that she shouldn't worry. I hope that was OK."

Spires was standing next to Johnson, his head bent forward and his hands knotted into fists.

Greene continued, "I told my guy to come home. I don't think it's a good idea to keep nosing around Chuk Ra Met. It's pretty remote but if we keep sending people there sooner or later someone will want to know why. That could endanger Mrs. Spires and the other woman."

Johnson was watching Spires. He wished he'd not used the speaker. Even though it was too late, he picked up the receiver so Spires could only hear what Johnson was saying. "Don't do anything."

Spires pounded his fist into his other hand.

Lucas glanced at him and then told Greene, "You're right about not drawing attention to that village."

When the phone call was over, Johnson turned to Spires, "Sergeant Major, maybe she decided to try and hide somewhere else." It didn't work.

"She wouldn't do that Colonel. The bastards got her. Michiko's dead."

There was little purpose in trying to put a good face on it, "You may be right, but there's not much we can do about it now, Sergeant Major. I'm sorry, but there's something I have to ask you and I need your best answer?"

He didn't even wait for the question, "She didn't tell them shit, sir. If she had, I'd have been nabbed when I got off the ferry in Okinawa. She didn't talk."

Colonel John Botts, Commander, Criminal Investigation Division, Pacific, put a secure call through to Mike Hurley. "Sir, it's a match. General Stanley wrote that note; no doubt about it."

"OK, thanks Colonel. I know your analyst knows not to talk about this with anyone."

"Roger, sir but I'll have a conversation with her just to make sure."

"Thanks for the quick work, John."

While Hurley was talking with Botts, McKeever got a visit from his J-2. He had clear satellite images of the estate and the four satellite dishes, as well as the antennas poking from the estate's roof. There were also images of a car, a limousine, and someone walking from the limo toward the house.

"What do you make of these, Bill?"

"This is some pretty sophisticated stuff, sir. I haven't a clue what a house in an otherwise residential neighborhood would be doing with communications equipment like this. We can get better imagery, more detailed, but the pentagon is going to have to free up some close-in, look-down satellite time to get the pictures for us."

"What's our priority?"

"Pretty low right now sir. Iraq, Iran, Afghanistan are getting the bulk of the time."

"So I'd need to call the Chairman?"

"Yes, sir."

"What about the guy heading toward the house?"

"Yeah, well other than telling you he arrived sometime between 3:00 PM and 3:15 PM, Japan Standard Time and left sometime between 6:15 and 6:30, I can't give you anything. Some of the more powerful stuff could pick up his face, but it'd be iffy, sir. He'd have to be looking up as the satellite was taking the picture. What are the chances?"

"OK. See if he's a regular visitor. If he is, that will confirm one thing for me. Come on back tomorrow same time and let's revisit the mystery man."

The phone rang on McKeever's desk as the J-2 was on his way out. It was General Kinney. "Admiral, we just got a solid match on the handwriting. Paul Stanley's in on this thing, whatever it is."

"Shit!"

"I know, sir. I didn't want it to be true either."

"OK, Lynn. We can't change what is. Get your three guys together and bring them to my office as soon as you can. We need to talk."

Johnson and Spires were restless hanging around the dormitory, but that boredom was to be short lived. Hurley called and told both of them to get to McKeever's office ASAP. The trip from Hickam to

Camp H.M. Smith was a short one and at 7:30 PM Mike Hurley closed the door to McKeever's office and filled Johnson and Spires in on what CID had found on the handwriting match.

Then McKeever added what he'd learned from his J-2, "The satellites showed the communication dishes where Spires said they'd be. Intel can't confirm what type they are or what the hell this guy might be using them for, but they definitely don't fit in with the rest of that neighborhood. I'm looking for some bright ideas. What's next?"

Spires and Johnson had talked about that very same question earlier. Hurley looked at Johnson with a look that suggested that if he had something, he should offer it up. Lucas said, "Sir, we need to proceed cautiously."

Admiral Chet McKeever was highly intelligent. He held an undergraduate degree from Ohio State University and the Navy had put him through a Masters Program in Nuclear Physics at Massachusetts Institute of Technology. In the thirty-five years he'd spent in the Navy, he'd been one of the few officers to walk down two pathways that the Navy valued perhaps more than any others. He'd been a naval aviator and flew over one hundred missions over North Vietnam, but, after the Masters Degree had been earned, he'd gone into submarines and had commanded one of America's most vaunted strategic weapons, an Ohio-class nuclear submarine. Chet McKeever was cool under pressure, self-confident and had trained his entire life to do what his country demanded of him as the Commander-in-Chief, US Pacific Command. However, at this moment, frustration and disappointment gave way to anger.

"Colonel, I have a two-star general on my staff who may be playing footsie with the *Yakuza.* The handwriting experts confirm that. Why the hell should I be cautious? I'm going to slam dunk the son of a bitch."

Hurley gave Johnson a be-careful-you-don't-go-too-far-out-on-the-limb look.

It was Cleve Spires who stepped in, "Well, Admiral, it's true you have a note and apparently General Stanley wrote it. So what's the charge going to be? He's guilty of writing a letter to some guy in Japan that talks about some shipments that are apparently on time. Seems odd, seems coincidental, but it doesn't really prove anything. Stop and think about this, sir. What are these guys really up to? What's the *Yakuza's* interest in these shipments?"

McKeever, Kinney and Hurley sat there.

Lucas said, "Sir, the Sergeant Major's right. We need more information and that information centers around this estate." He pointed to one of the satellite photos with Fujiwara walking toward the house. “If we can listen in on what’s going on there, we’ll know what they’ve got planned. Maybe we’ll even find out what the hell General Stanley’s involvement is.”

McKeever got up and walked over to a wide window with a breathtaking view of a luscious Hawaiian hillside sloping down toward Pearl Harbor and the ocean beyond. He was quiet for a long time while he struggled with his next decision. He could confront Stanley right now and find out why he was writing notes to this guy in Tokyo. Or he could elevate this thing to Washington, get the Chairman involved, maybe even the Secretary of Defense. No one wanted to break in on his thoughts, but Spires finally had enough of the quiet.

“Sir, I don’t want you to think I’m trying to teach an Admiral the principles of war, but it seems to me that *surprise* is a key here. They had it on their side until we found that note. Now we know they’re up to something and they don’t know we know. We need to give them a dose of their own medicine, if you know what I mean.” McKeever did.

“All right. I’ll make a call. That’s it for tonight.”

The red phone on the desk rang just once before the Army Colonel, the Chairman’s Executive Officer, answered it. Caller ID told him it was Admiral McKeever on the other end of the line. “Good afternoon, sir. It’s Colonel Terry Sweet.”

“Terry, I need to speak to the Chairman. Is he around?”

“He’s on the hill, sir. Should be just finishing up his testimony over there. May I take a message?”

An hour later, Air Force General Jonas Pastor, Chairman of the Joint Chiefs of Staff, placed a call to Admiral Chet McKeever from the welcome solitude of his sedan while traveling back to the Pentagon from Congressional hearings.

"Chet, how's things in Paradise?"

McKeever didn’t waste time; there was little point. "Sir, something’s up with the China-Vietnam arms sale."

McKeever couldn't see it, but Pastor winced. Since McClint’s suicide, the media had played the sale and every detail of it out like a soap opera. Without exaggeration, he’d been asked at least one hundred times if he had known McClint was going to do something like that, would he have still recommended the sale to Congress? It was like being asked if you beat your wife often. There was no way he could answer it without coming off poorly. One editorial cartoon had pictured him as the grim reaper, another as Teddy Roosevelt trying to sell a big stick to a Chinese guy.

"This ammo sale is taking on a life of its own, Chet."

"Yes, sir. I know."

McKeever laid out what he had. When he was finished, Pastor's first question was one McKeever had anticipated, but not expected to be first. It was a matter of priorities and McKeever lived and worked nearly eight thousand miles from Washington D.C. Pastor was inside the beltway.

"Is Spires credible?"

"Sir, I wouldn't have bothered..."

Pastor interrupted, "Chet, if I start repositioning satellites, I've got to go to the National Security Advisor and let him know why. I'm not going to do that unless you can convince me that your guy is credible."

"Sir, Spires is a former Army Command Sergeant Major, convicted and sent to Leavenworth for ten years. He is also a fugitive from a double murder charge in Thailand. What I can't get around is the fact this man brought us a note in my J-4's handwriting and I think the note's about those god damned arms sales. Spires didn't have to do that, sir. That gives him credibility in my book."

"OK, Chet, OK. What do you want?"

"I want some close-in look-down satellite shots of this estate in Japan and I want some eavesdropping."

Silence. McKeever knew the line wasn't dead. He waited.

"First let's take some pictures, then we'll see about the other."

"I'll take it."

"OK." There was a brief pause and then a final question from the Chairman. "Chet, how many people know about this?

It was a good question. McKeever went over it in his head. When he had the number he said, "Six, sir. Six people know about this."

"Are they all reliable?"

Another good question and if he answered it honestly, he could only vouch safely for five of them. "Sir, there's a woman, a Japanese woman, who was helping Spires. She's gone missing. Spires is sure she's been kidnapped and murdered by the *Yakuza,* but he's also sure she wouldn't give anything up.

"Shit. That's a problem Chet."

The obvious got the obvious reply, "Yeah."

The phone rang at about 4:00 A.M. in Admiral Chet McKeever's quarters on Pearl Harbor Naval Base. The call was from the Chairman of the Joint Chiefs of Staff. "Chet. I need you to get here and bring the people who know about this estate in Japan with you. We got some satellite photos in late last night and the analysts are going crazy with them. I haven't let the National Security Advisor (NSA) know about any of this yet. I'm going to do that while you're in the air, but I'm ready to ask him for permission to do some eaves-dropping. I want you here as reinforcements. Andrews Ops (Andrews Air Force Base Flight Operations) will know where you need to go when you get here."

Things were ratcheting up. An hour later the Commander-in-Chief Pacific Command's personal 757 taxied ahead of five commercial flights already lined up for departure from Honolulu International Airport. By the time the pilot had the nose pointed down the runway, he had his clearance to takeoff. He released the brakes, jammed the throttles forward, and the jet sprang off the reef runway using less than half of its ten thousand feet length. McKeever, Hurley, Johnson and Spires settled back in the overstuffed seats. General Kinney had the unenviable task of staying at home to keep an eye on Paul Stanley.

Chapter Twenty-nine

McKeever's party arrived at Andrews Air Force Base in the middle of the night. A Chevy Surburban and driver were waiting planeside. The car had barely started to move when the Admiral asked, "Where are we going?"

"The White House, sir."

Spires heard that, and for the first time felt that his credibility wasn't at stake. The idea that they were on their way to the White House to meet with---Who?---Hell, what did it matter? The meeting was at the White House so it had to be somebody way up there, maybe even the President. McKeever didn't enjoy the same sense of relief. On the long flight from Hawaii he'd speculated who he would eventually wind up talking to. He'd served no fewer than four tours in the Pentagon and his last one had been as the Navy's top Admiral for Legislative Affairs and that assignment wasn't that long ago. One of the first lessons he'd learned during his first tour there; always know who you're meeting with in Washington and anticipate what they want. He didn't have either answer well in hand and this meeting was at the White House for god's sake. He thought about asking their driver, but gave that up. Hell, he was just a driver. He knew to take them to the White House, anything beyond that he wouldn't have a clue.

When the Suburban pulled under the portico at the White House, a Secret Service agent met them. McKeever asked the agent escorting them down the corridor, "Who's here?"

"Sorry, sir. I just came on duty. I know Mr. Munson's in there. Other than him, I don't know."

Now it didn't matter. They were at the entrance to the Situation Room. The agent put his palm on a lighted panel. The unlocking mechanism buzzed as the scanner read his fingerprints and allowed the door to unlock. He pulled the steel door open. Spires was the last one in and the agent closed the door behind Spires, without entering himself.

Admiral McKeever quickly took inventory. There were more than he expected.

General Pastor broke away from the group he was with. "Chet, thanks for getting here so quickly. The satellite photos are still coming in, but what we've got sure has us scratching our heads. The best pictures came in about two hours ago. The analysts are going over them now. We expect a full report within the hour. I briefed the Secretary of Defense this afternoon. Munson brought in the Secretary of State. I didn't know he was going to do that, neither did the SECDEF. Munson tells me the President won't do anything unless SECSTATE is in on the discussion. I had no choice..."

McKeever was getting a Washington apology from his boss, a form of apology that omits the words "I apologize". In the middle of it, Tim Munson, the National Security Advisor, called them to order. He introduced all the Washington-based people; McKeever introduced Hurley, Johnson and Spires.

Roger Levi, the Secretary of State, was a bit of an anomaly. Normally Secretaries of State go into academics after they've left office. Levi broke this tradition. He got the job because he was an academic. As Dean of the Kennedy School of Government at Harvard, he was renowned for his publications on government responsibility in international relations. Roger Levi brought an effete academic snobbery with him to Washington and he was renowned for using it in his role as Secretary of State, a position that allowed him to test the theories he'd written about for so many years. He zeroed in on Spires, someone he took to be an intellectual inferior, someone he thought had no business in the rarified air of the White House.

"Mr. Spires, I'm told we have you to thank for bringing this issue with the arms sale to our attention, but I find your actions to be rather curious. For instance, there is a military installation in Tokyo, Yakota Air Force Base. Why not turn yourself in there? Why go to Okinawa? Why Colonel Johnson? What's your connection to him?"

McKeever bristled, but before he could open his mouth Spires answered the question.

"I trusted Colonel Johnson to do something with the information I'd stumbled onto. I didn't know anyone at Yakota. If I had gone there, they would have arrested me for the bogus charges in Thailand and none of this would have surfaced. I think I made the right decision. After all you are here at midnight aren't you, sir?"

A chuckle spread around the room, everyone laughing except Levi.

"I'm here because, quite frankly I question your credibility. I find it difficult to believe that any man is as magnanimous as you appear to be..."

That was it. McKeever had heard the rumors about this asshole.

"Mr. Secretary, with all due respect," there was little respect in his tone, "this is pointless. Sergeant Major Spires' credibility is not the issue here. Stick to the facts. I've got a note that my J-4, a highly respected Army Major General, sent to some guy in Tokyo who is visited regularly by the man we think heads Japan's organized crime syndicate. We think they are meeting about the stuff we sold to China and Vietnam. I'm sorry it wasn't Mother Theresa who delivered the note to my Headquarters, but she's not in this business. The fact is, we know something is up. What the hell are we going to do about it?"

Pastor smiled and looked at Munson, "I agree with the Admiral. It isn't important how we found out or who told us. The fact is we know and we..."

Levi roared, "What do we know General? Both of you keep saying that. Well, what exactly is it that we know?"

The door opened and a man with a briefcase stepped in. Munson resumed control of the meeting. "Gentlemen, perhaps the answer to the Secretary's question just walked in. This is Jim Crane from the National Security Agency. He's been analyzing the latest satellite pictures from Japan. Let's see what he's got."

When it came to interpretation of satellite imagery, there was no one better than Jim Crane. He'd been doing it since U-2 and SR-71 spy planes and satellites were first used to take high-altitude pictures. Jim Crane had sat in the Oval Office with President Kennedy. Together they'd gone over the U-2 pictures of Russian missiles in Cuba. Since that time he'd been there with every President when they needed an expert to tell them what was in a high-altitude, grainy and blurry photo of some obscure point on the ground. While he unlocked the manacle that shackled the briefcase to his left hand and worked the combination on the briefcase he talked. "This is the damndest thing I've seen in forty years in this business. I'm still not sure what I'm looking at.

He threw a slide on an overhead projector. "We've come at this place from all angles. First, this is a completely residential neighborhood. It's a ritzy neighborhood, especially for Japan, but the bottom line is it's just a residential neighborhood. But this guy has got some industrial-strength communications gear, pretty sophisticated equipment. I know a lot of people who work out of their house and do some pretty important stuff, but none of them have anything like this." Crane knew Admiral McKeever from some work he done in PACOM. He looked at him and said, "Hell, Admiral, this stuff is as good as anything you've got at Camp Smith. I don't know what the hell he could be using it for."

The next slide zeroed in on the four dishes that Cleve had sketched when he'd ventured onto the estate. "He's got communications capability with nearly all of the Pacific Rim with these babies."

One-by-one Crane pointed to the dishes. "This one, oriented in a northwesterly direction, is likely communicating with the Korean Peninsula. This one, aimed almost due west---well, that's covering China, probably most of the country, and that's a huge area. This one is pointing southwest and could cover Vietnam, Laos, Cambodia, Thailand, Myanmar---any of those countries in Southeast and Southwest Asia. This last one is aimed due south and could cover Okinawa, the Philippines, and probably most of Malaysia and Indonesia. He might not be able to reach Australia or New Zealand, but, hell, if atmospheric conditions were just right, who knows."

He changed slides, and a close up of one of the dishes appeared on the screen. "But you know what I find really interesting about all of this is this little gizmo here." He took a laser pointer from the briefcase and traced a red circle around the antenna extending from the dishes' center.

Munson said, "An antenna, what's so unusual about an antenna?"

"More than an antenna, sir." Crane took aim and laid the red laser on the very end of the antenna shown on the screen. "That thing right there. Each dish has one of these. It's a scrambler---kind of like the ones the cable companies use to prevent piracy---but this one is much more sophisticated. I've not seen one like this, but I know what it does. It's got a wide bandwidth and it switches frequencies automatically at a tremendous rate of speed. It has to match with a scrambler on the other end of equal sophistication. This is real secure communication and it doesn't fit the environment where you'd normally find stuff like this. I mean I know why Admiral McKeever or General Pastor might want secure commo like this, but this guy---I'll say it again, I have no idea why this guy would want or need stuff like this."

Hurley asked, "How much money are we talking about here?"

"Best I can do without a full-blown work up, and making some assumptions about the computers this guy might have coupled up with these dishes---I'd guess three to five million dollars," he paused and then added, "per dish. And remember this stuff isn't any good unless it's got equipment just like it somewhere out there to talk to."

Tim Munson asked, "Any more questions?"

There weren't. Jim Crane had done his job. He left the slides he'd used with Munson, gathered his stuff and left.

"OK, Gentlemen, where were we?" He looked at Levi, who shook his head. Pastor answered the question, "We need to eavesdrop on that estate."

"It's in Japan," came the response from Levi.

"It's our guns and ammo," responded Pastor.

"No, it's not. We sold it to the Chinese and Viets, remember?" Levi thought he'd won one.

Munson didn't think so. "Yeah, and now the *Yakuza* has an interest. Roger, do you think for one minute that if something happens to that stuff and it gets into the wrong hands the press is going to blame the Chinese and the Vietnamese? Hell, no. It's my neck, your neck and the President's neck that they'll be coming after. We can't treat this like it's a fucking garage sale. If we do we'll wind up getting this stuff rammed up our asses."

"*We* didn't approve these sales, Congress did."

"I know that, you know that and the President knows that. No one else will see it that way. I'm going to call CIA and have them get some surveillance on that estate."

"I'm going to tell the President?" Roger Levi had no idea how much he sounded like a second-grader threatening to tell the teacher that little Timmy Munson had just taken a piss on the playground in public.

"No you're not, Roger." They glared at one another. "That's my fucking job."

Chapter Thirty

Three hours after they'd arrived in Washington D.C. they all found themselves back aboard McKeever's jet and headed to Hawaii. The flight was going to take about ten hours. McKeever and Hurley turned in. They would need to sleep because each had duties to tend to when they got back to Honolulu. Spires was too pumped to sleep and Johnson, who was still Spires' designated watch-dog, didn't have anything to do when they got back, except keep an eye on Spires. While the two flag officers slept, they speculated on what was going on in Japan. The more they speculated the wilder the scenarios got. Finally Johnson said, "This is nuts. We've got World War III starting and all we know for sure is that two guys in Japan are interested in some old weapons and ammo we sold."

The President's National Security Update was over. Munson waited for the last participant in this three-times-a-week ritual to depart the Oval Office and then captured a few moments of the President's time in between appointments. It was time alone with the President that he didn't get very often these days. President Wilson Glover won on a domestic agenda that included jobs, education, taxes and crime. National security came in fifth after these things unless, of course, there was some urgent reason to bump it up, and that hadn't been the case for quite some time now. That made Tim Munson's job one of the toughest in Glover's administration.

"Mr. President I have asked the CIA to do some work in Japan."

"And what kind of work might that be, Tim?" Glover's head never looked up from the stack of papers he was shuffling thorough on the desk in front of him.

The President's apparent preoccupation with other matters didn't bother Munson. He knew he'd get his boss's complete attention as he went on. "We're going to listen in on some very sophisticated communications equipment that apparently belongs to a private citizen in Tokyo."

The President stopped shuffling long enough to ask. "And the reason you are doing this?"

"The arms sales to China and Vietnam."

"Oh, Christ!" Now he had him. Glover detested international politics and policy. There were just too many aspects of it that were completely out of his control. The arms sales, not just this one, but the first one as well, were a perfect example. The first one had gone virtually unnoticed except for some editorials in the papers. Glover hadn't really worried about them because so few Americans read the papers these days. As long as "60 Minutes", "Date Line", or Brokaw, Jennings or Rather hadn't come at them, Glover hadn't worried about it. But this second sale and McClint's suicide, well, his administration had begun to look like the world's supplier of cheap guns and bullets. With this second sale politics had suddenly become policy. The Glover Administration is open for business to sell guns and bullets, come and get yours while the supply is still good and the price is right.

Munson tried to put what they were doing in Tokyo in some sort of perspective. "Mr. President, we're just on a fishing trip right now. We're not sure what this guy is up to, but we've got some credible information that he has some interest in these shipments. We're trying to find out exactly what that interest is."

"Who's *we?*"

"McKeever in the Pacific, Pastor, Secretary DuPray at Defense and Secretary Levi at State. We all agree this surveillance is the right thing to do. Levi's a little squeamish, but if you were to press him he'd tell you it's the next step."

"How did we get ourselves into this?"

Munson wasn't sure if the President was asking how they'd gotten into the business of selling to the Chinese and Vietnamese or how they got into pursuing surveillance of Seito Yamamoto. Answering the first question was much more complicated than answering the other one. Munson took the easier one. "A source intercepted a note..."

The answer started out sounding like one Glover's Press Secretary had crafted for the boys in the press room. "Tim, don't play around with me. Who's the source?"

"Mr. President, do you really want to know..."

"Yes, I do."

"The source, Mr. President, is an American the Thais want to charge with murder, but he..."

"What?" This was getting worse by the minute for the President.

"But he claims he didn't..."

"He claims he didn't do it. Right? What would you expect? Christ All Mighty..."

This time Munson interrupted the President. "Mr. President, give me some credit. Give your senior advisors some credit. I've met this guy, talked with him. So have McKeever, Pastor, DuPray and Levi. He's credible and he's brought us some information we can't disregard. Surveillance is the next logical step.

Munson let this sink in and then added, "Mr. President, we can't turn our backs on this. Remember how everyone dissected the Bush administration after 9/11? They knew this in advance or they knew that. This is like that Mr. President. We know something but we're not sure what we know. We need to find out more. If the pieces fit together, then we'll come to you. If they don't, then I won't bother you again about this."

Glover got up from behind the huge desk that dominates the Oval Office and walked over to the glass doors that lead into the Rose Garden. He stood there for a moment staring into the distance. Wilson Glover and Tim Munson had been in politics together for a long time, since Glover had been a state representative in the Michigan Legislature, but none of that mattered now. When Glover turned, he pointed his finger at Munson and very calmly, very dispassionately told his old friend, "OK, Tim but if this thing blows up, you'll be the one who takes the heat."

"I would expect it to be no other way, Mr. President."

The C-141 was low on its final approach to Yakota Air Force Base on the outskirts of Tokyo. It was 6:00 AM Japan Standard Time on 13 June. At 6:05AM the first of a dozen complaints was received at the base's Public Affairs Office. Quiet hours were from 9:00 PM to 9:00 AM. No flights were supposed to land during these hours, part of a ridiculous agreement that the Air Force had worked out with the surrounding communities to placate them. Later there would be follow up phone calls to each of the complainers apologizing, but telling them the landing was necessary at that time due to an on-board emergency.

The truth of the matter, however, was that there was no emergency. This flight carried a priority designator that required Yakota to expedite the flight's arrival. In fact, a declared emergency by another aircraft wanting to land at Yakota would have been the only thing that could have delayed this particular flight.

By 6:30 AM Pete Charles had deplaned and gotten his equipment moved to an empty hangar on the sprawling base. He was anxious to get started. It was a chicken-and-egg-thing. Either this job had been perfectly created for Pete Charles or Pete Charles had been perfectly trained to do this job. Third generation Japanese-American, he was as fluent at speaking, reading and writing Japanese as any native and he was one of the CIA's best surveillance experts.

The hangar the Air Force had given him to work out of was isolated on the west side of the base, so he had to walk a few blocks before he was able to hail a base cab to take him to the main gate. From there he took a civilian cab to one of a half dozen truck rental agencies he'd found on the Internet before leaving the US. There he presented a Japanese driver's license listing a fictitious Tokyo address as his residence. He rented a panel truck for two days.

By 2:00PM he was parked on a side street bordering Yamamoto's estate and was ready to begin listening to the traffic coming into and out of the satellite dishes. He wanted to tap into the signal at the receiver/transmitter inside the house rather than at the satellite dish. If he tapped the signal at the satellite dish, he would weaken slightly the signal received at the receiver/transmitter. A drop in signal strength to a skilled operator inside the house might betray his presence. He had a satellite image of the grounds that he used as a map of sorts. So he knew approximately where on the estate the dishes were located, and from that he knew the general location of the residence. He had a handheld scanner that worked like a homing instrument and it fixed on the dishes easily, but as he moved the scanner toward the house where the receiver would be located he lost the signal. That shouldn't have been. He adjusted his equipment and tried again with the same result.

After half an hour of adjustments, he was satisfied that his equipment was working as it should. The problem must be at the house. He took his earphones off, stepped out of the truck, locked it and set off to find some vantage point where he could get a look. Two blocks away he found an apartment building, took the elevator to the top floor, picked the lock on the door to the roof and looked down at the house through binoculars. The place appeared to be made of wood, so his equipment should have easily penetrated, unless---he thought for a moment---unless the walls were lined with something that he couldn't see. He concluded that was it; the walls were lined, probably with lead. If he was going to listen in on the communications going and coming over these four dishes he was going to have to do it at the dishes' antenna, and that was risky if someone was watching signal strength inside the house.

Risk of detection is a field agent's call. Charles knew this mission was high profile, not so much by what he'd been told, which was damn little, but more by the fact that he and his small pile of equipment were the only payload on the Air Force cargo jet that had flown him here. He looked at his watch. His first report was due back to Langley in less than two hours, but his problems weren't over.

The first signal his equipment detected came at 4:30PM. The interceptor fed the signal to a recorder and the recorder fed into a decipherer. This device that looked like a regular desktop computer was the product of billions of CIA dollars and it contained every code known to the US intelligence community. Charles himself had pulled scrambled stuff out of foreign embassies around the world and this little genius had decoded it flawlessly. That was what was now puzzling Pete Charles. Here's some Japanese Joe Six-Pack with this kind of equipment in his fucking backyard and Charles' equally sophisticated equipment that should have easily unscrambled the code wasn't working at all.

He looked at his watch. "Shit!" His first deadline to report back to Langley was one hour away. He tried everything he could think of for the next half hour and failed miserably to get anything useful. Frustrated with his first day's failure, he closed up shop and headed back to Yakota. From a secure phone inside US Forces Japan's Operations Center, he called his boss, Doctor Cecil Parker, at CIA Headquarters.

"Cec, it's Pete. Got a problem here. Well, two actually. One's mine and the other's going to be yours. First, I've got to take the signal at the antenna, but, bigger than that, these guys are using an unknown cipher."

"Unknown?" How's that possible?"

"Well, that's a good goddamn question. I've checked my equipment up one side and down the other. It's all working just the way it should. The code these guys are using isn't programmed in so I'm just getting junk. I'm going to stream you the recording I've taken. Can you put the cipher team on this and see if they can crack it?"

"Done."

"How long, Cec? I'm parked right next to the place. The intel report I read says 'no security'. I didn't see any, but I find it hard to believe. I'm going to lay off the dishes until I hear from you. In the meantime I'll use the 'phones'. That means I got to stay close to the place and, to make matters worse, the back of the place, where the communications equipment is, has some kind of lining, probably lead, that keeps me out in the cold. The only thing that's got a chance of working right now are the 'phones' and then only when there's conversation in the front of the house. It's not the best situation I've ever been in, Cec. The quicker I get that code deciphered, the quicker I can get on with what I need to do here."

"I'll get the crypto guys on it soonest. I'll call you when we've got something."

Cato Fujiwara's limo swung onto the estate and pulled to a stop in its usual place. The routine was established. One bodyguard went ahead. After a brief delay, Fujiwara and the second bodyguard followed. By the time Fujiwara got to the front door, the first bodyguard would have it open and Fujiwara would proceed to Yamamoto's office at the rear of the house, but Cato Fujiwara was getting tired of this routine. He was ready to proceed with the takeover of Japan. They'd been at this planning crap for the last five years. For the last year, Yamamoto had insisted on these frequent, face-to-face meetings and, as if the long trip from downtown Tokyo wasn't enough, when he got there, Yamamoto would drag him through a detailed litany of questions that long ago had become quite immaterial to Cato Fujiwara. They would not only discuss which industries they'd take over, Yamamoto would push him on details like how many men would be used, what weapons they'd have and even which entrances they'd enter through. Timetables had been worked out for each location, nearly a thousand of them. This wasn't the way Cato Fujiwara was used to operating. Normally he would just tell someone to take over Mitsumo Industries and they would see to it, or else.

Yamamoto had noticed Fujiwara's growing impatience. He feared he would lose him before everyone else was ready. Now he didn't have to worry about that anymore. Last night he'd gotten confirmation from the Philippines that they were ready to go. The last country had finally fallen into place when the associate there reported that the National Police of the Philippines had finally been confirmed as an ally. This had taken the last three years to accomplish, millions of dollars in bribes and nearly a dozen assassinations, but the Chief of the National Police had finally delivered his organization to the *association.*

Today, Seito Yamamoto greeted his visitor on the walkway in front of the door. This departure from the routine didn't go unnoticed by Fujiwara. Neither did it go unnoticed by the boys and girls who analyze satellite images. Fujiwara's daily arrivals and departures had been well documented. Today, however, was the first day they'd gotten pictures of anyone from the house. Even more importantly, on the other side of the estate, parked in a different location and in a different rental van, Pete Charles's ultra-sensitive microphones began listening in.

The two men bowed. "Well Seito, this is unusual. To what do I owe the honor of an early reception?" Yamamoto was smiling broadly. "I'm going to guess that you have good news."

"I do, Cato. Our years of hard work are about to pay off. We are close--- very close to our jumping off point."

They began to move toward the house.

"I don't suppose you've located Spires." It was a loose thread and Yamamoto didn't like loose anything.

"No. He's managed to escape from Japan, I'm certain. I've tripled the reward for his death, but still nothing. Our contacts in South Korea are on the look out."

They stepped into the house.

Charles heard the other voice reply, "Well, it doesn't matter."

They headed down a hallway toward Yamamoto's office in the rear of the house.

Charles heard the first voice, the one that had inquired about Spires, say, "We will begin Operation Light Switch on the fourth…"

"Shit! What the hell happened?" Pete Charles twisted the sensitivity knob on his "phones" to their maximum sensitivity. The static in his ear increased to almost an unbearable volume, but that was all his adjustment got him, loud static.

"The fourth of what? God dammit!" He'd lost them into that part of the house where the lead lining protected them from intrusion. They'd withdrawn to their cocoon and were invasion proof by anything Pete Charles had at his immediate disposal. Disgusted, he threw his headphones onto the makeshift desk he'd set up in front of him, using his computers' travel cases. He closed up shop and headed back to Yakota. He had something for them but it had just missed being the whole enchilada.

"Cec, it's Pete."

Dr. Cecil Parker was waiting for his call. "Any luck today?"

"Got some stuff with the phones, but these guys are lucky. You'll know what I mean when you hear the stream I'm sending to you. Any luck on your end with the cipher these guys are using."

Parker replied sheepishly, "No."

"You're shittin' me. What the hell's the matter with those geniuses. They broke China's national code but they can't break this mickey-mouse operation..."

Now a little miffed, Parker replied, "Come on, Pete. You know better than that. We're busting our asses here, but this isn't like anything we've ever seen before. I don't know who wrote this code for them but it's got our computers spinning their wheels."

"So what do I do?"

"Low profile. Stay off the dishes until we get their cipher unlocked. Use the 'phones' as you are able, but word from the National Security Advisor is that if you get caught listening in on this guy, you should swallow the cyanide pill. Understand?"

There was no cyanide pill, but Charles almost wished there was. What Parker was telling him was that if he was caught, the US government wouldn't own up to any involvement in Charles' being there. He'd be treated as a private citizen breaking the law and the Japanese could do with him as they may. Charles simply replied, "Yeah, OK."

Chapter Thirty-one

Admiral Chet McKeever, Lieutenant General Lynn Kinney, Brigadier General Mike Hurley, Colonel Lucas Johnson and Private (Retired) Cleve Spires sat in a semi-circle at PACOM's video-teleconference center. In front of them was a large screen TV, and on it they could see, at the Pentagon, the Secretary of Defense, John DuPray and the Chairman of the Joint Chiefs of Staff, General Jonas Pastor and, at the White House, National Security Advisor Tim Munson who was joined by Secretary of State Roger Levi. The video-teleconference system in use was secure and Top Secret information could be discussed without fear of compromise. VTC's were huge time-savers. In fact McKeever had wondered why they hadn't used it earlier, when Spires first stepped forward with his information. He'd finally figured it was because no one in Washington wanted to trust Spires' credibility without looking him in the eye and deciding for themselves. Apparently everyone was satisfied. Now video-teleconferences could be used.

Munson began, "OK. There's something called Operation Light Switch set for the fourth of something and they're interested in Sergeant Major Spires." He could see Spires on the screen in front of him. "Sergeant Major, any idea why the interest in you?"

Everyone was calling him that now, *Sergeant Major.* It bothered him a little, but he wasn't sure why. He'd have to think that through later when there was time. For now, he answered Munson's question honestly, "No, sir, unless they think Driscoll told me something before he died."

"Did he?"

The question rankled Spires a little. He'd been through the Driscoll death scene time and time again. Munson had heard the story at least twice. He gave it to them again.

General Kinney, impatience marking his voice, offered, "May I suggest that Sergeant Major Spires isn't the issue, he's given us what he knows. What we don't know is anything about this Operation Light Switch. It's time we turned Stanley to see what he knows.

Maybe he can put two and two together for us." Admiral McKeever and General Pastor nodded in agreement.

Roger Levi asked, "What if Stanley doesn't know anything?"

John DuPray added, "Worse yet, what if knows something, but doesn't cooperate?"

Munson answered their questions. "Then the pressure will be on over at CIA to get the cipher code these guys are using on those satellite dishes cracked. We still have a guy standing by in Japan." Munson saw McKeever nod in agreement. "Admiral, you have a plan on how to spring this on your boy?"

"I do."

"OK then, enough said." Munson and McKeever both caught glimpses of Levi and DuPray shaking their heads, but McKeever appreciated Munson's hands-off approach. Plenty of times before he'd seen some Washington insider use a situation like this as their chance to grab a headline. He'd seen them interfere and, on occasion just plain take over, only to screw something up that could have been more efficiently handled by someone who really knew what was going on. McKeever knew Paul Stanley and he thought he knew of a way he could get to him. Munson trusted him and McKeever liked that.

Munson closed by asking, "When do we reconvene, Admiral?"

"Tomorrow, same time, same channel?"

Munson said, "See all of you then."

Admiral McKeever placed a call to General Peter Rentz, Commander-in-Chief, Special Operations Command.

"Pete, got a problem here and I need your help."

"Chet, if I can..."

"Paul Stanley's a friend of yours, right?

"He is."

"Well, he's in a heap of trouble..." McKeever laid it out for him.

Rentz listened to the incredible story spun by the CINCPAC. When McKeever was through, Rentz was too stunned to ask any questions except, "What can I do to help?"

"How quick can you get here? I'm going to hit him cold, right between the eyes with this thing. I'd like you here when I do that. If he clams up, I want you to help me break him down. I've got to know what the hell he's up to. I suppose I need to stay within the Uniform Code of Military Justice as much as possible, but if I need to trample on his rights a little to get at the truth, I'm not afraid to do that, Pete. I want him to talk to us about this. You're his friend. If he makes the bad choice to dummy up, I'll need you to help me make him see the light."

"It's nine, maybe ten hours flying time from McDill to Hawaii. Give me twelve hours. I'll come straight to your office when I get there."

"There'll be a sedan and driver waiting for you at Hickam---and thanks Pete."

"How close are you to cracking it?"

Dr. Cecil Parker had headed up the CIA's cryptology department for twenty years and he hated it when people asked him a question like that. It showed a complete lack of understanding of what he and his team of experts do. It made it sound like cracking an encrypted message was as easy as cooking from a recipe; add the ingredients, stir and place in the oven. One-hour later it's done.

"It's not easy to say."

"Dr. Parker, this is very important..."

"Mr. Munson, I know how important it is. If it weren't, you wouldn't be calling me right now. I've got my entire team dedicated to this. The computers are running twenty-four hours a day but we still don't have it."

"But you cracked the Chinese code..."

"We got lucky."

"What do you mean you got lucky?"

"Look, this business is about sixty percent science, thirty-nine percent analyst's experience and one percent luck. The computers do the work; they run iterations of the code trying to detect patterns that can then become language. Analysts check each of these iterations just to give a level of human experience to the science. We got lucky on the Chinese code because one analyst saw a pattern before the computers did and he ran a special program to test his theory. I've seen guys try to beat the computer before, but I've never seen one actually do it until then. He saved us a week, maybe two, in figuring out their encryption. You all thought we were heroes. Well the analyst certainly was, but he was also very lucky."

"Is this guy working on this code?"

Parker rolled his eyes. "Yes, sir, he is."

Munson had made his point; he needed this code cracked. "OK Dr. Parker. Keep at it. We are going to need this as soon as you can get it."

"I understand sir. I'll stay in touch."

It was 7:00PM. Paul Stanley was just putting things into his briefcase and preparing to leave the office when the phone rang on his desk. The line that was blinking was the extension reserved for the CINC or the DCINC. He had no way of knowing which one it was. He answered, "Stanley, sir."

It was the CINC. McKeever said, "Please come to my office immediately."

He recognized McKeever's voice. "Yes, sir." The line went dead. McKeever, he thought, sounded pissed about something. Stanley took a moment to figure out what was going on. Rarely did this sort of thing happen with McKeever. He'd gotten calls like this one, but always before it was the DCINC that was on the line, upset about some bullshit thing or another. McKeever delegated management of the staff to Lieutenant General Kinney.

Stanley didn't like getting on either McKeever's or Kinney's dark side. However, he could handle both of them, and had done so, quite nicely, on many previous occasions. What was bothering him now, as much as whatever McKeever's problem might be, was that this summons to the front office was getting squarely in the way of his social life. He was to meet Tricia Smyth in a couple of hours. These meetings, which occurred once or sometimes twice a week for the past year, were something that he'd found himself looking forward to. Theirs was purely a sexual relationship. He'd been in two failed marriages and wasn't looking to test those waters again. She'd been married and divorced four times and amassed quite a tidy little income by way of alimony. Her last divorce had reaped a house on the slope of Diamond Head with an absolutely magnificent view of the ocean from the bedroom. Stanley liked it because he could look out to sea while he banged her. Frequently he'd see a ship on the horizon and he'd fantasize that someone on the ship had a telescope trained on them as they made love. He'd told her about this once and she'd said, "Well, let's give them a real show," and gone down hard on him. She required nothing of him except his complete participation in their act of lovemaking. He wanted nothing more from her than the same, as well as her discretion, of course.

He didn't want to cancel their date. He rolled the dice and didn't call her, thinking he'd be in and out. He reasoned, after all, that it was 7:00PM and the CINC had a life outside of the office, too. Whatever it was that he was pissed about, it wouldn't take long to tell Stanley, who could go have his daliance this evening, and then, take care of whatever the hell it was that was bothering McKeever in the morning.

When Stanley got to the front office, the CINC's Exec was waiting for him. He ushered Stanley into the CINC's office and closed the door behind him. Stanley scanned the room. McKeever was at his desk. Along one side of the office was Kinney, Hurley, a Colonel he didn't know and an African-American civilian he didn't know. Then he saw Pete Rentz sitting in an easy chair in front of McKeever's desk. When he saw Rentz a wave of relief washed over him and he knew he'd made a mistake by not calling Ms. Smyth. Rentz was in town and Stanley thought he and McKeever were playing a little trick on him. *Very funny. They made me run down here like a school boy, thinking I was in trouble.* Stanely assumed now that they would be spending the evening together probably over dinner, wine and a cigar. Perhaps this entire group would go.

He needed to get hold of Tricia and beg her forgiveness because he wanted to dip his pen in her inkwell again; it just couldn't be tonight. He'd call her, but before he could get to that he'd need to say hello. "Well, I'll be damned. General Pete Rentz. It's great to see you, sir."

McKeever commanded, "Sit down General. There are some things we have to discuss."

Stanley knew a command when he heard one, but the joke should be over. He responded to McKeever, "Sir?"

"You heard me, sit down."

Stanley sat. McKeever wasted no more time.

"General Stanley, you are in some very serious trouble..."

Stanley went deaf, his hearing paralyzed, and he had a sinking sensation in the pit of his stomach. Oddly, he thought of Tricia again. He thought how much he was going to miss seeing her tonight. McKeever was rattling on but whatever he was saying, Stanley wasn't getting it.

"What is Operation Light Switch?"

The question jolted him back to reality. Tricia Smyth flew out of his mind. The question stunned him. He blurted out the first thing that came to his mind, "How do you know about..." He caught himself, a little too late.

McKeever snapped, "Meet Command Sergeant Major Cleveland Spires."

"But INTERPOL..."

Kinney fired on him next, "Cut the crap General. I called INTERPOL, the office in Tokyo, the one you said your friend worked for; no one there has ever heard of you."

McKeever continued, "We know about Seito Yamamoto and Cato Fujiwara too." He produced satellite photos of the estate.

Desperation swept over Stanley. He tried to figure out how they knew.

"And we know you know them." He produced Stanley's note to Yamamoto.

The note, the damned note Yamamoto had asked him to send. But how had they come by it? He quickly ran McKeever's last statement through his brain, *"and we know you know them."*

There was a slip up there, a small one, but nonetheless a mistake. It told Paul Stanley that they might be pretending to know more than they, in fact, knew. *"Them", I don't know "them". I don't know Fujiwara.* These bastards were trying to nail his hide to the barn door. He could keep handing them nails or he could shut up and not give them shit.

"I'd like an attorney present before we continue this."

McKeever lost it. "An attorney! You fucking bastard! You can talk to your attorney from your cell at Fort Leavenworth."

Rentz was on. It had suddenly become his turn. This was exactly why McKeever had asked him to be here. McKeever wasn't going to break through. None of them could. Paul Stanley was a tough old soldier and he wasn't going to be pushed around. It would take a friend, someone he trusted to break through the wall that Stanley was building right now and Rentz knew if he didn't get on with his part of this interrogation right now, even he wouldn't be able to break through.

"Admiral, would you give General Stanley and me some time alone?"

McKeever was fuming mad at the man in front of him, but he was in control sufficiently to remember that he'd had the foresight to bring Rentz here for exactly this type of situation. Still anger gripped him strongly enough that he sneered at Stanley, "I trusted you, you bastard."

Stanley stared straight ahead, looking through McKeever at some point on the wall behind his boss. McKeever got up and left; the others filed out behind him. Rentz closed the door.

"Paul, what have you gotten yourself into?"

"Don't worry General, I won't tell them about the whore." His tone was caustic. The wall Stanley was building around himself was nearly complete.

Rentz stared at him for a moment and then went to the office door and opened it, "Would you all come back in here for a moment please?" After they'd all filed back in, he closed the door, walked to the front of McKeever's desk and leaned back on its front edge. "There's something I need to tell all of you, and you may do with it as you please. Thirty-five years ago, I was the Cadet Captain of the Brigade at West Point. General Stanley was a yearling. One evening I broke the Code of Honor that we lived and died by at the Academy. I brought a woman into my room, a woman I was going to pay for sex. To add to my disgrace I was too drunk to care. Paul---General Stanley--- saw the TAC Officer coming across the parade grounds, warned me and then diverted the TAC so I could get the woman the hell out of there. He's kept the truth of that night a secret between him and me all of these years. He's a true friend, but if the truth were to be known, I should have been busted out of the Academy. I never should have been commissioned. I don't deserve to wear this uniform, much less wear these stars on my shoulder."

He paused. The room was soundless until he spoke again. "Now could I ask you to leave us again for a few minutes while Paul and I talk."

When they were gone again and the door was closed, Rentz walked over and put his hand on Stanley's shoulder, "You know they say confession is good for the soul. Paul, what I did was wrong . I've had to live for thirty-five years with the guilt of knowing I should have been busted out of there. Every time I got a promotion, every time I was selected for school or command, it was a bittersweet thing, because I knew the truth of that night all those years ago. Well, I guess I don't feel quite so guilty now."

Rentz was through. He shut up. The silence closed in on Paul Stanley like a shroud. Fully five minutes passed without either speaking.

"You think I should tell them what I know?"

"I do."

Tricia Smyth called Paul Stanley's office, looking for him. She was going to give him a piece of her mind. No one had stood her up since high school and she wasn't going to let Paul Stanley get away with it now.

"When will he be back?"

"Just a minute ma'am. The Navy Yeoman put her on hold and called the Deputy J-4, Colonel Paul Sloane. Sloane had him forward the call to his extension.

"Tricia, Paul Sloane."

"Don't try and cover up for him Paul. Where is he? I'm going to give him a piece of my mind…"

"Tricia, he's been medevaced to Walter Reed. He had a heart attack last night. It's pretty serious, I'm told. He may not even return to duty."

"Oh---well---I see." There was an awkward pause. "Well, if you talk to him ask him to call me."

Sloane thought he was telling her the truth. It was the story he'd been given last night sometime around midnight when the DCINC woke him. The truth was, however, that Paul Stanley was on his way to Fort Leavenworth and the US Military Disciplinary Barracks. The charge was treason, but the court martial would have to wait. More important matters were at stake. Paul Stanley had just revealed to them plans for revolts across the Pacific Rim, revolts that would change the way the world would do business, if it could do business at all, in that part of the world. No, dragging Paul Stanley through the humiliation of a court martial wasn't the priority. What had to be the priority was getting this information in front of the National Command Authority and figuring out how in the hell the US was going to deal with what it now knew.

Chapter Thirty-two

Stanley wasn't handcuffed as he was led from McKeever's office, but a goliath of a man, Marine Corps Gunnery Sergeant Bart Atherton, escorted him to a waiting sedan. Atherton's orders were to stay with Stanley until he'd turned him over to two Air Force Security Policemen on board a waiting airplane at Hickam Air Force Base. The Security Police would take over from there. Atherton understood his mission and how unusual it was. Beyond that he had no idea what was going on and no one was going to clarify it for him. He was told he could not discuss this with anyone.

McKeever stood at the window in his office and watched the sedan pull from underneath the portico in front of his headquarters. Then he went back to his desk and put a call through to General Jonas Pastor, Chairman of the Joint Chiefs of Staff. McKeever suggested Pastor gather up Levi, DuPray and Munson and in an hour they could convene a secure teleconference and decide what they should do with the information Paul Stanley had given them. Pastor insisted that McKeever get on his airplane and return to Washington as soon as possible. They would reconvene in the White House Situation Room as soon as McKeever and his contingent got there.

McKeever didn't like wasting the ten hours it would take to fly to D.C. They had hatched a plan, he and Rentz, but they needed to get cracking on it, if the President approved. "Why waste time, Jonas? We can lay this out for you and you guys can brief the President. We'll be available on VTC as you need us."

"No way is the President going to want to talk about this over a VTC. No way is he going to believe what you've just told me or entertain any course of action without standing face-to-face with you and your guys, Chet. I'll gather everyone up here. A sedan will be waiting on you at Andrews. Come straight to the White House. It'll be the same group as last time, but you can bet it will be a tougher discussion, my friend. See you in ten hours."

Johnson and Spires were together in Johnson's room when the call came in from Hurley, telling Lucas to grab his gear. He would be going to Washington, along with McKeever, Rentz and himself to brief the President on what Stanley had given them.

"What about Sergeant Major Spires," Johnson asked.

CINC wants him back at the Disciplinary Barracks to keep him out of sight.

Johnson looked at Spires, who was able only to hear one side of the conversation, and then told Hurley, "Sir, that stinks."

"Colonel, I don't have time..."

Johnson swallowed hard and interrupted his superior, "Sir, I have a suggestion. If all you want to do is keep him out of sight, my father-in-law has a cabin in the middle of nowhere. That would be a better place than Leavenworth."

Spires had heard enough now to put it all together. He slumped in a chair and shook his head at the thought of going back to that place.

Johnson continued, "Send that Marine Gunnery Sergeant with him to keep an eye on things, if you're worried he'll try something. Just don't send him back to prison; he doesn't deserve that, sir. You and I both know that and I think the CINC does too, if you can offer him a reasonable alternative."

Time was wasting. Hurley told him, "OK, I'll see what I can do. You're sure this place is secure?"

"Yes, sir. I've spent a lot of time up there and I've never seen anyone stumble on to the place."

"All right. Bring Spires with you. One way or the other, he's leaving Hawaii and getting out of sight. You'll know the answer when we get to the flight line. Thirty minutes. Don't be late."

"Where are we?"

"Forty-eight, maybe seventy-two hours, we should have it.

"No longer." Munson hung up and turned to John DuPray, Roger Levi, Jonas Pastor, Chet McKeever, Mike Hurley, Lucas Johnson and Pete Rentz who were with him in the White House Situation Room, "Nothing yet. Dr. Parker says two, maybe three days."

"Shit!" DuPray's comment pretty much summed up what everyone else was thinking.

Pastor said, "We have to assume that the *fourth* refers to the fourth of July."

Sides in the debate were shaping up. Those in uniform nodded; DuPray and Levi were shaking their heads.

Levi contended, "What difference does it make whether it's the fourth of July or the twelfth of never. We can't put a military solution out there. It's too many countries, too far away, and, if you're right, General, too little time. We have one option and that is to let the leaders of these eight countries know what we've found out. These are civil wars gentlemen, and they are going to have to take care of them by themselves. The United States just can't go around the world sticking its nose in fights like these."

DuPray agreed.

Pastor shot back at his boss, "Well, I don't. We have one big advantage, surprise. We can turn that right back around on these bastards and use it on them just like they're planning to use it on us. This is like knowing the identities and intentions of each of the nineteen hijackers before September 11th. What would that day have been like if we'd have known who they were and what they were up to?"

Levi would have none of it. "You can't be serious General. That was nineteen people, four airplanes, all departing from the same airport. This is eight countries, tens of thousands of people, in thousands of places. There is no military option that has even a remote chance of success." He said it with the scorn of a professor challenging the work of an undergraduate student trying to disprove the validity of some long-held theory. For the student's indiscretion, the punishment was to be public humiliation.

DuPray shot a glance at Pastor and said, "You're on your own here, Jonas."

Pastor looked at his boss, shrugged then focused his remarks on Tim Munson, the National Security Advisor, the only civilian in the room whose position on this matter was apparently up for grabs. "We think we can put some Special Ops folks on the ground in four of the countries, in certain key locations and let the bad guys walk into a buzz saw."

Munson asked, annoyance in his voice, "That might have a chance if we knew when, but we don't. The fourth of what, Jonas? That's still the question."

"The fourth of July, the fourth of August, the fourth of September. It doesn't matter, if we do this right. As long as their presence remains a secret they can stay there for as long as it takes. These forces are trained to survive like that, Mr. Munson."

Levi pushed, "What four countries?"

"Japan, South Korea, Thailand and the Philippines. We'll need to get the cooperation of the existing governments. I don't know why they wouldn't cooperate when they see what's at stake."

"And the others, what about them?" Levi asked with impatience.

"What about them, Mr. Secretary? China, Vietnam, North Korea and Malaysia have never been friendly towards the United States." Pastor's tone had become sarcastic to match that of his adversary. "If we're lucky enough to find out exactly when Operation Light Switch is to occur, we let their leaders know at the eleventh hour what is going to happen. We time it so we don't jeopardize our operation. These countries have plenty of mechanisms to deal with these kinds of things. On the surface they may look more moderate than they once were, but when you get right down to it, all four are still police states. They'll have ways of dealing with revolt. They all have plans."

Levi persisted, "You don't know that they have plans..."

Munson held up his hand and interrupted, "General, how the hell would you disguise the movement of all of these troops?" Pastor, McKeever and Rentz all got a mental charge from the Security Advisor's question. Questions meant interest. Good questions like this one meant he thought their proposal had a chance.

"Well, sir, it's fewer troops than you might think, probably not more than three thousand..."

"Impossible!"

Munson shot a look at Levi. "Mr. Secretary, last time I checked, you were the expert on foreign affairs of State and General Pastor is the President's top military advisor. Let him talk, Roger."

Pastor looked at Munson and nodded, "Our troops will go in on scheduled airlines. Once we get them in the country then we'll use military air to supply them."

He paused briefly to judge Munson's reaction, but it was too early. There was a downside and Pastor decided now was the time to lay it out. "But there is one other critical point. We have to keep this operation secret. Admiral McKeever, General Rentz and I have discussed this at some length. Those of us in this room, and the President, of course, are the only ones who can know what we are doing."

Levi jumped to his feet. "That's illegal. Congress has to approve the use of military troops overseas. I'm not going to be a party to anything..."

DuPray interrupted, "General Pastor, I would have appreciated the courtesy of knowing what the three of you have conspired...

Munson commanded, "Sit down, Roger. Shut up, John. We have a very real threat to deal with here. This isn't the time for us to cut ideas off short or to get upset about protocol." Levi sat down but it was obvious he didn't like the way Munson had cut him off. DuPray was red in the face, a result of anger and embarrassment. Both secretaries glared at the three four-stars.

Pastor ignored them and focused his remarks on Munson, whom he was beginning to think of as an ally. "If you tell Congress what we're proposing, there will be opposition and the opposition will be smart enough to know that all they have to do is leak what we are proposing to the press. That ends this military option, Mr. Munson. If this makes it to the nightly news, our troops will be sitting ducks. I won't do that to them," he turned and stared down Levi and DuPray, "and you shouldn't either." It was a warning to his two opponents.

Tension hung over them, especially Munson, who knew he was the swing vote in determining what recommendation would go to the President. When the door opened, it startled all of them. The President of the United States walked in. He looked at Munson, "Your secretary said you were down here and when she said she didn't know what the subject was, I thought I'd better check in, Tim." He looked around the room. "Is this about your little foray into Japan?"

"Yes, Mr. President, it is."

"Well then I'm going to draw two conclusions. You tell me if I'm right. First, we didn't get caught. If we had, I would have read about it by now. Second, we found something out, and looking at who's here and the looks on their faces, it isn't good is it?"

"No, Mr. President it isn't. We're trying to decide what to recommend to you."

Glover picked up the phone and dialed his Chief of Staff. "Leo, cancel everything today. Give my apologies; tell them I've come down with something. If you need me I'm in the situation room, but don't call unless it's important because the reason I'm down here apparently is." He hung up. "OK, gentlemen, let's get started."

Munson brought the President up to date on the revelations provided by Paul Stanley's confession. Once the background was out of the way, he moved on to the debate they were having over the military solution to the situation. Glover twisted uncomfortably in his seat. "How do we know this General Stanley is telling the truth?"

Rentz answered, "He is, sir. First, there's no reason for him to lie. Second, how could he make up a story this incredible and third, he's a friend..."

"General, the fact that he's your friend doesn't do much for me." He looked around the room. "Have any of you considered my political liability? Have you considered what would happen to me---to us---if I send US Forces into something like this without going to Congress first?"

Roger Levi sat up, "That's exactly what I told them, Mr. President." He gave Pastor a smug look.

Pastor wanted to smack the smart ass, but instead told the President, "Sir, you can't disclose this military option to the Congress without guaranteeing a security leak." He shot McKeever and Rentz a quick look for confirmation and found it in their nods, "If you do that, we withdraw this as a military option."

"Are you threatening me, General?"

"That's certainly not my intention, Mr. President. Neither is it my intention to set our troops up for failure."

Glover glared at him. Though Munson had covered Roger Levi's tell-them-everything-and-let-them-sort-it-out option, Levi gave it to the President again as if it were his only logical choice. It was the President's out from this very tenuous situation. "He's right, gentlemen. These are civil wars. We can't get involved."

Pastor offered, "Mr. President, what if we warn them and the rebels succeed in spite of our warning. That's possible you know. They're close to kicking this thing off, maybe as close as twenty-three days. According to Stanley, they are well organized. What's the impact on Wall Street, on the American people? Could you say we did everything we could with the information we had at the time?"

Glover was twisting in his seat again. So was Roger Levi.

Tim Munson thought the military option had merit. Despite the imbalance of forces, it was a good option. We didn't have to beat them everywhere, just in certain places, to preserve the existing governments. He was grateful for Pastor's input. Nothing, he thought, would be worse than being in this situation without a military option. Now the trick was to figure why the military option was better than the one proposed by the Secretary of State.

He asked himself, *"What if these coups succeed?"* He tried to see the future, and he didn't like what he was coming up with. When he spoke it was directly to the President, "Mr. President, you are on the point of the spear here and none of us can change that. There are plenty of precedents for you to order our forces overseas on your authority as the Commander-in-Chief. Certainly there is a clear and present danger to our national security interests. We've sent troops into Haiti, Rwanda, Burundi, Liberia, and Bosnia with a lot less at stake than we have here."

The President shot back confidently, "Those were humanitarian missions. We went in there to save lives. Congress was consulted. There's no comparison, Tim. We're intervening directly in the governmental issues of other countries in this case---it's more like Vietnam and Korea than Rwanda or Haiti."

The President stood as if the discussion was over. Pastor, McKeever and Rentz began folding their tents. The President had taken the easy way out and gone with Levi's option. But Munson wasn't finished. He didn't like the President's walking out as casually as he'd strolled in. "Mr. President, you can walk out of here and be like any other politician in this town or you can stay here and act like the Commander-in-Chief." Glover strode toward the door.

Munson, calmer now, but still assertive, called after him, "If you turn your back on this thing and this *association* that Paul Stanley told us about succeeds you will be known in history as 'the man who let the world down'. You will kill the US economy. Last year we did nearly 300 billion dollars in exports and 400 billion dollars in imports with Japan alone. I know businessmen bitch because the balance is wrong, but what's the impact on those businessmen if the numbers drop to zero in both columns?"

President Glover stopped at the door, his hand poised on the handle. He turned and looked at Munson. Munson had his attention now. Pastor, McKeever and Rentz held their breath. If he walked through that door, they were through. Munson continued, "Mr. President, two-thirds of the world's population lives in Asia and the vast majority exist well below America's poverty line. These bastards and their revolution just might make things better for them in the near term---when you're at the bottom of the barrel it doesn't take much to make you feel like you're making progress. So these guys improve the lives of millions of people for a while, and these millions of people are willing to overlook the fact that one of their basic fundamental rights has been taken away. You remember the one Mr. President---the one that caused us to revolt against the tyranny of our British oppressors. We wanted the freedom to trade with whoever could pay a fair and reasonable price for the goods we were producing. We wanted competition."

Glover was an historian and Munson's logic worked that angle. "Now it's a fair question to ask ourselves, Mr. President, whether the citizens of this utopia will put up with the oppression this group of men will impose on them. I think that they will---*we did* before we finally revolted against British tyranny and presented King George with the Declaration of Independence. So, the next issue becomes the survival of our economy. Can our economy, can the economies of the rest of the world afford to wait until the average citizen in this *utopia* realizes that greater prosperity lies in greater freedom? Again, if you use our experience as the barometer, that could take decades. Our economies and others around the world won't survive as we know them today."

"Now let's jump ahead a few decades---when the people of Asia finally realize how they're getting screwed. What happens when they revolt like we did? How will the government that we let take hold handle revolt? King George did not deal magnanimously with us. But the soldiers and weapons that King George turned on us are inconsequential, compared to the weapons that these men have at their disposal. Remember what General Stanley told us. They aren't afraid to use genocide as a means to their end. They could make the work of the Khamer Rouge in Cambodia look like child's play. Their weapons will be potent---perhaps even nuclear, biological, or chemical. We have learned well how to kill large masses of people with great efficiency since the days of Red Coats marching in straight lines and patriots sniping at them from behind trees and stone walls. My prediction is the governments that we allowed to come to power will not hesitate to use weapons of mass destruction against their own people in order to retain their grip on them. And they won't care one whit about the effect of these weapons on the global environment."

Glover had returned to his seat. Munson finished, "Mr. President, I've heard you say many times that knowing history isn't any good unless you can take its lessons and project them into the future. Sir, if you see something wrong with my prediction, please tell me, because I don't like the conclusion I've come to."

Munson's picture of the future stunned everyone in the room. The disdain that had marked the President's face earlier was gone now. Munson offered a final and equally sobering prediction, "Your lot is not an easy one, Mr. President. Your domestic agenda will suffer from this crisis because attention will revert back to defense. The questions will arise again. You will likely be accused of reducing defense too much. Your critics, and there will be many, will say the reductions led us into this predicament. They will point their fingers and say you had no foreign policy. If you did, this never would have been allowed to happen. But if you allow fear of these criticisms to lull you into inaction, if you choose to allow matters to unfold without our direct influence, when we had a chance to do exactly that---influence events, change outcomes---you will likely end up without an agenda, domestic, foreign or otherwise. After the economy collapses, there will be little remaining to worry about, Mr. President."

The room fell utterly silent. All of them, even John DuPray and Roger Levi, gave Glover the time to think. Finally Munson pressed him, "Mr. President, what do you want us to do? If you choose a military option, time is of the essence."

Again there was no response. Glover could feel their eyes focused on him. He regretted ever having broken in on them, not that it would have made any difference. It was a decision that he and only he could make. His head ached at the back of his skull in rhythm with his heartbeat. He wanted to go to the residence and lay down for a few minutes.

"Mr. President, we need a decision and we need it now. We're going to have to begin getting our forces ready if you approve this."

"I have no choice, do I?" He got up and headed again towards the door.

Munson called after him, "None, Mr. President, that doesn't abdicate our responsibility as I see it in this situation. You'll need to call our allies. We should go over the things we need to tell them and the conditions of our help."

"You work out the script, Tim. Have the communications room schedule the calls beginning at 7:00 tomorrow morning. If we have no choice, we should get on with it, I suppose."

When he was gone, Roger Levi said, "He hasn't approved this. You can't…"

Munson snapped, "Shut up, Roger. He has no stomach for this kind of thing. We've gotten his approval as much as we're going to get it. Do you agree Mr. DuPray?"

"Well, I, uh, I…"

Munson interrupted him. He sounded disgusted, "Never mind John. You don't have to incriminate yourself, you either, Roger. I take responsibility for interpretation of the President's comments." He looked at DuPray and Levi but made it sound like his comments were intended for all, "I shouldn't have to remind any of you how sensitive this information is. No leaks, gentlemen."

Pastor, McKeever and Rentz shared glances. Over the years they had seen political appointees squirm when historic decisions had to be made, and this was clearly in that category; it had to be one of the most historic Presidential decisions ever made. But later, when the three four-stars talked it over among themselves, they agreed that they had never seen two more gutless cabinet members. Levi and DuPray were like earthworms when the rock they've been hiding under is suddenly lifted and the sunlight hits them. They couldn't get out of sight fast enough.

Tim Munson, however, was a different matter. For as much as they disliked the Secretaries of State and Defense, all three held the National Security Advisor in the highest regard.

Chapter Thirty-three

Cleve Spires and Marine Corps Gunnery Sergeant Bart Atherton arrived at Hill Air Force Base, Utah aboard a US Air Force Learjet in the wee hours of the morning. A shuttle bus took them to the Base Exchange where Cleve collected some reading material while Atherton called Enterprise Car Rental. Twenty minutes later Enterprise's agent met them in front of the Exchange, Atherton completed the paperwork on the rental and they were on their way. Their destination lay still three hours away, a mountain cottage owned by Lucas Johnson's in-laws, about twelve miles outside White Birch, Utah, a thriving town of one hundred souls.

McKeever wanted Spires isolated and that was what he got. Johnson had assured McKeever that where they were going was miles away from civilization. There were no phones of any type; cell phones wouldn't operate in this rugged and remote terrain. Even radio reception of commercial radio stations was difficult; television was an absolute impossibility. Atherton's instructions were to stay there with Spires until told otherwise by either the CINC or the DCINC.

They had hardly spoken on the flight into Hill. Quite honestly, Cleve Spires was miffed that he hadn't been allowed to accompany everyone to Washington. He thought he'd earned that right. Atherton, on the other hand, a highly respected satellite photo analyst in CINCPAC's J-2 shop, wasn't fond of getting what seemed to him like guard duty again. Their silence continued for the first thirty minutes of the trip to White Birch. Finally Atherton asked the question he'd been dying to ask since he'd met Spires, "Did you kill Driscoll?"

"No, I didn't." There was a pause. "Why would I kill the guy who could have cleared me of the charges that sent me to Leavenworth for ten years?" Does that make sense to you Gunny?"

"No." Atherton drove on for the next several miles just thinking.

"So, you didn't kill that kid on Okinawa either?"

"No, I didn't. I think maybe Driscoll did. The evidence..." He flashed back to the court martial. "The evidence was all circumstantial. There were no witnesses, nothing that linked me to that airman, except my fingerprints on the murder weapon. Hell, I handled fifteen or twenty of the pistols in the First Battalion's arms room the day before that kid was killed. That was part of my job as Group Sergeant Major. And the money---I don't know where that came from---probably Driscoll too. Hell, look at the money they found in his accounts after he was killed. The ten-thousand dollars he sent to me must have been chicken feed for him, just the cost of doing business."

Atherton drove on some more. Spires could tell the Marine wanted to know more. Something was troubling Atherton and he wasn't sure what it was. In trying to figure out what Atherton was fishing for, Cleve Spires became reflective, "You know, I *could have* killed Driscoll. That son of a bitch cost me ten years of my life. For ten years I never saw my wife, I missed my son growing up, my father died, my career---up in smoke---all of it gone because Billy Driscoll framed me. But I didn't; I didn't kill him."

Atherton swung off of the highway and pulled to a stop. "Look, for what it's worth, I believe you on both counts, but I got this duty handed to me by the CINC. He wants me to keep an eye on you."

Spires said, "OK. We're going to be together for a while. We probably need to be honest with one another. So what's on your mind?"

Atherton stared out the windshield, "This would be a mission that I could fail at very easily, Sergeant Major. We're headed into some of the most rugged terrain in the states. I know you know how to survive in it. So do I. If you wanted to get away from me, that wouldn't be very hard to do." He turned and looked directly at Spires, "But you know I'll come after you."

The thought of just walking away from the cabin and back to civilization had crossed Spires' mind, but there were two problems. First, there was too much at stake. When he'd come forward on Okinawa, he committed to this course of action. He could only hope that those in authority would look on his actions favorably when this was all over. The second problem he was facing was that he liked Atherton's honesty.

Atherton said, "Tell me you're not going to try anything. Tell me that and I'll believe you just like I believe you about these murders."

The reply, almost without hesitation came, "I'm not going anywhere Gunny. You have my word on that."

Atherton extended his hand and Spires took it. Atherton pulled back onto the highway and drove on. Atherton's curiosity got the best of him five miles down the road. He'd seen Spires in the CINC's office the night he'd escorted Stanley to Hickam. "What's the link between you and General Stanley?"

"No link," there was a pause, an awkward moment, then Spires added, "and don't ask me anything else about why or how I came to be in Hawaii. I can't answer that Gunny."

Atherton liked Spires' directness. "Aye-aye, Sergeant Major."

Chapter Thirty-four

The phone next to Tim Munson's bed rang. He had the ringer volume turned full volume because he knew he was a heavy sleeper, but this night he'd had trouble falling off. He looked at the alarm clock, 2:00A.M. He'd been asleep no more than fifteen minutes.

"Mr. Munson, it's Cecil Parker. We've got it. I've passed the program to Pete Charles in Tokyo. He should be on his way to the estate now to try it out."

"Great. You guys are heroes again."

"Yeah, well, thank you, but there is a risk to what Charles is doing. The house is lined with something, probably lead. He's going to have to intercept the signal at the satellite dish rather than the receiver inside the house. If these guys are sharp, and we shouldn't underestimate them, they'll see a drop in signal strength at the receiver and suspect something. I've told Charles to be very cautious."

"Let me help you out in that regard, Doctor. Your man got us a partial date, the fourth of something. I need to know the *something.* If he can get that for us, then he should get the hell out of there."

"Yes, sir. I'll pass that along."

Inside the communications suite Seito Yamamoto's manservant, Aieto Fukora, sat at the control panel adjusting knobs and watching the signal strength indicator. It was a full two points below its normal reading of five. The signal was still plenty strong and communications were being received and sent without any problems, but Fukora was afraid this suddenly weakened signal could be a sign of an imminent malfunction. They were at a point where any break in communications would be a disaster. The *association* employed two technicians, full time, to service their communications equipment. One of them was in China looking after a small problem the Chinese associate had been having, so only one was available to Fukora this day. Thirty minutes after Fukora's call he arrived at the estate.

Pete Charles had been listening in steady for just over an hour. He figured it was better to do it this way than switch on and off. He might get lucky and if they weren't paying close attention inside the house a steady drop in signal strength would be less obvious that a signal strength that was fluctuating.

The missing piece of information came in from the Philippines. Message traffic had been brisk. He intercepted no fewer than half a dozen messages in the brief time he'd been intercepting. As the scrambled messages fed into his descrambler, it would unscramble them using the cipher that Parker's team had provided him and then record the message in unscrambled, clear text. Charles listened to each message he'd intercepted thus far. The seventh message gave him what they were looking for. In his earphones he heard the recorded message say, "I have just learned that President Lopez will be out of Manila on the fourth of July. This will make things more difficult that day, but I am working on a plan. Details will follow later."

Gottcha! He took the tape out of the recorder and put it in his pocket and then switched off his equipment and began packing up, glad that he didn't need to press his luck any further.

Inside the house both Fukora and the technician saw the needle on the signal strength indicator swing abruptly to five. They froze on it for a few seconds to be sure it was going to stabilize there.

"What did you do?"

"Nothing." The technician scanned all of the controls in front of him. "I did nothing that would have caused that jump." The technician thought for a minute more then said, "Come with me, can you?"

"Yes, of course."

As they headed for his truck he explained to Fukora his theory. The signal was being intercepted at the antenna, or in some way interrupted there. He wanted to take a swing around the block and perhaps a few of the adjoining blocks to see if he could see anything that could account for what they'd seen on the signal strength indicator.

Two hundred yards ahead of them Pete Charles turned his rental truck to the right and headed back to Yakota to forward his intercept. When Fukora and the technician got to the same intersection they went straight ahead.

Chapter Thirty-five

President Glover left the White House residence at 6:45AM on June 24th and made the short walk to the Oval Office. Munson was waiting for him. "Pastor was right. Operation Light Switch is scheduled for the 4th of July. We don't have much time, Mr. President."

At 7:00AM precisely, the phone rang on the President's desk as the White House Communications Room transferred in the secure call from the Prime Minister of Japan. When Glover gave him the basic outline of what had been uncovered, the Prime Minister was skeptical.

"President Glover, put yourself in my position. How could something this big be going on for this long without anyone suspecting. You must admit it does seem all too preposterous. Can you send someone with the proof you have? May I see the satellite photos and listen to the intercepts? Perhaps then I can…

"I understand Mr. Prime Minister. Let me see what I can arrange. I will be back in touch. In the meantime I don't have to tell you how sensitive this information is."

"Of course. You may count on my complete discretion."

Glover hung up the phone. "Dammit! The others will be just like him. They'll want to see the proof and even then…"

"Mr. President, let me work this out."

"Hell, Tim, you can't go out there and line these countries up. Everyone will want to know what you're doing. It'll leak…"

"No, sir. I know I can't go but let me work out the detail of who should go. I'll work with Defense and State. We'll find someone who won't draw attention."

Lucas Johnson was working at his desk when his Operations Officer and Executive Officer showed up at his doorway. Lieutenant Colonel Dave Ellison, the Exec, had a piece of paper in his hand. "It's a warning order, sir." Johnson's face registered relief. He'd returned from the meeting in the White House with instructions that he could not do anything, until he'd gotten the word through official channels. The warning order was what he'd been waiting for.

"Good. We can talk about this thing now."

"You know about this?"

"I do. The First Battalion will have Thailand. They're the lucky ones. There's an outfit in the Royal Thai Army that can help them, the Tiger Brigade." He opened up his planner and thumbed through some pages of notes. "Darrell Greene needs to meet with Colonel Pramrashorn Saraveet. No one else in this dog fight will have that kind of help."

Johnson was looking down into his planner and didn't notice their bewilderment. No one knew how he knew any of this. He continued, "Second Battalion draws Japan. Dave, you're going to lead an operational team into Cato Fujiwara's headquarters in Tokyo. Do you know who he is?"

Lieutenant Colonel Dave Ellison, Johnson's Exec replied, "No, sir, but..."

"President and CEO of an organization known as the *Yakuza.* Ever heard of *it*?"

"Yes sir, Japan's mafia, but..."

"Right. I'll be in Japan with you. I'll lead an operational team against a man named Seito Yamamoto. Both of these guys are key to what's going to happen out there. Does that thing," he pointed to the Warning Order, "tell us when the op kicks off?"

"The fourth of July, sir," answered the Operations Officer.

"Great! They filled in the blank. All right. The Third Battalion gets the Philippines. We're under two weeks and there's a lot to do. Let's go to the Ops Center and get busy. From this point on we don't talk about this operation outside of the Ops Center. One leak and it's over."

Ellison blurted out, "Sir, how the hell did you know about this?"

The question brought Johnson back to their level. He'd been moving at the speed of light. They on the other hand had just scanned the Warning Order quickly. "Sorry guys, I'll explain downstairs." He stood up to follow them to the Operations Center in the basement when the secure telephone on the credenza behind his desk rang. "You two go ahead. Get the staff together. I'll be right down. Close the door please, Dave." He picked up the phone and said, "Johnson."

Admiral Chet McKeever said, "Lucas, it's McKeever. Listen, I just finished a video teleconference with the National Security Advisor and General Rentz. We want you to be a Presidential envoy."

Of all the things that he might have anticipated this call to be about, this was not one of them. Lucas had learned long ago that when surprised, it's better to shut up and think rather than blurt out the first thought that comes into your mind. In this case that first thought was, *Presidential envoy! Admiral you must be smokin' dope.* Silence pervaded the secure telephone connection.

"Lucas?"

"Yes, sir."

"Listen son, the Prime Minister of Japan wants to see and hear the stuff for himself. He won't be the only one. The others will want to see it, hear it, touch it---I guess I can't blame them. If I were in their shoes I'd have trouble believing us too. We need someone who can travel around without drawing attention, but that someone needs to know what the hell is going on. We think that someone is you. The President has agreed."

"But sir, we just got the Warning Order. There's a ton of work…"

"How's your Exec?"

Ellison was good. That was why he was the Exec. He could do what needed to be done. "He's good, sir, but he doesn't know what I know..."

McKeever interrupted, "OK, then that's that. Mike Hurley will keep your Exec on his toes. Lucas, we need you to do this. You're going to build this coalition. If you fail, this op can't go forward and we'll have to go to Levi's scenario. But if you pull it off…" He let Lucas fill in the blank. "There's a video teleconference at 1:00PM today, your time. Munson, Levi, DuPray, Rentz and I will hook up with you and go over your script. Munson and Levi can fill you in on the personalities you'll be dealing with. Your plane will be standing by. There's no time to waste, Lucas. I don't have to tell you that. Japan, Korea, Thailand and the Philippines will be your rotation. We'll see you at 1:00."

Lucas Johnson was the only passenger on the 747. On the outside, it looked like a standard commercial jetliner. On the inside, it was a flying communications center with private accommodations at the rear. This was one of the airplanes the President might use in the event of some cataclysm that would make his occupation of a land-based command center hazardous. On the flight to Japan, he went over his notes from the video teleconference. After three hours he had his script and his notes down cold. When the flight deck advised him there were still nine hours of flying time remaining he went to the private sleeping accommodations that were on board, but he couldn't sleep. His mind kept working the script and every possible question he could be asked over and over again. An hour out of Yakota he showered, shaved, got dressed and resumed his silent rehearsal.

"Colonel Johnson." Japan's Prime Minister extended his hand in the western manner of greeting. They were alone in his office. Lucas was prepared to bow in the eastern manner and this departure from the over-practiced routine he'd expected took him by surprise. He shook the Prime Minister's hand, but bent forward awkwardly in a kind of hybrid handshake-bow. He was nervous and uncomfortable in this unfamiliar role and the Prime Minister could sense it. "You are nervous. Don't be. Few warriors can also be diplomats. Your President trusts you to be both."

The Prime Minister's English was superb and his way was an easy one. Lucas began to relax. "Thank you, Mr. Prime Minister. President Glover sends his regards."

"I understand you have some photos and recordings for me."

From this point on, Lucas was thankful for the silent rehearsals he'd gone over and over again on the plane. The briefing was precise and concise. When he was finished, the Prime Minister asked the question everyone had anticipated, "Tell me Colonel Johnson, why shouldn't I simply apprehend the Minister of Foreign Affairs and publicly expose him as a traitor?"

"Sir, you could certainly do just that. If this plot was limited to just your country, it is what President Glover would suggest that you do. However, there are several points he wants you to consider. First, there are seven other countries whose existing governments are at stake. Three of them, I believe, you would count as your allies, as does the United States. Second, our information is at best, sketchy. Our informant has given us some names, which I have passed to you, but the truth is, we don't know how complete this list is. There is little time for us to gather more information, and trying to gather more information might tip them off. If they know that we know, Mr. Prime Minister, the assistance we are offering you will be too little, too late, I'm afraid."

"Who is your informant?"

Their strategy had been to withhold details on Stanley unless asked. Now he'd been asked. Lucas gave him Paul Stanley's name and background.

"And what will your President do with this informant?"

"He is in prison awaiting trial which can't begin until we have settled the matter at hand here in Asia. I'm sure you understand why. He is charged with treason and he could be sentenced to death if he is found guilty. If the court-martial doesn't sentence him to death, General Stanley probably would not survive the length of any prison term he might be sentenced to serve."

"What are the conditions of your country's assistance, Colonel Johnson?"

"You must tell no one of your agreement to our assistance."

"But how will the people of Japan know on that day that your Special Forces soldiers are here to assist. How will you communicate..."

"Sir, the operational plan calls for specially equipped US Air Force planes to block the signal of key radio and television stations across Japan. The blocked signal will be replaced by a signal originating from the aircraft and we will announce on Japanese television and radio what is happening."

"You have such technology?"

"We do. We used it in Haiti in 1995, and although the circumstances weren't quite as dire, it worked out very well for us. We used these aircraft to relay in the World Cup Soccer Tournament in an effort to take the Haitian people's minds off their troubles. We believe it will work in this case as it did then."

"Your Pentagon has a reputation for trying to forecast the price of conflict. What have you forecast for casualties on July 4th?"

"Mr. Prime Minister, if that has been done, I don't know about it. I think President Glover would have wanted me armed with that information, if we had it at our disposal. Things have happened very quickly for us, as they are happening now for you. If it is of any reassurance, our forces will only be armed with small arms. The enemy is not intent on killing people and destroying buildings, neither are we. I believe you are familiar with the training our Special Forces receive. All of them are small arms experts."

The Prime Minister sat down at his desk and stared into the top of it.

"Your President Glover---has he talked of his political future after this is over?"

This question was not one that anyone had foreseen, but it was a good one for him to ask. It was a political question and not one that Johnson thought he was qualified to answer, but he'd been there when the President asked if anyone had ever considered his political liability. Johnson answered, "Just as you are not permitted to tell anyone here in Japan about what is going to happen on the 4th, President

Glover may not tell Congress. He is aware of the political liability that decision carries with it. He believes that what is at stake in Asia is more important than his political future."

"Your President is," he was looking for the term, "how do you say it, he is a real stand-up guy."

Lucas smiled, "Yes, he is, Mr. Prime Minister."

He'd been there only about an hour and a half; hardly sufficient time for a leader of one of the world's leading countries to make such a momentous decision, but both men knew a decision was expected. Lucas fell silent and let the Prime Minister think.

"Colonel Johnson, I am the first leader with whom you have spoken, is that correct?"

"Yes, sir. You are the first."

"Very well. You have my agreement to your plan providing South Korea, Thailand and the Philippines subscribe to it as well. I won't keep you. You have a schedule to keep. You have my word that I will take no action for the next forty-eight hours. In that time, I will expect to hear from your President as to the results of your travels. If I have not heard from him by then, I will be forced to take matters into my own hands."

"I understand, Mr. Prime Minister. We will be in touch."

On June 25th, Lucas Johnson was somewhere between Thailand and the Philippines. The coalition he'd been tasked to forge, the agreement he'd been sent to secure, wasn't yet complete, but US forces continued to get ready. Brigadier General Mike Hurley, who had become the Joint Task Force Commander, issued a message to the First Special Forces Group at Fort Lewis, Washington; the Fifth Special Forces Group at Fort Bragg, North Carolina; the First Seal Unit in Coronado, California and the 352nd Air Force Special Operations Squadron at Eglin Air Force Base, Florida to recall all of their personnel and go into a pre-operational lockdown.

The secrecy of American plans now became a vital concern. No one worried about any of the Special Forces themselves breeching security. It was their wives, mothers, fathers, relatives and friends, who all lay outside the span of the Defense Department's control, that was the source of worry. All one of them had to do was complain publicly. It had happened before. During Desert Storm, morning news shows carried stories of pregnant, near-term wives who were going to have to have their baby while Daddy was boarding a flight to Saudi Arabia. There were stories of parents who had to face high-risk surgery while their sons and daughters moved off to war. Hurley's all time favorite was the single parent who loved being a soldier, but now was faced with a deployment, and was concerned about what to do with her children. If the networks picked up stories like these, they needed an answer. Hurley called the Public Affairs Officer on the Joint Staff, and together they worked out a cover story about a routine exercise, not expected to last very long, but one that has been in the planning for a long time: the Department of Defense regrets the hardship, blah, blah, blah.

The first troops were scheduled to depart on June 26th aboard regularly scheduled commercial flights. The last troops would be in place by June 30th. Four days to move just over three thousand troops on one hundred and fifty flights. They were going to travel as tourists, businessmen and students, using regular US passports. If Lucas should happen to fail, they would simply return in the same manner. If he succeeded, supply flights would begin departing the US on June 27th.

Each operational team had a schedule. It had been fairly easy to construct for those teams operating in Korea and Japan. US Air Bases at Osan, South Korea and Yakota, Japan would be the rendezvous point for them to meet the flight that brought them their warfighting gear; their communications equipment, weapons, ammo and other sundry explosives. They had credit cards and cash to make local purchases of whatever else they might need.

Supplying the operational teams in Thailand and the Philippines was a bit trickier. The US didn't have American-controlled bases to fall back on in either of these countries. Starting on the 27th of June and lasting until the 3rd of July, there would be a steady stream of US military and commercial charter cargo aircraft landing at Utupao Air Base in southern Thailand and at Cubi Point Air Base in the Philippines, about seventy-five miles southeast of Manila. The story was that these aircraft were carrying humanitarian supplies, and the people meeting them were missionaries who would distribute the supplies throughout the country.

This is the kind of thing that Special Forces troops trained to do. Hurley had every confidence in them. It was the news leak that scared the hell out of him. He was never more than a minute away from CNN or an all-news radio station. If the story broke, that was it for Operation Lights On.

South Korea had gone very much like Japan. The last question he'd gotten from the South Korean President was, "What did Japan agree to?"

When Lucas told him, the South Korean President nodded and commented, "Most prudent. I will offer you the same assurances, the same length of time and, if you can get everyone to agree, we will move forward."

In Thailand, the Prime Minister had met him at the airport in Bangkok and taken him directly to the King. Though it was a parliamentary monarchy, in Thailand the King was the final word. In the mid-nineties, the Kingdom of Thailand had been shaken by violent civil unrest sparked by the rigid conservatism of the majority party in Parliament and the extreme liberalism of the minority parties. The King publicly humiliated the leaders of both sides, and told them they had twenty-four hours to reach compromise and end the violence occurring in the streets or he would take matters into his own hands and that would include throwing all of them in jail. They reached compromise within a matter of hours.

Lucas found King Rama XXII to be extremely likeable, despite his vast powers. He'd been educated in the US, at Princeton no less. When Lucas told him how they'd first found out about the plot, he remembered the death of Billy Driscoll and the prostitute. "Too many of my people are too poor. They are so easily exploited by evil, all because they are trying to become wealthy. Driscoll, what I know of him, was an exploiter of women; it sounds like this man Spires did Thailand a favor."

Lucas clarified, "Your majesty, Cleve Spires didn't kill Sergeant Major Driscoll. Someone else did and made it look like Spires. Perhaps when this is all over..."

"Perhaps when this is all over I can meet this man Spires and judge him for myself."

"I know he would appreciate that opportunity very much, your majesty."

The King agreed to the same conditions that Japan and Korea agreed to.

The last link in the chain remained, the Philippines. One of the things that Lucas had always enjoyed about his work was the travel, and especially the trips to Asian countries. He'd found the cultures there and the people to have a distinct gentility. He thought that it was somehow a result of their ancient histories and cultures, so full of time-honored traditions. In America, nothing was truly old like it was in this part of the world. Ancient temples were still used daily for mystic, holy ceremonies. Priests and monks used priceless antiques to perform the rituals of these ceremonies; none of it changed for centuries. Visitors were welcomed with a warm civility, even in Japan and Korea, as industrialized as they had become, even in China, a country swept up in social and economic changes.

But this was his fifth or sixth trip to the Philippines, and as many times as he'd been here, Lucas Johnson had not found anything genteel about the place. Maybe the Philippines weren't old enough to have a gentility of their own yet. Maybe it was the diversity of the Filipino people, the many cultures and religions that blended here, that made the place so different from the other countries of the Pacific Rim. Lucas thought the Philippines was like the American wild west of a hundred and fifty years ago. Manila was an oriental Dodge City and Subic Bay was Abilene. Everything in between was badlands with rattlesnakes under the smaller rocks, and robbers and rustlers behind the big ones.

The armored van and driver that met him at Aquino International Airport foreshadowed that this visit was probably not going to make him feel any different. The van was dirty. The driver was basically uncommunicative; when he did say something it was in short, unintelligible guttural grunts.

Munson had warned him about the Philippine President, Theodore “Teddy” Ferdinand Lopez. "Don't to be fooled by this son of a bitch's smooth English and the fact he's a West Point graduate. You are authorized to play diplomatic hard ball with this pecker head if you need to---you can do or say whatever you think is needed to make the guy understand his country is included in this coalition simply because when this is all over, we may need every friend we can get in the Pacific Rim. The fact of the matter is, the place is a shit hole and always has been. Lopez likes his power and he doesn't want to lose it, so make sure he understands that if he tips our hand we'll make sure he comes out the big loser. If you can scare him badly enough, he'll do whatever he needs to stay in power.”

Lopez had confounded US military and political leaders for the last six years. A majority of Congress branded him anti-American. The international community accused him of corruption and carrying out a string of human rights abuses against political enemies---but no one had proven it.

On the plus side, the country had actually stabilized somewhat under his leadership. The many political and religious groups that once threatened to fragment the country and replace government with anarchy were as inactive as they'd ever been. Some American, Japanese and Taiwanese industry had moved in and invested in the old Subic Bay Navy Base, abandoned in 1992 by the US. That investment alone had caused nearly a 25% growth in the stagnant Philippine economy. So the average Filipino, who believed he was leading them to a more prosperous future, loved Teddy Ferdinand Lopez.

At the Presidential Palace, Lucas was unceremoniously checked with a hand-held metal detector and told to have a seat. Lopez kept him waiting for an hour.

"Mr. Johnson, the President will see you now. Follow me, please." He was led down a long hallway lined with paintings of past Philippine presidents, into an office that could only be described as garish. Lucas thought it somehow fit the image, as it had been described to him, of the man he was about to meet.

Johnson extended his hand. There was no firmness, no pleasantness, only disinterest expressed in Lopez's handshake.

"Mr. Johnson, why does your government trust such a seemingly important mission to just a Colonel?"

This son of a bitch really doesn't mince any words.

Lucas let go of the cold fish, and also decided to drop the pleasantries, "President Glover needed someone who could travel without drawing attention..."

"Well, he certainly has accomplished that." He was smiling now at Johnson, enjoying belittling him.

For the moment, Lucas overlooked his rudeness and stuck to business, "If I may, I would like to show you some rather startling photos taken by our reconnaissance satellites."

Lopez took the photos from Lucas and hapahazardly thumbed through them. When he was finished he tossed them in the middle of the massive mahogany desk that was the focal point of the room. "This is your proof of a revolt?"

"I have some..."

"Oh yes, recordings. Tell me Colonel, why is your country doing this?"

"Mr. President, forgive me, I don't wish to be rude, but this is a matter of the gravest importance to your government. I find it hard to believe you aren't interested in what I have brought."

The smile turned to frown. Lucas could see Lopez's hands clinch into fists.

"You are impertinent, Colonel. If you don't apologize, I will terminate this conversation now."

Lucas was pissed, but kept his composure. In a level voice he said, "Mr. President, it would be most unfortunate if you chose to do that. In all likelihood you would find yourself replaced at best, dead at worst, and my money would be on your death. You, sir, are surrounded by revolution, and you're acting like the rebels are just so many pesky mosquitoes."

"So you say, but tell me Colonel, if this danger is so real---if this threat is so imminent, why then doesn't your President talk with me about this? If it does not require his personal conversation with me, why should I listen to his emissary who is just a Colonel?"

"It's not the messenger that's important, but the message. Before you dismiss me, you should listen to some of these tapes."

Lucas slammed one into the hand-held tape player and turned the volume up.

"That, sir, is the voice of your Minister of Defense. He is talking to a Mr. Yamamoto in Tokyo. The government they are talking about is yours. Their instrument of revolt is your military. The operation will begin on the fourth of July."

Lopez shut up and listened for the next several minutes and then announced, "I will arrest my Minister of Defense. Thank you for bringing his disloyalty to my attention."

They were back to that. The anticipated response, but this son-of-a-bitch wasn't asking a question, he was telling him what he was going to do. Lucas judged it was time to play a little hardball. "Mr. President, that would be unwise for several reasons. First, you would in all likelihood not stop the *coup* currently threatening your country. You will remove your Minister of Defense but someone else will take over from him. You have no idea how deep this revolt runs in your military. In fact, Mr. President, you didn't know anything about this revolution until we brought it to your attention. I have more information Mr. President, but I will not show you anything more if you choose to act so rashly."

"You forget where you are..." Lopez was beginning to bluster.

It was Lucas' turn to interrupt. He held up his hand. "Mr. President, this may be hard for you to understand, but you should try. The US does not care one bit about your country economically or militarily."

"You impertinent bastard..."

"Call me what you will, Mr. President, it does not change the fact that your country represents only political capital for us. If you fail to cooperate with us in the effort to defeat these rebels, we will leave you to your own devices, which, I assure you will be insufficient to defeat the revolt facing you. Remember, I have an idea how deep the disloyalty runs in your military---you do not. If you do something stupid, you will make an enemy of the US forever, but more importantly, President Lopez, for once you might want to consider your actions as they relate to other countries in the region. If you spoil our element of surprise, you will also spoil it in Japan, South Korea, and Thailand as well."

Lopez was seething as he spit something out in Tagalog.

Johnson continued unrelenting, "If you spoil our one edge, our only advantage, the US will make your impertinence well known to everyone in the region. You will have no credibility with us and, more importantly, if by some miracle you manage to survive, you will lack credibility with the other nations of this region, regardless of who survives. Make your choice very carefully, Mr. President. It will have lasting effect upon your country and you personally."

Lucas was staring at the President now. He was not cowed at all by this man. Few people had ever pissed off Lucas Johnson as badly as President Teddy Lopez of the Philippines.

"You are blackmailing me, Colonel Johnson."

"Call it what you will, Mr. President. If I have your agreement, I will share more information with you. If you aren't interested, then I will..."

"Show me what you have."

"Your agreement first, Mr. President."

"What have the others said?"

Lucas recapped for him. Lopez stood in front of his massive desk with his back to Lucas for what seemed an interminable length of time.

"You have my agreement."

"And I have your agreement that you will not discuss this with anyone else?"

There was no response.

"Mr. President we have no agreement until I have your answer."

"Yes...Yes...all right."

Lucas simply nodded. He didn't trust Lopez. He had wrung an agreement out of him; he had built the coalition, but he told McKeever and Munson over a secure satellite connection exactly what had taken place in Lopez's office. So far Lopez was the coalition's weakest link. If surprise was going to be lost, Lucas' money was on Lopez to be the guy who would spoil it.

Chapter Thirty-six

It was noon on the third of July in Washington D.C. In the Pacific Rim, the clock was just about to roll over to the fourth of July. Glover sat at his desk in the Oval Office while Tim Munson nervously paced back and forth in front of him. The cat was about to be let out of the bag.

Each of the first three calls went almost as Munson and Glover had thought they would. Glover didn't debate the validity of his information with his counterparts from China, Vietnam and Malaysia, although in each instance that was exactly what each had wanted to do. Glover chalked it up to natural instinct to deny news like this as too improbable, too radical, simply impossible. After all, that had been what he'd wanted to do. When they started, Glover would interrupt them and advise, "You don't have the time to debate with me. If you want to debate with someone, try one of these people…" and then he would give them the names of their countrymen implicated by Paul Stanley's confession.

North Korea was the last call to be made. It took an unexpected turn. The White House operator had placed it when Munson told her to, but when the call wasn't forwarded into the Oval Office, Munson became impatient and called the communications center back.

"Is there a problem with the North Korean call?"

"Uh, Mr. Munson, Uh…"

"What is it?" he said, the impatience rising in his voice.

"He doesn't want to talk to you."

"What?"

"They told me that he was busy and didn't want to talk to you. I'm sorry, Mr. Munson…"

"You dumb, fucking bastard!" It was his first thought and he hadn't intended to say it aloud; it just slipped out.

"Sir?" The operator thought he meant her. Munson started to laugh.

"Sir, what did you call me?" There was a rising indignation in the operator's voice.

"No, not you." He was laughing harder now. He'd gotten a mental picture of this little dwarf sitting in his palace in North Korea playing with himself while the North Korean Army is outside about to burn the damned place down. It was comedic. He couldn't stop laughing. Glover stared at his National Security Advisor. Munson covered the mouthpiece of the phone, "He doesn't want to talk to you Mr. President. He's busy." Glover saw the irony and broke into laughter. Munson's hand was still tight over the mouthpiece so the operator couldn't hear the laughter.

Indignant at Munson's language, but accepting that his remark hadn't been intended for her, she asked, "Shall I keep trying?"

His hand remained clasped over the mouthpiece, "She," he paused to laugh at the absurdity of the little prick's indifference, "she wants to know if she should keep trying."

Glover howled.

The operator thought she'd somehow lost the connection. "Mr. Munson?"

Munson gathered himself. She wasn't the butt of their joke, but she'd been the perfect straight man.

"Yes," he strained to keep his voice under control. " I mean no. If he's too busy to talk to the President, then we don't want to interrupt his busy day." Glover erupted again; only this time the operator heard him through her earpiece. She'd handled many presidential calls before but never one like this.

"If he calls back, shall I put him through?" Again, it was the perfect straight line.

"No. If the idiot calls back, just tell him it's too late." He barely got it out before he cracked up. Glover heard the answer, imagined the question and put his head down on his desk, near tears.

The city began to wake up, and with that came noise, not that Beijing was ever without noise. That was, of course, impossible in a city of this size, a population measured in the tens of millions and half of these possessing motor scooters powered by cheaply built, two cylinder gasoline engines that provided amazing miles per gallon but also produced most of the pollution that clouded the sky. The predawn sky on the fourth of July was the same as it always is when the dawn of a nice day breaks over Beijing; a kind of murky piss-yellow sky hung over the city. Eventually it would become sunny, but not until the sun climbed high enough so that its rays could burn through the haze and smog.

People living around Tienemen Square were accustomed to all of this: the noise and the acrid air, a pungent mix of garbage, industrial pollution, gasoline fumes and cooking odors. If cities could have a heart, Beijing's would be Tienemen Square.

This morning, however, the noises were different. Loud pops recurred on schedule, which distinguished them from the random backfires of the motor scooters that were now finding their ways onto Beijing's crowded streets. Those with some curiosity and an eye for detail timed the interval. When they'd first begun, the pops were three to four minutes apart. Now, a half hour or so after they'd begun, they were occurring at about two minute intervals, as if the mechanism that was creating them had reached a maximum peak of efficiency after some warming up and now was functioning exactly as it should.

Older residents living in the sector of the city reaching out a mile on each side of the huge square tended to stay inside. The older ones knew what the sound was. Curiosity, however, is an affliction of youth, and as the sun rose and brought full light to Beijing, the crowd forming around a place in the center of the famous square was a fairly young one that grew bigger with each passing minute. Periodically a truck, with its horn blasting and a loud speaker blaring, would part the gathered masses and roll into the cordoned-off center of the Square. The incoming cargo was human, officers, many of them high-ranking, from the People's Army or Air Force. Sometimes there were as few as two or three, other loads carried twenty to twenty-five. All had their feet shackled and their hands bound behind their backs. Some fell from the high bed of the truck and hit the ground like a sack of grain. Guards were intolerant of this kind of clumsiness, of any talking or lagging behind, and would prod their prisoners with bayonets, forcing them into a line that moved forward at a slow but steady rate. Nearly all of the prisoners had puncture wounds from the prodding bayonets. If an artery or a vein gushed blood, it was of little consequence. Once this human cargo reached the other end of the queue, blood lost while waiting in line wouldn't matter.

Spectators didn't stay long, usually just through one volley; the more jaded would stay for two or three. Few lasted longer. Six at a time were moved from the head of the line to a point directly at Tienemen's center. The stone there was now drenched in the blood of those who had gone before. Unceremoniously, the prisoners were made to kneel. If they didn't bow their head forward, their executioner, a People's Army soldier, would bang it with the butt of his rifle until it was canted downward at a seemingly contrite angle. This had less to do with any final act of contrition and more to do with the safety of the spectators who literally ringed the execution square.

An unarmed soldier would bark two commands to the six executioners. At the first command the executioners would take aim at the back of the head in front of their rifle barrel, careful to aim the muzzle down at about a forty-five degree angle. At the second command, the six would fire in unison, their prisoner falling forward behind the bullet that killed them. As the bullets impacted the ground, they sent stones spraying up to fifty feet in front of the massacre. Twelve soldiers stepped forward, two per corpse, one grabbing the bound feet while the other took a grip under the arms. In ugly unison, they moved the corpses to a stack of others located about ten yards from the line of execution. All of their uniforms were completely bloodstained, indicating that they took turns handling the bloody head-end. Occasionally the single bullet would miss its mark, however slightly, usually the result of some spastic attack of panic by the prisoner. This caused a momentary delay in the orderly process they'd established as the executioner chambered a second round, more carefully positioned the rifle's muzzle and pulled the trigger a second time. This disruption to their efficiency would trigger catcalls from the clean-up crew who would jokingly cast aspersions on the executioner's ability as a marksman. The humor amidst all of this blood and gore provided a true commentary on the value of life in this country.

Trucks repositioned near the stack of corpses after they unloaded their live cargo. Six soldiers in equally bloodstained uniforms loaded corpses into the truck. The supply of bodies into the stack always exceeded the transportation assets to remove them. A stack of corpses was always waiting; this provided a not-so-subtle message of who was in charge of the country and what price any one challenging the government would pay. The Premier had personally directed this small, but very noticeable detail.

A gallows with three nude corpses hanging from it stood at one end of the cordoned off area. Stones, kicked up by the executioner's bullets, landed near the base of the gallows, as if the executioners were in some grotesque way further mocking the traitors who hung there. This bit of symbolism was the genius of the People's Army two-star general who'd spent the first half hour or so of executions carefully moving the line of execution to exactly the right place. He'd been promoted to that rank only four hours earlier by the Premier himself, and was further promised another two-stars if the existing government survived.

A huge sign labeled the three hanging corpses as "Traitors to the People's Republic". The finer print read, "Hung here to watch their fellow traitors die". The true fact of the matter is that these three were dead before they'd been hung up there: Paul Stanley's colleague, China's Minister of Culture; the Chief of Staff of the Peoples' Army and the Chief of Staff of the Peoples' Air Force. Their eyes were gouged out, their genitals mutilated, a fine red line of blood ran from their ear canals, the result of needles being slowly pushed far into the inner ear. All three had died slow, horrible deaths and in the process vomited names and their names had in turn given up names so that the execution line in Tienemen Square was never without a wait of at least a few minutes.

At noon, the Chinese government let the first television cameras into the Square. No attempt was made to cover up the horror happening there. The government took the position that it was accountable only to itself, and this was the price of survival. Pictures began streaming out of Beijing for all the world to see. The problem was that in seven other countries in the Pacific Rim, people were too busy with events at home to care about what was happening in China.

Vietnam handled Glover's news in a similar but much less public manner than China. Hundreds of executions occurred, many of them on the grounds of the old Presidential Palace in Ho Chi Minh City. The high walls around the palace kept prying eyes out, but the volleys of fire could be heard for blocks. Trucks arriving with live cargo and departing with corpses were telltale evidence of what was going on inside.

In Malaysia, the Prime Minister chose to hunker down along with his cabinet. In an emergency cabinet meeting called at 1:00A.M. Japan Standard Time, he confronted his Minister of Defense, Malaysia's member of the *association*. That man was now in his death throes in a nearby prison where some rather ghoulish steps were taken to get him to talk. First his seven children were summarily executed in front of him. They made him watch while his wife was gang raped and her throat slit. Then his tormentors turned their attention to him. He'd added more names to the list Glover had supplied, but little life remained in him now. At 5:00A.M. the Prime Minister went on TV, denounced the rebels, publicly announced the names of their leaders and put a bounty on the head of every rebel. By 6:00A.M., the time when Operation Light Switch was supposed to kick off, there was little fight left in the Malaysian rebels. By noon, the Prime Minister announced an amnesty plan for every officer in the Malaysian Army in the rank of colonel or below if he swore an oath of loyalty to the existing government in the next twenty-four hours. Martial law was imposed in Kuala Lampur, and by nightfall the streets were empty and quiet.

In Pyongyang, North Korea, someone jabbing him with the barrel of a rifle rousted the Premier out of an alcohol-induced sleep. The three Filipino girls, naked, drunk and asleep with him screamed as they were led one way, while Kim was escorted in another. At noon, the North Korean Ambassador to Japan, Stanley's colleague, announced that he would lead the country to change. There was no mention in his remarks about the *association* or North Korea's part in anything called Operation Light Switch. When asked what happened to Kim Jong Il, he merely said, "He is unavailable for comment and will have no part in the operation of North Korea's government from this day forward."

Mid-day in the Pacific Rim is mid-night in the US. While all of this was happening in the broad daylight of the fourth of July in the Pacific Rim, America slept. She would awake expecting a peaceful holiday, a time to relax, enjoy friends, family and just take things easy. It was good that she rested, because when she would awake she would need all of her energy for the days, weeks and months that lay ahead of her.

Chapter Thirty-seven

Cleve Spires could hear Atherton spinning through the stations on the battery-powered radio, trying to find a station that would reconnect them with civilization. He wasn't having much luck, but Spires admired his doggedness. This was a ritual with Atherton; he'd try and find a station four, sometimes five times a day. Most of the time he struck out. Since they were tucked half way down a mountainside with mountains surrounding them, few radio waves strayed near the cabin, and when they did they didn't stick around very long. The longest he'd ever held a station was ten minutes and then he'd strained to hear and had to fill in blanks of two or three seconds. That had been three days ago.

Despite the natural beauty of where they were, Atherton hated their isolation and he'd been vocal about that. Spires suffered in silence. He hated it even more. Liott and Daniel were constantly on his mind. He knew about the danger ahead for Thailand and he knew what the US was planning to do about it. He'd even asked Admiral McKeever to allow him to be a part of the US force placed on the ground in Thailand, but the Admiral had rejected that idea immediately. In retrospect, he'd even gone so far as to regret Johnson's intervention on his behalf. If he had gone to the Disciplinary Barracks as McKeever had first suggested, at least he would have had access to radio and television.

In the other room, he heard Atherton mutter, "Shit!" He heard a few more stations come for a second and then fade to nothing. He looked at his watch, it was nearly 6:00AM Mountain Standard Time on the fourth of July. Atherton would give up in a minute and they would start their day without knowing what the hell was happening in the world.

Lieutenant Colonel Darrell Greene had made his first contact with Colonel Pramrashorn Saraveet on June 30th. Saraveet had trouble at first believing what Greene had to say, but that had been anticipated. Greene told Saraveet, "Go to Chuk Ra Met. There is a woman there. Her name is Sanji."

Saraveet shot back, "You know about her?"

"I do. Sergeant Major Spires knows she is safe in Chuk Ra Met. He's asked us to check on her and we did. Spires arranged for her to hide there. A driver by the name of Tradip brought her there from Bangkok. She will tell you that no one else knows where she is except Spires and another woman by the name of Tomichi, Michiko Tomichi. Sergeant Major Spires says to believe everything I tell you. When this is over he wants to come home to his wife and son."

His facts were right and they were facts that Cleve Spires wouldn't give to anyone that he didn't trust. That was good enough for Saraveet.

Next, Saraveet met with his officers, first individually and then in a group. They weren't part of what was about to happen in Bangkok. Tucked away in Korat Province, two hundred and fifty miles from the center of revolt, revolution's tentacles hadn't reached the Tiger Brigade yet. He gave his officers a choice. He was very clear about what was at stake. If they succeeded, little changed. If they failed, they'd be marked for elimination. To the man, they chose to oppose the rebels. Darrell Greene watched Saraveet and his officers as they went through this decision process. Initially, he was concerned that someone would bolt and compromise their secret presence in Thailand. Later, he watched in awe and admired the rapport Saraveet had with his officers and their men.

By the second of July, the Tiger Brigade had infiltrated Bangkok. Their mission was as symbolic as it was key. The Tiger Brigade, an element of the Royal Thai Army, was to defend the Royal Palace against the rebel force. More than anything else, the King and the Palace represented the current government of Thailand: eliminate them and the rebels could claim that they were now in control.

The rebel's plan called for two columns of tanks and armored personnel carriers full of troops to surround the palace. Once they'd encircled it, the troops aboard the armored personnel carriers would dismount, invade the palace grounds and capture the royal family. The palace was guarded, but the guards were ceremonial for the most part. They were armed only with pistols; they carried only minimal amounts of ammunition. The rebels would have had an overwhelming advantage in numbers of troops and firepower. What they hadn't planned on was Paul Stanley's defection. Darrell Greene and Pram Saraveet knew exactly what they had planned. More importantly they knew exactly what they had to do to counter it.

Greene gave Saraveet his best explosives expert, who had spent the last two nights working with some of Saraveet's soldiers disguised as laborers working on sewer lines. What they were really doing was installing the latest anti-armor mines along the routes the armored columns would use to approach the palace. These mines were discriminate, meaning that they weren't active until a switch on a remote unit activated them. The mines were attached to the bottom of manhole covers conveniently located every fifty meters or so down the center of both avenues.

At 6:00A.M.on the 4th , the sun was just beginning to peek above the horizon when Greene's spotter, located on the roof of the Palace, saw the first column moving forward. A minute or so later he saw the first signs of the second column. Patience now was the key. He alerted Saraveet by radio that the columns were in sight. The Tiger Brigade soldier standing next to Saraveet held the remote unit that would activate the mines. The spotter let both columns advance until their lead tanks were less than a hundred meters from the palace, and then he whispered into his radio, "Now."

Saraveet nodded to the soldier next to him who flicked a switch; a red light glowed on the top of the remote control unit. Ten seconds later, with near simultaneous precision, the lead tank of each column rolled over the rigged manhole covers closest to the palace. Direct pressure on the mines wasn't necessary for detonation. The tank treads were actually on either side of the charges that they detonated. Vibration from the tank's engine and its treads on the roadway set the mine off. Within seconds of this first blast, others down the two armored columns began to detonate as the tanks or armored personnel carriers rolled over the rigged covers. The explosions were so close to one another that it almost seemed to be just one explosion. Windows for two blocks were shattered, including many in the Royal Palace. For many more blocks the shockwave rattled windows, shelves and their contents.

The rebel's neat, orderly advance was immediately reduced to chaos. Tanks and armored personnel carriers were reduced to flaming hulks that momentarily would become lethal fireworks as the ammunition inside cooked off in the fires that consumed them. The unlucky crew members and passengers in those vehicles hitting the mines perished almost instantly. The more fortunate were trapped in vehicles between these infernos. Doors and hatches flew open and troops flooded out, moving at random along whatever path they thought would allow them to escape the growing inferno around the long column of armored vehicles. These rebel troops thought safety lay beyond the flames. It didn't. The Tiger Brigade saw to that.

Saraveet's men began to close in on either side of the two columns, collapsing tighter and tighter down on the rebels, driving them to a position between the two avenues they had once thought they could so convienently use. Warning shots were fired over their dazed heads as Saraveet's troops commanded them to throw their weapons down and surrender peacefully; the rebellion had no chance of success. For the most part they complied; the few who didn't were shot. Fewer than ten chose to die like this. The death toll in the still-burning tanks and armored personnel carriers would drive the human cost of this engagement considerably higher, but this was war. As wars go casualties and fatalities were low.

Saraveet called the fire department as soon as he was convinced the scene at the Palace was stable. The first unit responded thirty minutes after the first tank had gone up in flames. Within an hour nearly every fire unit in Bangkok was at or on its way to the Royal Palace. In a city with a population density of Bangkok's, fires like this were always terrible and this one would get worse before it got better.

The tanks carried as part of their basic load of ammunition some old white phosphorous rounds, a particularly nasty anti-personnel ammunition. Upon impact the bullet's warhead would explode and spread white phosphorous for twenty to twenty five meters in every direction from the point of contact. Upon contact with air, the white phosphorous would burst into flames, and from that point on it was almost impossible to extinguish. It would burn anything or anyone in its path with white hot intensity. The burning rubble which now surrounded these rounds kept most of the white phosphorous contained inside the flaming wreckage. However, one round cooked off in the tremendous heat. The propellant sent the phosphorous-filled warhead flying out of the wreckage through an unluckily open hatch. The warhead shot skyward almost as if it had been shot from the tank's cannon. The trajectory of the round carried it a distance of three blocks eastward and two blocks in a southerly direction and it impacted nearly in the middle of a two block long splinter village.

Bangkok abounds with these splinter villages. They are the temporary homes of construction workers who work on projects throughout the crowded city. They're built to last only the duration of the project and out of literally any material that can be found. This particular splinter village, not Bangkok's largest, but certainly not the city's smallest either, held nearly five thousand people on the morning of July 4th. Half of them died. Twenty-five hundred of Bangkok's poorest men, women and children never had even the slightest chance to escape the flash inferno that erupted and burnt itself out before the first available fire truck could even get close to it. A local TV station captured the horror entirely on film.

Thirty thousand feet above Bangkok, an Air Force RC-130 was flying wide lazy orbits. The pilots saw the two long lines of burning armored vehicles. They saw the white phosphorous round emerge from the middle of one of the columns of fire, and they saw the fire created by the impact of that round. They were too high to see what it had hit, but they commented to one another about how quickly the fire had spread. The pilot-in-command punched his intercom button and alerted his crew, who were hard at work at consoles in the aircraft's mid-section. "It's started. Looks like Bangkok's on fire. Get ready to block on my mark." Two minutes passed. The pilots watched the fire in the splinter village spread to nearly four times its original size. "On my mark." Thirty seconds later, "Mark."

Every radio and television station in Bangkok and its suburbs went to dead air. Technicians and engineers on the ground scurried around trying to find the difficulty.

Two minutes after he'd blocked their signal, the colonel alerted his crew again, "On my mark begin broadcast." Thirty seconds elapsed and then, "Mark."

Radios and televisions came back to life, but not with familiar shows and personalities. The audio and the picture came from the rear end of the C-130, where a US Air Force airman, speaking in Thai, told them, ""Citizens of Thailand, today a military operation has begun with the full cooperation of your country's government. Enemies of your freedom will attempt to capture the King and Queen and to take over other government offices. They may even attempt to take over your place of business. The United States, with the full cooperation of your government, has placed Special Operations forces in your country to help defend against rebel attacks."

"Remain at home. Travel today only as necessary. If you encounter US Forces, give them your complete cooperation. They are there to protect you from harm. Please stay tuned for an announcement from His Highness, The King."

The videotaped announcement was quickly cued up. Their beloved King reassured his countrymen, "Citizens of Thailand. As you hear this, know that I am safe, as is the rest of the royal family. I assure you this message is real. I am under no coercion by anyone or anything except the urgency of time and the laws of morality. There will be an illegal and immoral attempt made this morning to take over the government of this country. The US is helping us to resist the rebels. I ask that you give them and members of the Royal Thai Army's Tiger Brigade your complete cooperation."

There was a pause while the King shifted forward and moved closer to the camera. "If you are one of the revolutionaries, I urge you to rethink what you are doing. You only know half of the story. The half that has been hidden from you takes away your freedom. There is a reason why the leaders of the revolution have not told you about this part of their plans. Can you trust leadership that would conceal such vital information from you?"

"By this time tomorrow night, it is my earnest hope I can speak to you on live television and tell you this threat is behind us and your government remains safe. In the meantime, please cooperate fully with US Forces. They are here as our allies and they are our best defense until I am able to determine how deep the roots of rebellion run. I assure you, your government will deal quickly yet fairly with the rebels." The TV screens and radio airways went blank, but only momentarily as the entire message would be rebroadcast again and again throughout the day.

By noon on the fourth of July, Darrell Greene, with a reinforced Special Forces Operational Team, secured the Royal Thai Army Command Center about ten blocks from the Royal Palace. There was one fatality; Paul Stanley's Thai colleague from the *association* was found with a bullet through his head. The Chief of Staff of the Royal Thai Army claimed it was a suicide, but later forensics would prove that the round that killed Stanley's associate came from the Chief of Staff's own .45 caliber pistol, the one taken from him at the time of his capture.

By 6:00PM, sooner than anyone had ever anticipated, the King of Thailand appeared on live television announcing the capture of rebel leaders. He declared that the current government was fully in charge of affairs of state. He credited the Tiger Brigade and the American First Special Forces Battalion as being the decisive force that turned back the rebels. He had with him, throughout the broadcast, Colonel Pramrashorn Saraveet and Lieutenant Colonel Darrell Greene.

Atherton was getting frustrated, and was about to give up on finding a station that would produce anything useful when he finally fixed on one and heard, "There are..." static interfered, "...firmed reports of mass executions taking place in Beijing and..." more static, longer this time, he was loosing the station, "...similar activity in Ho Chi..." And then it was gone. Atherton filled in the blanks, *confirmed reports of mass executions in Beijing and the same in Ho Chi Minh City*.

He got up and headed for the front porch, where he thought Spires was probably sitting. The two met one another in about the center of the cabin. Atherton asked, "Did you hear that?"

"I did. Can you get it back?"

Atherton fiddled with the dial some more but got nothing. "This damned thing." He threw it into a stack of pillows on the sofa next to him. "What's going on, Sergeant Major? The Chinese and Vietnamese are killing people. Why?"

"It's started, Gunny."

"What's started?"

Spires turned around and looked at him. "Well, it's time you knew..." Spires told him his story.

Midway through Atherton interrupted him, "Sergeant Major, let's go into town. This is history in the making. Sounds like you're a part of it. If I can't be a part of it, I'd at least like to see what I'm missing."

On the thirty minute drive into White Birch, Spires finished filling Atherton in. As they pulled into the parking lot of the Moose Breath Bar, Spires said, "That's it. You know as much about this as I do."

"What do you think will happen to General Stanley?"

"Court-martial."

It wasn't odd that the Moose Breath was the only thing open in this town of never more than two hundred. What *was* odd was that it was open at all. Inside, they found a bartender, one old guy in the corner with his head down on the table and a half-gone bottle of George Dickel in front of him. ESPN Classic was on the TV, replaying some USC-Notre Dame football game that at some point in sports' history was pivotal but was truly now insignificant in light of what was going in other parts of the world.

Atherton asked the bartender, "Not much going on in town this time of night, is there?"

Without looking up he muttered, "Nope."

Undeterred by the indifference, "You're open. How come?"

This time the bartender looked up. He pointed to the guy at the table in the corner. "He's the owner. As long as he's here, we're open."

"But he's asleep."

"Long as he pays me, know what I mean?" The bartender flashed a wry smile, indicating that he wasn't as stupid as he looked, and with that Atherton decided he'd gone about as far with White Birch logic as he wanted to.

"Buy you a beer, Gunny?"

"Sure, Sergeant Major." Atherton saw the TV remote control laying on the bar and he gravitated to a seat directly in front of it. He picked it up, pointed it at the TV and flicked through a few channels until he came to CNN. A commercial was in progress. The bartender had a disappointed look on his face, as if the outcome of the rerun was important in the present. Atherton caught the look and hoped the guy knew he'd been watching a replay.

When CNN returned to what they did best, they didn't disappoint the audience at the Moose Breath Bar. The three who were conscious watched the guards at Tienemen Square peel six men off the head of the line, move them to a spot and kneel them down. The camera panned back and the executioners came into sight. There were fifteen, maybe twenty seconds to anticipate what was going to happen next. The sound equipment picked up the soldier who barked the two commands that proceeded each execution, but the three at the Moose Breath had gone deaf. The video was so graphic, the action so grotesque, that the audio feed was lost on them until the shots, which sounded like a single shot. The audience at the Moose Breath Bar flinched as the six victims rocked forward and onto their sides. The camera had panned in close enough for them to see the blood erupt from the front of the victims' heads, as the bullets that had just scrambled their brains emerged out of the other side. They saw the stones fly up. The camera panned to the three corpses hanging from the gallows.

The bartender, who was least prepared for what they'd just witnessed said, "Jesus, what the hell is going on over there?" He looked at Spires and Atherton, not expecting an answer. Imagine his surprise when they filled him in.

If Thailand had gone well, Japan was even easier. At midnight on 3 July, Japan Standard Time, Lieutenant Colonel Dave Ellison and Colonel Lucas Johnson led simultaneous raids on Cato Fujiwara's penthouse residence in Tokyo and Seito Yamamoto's estate on Tokyo's western fringe. Ellison's raid was completely unresisted. He found Cato Fujiwara working at his desk. The top five floors of the skyscraper were completely unoccupied, except for a couple of accountants who immediately threw down their pencils and stopped manipulating their calculators at the command of Ellison's soldiers. Apparently all of his minions were out preparing for their morning takeover of Japan's governmental offices and major corporations.

At Yamamoto's estate, Johnson's team kicked in the front door at about the same time helicopters landed Ellison on the skyscraper. They were prepared for more, but all they really expected to net from this raid was Fukora and Yamamoto. The world would marvel at what they found.

The man-servant Fukora was killed outright as he charged to the front of the house with a 9mm pistol in his hand. Yamamoto was more cunning. He grabbed a sword and ducked through a door leading to the estate's sprawling basement. Johnson and his team searched the remainder of the house's main floor and found only the big friendly Doberman. One of the team secured it in a room while they regrouped.

"He could have gone out a window."

"The guys outside would have gotten him and we would have heard." The estate was surrounded by a reinforced Operational Team. Lucas asked, "Does this place have a basement?" They quickly organized a search, and within a minute the call came over their radio earpiece, "I've got the door. Rear of the house near the communications suite."

Johnson said, "Roger that. Wait for us. We'll go down together."

At the top of the stairs Johnson told them to put on their night vision goggles. When he had a thumbs up from each, he turned off the lights at the top of the steps and the basement fell into complete darkness.

When the lights went out, Seito Yamamoto flinched. He couldn't see anything. His hand tightened around the old sword he'd taken with him. It gave him some reassurance, as did his ability to see at least the outline of the stacks around him, as his night vision began to adjust to the total darkness in the basement.

"Jesus Christ."

Johnson's hackles went up on his neck: he waited to hear more, but it didn't come. He said into the radio mouthpiece positioned in front of his lips, "What is it?"

"Sir, do you know what these stacks are?" He recognized the voice now. It was his youngest team member.

"Yeah, they're gold. Now get your mind on what we came down here for."

The technology was amazing. With the exception of some loss of depth perception, they were able to see in that pitch-black basement. They had split into two teams of two men each. They were moving down parallel aisles. Johnson warned the other three members of the search party, "Keep a good interval. Yamamoto's probably alone down here, but he knows this place better than we do. Don't let him get two of us with one bullet." They spread out more. About every ten meters, they would come to a cross aisle that intersected the aisle they were proceeding down at a right angle. As near as they could tell, the damned place was full of gold ingots in neat stacks that reached from floor to ceiling and went on for as far as---well, as far as night vision goggles could see. Amidst this vast wealth, all Lucas Johnson could think of was how many hiding places these stacks created for Yamamoto.

Yamamoto heard his footfalls before he could make out the shadow. Lucas Johnson was close to him now. Like a cat, Yamamoto moved back into the shadows of a crossing aisle and let Johnson pass. Then he stepped out behind him and raised the sword high above his head. He drew an aim for the middle of the form, imagining that to be about in the middle of this intruder's shoulder blades.

Just as Yamamoto lunged at Johnson's back, a shot ripped through the back of Yamamoto's head. The impact of the round and the tumbling effect as it moved through his skull scrambled his brains. As he instantly lost all motor coordination, the sword drooped harmlessly downward while the impact of the round carried him clumsily into Lucas Johnson who had spun around out of instinct as the shot rang out. The hackles on Johnson's back weren't just standing now. They felt like they were crawling all over him. Yamamoto was dead by the time he collided with Lucas, but the impact of the round propelled him enough and his weight was dead enough that it knocked Johnson backwards and he fell. Yamamoto fell on top of him. All Johnson could say was, "Shit, I needed that son of a bitch alive."

The young Green Beret who fired the shot thought Johnson was pissed at him for killing this guy.

"I'm sorry, sir. Is that Yamamoto?"

Before Lucas could answer, the soldier went on. "He got behind you. Must have come out of here," he pointed to a crossing aisle. " I didn't have time to warn you. By the time I could see him in my goggles, he had the sword up. I just let him have it. I'm sorry. I didn't know what else to do."

Johnson was getting his feet back underneath him.

"It's OK, Sarge. If it weren't for you, I'd be a shish-ka-bob right now. Sergeant Major, turn the lights on and let's check this place out and see if anyone else is in here."

There wasn't.

At precisely 6:00AM another group of RC-130's in orbit over Japan began transmitting a message over Japanese national television very similar to the one in Thailand. Operational teams were deployed and waiting at government offices throughout Tokyo. and at the corporate headquarters of Japan's fifty largest corporate headquarters. In most locations, no one ever showed up to oppose them. Pete Rentz had predicted that once the shooting started, the men would quickly be separated from the boys. He also predicted the *Yakuza* would be more boys than men, but even Rentz was surprised at how easily they had given in. By noon, the Prime Minister went on TV and assured the Japanese people that his government remained firmly in control. He announced that Cato Fujiwara had been taken into custody and was likely to be charged with treason.

Seichu Mori, Japan's Minister of Industry and Technology sat at home as he'd been instructed in the television broadcasts from the C-130. He felt a little quesy when he heard Cato Fujiwara was in custody. The two were illegal business partners, had been for many years. Together they'd made millions from insider information that Mori came by in his cabinet position. He knew what industries were going to get which lucrative government contracts, what technologies the government was going to underwrite next and he knew all of this months before the general public. He would simply tell Cato Fujiwara, who would then invest both his money and Mori's appropriately---and, of course, illegally. On one hand, he was sad to think the cash cow might have died. On the other, he was concerned Fujiwara might incriminate him. Seichu Mori kept a close ear to the news.

Tim Munson sat at his desk in the White House and bit his lip. Jonas Pastor was on the other end of the phone line and he was pissed. "That little prick put us all at risk. We need to do something about this and we need to do it right now."

"Jonas, I know you're mad. I am too, but the bottom line is that it worked as well in the Philippines as it did in Thailand and we can't complain about that."

Munson was right. So was Pastor. Teddy Lopez put the whole thing at risk and for that he *was* a prick. But the Major General he'd confided in either wasn't a rebel, or he was, but he was more of an opportunist, so he crossed back over to the government side. At any rate, unbeknownst to the US Special Forces in the Philippines, two brigades from the division commanded by the Major General that Lopez had trusted, reinforced them. The rebels were crushed quickly; many died, some shot in the back. Philippine soldiers fighting for Lopez counted only a few wounded. There were no American casualties in this brief little war in the Philippines.

Once his government was secure, Teddy Lopez turned his thoughts toward revenge. Unlike China and Vietnam, however, his revenge would not be played out in front of prying eyes. Five hundred men, mostly high ranking officers in the Philippine Army were rounded up by 6:00 PM on the fourth of July. They were now on their way to a ship that would transport them to a remote island three hundred miles away. There each would dig a hole deep enough that they could stand in it with only their head protruding above the ground. Their guards would then fill in the holes.

The officer-in-charge of this miserable detail asked, "What shall I do if they don't dig?"

Lopez screamed at him, "Then dig for them. I don't care how you do it. Shoot their balls off if you'd like. But don't kill them. I want them alive when you plant them in their holes. I want these bastards to suffer."

One hundred soldiers were handpicked to guard the five hundred rebel prisoners. They could never talk about what they would see or do. For their silence they would receive a cash reward and rapid promotions. Lopez's last instruction to the officer-in-charge was, "Call me when the last has died. I want to come to this field-of-heads and see if any are smiling now."

For those Lopez ordered buried, it would be seven days of agony before that call would come.

Chapter Thirty-eight

At 2:00AM on the fourth of July the bartender at the Moose Breath announced that it was closing time. CNN was just beginning to report on events taking place in Japan, South Korea, the Philippines and Thailand. Atherton looked over his shoulder and pointed to the owner, who was still asleep with his head down on the table, "What about him?"

"I leave him just like that, almost every night."

Spires said, "Listen, we've been out of touch for the past couple of weeks. Where we're staying we can't even get radio. What's it worth to you, just to lock us in here?"

"Naw, Mister, I can't do…"

Spires produced a roll of bills, and placed a hundred dollars on the bar. The bartender glanced back at the sleeping owner, "He won't like it if he wakes up and finds the two of you…"

Spires put another hundred on the bar and said, "Don't worry about him. We'll work it out with him. We're honest men. We'll pay you for whatever we drink---give you a deposit up front," he added fifty to the pot. The bartender took all two hundred and fifty dollars and stuffed it down into his jeans' pocket. "One more thing before you go," Spires said, "sell me twenty dollars worth of quarters. I've got a couple of phone calls I need to make."

The bartender counted out the change, after which Atherton followed him to the door and turned the lock behind him. Then they both sat glued to CNN. When Spires heard the fighting in Thailand had largely been confined to Bangkok, he looked at Atherton and said, "I'll be back in a few minutes. I'm going to make a couple of calls."

The military theorist Clausewitz coined the term *the fog of war* three hundred years ago in his treatise *On War.* Certainly the smoke and haze that hangs over a battlefield after thousands of soldiers have fired their cannons and their muskets at each other, was part of what Clausewitz was describing. But there was a second meaning to

Clausewitz's term and it has to do with the fuzziness surrounding the picture of war when tactics and politics become mixed together.

The *"fog of war"* settled over South Korea, the Land of the Morning Calm, on the fourth of July. It didn't matter that things had gone so well in Japan, Thailand and the Philippines. In South Korea, things would go horribly and desperately wrong. The root of rebellion was deeper there than elsewhere. The intelligence information that Paul Stanley's confession had yielded had been good, objective information. What was missing was the subjective information. What the US had no way of gauging was the resolve of the South Korean rebels.

In the other countries, when the rebel chain of command lost one of its links, the entire chain simply disintegrated. In South Korea, when the Chief of Staff of the South Korean Army heard that Lee Pak Son, the South Korean associate, had been arrested, he took charge. One phone call was all it took to trigger a horrible chain of events that would blight the Seoul landscape for years to come, and take a terrible toll on two countries' governments. He called the Chief of Staff of the South Korean Air Force and between the two of them, they made the decision that if they couldn't surgically take over the seats of power, then they'd pulverize them and pick up the pieces later. It didn't matter how small those pieces might be or how many innocents might die from collateral damage. Fifteen minutes after that call the first aircraft made its run on Blue House, the South Korean President's residence.

On the roof of Blue House, US Army Special Forces Sergeant Jesus Ortega aimed his shoulder-fired ground-to-air missile at the oncoming jet. He heard the intermittent ping-ping-ping in his earpiece that told him the missile had not yet locked on to the target. He saw the jet launch two missiles at him, at Blue House. The ping-ping-ping changed to a steady tone and he pulled the trigger; the launcher recoiled as the missile raced out of the tube. He felt the impact of one of the two missiles fired at him. It hit the building he was perched on top of, but the strike seemed to leave the residence structurally sound, at least the part he stood on. The second missile missed its mark; he felt nothing. This assessment of his opponent's marksmanship was made in a split second. He never took his eyes off the aircraft that had fired at the residence. He saw his missile hit its mark. His prey erupted in smoke.

Inside the cockpit, the pilot couldn't feel his legs. The smoke around him was so thick he couldn't see his instrumentation, but if he looked up and forward through his windscreen, he could make out Blue House to his front. His plane was mortally wounded and so was he. The cause was just. This South Korean government was too easy on those who didn't think the way he did, the way the generals thought. He pushed the stick forward and aimed his aircraft at the front door.

Ortega saw it coming. He was inside the pilot's mind as he saw the plane nose downward, but there was nothing he could do; there was no time to grab another launcher, aim it, fire it and expect the missile to change the course of the plane. He keyed his radio and said, "He's going to hit..." His transmission ended as the ball of flame that engulfed the South Korean President's residence vaporized him. Twenty members of the Special Forces operational team assigned to defend Blue House perished. So did the South Korean President, his wife and two children, who'd refused all pleas for their evacuation to safer ground. It had been the South Korean President's way of showing confidence in the American forces. It had been his way of showing his confidence in the decision he'd made to accept their help.

Other aircraft swarmed the skies over Seoul, and in the beginning they were all flown by rebel pilots. Each Special Forces Team deployed at various locations throughout Seoul, had a supply of missiles like the one Ortega had used. Not all of them found their mark. Three did and now three fires raged in Seoul where the aircraft had crashed. The odds were working against the Americans. For every aircraft they managed to shoot down, two replaced them in Seoul's airspace.

The Commanding Officer of the Fifth Special Forces Group, a Colonel, like Lucas Johnson, listened and responded to the radio traffic bombarding his command center. The rebels had achieved air superiority, and because of that, his teams were getting their asses handed to them. He needed to turn that around right now. He had an ace back; he only hoped he hadn't waited too long to play it.

The phone rang in the command center. The Commanding General, US Forces Korea, was standing next to it when it rang, but the watch officer picked it up. When the watch officer told the general who it was, he told him to put the call on the speaker, it would save time. Everyone in the room could hear the problem first hand; they could also hear anything the four-star general might want done to solve it.

There was no panic, but everyone in the command center could hear grave concern in the voice of the Fifth Special Forces Commander, "Sir, I need something turned on these aircraft. I've lost four teams so far..."

The Commanding General had a decision to make. He had aircraft available, just minutes away at Osan Air Force Base. He knew there were a dozen of them sitting on the ramp, armed, fueled and ready to go; others could be ready in less than an hour. Their intended purpose, until today, had always been to defend Seoul from North Korean invaders. That was the mission of US Forces Korea, but this wasn't an invasion. This was civil war. He had no direct authorization to commit his forces against South Korean forces.

The General didn't hesitate; US forces were dying, and the President, his Commander-in-Chief, had ordered them there. The President wouldn't want these troops to die like this when he had something that could protect them. He called the Seventh Air Force Command Center at Osan Air Force base and ordered every available fighter scrambled. Their target was easily described, any South Korean military aircraft in the skies over Seoul.

Seoul, Korea is a big city, one of the five largest in the world in terms of population. Its physical size is also impressive, but not when it comes to air-to-air combat. Within thirty minutes of the General's call to Osan, nearly thirty aircraft crowded into the airspace above Seoul, and that number would grow to as many as fifty in a couple of hours. The rebel aircraft no longer had the luxury of rolling in hot on lightly defended ground targets. Now they had to deal with aircraft superior to theirs and flown by pilots who were generally superior. This diversion allowed the Special Forces teams on the ground to redirect their energy back to defending the targets they'd been assigned, against the threat they'd anticipated. At those targets not yet destroyed by rebel aircraft, US forces proved to be formidable. However, the war taking place over their heads now was having its own horrible effect. The city of Seoul was becoming an inferno fueled by shoot-downs that crashed with their heavy loads of jet fuel and explosives into her heavily populated neighborhoods. By 10:00AM every fire station in Seoul was committed to one fire or another, but the jets continued to streak across the sky, putting on an aerial acrobatic show that no one saw, because they were too busy fleeing the fires that were consuming the city. By 10:00AM the number of fires to be fought outnumbered the available fire trucks and fire fighters available to fight them. Untended fires burned furiously out of control, devouring city block after city block inside Seoul.

As daylight ended, so did the aerial acrobatics. The General had by now gone ahead and committed the Second Infantry Division to the ground war effort. US Special Operations Teams were being reinforced in a priority determined by the Commander, Fifth Special Forces Group. For the moment their mission was accomplished. The rebels weren't in charge of anything, and the South Korean Vice President and his cabinet, minus Paul Stanley's colleague, Lee Pak

Son, were now safe in a secure bunker on Yong Son, a US Army installation in the heart of Seoul. They would have to wait and see if the rebels had any more fight left in them. They would have to wait and see if the aircraft would return to the skies in the morning.

Cleve Spires dropped five dollars worth of quarters into the pay phone at the operator's prompt. On the fifth ring a sleepy Ida Spires picked up the receiver.

"Mom, it's Cleveland."

There was a silence while her mind came to grips with who she was talking to.

"Cleveland. Thank God. Where are you? Are you all right? Where have you been?" The questions spewed out of her at rapid-fire rate. He let her go on until she ran out of them.

"I'm safe. Probably best not to say where I am over the phone. The police may have your line tapped. I can't stay on the line too long." He'd become adept at being a fugitive and had survived this long; he wasn't about to become careless at this point. "I don't want you to worry. I'm not sure if I'll get home to see you. There's a lot going on right now. Have you been watching television?"

It was a strange question from him. He knew she didn't watch it very much. "Cleveland, you know I don't…"

"Mom, turn it on. You'll see what I mean when I say 'there's a lot going on'."

"Cleveland, I don't…"

"Mom, have you seen Wanda?"

"Yes, yesterday…"

"Good. Is she all right?"

"She's worried about you. I'll call her and let her…"

"Let me do that, Mom. I owe her that much…" his voice trailed off.

"Cleveland…"

"I've got to go Mom. I don't want them to trace this call. It's still not safe for me. Just remember that I'm OK." He hung up and stood there for a minute while he screwed up his courage to call Wanda and when he was ready he dropped another five dollars in quarters into the slot.

She answered on the third ring. "I'm sorry to wake you."

She recognized his voice immediately.

"Wanda, don't talk just listen. I can't stay on the line long. The police may have your phone tapped. I'm safe; just know that. I know you don't understand and I can't even begin to explain it in this phone call. I'm not coming back to Cleveland like I told you I would. I can't. Maybe someday I can explain to you, but not now. There's not time. I know it doesn't seem like it, but I've actually put my life back in better order. There's just so much going on right now, that it's impossible for me to explain that to you. My life now is elsewhere, but I wanted to call and let you know that I will never forget you, what you did for me. If it weren't for you Wanda..."

She found her voice, "Where are you Cleve? I want to come to you."

"I can't tell you that. It's not a good idea for you to see me. What we had is over. It has to be. I can't explain over the phone. It would take too long and they're listening."

"Who's listening?"

"The police."

"Cleve, don't be..."

"Wanda, I've got to go."

"But..." she heard the click and then the dial tone. She felt sick to her stomach.

In White Birch, Utah, Cleve Spires sat down next to Atherton at the bar. He stared at the bar top. Atherton was watching the first reports on the fires in Seoul, but it wasn't long before he noticed Spires wasn't watching television. He was staring at the bar. "You all right, Sergeant Major?"

He swiveled his head toward Atherton, "No, Gunny, I'm not all right. It's a shit hole world."

The Commander of the Fifth Special Forces Group turned in his casualty report by midnight on the fourth, Japan Standard Time. Three hundred of his soldiers had been killed-in-action. Nearly everyone else who had survived death had been wounded. Twenty-five members of his command were missing-in-action. President Glover was given these numbers exactly one hour before he was to appear before the nation in a televised press conference. He put his elbows on his desk and cradled his head in his hands, looking down at the terrible numbers and asked Munson, "How many South Koreans, Tim? How many of them have died?"

Munson didn't know for sure, but he'd seen the pictures of the scenes in Seoul. He shook his head. When the President looked up he said, "We don't know for sure. It will be days, weeks before we know that."

"Take a guess."

"Mr. President, Seoul's on fire. The number could run in the tens of thousands."

The President returned his head to the hand-cradle that had held it earlier. "How do I tell America about this?"

Chapter Thirty-nine

When the phone rang, Ida Spires' hope was it was her son calling her back. It wasn't. The call was from a nearly inconsolable Wanda Cheevers. The two women cried together over the telephone and tried to piece together the pieces of their two separate, cryptic phone calls from Cleve. He'd told them he was safe, but they didn't believe him. How could he be safe, if he was still running from the police?

When she'd hung up, Ida took her son's advice and turned on the television. She was shocked by what she saw there. It was the fourth of July. It was supposed to be a happy time. Instead, the day reminded her more of September 11th. She remembered how lonely and isolated she'd felt that day. Today that feeling returned but with much greater force.

Ida Spires and Wanda Cheevers had no one else except each other at this point. She redialed Wanda's number. When Wanda answered Ida asked, "Have you see what's on television?"

"No, I was going to take a shower…"

Ida said, "Wanda, it's awful. We're at war. It looks like it's a world war."

"What?"

"Cleve told me to turn on the TV. I did. That's what's on; we're at war."

Wanda was speechless.

"Can you come over? I need to be with someone right now. Wanda, please come. Spend a few days with me."

"Give me a few minutes to put together a few things and I'll be right over, Ida."

"Thank you, Wanda. Please hurry."

They were both sitting in front of Ida's television when CNN's coverage of events in the Pacific Rim was interrupted by a special news bulletin; President Glover was about to convene a press conference. The White House pressroom was jammed with reporters, all talking among themselves. An empty podium stood at the front of the room. French doors at one side of the room, near the podium, swung open and the President of the United States stepped through them. Immediately the room hushed.

Glover took fifteen minutes to explain the rebel plot and the decision that he and his administration had wrestled with for days. His words were carefully chosen, he delivered them well and when he was through he asked for questions. The room broke into a din of shouting as every reporter, even the ones in the back of the room, expected him to call on them first despite the fact that there is a protocol for such things. Glover tried to ignore the chaos and go with the protocol. The senior correspondent in the room was right in front of him and he pointed to her. Already on her feet, she asked her question. He saw her lips move, but he couldn't hear her. The din continued. He looked at his press secretary who started to move forward, but Glover motioned him back. The President stepped away from the podium. For a minute the din continued until the reporters began to organize themselves. They grew quieter and quieter until the room was completely silent.

Glover stepped back to the microphone. "I will stay here and answer as many of your questions as I can, but we are an orderly society, we Americans, and we have clear rules for how we treat one another. I ask that you abide by those rules here today, and I ask that you abide by those rules as you report your stories going forward. You are going to hear some things today that you may not like. Over the past few days, I have had to make some decisions that I didn't like. Nonetheless, I made them and I stand by them. I'm here to explain those decisions to you. Now, Ms Luce, may I have your question again please."

This time there was order. The senior correspondent stood and asked her question. "Mr. President, exactly when and how did we first come to know about all of this?"

Glover glanced over at Munson standing in the wing. Munson nodded. The question was anticipated. An answer had been worked out. "We had two sources of human intelligence. One led us to Japan and the center of the rebel plot. The other supplied us details of their tactical plans."

She asked in follow up, "Can you tell us the names of your sources, Mr. President?"

Again the question was anticipated. Normally, intelligence sources weren't disclosed, but these weren't intelligence agents. Paul Stanley was going to be court-martialed for treason. He could get the death sentence. Spires would be a material witness in the trial. It was all going to come out anyway. There was no reason why it shouldn't come out now.

The President responded, "Sergeant Major Cleveland Spires led us to the information in Japan, and supplied us with information that implicated Major General Paul Stanley as an accomplice to the revolts. General Stanley gave us big pieces of their tactical plan. He was, as I said, their accomplice, and he is now in custody at the US Military Disciplinary Barracks in Fort Leavenworth, Kansas, where he is awaiting trial."

Normally, one follow up question is all any reporter gets and that rule generally includes the senior correspondent, but she pressed her luck. "Where is Spires?"

Glover didn't know, and even if he did, he wouldn't have disclosed his location. "I can't answer that."

When Ida heard the President say Cleve's name her heart raced, every nerve in her body stood on its end. She leaned forward and put her head in her hands and said a silent prayer of thanks.

The phone rang. In tears, Ida answered it; it was a local reporter. He knew the Cleveland Police wanted Cleveland Spires for murder. He'd found her number in the phone book. He asked a couple of questions and she politely answered them, but, when it was obvious that he had a million others, she asked him to call back later and hung up. She'd no sooner put the receiver down than it rang again, another reporter, same questions, same wanting to ask more. At the third call, she disconnected her phone. Her son was safe. That was all she cared about at the moment.

At the Moose Breath Bar, the sleeping owner awoke just as the President's news conference came on. At first, he thought they had broken into the place. He'd begged Spires and Atherton not to hurt him. When they said they had no intention of doing anything like that, that they'd just talked his night bartender into letting them stay there to watch the breaking news, he was so relieved that he put a beer in front of each and asked, "What the hell's going on over there?"

Atherton undertook the job of bringing him up to date, and just as he was finishing, he heard the President say Cleve's name. Cleve heard it too. They exchanged glances. It wouldn't be long before one of the news services came up with a photo of Cleve Spires, and, if the bartender from the night before or this old codger recognized him, it wouldn't be long before the press would be here in White Birch. Neither wanted to leave the news reports; both knew that is exactly what they had to do. It was time to get back to the seclusion of the cabin.

"Where ya' goin'," the bar's owner, now wide-awake, called after them.

"Gotta' go," and the two scrambled out of the place, into their rental car and got out of town as fast as they could. The owner returned to where Atherton and Spires had been sitting, and poured their two half-finished beers into a glass and settled back to watch the rest of the President's press conference.

Glover fought back the impatient urge to tell them exactly what he was thinking.

"What will you say to the families of the US soldiers who have died in this war?" He thought, *My God, what a question. What would you expect me to say? How would you expect me to feel? I ordered them there.* He answered, "Their sons were heroes and a grateful nation thanks them." As he said it, it all sounded so trite to him. The same words Reagan used after the Marine Corps Barracks bombing in Beirut, used again by George H.W. Bush after Desert Storm. Bill Clinton had uttered them after Somalia as did George W. Bush during action in Afghanistan and Iraq. Now it was his turn, and he couldn't be more creative, more eloquent than any of his recent predecessors.

"What will you say to the people of South Korea?" *Why do I need to say anything? They were in trouble; we tried to help. It's the South Korean government that must explain things to the South Korean people, not the US government.* He answered, "The United States expresses its deepest regret for the losses suffered by the people of Seoul. They are a courageous people. They arose like the Phoenix from the ashes of war once, so shall they rise again."

"How will you answer complaints already coming from Capital Hill that you violated the War Powers Act by committing troops without Congressional approval?" *Those bastards should sit one day in the Oval Office.* He answered, "Surprise was critical to our success. Without it we had no military option. So it was important that as few people as possible knew what we were planning."

A follow-on question, "You didn't trust Congress to keep the operation a secret?"

He gave an honest answer, perhaps one he should have considered a little more carefully, "I didn't even trust everyone on my cabinet to keep this secret." With that disclosure, a resentment that had already begun to simmer on Capital Hill suddenly boiled into a maelstrom.

Glover stood at that podium for two hours, answering every question he was asked until Tim Munson stepped up, covered the microphone with his hand and whispered to him, "Mr. President, they will have you up here for the next week. You've done your share. Leave and I will explain that I have called you away for an important phone call. Let Defense handle the press from here on out."

Glover looked at him. Munson could see tears welling up. The two had known one another for years, but Munson had never known a deeper respect for his old friend. He also knew that he had to get the President out of here and into the privacy of the restricted inner sanctums of the White House. There President Wilson Glover could openly weep and be surrounded by friends who would understand the tears.

Wanda stayed the night with Ida. They went to bed on the night of the fourth of July with the street in front of the house clogged with reporters and the fleet of trucks that haul their technology around. She had reconnected her telephone long enough to make a call to Lee Shaw asking him for help. He'd made a quick call, and now the Cleveland Police were watching both her front and back doors in order to keep the press from ringing doorbells or knocking on doors. Shaw told her to stay inside, and he would be over first thing in the morning. Together they would go outside and face any press that stuck it out through the night.

On the fifth of July, the Senate Majority Leader, a Republican, made the preposterous assertion that since President Glover had not sought Congressional approval for what he'd ordered, he was little more than a murderer and a thief, robbing America of tax payer dollars to fight a war that only he had decided was necessary and killing three hundred of America's sons in the process. "A murderer and a thief shouldn't be allowed to sit in the White House. Wilson Glover should be impeached and then tried in our criminal courts." It was American politics at its best, or perhaps its worst.

On that same day Lee Shaw arrived at Ida's house at 9:00AM. On his way in, he'd alerted reporters that Mrs. Spires would issue a prepared statement and take a few questions at 11:00AM. Together, Shaw, Wanda and Ida spent two hours putting together a statement. Ida asked him to read it for her.

"Ida," he said, "I'm happy to do that, but it's you they want to hear from, and they won't rest until they've done that. I'll be there with you the entire time, but I really think you'll get rid of these people faster if they can hear from you."

Promptly at 11:00AM, Lee Shaw led Ida Spires and Wanda Cheevers down the front steps of her house and stepped to a makeshift podium that had been erected at her front gate. Confidently, Shaw stepped up to the microphones. "Ladies and gentlemen, my name is Lee Shaw and I am an attorney representing the Spires family. Mrs. Spires has a statement she would like to give to you and then we'll take your questions."

A reporter from somewhere in front of them shouted, "Who else is with you? Who's the other woman?"

Shaw answered, "Accompanying Mrs. Spires, is Ms. Wanda Cheevers, a family friend. Please be so kind as to address your questions to either Mrs. Spires or myself."

Ida was a strong woman, but she'd never done anything like this in her life. She was scared to death, and her voice quivered and her hands shook as she awkwardly held the piece of paper and read what she and Shaw had written. When she was finished, it was a replay of Glover's press conference all over again, bedlam as each reporter tried to get his question answered first. Shaw moved Ida away from the podium and waited until they settled down. After a few minutes he stepped back up to the podium and pointed to a reporter in the front row who shouted his question over a din of others. Lee turned to Ida, "Did you hear the question?"

She nodded and stepped to the podium. "Of course I'm proud of what my son did. It looks to me like he was the key to all of this."

"What about the murder charges?" The question came from somewhere in the middle of the crowd.

Ida bristled, and Shaw was about to tell her not to answer, when she leaned forward and spit into the microphone, "My son didn't murder anyone, not ever. If any of you knew him, you'd know that."

"We'd like to get to know him, but nobody knows where he is. Tell us, Mrs. Spires." They fell silent, waiting to see if she would give them that one scrap of information that would lead them to her son.

"I don't know where he is."

"Have you heard from him, then?"

"He's called. He said he was safe."

"Safe from what, Mrs. Spires?"

She didn't know how to answer. She didn't want to tell them he was safe from the police. She knew the kinds of questions she'd get then. She was confused, angry and frustrated. She looked out into their faces and didn't like what she saw there. These people didn't want to get to know her son. These people wanted a story. To them Cleve Spires was simply their job. She hated them in that moment, and she cursed herself for putting herself in front of them. She began to cry. Shaw stepped forward and whispered, "Ida, are you all right?"

She shook her head. Shaw ended the press conference, and he and Wanda helped Ida back into the house. The crowd of reporters in front of the house thinned slightly after that, but Lee Shaw's law office that afternoon was deluged with phone calls and visits from reporters. One of them found out Wanda Cheevers owned the Blue Note Bar and that night, though Wanda wasn't there, the place was packed---with reporters.

On the sixth of July some of the troops who'd been in the Philippines, Japan and Thailand began to arrive back at their home stations. Bands played, flags waved and commanders boasted. Some local coverage lasted for several days, but national news coverage of the returning heroes was not sustainable. News events in other parts of the world and the political rage in Washington were the bigger stories.

The news from Japan and South Korea on the seventh of July infuriated Americans and added fuel to Congress's growing battle with the President. This short war that seemed so just, so necessary for the preservation of peace and the way of life for millions of people in so many countries, was having an unforeseen aftermath that was every bit as terrible as the war itself.

In Tokyo, Seichu Mori, called a press conference and denounced Japan's Prime Minister for allowing Americans to interfere immorally, if not illegally, in Japanese affairs of government. He told the Japanese people about the eavesdropping American intelligence had done, without bothering to ask permission. He speculated on what other things they might be snooping into without asking. He concluded his prepared remarks by saying, "America thinks she is invincible. Americans think they were put here to save the world. As a people, we Japanese have thrived on our own wits, our own devices, and our own beliefs for thousands of years. We don't need America, and her intervention was wrong. People of Japan, you must demand a vote-of-confidence in the Prime Minister's government. I know I have no confidence in it, and I must believe that you also lack confidence. The current government is not dedicated to watching after the best interests of Japan. Remove from power this government, this man, that has allowed America to invade us."

Seichu Mori did a good job. Editorials in support of him appeared in major newspapers across Japan. He became the "hot" interview, and it was fortunate for Mori that he had been so successful in getting the spotlight, because his life literally depended upon it. Cato Fujiwara may have been in prison, but that didn't mean he was without influence or access to those who could extend his influence. A friend of Cato Fujiwara's with a message had visited Mori on The fifth of July; "Cato needs your help. It would be best for you not to fail your old friend."

Events in South Korea were equally as frustrating to Americans. In Seoul, a compromise was struck. At the request of the South Korean Army and Air Force Chiefs of Staff, Lee Pak Son had been released from prison. By now, news of the *association* and its ultimate goal was well publicized. The fragile egos of the two South Korean generals were badly bruised. Son had worked a deception on them. They thought they were fighting for the liberation of South Korea from a weak President. Instead, if Son's plan had worked, South Korea would have been subordinated to the *association.*

So when Son was handed over, the Army Chief of Staff, in full view of reporters, took out his .45 caliber pistol, put it to the head of the still handcuffed Lee Pak Son and pulled the trigger. Then, in a press conference, the Vice President along with the two Chiefs of Staff announced that they had formed a new government that would be headed by this triumvirate. This was a matter of necessity and expediency. While the planes hadn't returned to the skies, and the ground war was now very localized to government buildings and certain corporate headquarters, things were stalemated. US Forces kept rebel forces out, while rebel forces kept workers from getting in. Nothing was moving forward.

All the while, fires continued to consume Seoul, a city now ringed by refugee camps created as burned out survivors fled their homes and businesses. It was still summer, but by October the temperatures would begin to tumble below freezing. By December, it would be rare to see a temperature above freezing. These refugee camps would become death camps if the government didn't step up soon. This triumvirate, however improbable, had to be the answer, and to the credit of the three men who formed it, each had to swallow a large piece of his pride to make it happen. The Vice President and the two military leaders knew they would have to get things moving again or each would lose the loyalty of their followers. Neither side knew where the majority lay; neither side dared to presume it represented the majority.

In Washington D.C., these events in Japan and Korea were portrayed as simply examples of Wilson Glover's flawed plan, a plan that could have been flawless, if he'd gone to Congress as he should have. At least that is how the Republicans were painting the picture. To make matters worse, Glover's own party was remaining ominously silent on the issue, a point that did not go unnoticed by the ever-vigilant press.

On the eighth of July, the US Air Force colonel who commanded Hill Air Force Base stopped his Humvee in front of the cabin where Spires and Atherton were hiding out. He brought with him a communiqué from Admiral McKeever to Gunnery Sergeant Atherton. The message told Atherton that as of his receipt of this message he was relieved of responsibility to account for the whereabouts of Cleveland Spires. The note also told both Atherton and Spires that on the ninth of July, two aircraft would arrive at Hill Air Force Base. One would bring Atherton back to Hawaii; the other would take Spires to Cleveland, Ohio, where he was to wait. His testimony would be needed in Stanley's court-martial. The colonel warned Spires, "The press is looking every where for you. Your picture has been on television. Everyone is looking for you Mr. Spires. I'd like to get you in and out of Hill as quickly as possible if we could." They agreed that Atherton and Spires would wait until very early the following morning to arrive at Hill.

At 4:30 AM on the ninth of July, Atherton pulled their rental car to a stop at the sentry post entering Hill Air Force Base. He handed his ID card to the air policeman who saw the name on it and bent down to look in the window. "Welcome to Hill Air Force Base, Gunnery Sergeant Atherton." He looked over at Spires, "You too, Sergeant Major. Flight Operations is expecting you." He gave them directions.

At Flight Operations, they were escorted into the VIP Lounge. The Air Force Master Sergeant told them their flight was in bound but still two hours out. The television was on and showing scenes from Seoul, which was still burning but in fewer spots. "There's coffee here for you and cold drinks in the refrigerator over there," he pointed to it. "If you should need anything else, just pick up the phone and I'll see to it. Enjoy your stay with us."

Atherton poured two cups of coffee and handed one to Spires, as both men settled into easy chairs to see what had happened in the five days since they'd seen a television. The footage from the Pacific Rim seemed to indicate the fighting was over. Both, however, were appalled at the political direction things had taken; there was sympathy in Japan against Cato Fujiwara's imprisonment, two-thirds of the ruling authority in South Korea, came from the rebel side and, in Washington, there seemed to be a ground swell of support for the impeachment of President Glover. Spires looked at Atherton and repeated, "It's a shit hole world, Gunny."

Thirty minutes before their flights were to arrive, CNN and the major networks interrupted their regular coverage for a special report. The picture on the screen shifted to a place Spires knew well. He didn't need the blurb at the bottom of the screen to tell him the reporter was outside the US Military Disciplinary Barracks at Fort Leavenworth, Kansas. Behind the reporter, the camera picked up an ambulance rolling out of the main gate with lights flashing, but no siren. The reporter filled in the details, "The ambulance you see leaving behind me carries the body of Major General Paul Stanley, who was found hanging in his cell this morning here at this high security prison. Official inside say an investigation is underway, but preliminary indications are that Stanley somehow used his bedding to fabricate a makeshift noose. He apparently was dead when guards brought him breakfast this morning. Stanley was in what the military calls pre-trial confinement, and was awaiting trial on charges that he conspired to destroy the government of the United States. Stay tuned to this station, as more details of this case are known, we'll keep you updated. I'm…"

Spires tuned out.

He sat there for a minute. Atherton looked at him, but could tell he was far away. He let him have his thoughts. When Spires got up, he went over to the phone, picked it up and asked the party on the other end, "Can this plane take me to Thailand?" Atherton heard this and turned around. There was a rather long pause, while the party on the other end of Spires' line said something, "Yes, I'd like you to check on that for me. If need be, contact General Kinney or Admiral McKeever at CINCPAC; I'm sure they'll authorize it." Another pause, shorter this time, then, "Thank you." He hung up the phone and turned to Atherton, "Stanley's dead, that mean's no court martial. I need to get home to my family."

Atherton nodded.

"They're all dead, Gunny."

"Excuse me, Sergeant Major?"

"Anybody who might have been able to clear me of these murder charges---they're all dead, except for Fujiwara. If they let that son of a bitch loose…"

"I'm sorry, Sergeant Major."

He was quiet for a minute and then he looked at Atherton, "Bart, you know what I told you a while ago?" Atherton had a puzzled look.

Spires clarified, "About it being a shit hole world."

Atherton nodded.

"Well, forget it. My wife and son are safe in Thailand. I'll see them soon. Nothing else matters." He was smiling now.

Atherton walked over to him and extended his hand, "Enjoy them, Sergeant Major. You've earned the right to choose your future. Good luck."

In Cleveland, Ohio, an unmarked government sedan picked up Ida Spires and Wanda Cheevers at Ida's house. Two government agents plowed their way past reporters, protecting the two women from physical contact with the reporters, but unable to protect them from the barrage of questions which didn't let up until the sedan's doors were closed and it pulled from the curb. Two blocks later, the agent driving looked in the rearview mirror and said, "It looks like a convoy behind us." The two women turned and looked out the rear window to see cars and vans full of reporters following them.

The government sedan led the way to the private parking garage underneath Lee Shaw's office building. It pulled in and was passed through waiting security, but the convoy behind them was denied entry. Some of the entourage of reporters found hard-to-find parking spots on the street. Others double parked near the parking garage entrance and waited.

In the parking garage, the government agents pulled into a parking space next to another sedan identical to theirs. The two agents driving Ida and Wanda got out and spoke to the two men and two women in the other car. As they finished talking they all looked at their watches. Ida and Wanda wondered what was going on. They thought they were going to see Lee Shaw, that he had arranged this transportation on their behalf.

When the two agents returned to the car, the one who'd been driving said to Ida, "We're going to take you to see your son, Mrs. Spires, but first we have to lose that trail of reporters we brought with us."

Ida smiled and cried at the same time. Wanda took her hand and asked the agent, "Where are we going?"

"To the airport, on the general aviation side. We've arranged some privacy for the three of you there. His plane will land in about an hour."

They waited thirty minutes just to make it look like the two women had business in the office building that towered above them. Then the identical sedan started its engine, backed out of the space and headed out of the garage. "They're a decoy. The reporters will follow them to nowhere. We'll wait ten minutes and then be on our way. We'll have you ladies there in plenty of time."

Cleve's plane from Hill Air Force Base was early. He waited for them in a private office that just happened to have a television. He turned it on and Paul Stanley was the feature story. The reporter was reading from a citation, "...is awarded the Purple Heart for injuries sustained while engaging a hostile enemy force during an ambush near Quang Tri City on 15 December, 1970..."

Spires' mind picked out the important information, "ambush", "Quang Tri City", "15 December, 1970". It took him a minute to piece it all together. It had been so long ago. He put his hand on his left shoulder and even through his shirt he could feel the scar tissue healed around the wound. *When was it?* His mind flashed back. *It was in December, 1970; I know it was. We were only ten clicks out of Quang Tri, that's why the DustOff got there so quick.*

The patrol had been thrown together quickly. A pilot reported seeing a group of Viet Cong moving through the jungle. He could see their weapons. The young captain had volunteered, as had the other fifteen men that had gone out in pursuit. A few of them knew each other, but for the most part the patrol was like a pick up game of basketball in the playground; whoever was available, whoever wanted to play, was good enough.

Spires hadn't like it. They were heading straight down a trail, moving very fast. He went forward and asked the captain to slow down. The captain told him, there wasn't time. Two hours after they'd left base camp all hell broke loose.

In his mind, Spires could see the jungle trail; he could see the young Captain pinned down in a withering hail of bullets, caught directly in the ambush's cross fire. He remembered tossing two grenades; one to either side of the trial, into the bushes he thought concealed the Viet Cong. The blast killed several of the enemy, but others were still there, just stunned from the flash-bang of the grenades. Spires rushed in with his M-16 on full automatic, spraying bullets over the downed Captain's head. He grabbed him, and as he was pulling him to safety, an AK-47 round ripped through his shoulder. He shot the guerilla that had shot him and gotten the Captain back to safety before loosing consciousness.

He asked himself, *Could that captain have been Stanley?*

He was pondering that question when the door opened. Ida and Wanda stepped into the room. They ran to him and he didn't know whom to embrace first. He didn't have to make a choice, the two women put their arms around him and the three of them held one another until Ida patted him on the shoulder and said, "Cleveland, you look fine." Wanda chimed in agreeing.

He looked at the televison for just a second. The story had moved from Stanley to President Glover's troubles in Washington. He turned back to them and said, "I am just fine."

One of the agents brought them coffee. They settled back while he caught them up on everything that had happened since he'd left Cleveland. Ida told him about the media circus that had been swirling around their house and the Blue Note Bar. Wanda said, "Business has never been so good, Cleve. Those reporters eat anything and everything." They laughed.

Wanda said, "When you called the other morning, I didn't think we'd ever see you again."

"I know. Things are changing very fast now. Have you heard about General Stanley committing suicide?" They nodded. "He was about my last hope of ever proving that I didn't commit these murders, any of them. This guy Fujiwara in Japan probably knows something, but the way things are going there I'll never get to him. I've decided the two of you were right after all. I need to forget the idea of ever proving my innocence. Look where it's led us. I started down a path to prove my innocence and found a road to war."

He looked at his watch. "I want both of you to understand that I love you very much, but what I'm going to say will hurt the both of you." He looked at them and could see tears welling up in his mother's eyes, "I'm going back to Thailand. I'm going back to be with Liott and Daniel. My place is with them and nothing else that is going on right now matters very much to me."

Ida said, "But Cleveland, you've worked so hard to prove you're innocent. The President..."

"Mom, you're right, I worked very hard and look at what has happened." He pointed to the television behind them. "President Glover, no matter what anyone else might say, did the right thing, but it's not right for me to expect that he or anyone else is going to help me now. They've all got bigger problems to deal with than me. Besides, Liott and Daniel are waiting for me. I know that now."

He looked at Wanda. She smiled at him through a thin veil of tears and nodded. She understood and she couldn't be angry with him.

Ida asked, "What about the murders in Thailand? Won't the police there arrest you?"

He glanced at his watch again. "I don't think so. The *Yakuza* was behind the killing of Billy Driscoll and that girl in Bangkok. While I don't think they can prove anything, I think they know I didn't do it. I think the King is going to pardon me and allow me to enter Thailand as a free man. I'll know that for sure in the next couple of hours."

"So when will you leave, son?"

"Thirty minutes, Mom. This plane will take me to Hawaii. Admiral McKeever will have his plane take me from there to Bangkok. From there, there's this cab driver I know," he smiled at the thought of Tradip and his flip-up sun glasses, "who'll get me to Chuk Ra Met. Between here and Hawaii, I'll find out about the charges in Thailand, but I'm pretty sure they'll go away."

"How can you be so sure?" Wanda asked.

"I have a friend, a very old and dear friend, Pramrashorn Saraveet. The King of Thailand just made him Chief of Staff of the Royal Thai Army. Admiral McKeever has asked him to intervene on my behalf with the King."

There was a knock at the door and Cleve said, "It's open." An Air Force captain in a flight suit stuck his head in and said, "Sorry Sergeant Major, but we're going to need to have you board in ten minutes, so we can meet our clearance time."

Cleve looked at the two women in front of him and then said to the Captain, "That's fine. I'll be with you shortly."

Ida asked, "Will the three of you visit?" He nodded. She began to cry as he stood up.

Cleve hugged Wanda first and whispered into her ear, "I owe you my life from here on out. I want you to know that, Wanda."

She cried and whispered back, "God bless you, Cleveland Spires," and then added, "I'll look in on your mother. We've become good friends, you know."

Imperceptibly, he squeezed her harder and said, "Then I owe you even more than my life. Thanks, Wanda." She left the room and waited while he said goodbye to his mother.

For a long while, neither mother nor son spoke. They held each other. It was Ida who broke the silence, "You've earned the right to be happy, son. Give Liott and Daniel my love. Tell them I want to see them again before I die."

He squeezed his mother harder and said, "Don't talk like that. As soon as I get back, I'll ask Daniel if he'd like to come visit. You won't believe the man he's grown into. Liott must care for her father, but we'll see what can be arranged. We'll call regularly and Wanda said she wants to see more of you. You two have become good friends, I'm told."

Tearfully she replied, "Yes, we have."

"That's good, Mom. I'm glad Wanda's in your life."

They held each other for a minute more and then Spires said, "I'd better go."

She buried her head in his chest. "I love you, Cleveland."

"I know that, Mom." He paused for a moment. "Always remember that I love you, too. Don't worry about how any of this turns out. Don't listen to what anyone might say about me. I've done the right thing, Mom."

"Yes, you did, Cleveland. Yes, you did."

Chapter Forty

On the eleventh of July, the first of too many C-17's touched down at Dover Air Force Base in Delaware at 7:00A.M. Its cargo was precious, fifty flag-draped coffins, the first fifty American servicemen killed in Korea to be repatriated. It was a perfect day for such an event. Steel gray skies prevailed and a light drizzle never stopped. Family members made their way to the huge hangar where their dead would be eulogized. Everyone moved slowly, their senses oblivious to the ugly weather, dulled by the disbelief created by sudden, unexpected death. Even the reporters and camera operators who ranged behind the cordons that held them at bay did what they needed to do more reverentially than they normally would.

President Glover and the First Lady were on hand as they would be on each of the next five consecutive days, as all three hundred slain in Korea made their way to their final resting places. So, too, would General Peter Rentz be there. Glover looked drawn and haggard, the change in him taking only days. He was under unrelenting pressure, some of it from outside forces, some of it generated in his own mind. In Washington, he was under pressure to capitulate his administration; here, in the presence of these heroes, Glover felt inferior, inadequate to say what needed to be said. Warriors, he thought, should be eulogized by warriors, and that was a class Glover didn't believe he was a part of.

After a few brief remarks, he made it his habit to turn the podium over to General Rentz. He was the warrior these grieving families needed to see, needed to hear. Rentz was an imposing presence, his uniform, always immaculate, with row upon row of decorations above each breast pocket, four-stars gleaming from each epaulet. The families gathered there looked up at him and he met their eyes as he gazed down at them from the podium. They were there in the initial stages of their grief to try and make some sense of the loss that had befallen them. Rentz felt it his obligation to try to provide them the reason for their loss. They were all connected by the death of the men who lay in the flag-draped coffins on the hanger's northern side.

Rentz's voice was wonderfully bass and resonant in the huge hangar. With an eloquence of tone and gesture, he told the assembled families what he thought of the unfairness of war. He told them of the friends he'd lost to wars since he'd been engaged in this profession of arms, and he confessed to them that his grief still fell short of theirs; the measure of the loss of a friend is never equal to the loss of a son, a husband or a father. Each day he spoke, he changed his words slightly. He didn't want this to be scripted. He didn't want any family to think he was just there to say words to them. But each day that he spoke, Rentz concluded with the same words; he never strayed away from them because he fervently believed them to be absolutely true.

"Never in modern history have so few fought so valiantly to protect so many. The world as we know it hung in the balance this past Fourth of July. Your sons, your fathers, your husbands saved it, and their legacy is that we will never forget what they did to protect our way of life, the way of life of the South Korean people and, ultimately, the way of life of people in every country around the world. They bring new meaning to the idea of service above self, they bring new meaning to the word *honor,* and as we go forward they will give new meaning to that all-ready famous day in our history, *the Fourth of July.* God has taken them into his loving arms and now he cares for them. May God bless each of you for giving America fine men like these."

There was no applause; other than Rentz's voice, the only other sounds that could be heard in this makeshift cathedral was a mother's sob, a father's sigh, a widow's cry or scream of a baby whose father lay somewhere inside one of the caskets. When the speeches were concluded President Glover, the First Lady and General Rentz came down from the makeshift stage. Lowered now to the level of the grieving families, they moved about the mourners as if they were family and all three joined in their tears.

On Capital Hill a bipartisan committee of the House of Representatives met for the first time to consider the matter of Wilson Glover's impeachment.

On the twenty-fourth of July, Lucas Johnson participated in an awards ceremony at the First Special Forces Battalion Headquarters at Torii Station on Okinawa, Japan. Tomorrow he and Lieutenant Colonel Greene were to depart Okinawa for Bangkok where they would join Pram Saraveet and the King of Thailand in a ceremony honoring the soldiers of the Tiger Brigade.

After the awards ceremony, Lucas joined the soldiers of the First Battalion and their families for a picnic at Torii Beach, a broad stretch of sand along the island's southwestern side. It was a bright, sunny and stiflingly hot day; the humidity was at ninety-eight percent. Lucas looked around him at the families enjoying their time together; he had a longing to be with his family.

At 4:00 that afternoon, he left the picnic and went to the Community Club at Torii Station where the Non-Commissioned Officers of the First Battalion were welcoming the battalion's new Command Sergeant Major, Boz Williams.

On the twenty-sixth of July, Cleve Spires waited in a broad grassy field on the edge of Chuk Ra Met. Overhead, the helicopter swung into a lazy turn to head into the wind as it set up for its approach. He watched it land, as he'd watched so many helicopters like this Huey, land in grassy fields in Vietnam a lifetime ago. When it touched down, Colonel Lucas Johnson hopped to the ground, walked hunched over for twenty meters or so, just to make sure he was clear of the still-turning rotors, and then stood up straight. As Johnson got closer, Spires saluted him. Johnson returned it.

"Welcome to Chuk Ra Met, Colonel."

In the background, they heard the pilots cut the turbine engine. The crew chief was outside holding the village's children back at a safe distance until the rotors stopped turning. After that, he and the pilots let them sit in the cockpit, crawl in and out of the passenger space and explain this marvelous machine to these wide-eyed youngsters.

"They don't get to see things like that up close very often." Spires put his hand on Lucas' shoulder. "Liott's got lunch ready. She's anxious to meet you, sir. Daniel's not here. He's gone to the States to visit my mother. Sorry you missed him."

As they entered the village, the villagers stood deferentially to the side of Cleve and Lucas's route, but they all extended their hand to Johnson as he passed. Cleve slowed while Lucas shook every hand. When they'd gotten through this welcoming gauntlet, Lucas looked at Spires with a grin, "Did you teach them that?"

"Yes, sir," he said sheepishly.

When they got to the village's center, Lucas Johnson met Liott. She embraced him and whispered in his ear, "Thank you, Lucas. You gave me back my husband." That touched him nearly to tears. He couldn't say anything, so he simply patted her back as he returned her hug.

Lunch was a community affair. Liott had prepared a huge table sagging with every Thai delicacy that she and the other village wives knew how to make. Everyone came and ate and some of the children went to get the helicopter crew, so they could partake as well. It was a wonderful time, filled with spicy Thai food and fresh fruit. Johnson persuaded Liott to tell him the story of how she and Cleve had met, fallen in love and were married here in this small village. Lucas laughed as Spires told him how hard it had been to win the approval of Liott's father. By the time lunch was finished, it was easy for Lucas to understand how Spires could have chosen to come back here.

When Liott excused herself to begin cleaning up the leftovers, that was Lucas' cue. "Sergeant Major, can we take a walk. There are some things I want to tell you." There was a certain foreboding in Lucas' voice that told Spires the news wasn't good. Lucas thanked Liott and a few of the other wives for the lunch and he and Cleve walked out of the village toward the rice paddies.

"What's on your mind sir?"

"Sergeant Major, the Secretary of the Army isn't going to reopen your court-martial. I'm sorry." There was a protracted silence between them. Cleve sensed this was really bothering Johnson. He was right. Johnson continued, "The politics in that fucking city are..."

Cleve interrupted him. "Sir, if that's the worst news you've got, then let's go back and have another papaya juice. It would have been nice to set the record straight, to get my rank back, my back pay and all of that, but I sure wasn't counting on it. So unless you've got anything else..."

It was Lucas' turn to interrupt. "Sergeant Major, there's more." He paused while he tried to think where he should start. "The news out of Washington and Tokyo these days isn't good. Congress is calling for President Glover's impeachment. General Pastor, General Rentz and Admiral McKeever have all been forced into retirement. Mr. Munson has had to resign as the National Security Advisor and that little prick, Levi, resigned and then went to the media telling them he tried to tell the President that force wasn't the way to handle the problem in Asia. DuPray hasn't resigned, but he's not saying anything to help the President. The entire Democratic Party is scared and they're hanging the President out to dry."

Spires didn't know what to say. He'd been out of touch since his arrival back in Thailand. No television, no radio, but lots of time spent in the peace and quiet of Chuk Ra Met. What Lucas was telling him was too much information, too fast.

"That's why the Secretary of the Army isn't acting on your court-martial. He's scared. The President went to the gutless wonder and asked him to reopen the case. He told the President 'no', some bullshit about 'It's not in the best interest of the country right now'."

Again, too much, too fast. They stopped walking and Spires sat down under a palm tree, leaned back against it, looked at Lucas and shook his head.

Lucas knew he was dumping a lot, but all of this was background for what he really came to tell Spires. "There's more Sergeant Major. Are you up for it?"

Spires nodded.

"The Japanese government has released Cato Fujiwara."

He had been prepared for this eventuality, but now that it had become reality, the anger shot through Cleve Spires. The bastard he was sure had killed Michiko, who knew the truth about his own innocence, had been let go. He came to life now. "They can't do that. That murdering son of a bitch, how the hell can they just let him go? How can they let that guilty bastard back on the street?"

"The Japanese government returned a no-confidence vote to the Prime Minister. He's gone. Seichu Mori is a likely replacement, and he's whipped the Japanese people into an anti-American mood that hasn't been seen since Pearl Harbor. Japanese courts aren't allowing any of the photos or tapes that we supplied them to be used as evidence. They say they were obtained illegally and therefore aren't admissible as evidence. Yamamoto and Fukora are dead. None of Fujiwara's men are going to testify against him and even if they did, prosecutors aren't sure any of them knew enough to make a case. He walked out of prison yesterday, all charges dropped."

"That's just not possible."

There was one last thing that Johnson wanted to tell him. "I'm retiring, Sergeant Major. The world's gone to hell in a hand basket and I don't want to be a pawn for the politicians that will be running it after this mess has settled down."

For a brief moment, Cleve Spires didn't blame him one bit. Johnson continued to talk, but Spires wasn't hearing him. The more he thought about Lucas Johnson retiring, the more the thought of it disturbed him. Cleve Spires had always considered himself a doer not a thinker. In the professional world in which he'd come of age in the Army, the officers, like Lucas, were the thinkers and the non-commissioned officers, like him, were the doers. The US military needed both types. Here was a good thinker, in his estimation, who was thinking about getting out at a time when the military had just lost three of its' best thinkers in Pastor, McKeever and Rentz. It didn't need to lose Colonel Lucas Johnson as well. Whatever anger he felt at what the Japanese had allowed to happen faded for now. He needed to become a thinker rather than a doer; he had to give Johnson something to chew on during the long flight back to Fort Lewis, Washington.

Johnson had stopped talking and sat down on the other side of the tree from Spires. They sat there back-to-back for a while, each gathering his thoughts.

Spires spoke up. "Lucas," it was the first time he'd ever addressed an officer on a first-name basis, "of all the things you've told me today, this is the worst news yet." He gave that a moment to sink in and then went on, "I don't like the way things have turned out any better than you do, but sometimes we don't know the true value of good men until a long time after they've gone. Look at Abraham Lincoln. You think anybody at the end of the Civil War thought Lincoln would ever be considered one of our best Presidents. Hell, he'd been dead fifty years or more before anybody started to give him the slightest credit for what he did, for the way he changed the country. It's going to be the same way with President Glover. But I'll bet if you were to ask President Glover, Mr. Munson, General Pastor, Admiral McKeever or General Rentz if they'd do anything differently, they'd tell you they wouldn't. They're all good men who acted responsibly and in the best interests of the nation they serve. The time will come when the world will recognize that."

They sat there for a while, each of them thinking about what Spires had just said. Then Cleve continued, "You're a good man, too, Lucas. If you retire, the military just looses another good man, a man who will act responsibly. If you go, men like John DuPray, Roger Levi and Stevenson, that gutless Secretary of the Army, benefit. They become more powerful because there's one less good man in the fight."

There was a thoughtful silence and Lucas said, "So, you're telling me…"

Spires held up his hand in a gesture that stopped Johnson in mid sentence, "Lucas, I wouldn't presume to tell any professional soldier to stay or to retire. Only you can reach that decision, you and your family. I'm just telling you to really look at your reasons. If you're thinking we somehow lost this last little war, I'd tell you to think again. Those bastards aren't in charge anywhere except in North Korea, and who gives a shit about that godforsaken country. We stopped 'em Colonel, we did our job, just like we've been trained to do."

Spires felt a huge amount of pride in the word *we,* meaning the collective Army, Navy, Air Force and Marine Corps team that had interceded in Japan, the Philippines, Thailand and South Korea. He thought of himself as a part of that team.

"But war doesn't always make peace. There wasn't much peace after Vietnam ended. Hell, as much as we patted ourselves on the back after Desert Storm, it took us twelve years to come to terms with Sadaam Hussein. And this war, this little skirmish, hasn't resulted in peace either. Good men have been disgraced because other men have used the perfect clarity of hindsight to make judgments."

Spires got up and walked around to Lucas' side of the tree. "If you're retiring because you just don't want to do this anymore, then pack it in, but I'm not sure I'd believe you if you told me that." He paused for a moment to consider what he wanted to say next; it would be a bit harsher. "If you're pissed at the way they're treating good men who acted honorably then I'd tell you I'm disappointed that you're not staying to fight for what's right. I'd tell you someone has to be the voice of reason when decisions are made to put troops in harm's way. I'd tell you someone has to be there to make sure the plan is sound. Who better than you, Lucas?"

Johnson hadn't expected any of this. Spires was inside his mind, pulling at every argument he'd wrestled with to reach his decision. In the remaining time they had together, not quite an hour, they speculated on what the Vice President would be like if Glover were to be impeached, who would take Munson's place and who would backfill for Pastor, McKeever and Rentz. When it was time for Lucas to leave and return to Bangkok, the two friends walked toward the waiting helicopter. They heard the turbine engine begin to turn as the pilot pulled the engine's starter trigger. They stopped about fifty meters short of the slowly turning blades as the engine popped into life and the blades began to turn faster. Spires extended his hand, "Thanks for coming Lucas. It is OK that I call you Lucas, isn't it?"

"I'm honored, Cleve."

The turbine engine was now at full idle as Spires leaned close to Johnson's ear and said, "Let me know what you decide."

Johnson nodded as he stepped off for his ride to Bangkok.

On the fifteenth of August, while enjoying lunch with Liott in Korat, Cleve learned that Seichu Mori had been elected Prime Minister of Japan.

On the twentieth of August, President Wilson Glover was impeached.

On the twenty-fifth of August, Cleve Spires received a letter from Lucas Johnson telling him he would not be retiring.

It was 9:00AM on the twenty-sixth of August. Liott and Cleve had already waited an hour to use the one and only pay telephone at the Korat bus station. Even though the tin roof protected them from the direct rays of the sun, it also served the same purpose as a radiator. Overhead fans turned lazily trying to provide some cooling movement of the air, but it was so hot and humid already that they were next to useless.

The Thai phone system wasn't very good, but they were lucky; the call to Daniel went through without difficulty. Daniel answered on the third ring. Cleve and Liott both huddled around it to say hello and to hear their son's voice, but Cleve knew that voice could be gone in a second. He cut right to it and asked Daniel if he'd confirmed his flight. Details of his visit with his grandmother could wait until the essentials were taken care of. If the line held, then he could tell them of his time in America.

Daniel told them he wouldn't be coming home. He'd enlisted that day in the US Army.

He heard his mother scream, "No."

He tried to reassure her. He tried to explain why.

Cleve interrupted him, "Daniel," but his son kept talking so Cleve shouted it this time, "Daniel, listen to me, stop. Talk to me son. Why did you do this without talking with me? Tell me the truth; your mother's not on the line now."

"Papa, the good men are all gone. There's no one left who can help…"

Silence filled his ear. Cleve wasn't sure if the line had gone dead or Daniel hadn't finished his thought. Cleve asked, "Daniel, what do you mean there's no one left who can help?"

"There's no one who can help you, Papa, except me. I'll help you get to the truth."

Cleve looked at Liott who'd moved away from him and was sitting on a bench, her head bent down. She was crying; he could see her head move slowly up and down in rhythm with her sobs. "Daniel, I don't...Daniel...Daniel, are you there?"

There was no reply.

Printed in the United States
1310800002B/262-309